warm nights in *Magnolia Bay*

BABETTE DE JONGH

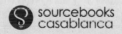

sourcebooks casablanca

Published by Sourcebooks Casablanca, an imprint of Sourcebooks
P.O. Box 4410, Naperville, Illinois 60567-4410
(630) 961-3900
sourcebooks.com

Printed and bound in Canada.
MBP 10 9 8 7 6 5 4 3 2 1

This book is dedicated to Penelope Smith. My ability to communicate telepathically with animals was a curse, not a blessing, until I found her book, Animal Talk. *It showed me how to summon the ability at will (rather than being smacked upside the head by incoming communication at the least opportune moment). When I later attended her classes in animal communication, her wisdom and mentorship literally changed my life. Thank you, Penelope, for showing me how to light my own small candle and keep it burning. I promise to add my light to the collective torch that all animal communicators carry, so that together, we can hold it high and pass it along.*

Chapter 1

"I HATE PEOPLE." ABBY CURTIS WADDED UP THE HEM OF HER yellow bathrobe and dropped to her knees in the ditch. A pair of green eyes stared at her from the middle of the culvert. "Here, kitty, kitty," she called.

The eyes blinked, but the kitten stayed put. Another stray dumped in front of Aunt Reva's house, and it wasn't going to trust humans again anytime soon. For a nanosecond, Abby thought about running back to the house to get Reva, but something told her the kitten would skedaddle the moment Abby turned her back.

Reva's dog, Georgia, a Jack Russell terrier/cattle dog mix, peered through the other side of the culvert and whined. The kitten spun around to face the dog and hissed.

"Georgia." Abby snapped her fingers. "Stay."

The frightened kitten puffed up and growled at Georgia. Abby didn't have Reva's way with animals. But with the little dog's expert help, she might be able to catch the kitten without bothering her aunt, who was in the house packing for a long-postponed trip.

Georgia whined again and the kitten backed up farther, her full attention on the dog.

Thankful the ditch had been mowed and recently treated for fire ants, Abby eased forward onto her belly in the damp grass. She reached into the culvert, ignoring the cool, muddy water that seeped through her robe and soaked her T-shirt and panties. Shutting out images of snakes and spiders, she scooted closer and stretched out farther.

Just a little bit more...

Georgia seemed to know exactly what to do. She fake-lunged

toward the kitten, who spat and hopped backward into Abby's out-stretched hand. "Gotcha!" Abby grabbed the kitten's scruff.

The kitten whirled and spun and scratched, but Abby held on, even when it sank needle-like teeth into Abby's hand.

"Shh. Shh." Abby got to her knees and stroked the kitten's dark tortoiseshell fur. A girl, then. Like calicos, tortoiseshell cats were almost always female. "You're okay, little girl. You're all right."

Abby's robe had come open in the front, and the kitten ped-aled all four feet with claws extended, scratching gouges in Abby's exposed skin. She held on to the scruff of the kitten's neck, croon-ing and humming. "You're okay, baby."

Georgia leaped with excitement, begging to see the kitten, who continued to struggle and scratch and bite.

"No, Georgia." Abby wrapped the kitten in the folds of her robe and held it close. It calmed, but Abby could feel its body heaving with every desperate breath. "Not yet. She's too scared."

If this catch didn't stick, Abby wouldn't get another chance. Abby's fingers touched a raw, bloody patch on the kitten's back: road rash from being thrown out of a moving vehicle.

God, Abby hated people. No wonder Aunt Reva had all but turned into a hermit, living out here in the boondocks alongside the kind of people who would do this. But then, Abby had learned that evil lived everywhere—north and south, city and country. She cuddled the kitten close, even while it tried to flay her skin with its desperate claws.

"Nobody's going to hurt you, I promise. Nobody's going to hurt you, not ever again." She could make that promise, because she knew Reva would keep the kitten or find it an even better home. All strays were welcome at Bayside Barn.

Abby herself was proof of that.

Disgusted with all of humanity, Abby struggled up out of the ditch, her mud-caked barn boots slipping on the dew-wet grass. She had just scrambled onto solid ground when a Harley blasted past, turned in at the drive next door, and stopped just past the ditch.

Uncomfortably aware that her bathrobe gaped open indecently and her hair hadn't seen a hairbrush since yesterday afternoon, Abby hid behind the tall hedge between Aunt Reva's place and the abandoned estate next door. Georgia clawed Abby's legs in a "Help, pick me up" gesture.

"Lord, Georgia, I can't hold both of you."

Determined, Georgia scrabbled at Abby's legs. One-handed, Abby scooped up all thirty pounds of the scaredy-cat dog. "It's only a motorcycle."

The sound of garbage trucks in the distance promised an even more terrifying situation if she didn't get the kitten into the house soon. She held Georgia in one hand and clutched the covered-up kitten with the other, jiggling both of them in a hopefully soothing motion. "You're okay. You're both okay."

The loud motorbike idled near the estate's rusted-out mailbox. The rider put both booted feet down on the gravel drive. Tall, broad-shouldered, he wore motorcycle leathers and a black helmet with a tinted visor.

Georgia licked Abby's chin, a plea to hurry back to the house before the garbage trucks ravaging the next block over ushered in the apocalypse.

"Shh. I want to go home, too, but..." If she fled from her hiding place, the motorcycle dude would notice a flash of movement when Abby's yellow robe flapped behind her like a flag. What was this guy doing before 8:00 a.m. parking his motorcycle in a lonely driveway on this dead-end country road?

The rider got off the motorcycle and removed his helmet. His light-brown hair stood on end, then feathered down to cover his jacket collar.

His hair was the only soft thing about him. From his tanned skin to his angular face to his rigid jaw, from his wide shoulders to his bulging thighs to his scuffed black boots, the guy looked hard.

He waded through the tall weeds to the center of the easement and pulled up the moldy For Sale sign that had stood there for years. He tossed the sign into the weed-filled ditch and stalked back to his motorcycle. The beast roared down the potholed driveway to the old abandoned house, scattering gravel.

———————

Quinn Lockhart sped down the long drive, a list of obstacles spinning through his head:

1. Cracked brick facade: possible foundation problems.

2. Swimming pool: green with algae and full of tadpoles, frogs—probably snakes, too.

3. Overgrown acreage: ten acres of out-of-control shrubs choked with vines and weeds.

He'd seen all this on his first and only inspection; he knew what he was getting into. Though he had never attempted to renovate and flip a long-abandoned house before, he knew he possessed the necessary skills to do it successfully. Hell. Even JP—his ex-business-partner and ex-friend he'd known since high school—had made a fricking fortune flipping houses. If all-talk, no-action JP could do it, Quinn could roll up his sleeves and do it ten times better. The sale of this polished-up diamond would provide the seed money he needed to start his own construction business in Magnolia Bay and, maybe even more important, prove his talent to future clients.

When his lowball offer was accepted, he hadn't known whether to whoop or moan. The hidden gem of this dilapidated estate could only go up in value. Located on a remote back road several miles outside Magnolia Bay and an easy hour to New Orleans, the place was a rare find he wouldn't have known about if he hadn't been dating the local real-estate agent who helped him find an apartment here after his divorce. But the next-to-nothing price and a small stash of cash for renovations had consumed every penny of the equity he'd received in the divorce. And he still hadn't quite convinced himself that leaving New Orleans to follow his ex and their son to her hometown was the best decision he'd ever made.

He reminded himself that moving to Magnolia Bay was the only way he could spend enough time with his teenage son. After years of working more than he should and leaving Sean's raising to Melissa, Quinn knew this was his last chance to rebuild the relationship between him and his son. Quinn was hoping they'd bond over the renovation, if he could convince Sean that helping out would be fun. So it wasn't just a business decision; it was a last-ditch effort to be the kind of father Sean deserved.

When Delia Simmons—his real estate agent—showed him this estate, a thrill of excitement and hope had skittered through him. This old place had good bones. Putting it back together again would be the first step toward putting his life back together again.

And when she told him the rumor she'd heard around town that the adjacent acreage between this road and the bay might soon become available as well... Maybe it wasn't a sign from God, exactly, but it sure lit a fire under his butt. With the right timing, he could use the money from the sale of this place to buy the strip of Magnolia Bay waterfront land that ran behind all five estates on this dead-end road.

He could subdivide the bayside marshland along the existing estates' property lines, then sell each parcel to its adjoining estate. If he had enough money, he could build nice elevated walkways from each estate to the marsh-edged bay; maybe even haul in enough sand to make a community beach complete with boat docks and shaded pavilions.

Maybe he was dreaming too big. But he couldn't stop thinking that with perfect timing on the sale of the estate and the availability of the waterfront land, he could make an easy-peasy fortune for not too much work. And—dreaming big again—the ongoing maintenance for five private boat docks would give him a steady stream of income doing seasonal repair work that he could depend on from here on out.

Quinn parked his bike on the cracked patio around back of the sprawling bungalow-style house and killed the engine. Expecting silence, he was assaulted by a loud racket of braying, mooing, and barking.

"Are you kidding me?" He walked to the hedge separating his property from the annoying clamor. When he'd toured the property with Delia, it had been as peaceful as a church. She hadn't warned him it cozied up to Old McDonald's farm.

Or, maybe more accurately, Old Ms. McDonald's farm. He'd glimpsed the crazy-looking woman hiding in the shrubbery with her wild mane of honey-brown hair, ratty bathrobe, and cowboy boots. How the hell would he get top dollar for a house with an eccentric animal-hoarding neighbor next door? He stalked to the overgrown hedge between the properties and bellowed at the animals. "Shut. Up."

The noise level escalated exponentially. "Fork it," Quinn said, forgetting that without Sean here, he could've used the more satisfying expletive.

The multispecies chorus ramped it up. Parrots screeched loud enough to make the donkeys sound like amateurs. Parrots? "What next? Lions, tigers, and bears?"

Fine. He would work inside today. Quinn planned to get the pool house fit for habitation in time for Sean's scheduled visit next weekend—unless the kid canceled again, claiming homework, football practice, school projects, whatever.

All great excuses, but was that all they were? Excuses?

Did his son really hate him so much that he never wanted to see him again?

The thought hit Quinn in the solar plexus with the force of a fist. If it had been a woman treating him that way, he'd have gotten the message and moved on. But this was his *son*. His heart. The kid was fifteen now, so Quinn had only three years of court-mandated visitation to compel Sean to keep coming around.

Three years suddenly seemed like a very short time, given all the inattention and absence Quinn had to make up for. And yet, it had to be possible for him to retrace his steps and rebuild the bridge between him and his son.

Quinn was a carpenter, after all. He knew how to build anything, even a rickety, falling-apart bridge. And he would rebuild this one, no matter what it took. The fight for Sean's time and attention generated its own list of obstacles, but Quinn had ordered the first round of obstacle-climbing tools online:

1. Cool guy furniture.

2. Flat-screen TV.

3. Premium cable and internet.

4. Xbox game system.

5. Paddleboards (secondhand).

Quinn knew of only one way to close the distance between him and Sean that compounded daily—worse than credit-card debt—because of his ex-wife Melissa's subtle sabotage.

He must become the best weekend dad he could afford to be.

"Got you another one," Abby announced above the sound of the screen door slapping shut behind her. "Saw her run into the culvert when I took the trash up to the road."

Reva came into the kitchen, dressed in Birkenstocks and a tie-dyed hippie dress, her prematurely silver hair secured with an enormous jeweled barrette. "Oh my Lord." She set her suitcase by the sliding glass doors and reached for the kitten. "Just this one? No stragglers?"

"She's the only one I saw, but I'll keep a lookout in case there are others."

Reva held the kitten like a curled-up hedgehog between her palms. Her magic touch calmed the kitten, who immediately started purring. Reva closed her eyes, a slight frown line between her arched brows. "She's the only one." Reva opened her hazel-green eyes, her gaze soft-focused. "But kitten season has begun, and folks'll start dropping off puppies next. Are you sure you can handle this place by yourself all summer?"

No, not at all. Abby had only recently mastered the art of getting out of bed every morning. But Reva deserved this break, this chance to follow her dreams after years of helping everyone but herself. "Yes, of course I can handle it." She glanced at the kitchen clock. "Don't you need to leave soon?"

"No hurry. My friend Heather will pick me up after she drops her kids off at school, so rush hour will be over by the time we get into the city. And the New Orleans airport is small enough that I can get there thirty minutes before departure and still have plenty of time. It's all good."

Abby gave Reva a sideways look, but didn't say anything. Abby knew her aunt was excited about her upcoming adventure, but equally afraid of reaching for a long-postponed dream she wasn't sure she'd be able to achieve. She might be stalling, just a little.

"What can I do to help you and your suitcase get out the door?"

"Would you get a big wire crate from storage and set it up for this baby?"

"Sure."

Cradling the purring kitten, Reva followed Abby through the laundry room to the storage closet. "Litter box is in the bottom cabinet, cubby for her to hide in is on the top shelf."

Abby hefted the folded wire crate. "Where should I put it?"

Reva closed her eyes again, doing her animal communication thing. "Not a big fan of dogs—or other cats, either. Wants to be an only cat." Reva smiled and stroked the kitten's head. "You may have to adjust your expectations, little one, just like everyone else in the world."

Not exactly an answer, but Abby knew Reva would get around to it, and she did. "She'll need a quiet place away from the crowd for the first few days. Let's put the crate on top of the laundry room table."

While Abby set up the crate, Reva gave instructions. "Take her to the vet ASAP; she's wormy and needs antibiotics for this road rash. You can use one of the small travel crates for that. But other than the vet visit, keep her in here until next week, Wednesday at the earliest. Then you can move her crate to my worktable in the den. That'll get her used to all the activity around here. When she's had all her kitten shots, you can let her out into the general population."

Abby put a soothing hand on her aunt's arm. "I'll remember." She knew that Reva secretly thought no one else could manage the farm adequately—with good reason. This place was a writhing octopus of responsibilities. Critters to feed, stalls to clean, and two more weeks of school field trips to host before summer break. Even in summer, there would be random birthday parties and scout groups every now and then. No wonder Reva was having a hard time letting go; hence all the detailed instructions on how to handle the newest addition to the farm's family. "I promise I'll take good care of everything."

Reva gave a yes-but nod and a thanks-for-trying smile. "I'll text you a reminder about the kitten, just in case."

Of course you will. Reva had already printed a novel-length set of instructions on everything from animal-feeding to tour-hosting to house-and-barn maintenance. Smiling at Reva's obvious difficulty in releasing the need to control everything in her universe, Abby filled a water bowl from the mop sink and placed it inside the crate next to the food dish. "All set."

"Call me before you make that decision."

"What decision?" Reva had returned to a previous train of thought that had long since left the station in Abby's mind.

"About when to let the kitten out. She might be more squirrelly than she looks. Let me check in with her and make sure she's ready. Don't want to have her hiding under the couch or escaping into the woods through the dog door." Reva paused with a just-thought-of-something look on her face. "But I'd totally trust you to ask this kitten if she's ready to join the herd. This summer at the farm will be a good opportunity for you to practice your animal communication skills."

Right, well. Abby didn't trust herself, even though Reva had been tutoring her since Abby first started spending summers here as a child. "I'll call first. I'd like to keep the training wheels on a little longer if you don't mind."

Reva laughed. "Training wheels are not necessary. You just think you need them. You're a natural at animal communication."

Abby didn't feel like a natural at much of anything these days. The fact that Reva trusted her to run the farm all summer attested more to Reva's high motivation to get her license to care for injured wildlife than to Abby's competency. Three months of an internship at a wild animal refuge in south Florida would give Reva everything she needed to make that long-deferred dream a reality. Abby was determined to help out, even though the responsibility terrified her. It was the least she could do.

Reva tipped her chin toward the open shelves above the dryer. "Put one of those folded towels on the lid of the litter box so she can sit on top of it."

Abby obeyed, and Georgia started barking from outside. "That's probably your ride, Aunt Reva. I've got this, I promise. You don't have to worry." She held out her hands for the kitten.

Reva transferred the purring kitten gently into Abby's cupped palms. The kitten stopped purring, but settled quickly when Abby snuggled it close. "About time for you to go, right?"

Reva gave a distracted nod. "Don't forget to make the vet appointment today. You want to go ahead and get on their schedule for tomorrow, because they close at noon on Saturdays. But call before you go. I don't know why, but everyone at Mack's office has been really disorganized lately. The last time I went in, they had double-booked, and I had to wait over an hour."

"I will make the appointment today, and I'll call before I go."

"Oh, and don't forget to drop that check off at the water department when you're out tomorrow. Those effers don't give you a moment's grace before cutting off the water." A car horn blasted outside.

"I won't forget." Abby put the kitten in the crate and shooed her aunt out the door. "I'd hug you, but I'm all muddy."

"I know I'm forgetting something." Reva glanced around the room one last time. "Oh well. I'll text you if I remember." She leaned in and kissed Abby's cheek. "Bless you for doing this for me."

"I'm glad we can help each other. Don't worry about a thing." As if Reva wasn't the one doing Abby a big favor by giving her a place to stay when even her own parents refused, for Abby's own good. They were completely right when they pointed out that by the age of thirty-three, she should have gotten her shit together.

After all, they'd had good jobs, a solid (if unhappy) marriage, a kid, and a mortgage by that time of their lives.

It wouldn't have helped to argue that up until the moment she didn't, she'd also had a good job (dental office manager), an unhappy relationship (with the philandering dentist), and a kid (the dentist's five-year-old daughter). Okay, so she didn't have a mortgage. Points to mom and dad for being bigger adults at thirty-three. Whoopee. It was a different economy back then.

After Reva left, Abby showered and dressed to meet her first big challenge as the sole custodian of Bayside Barn—ushering in three school buses that pulled through the gates just after 9:00 a.m.

When the deep throb of the buses' motors vibrated the soles of her barn boots, Abby tamped down the familiar flood of anxiety that rose up her gut like heartburn. The feeling of impending disaster arose often, sometimes appearing out of nowhere for no particular reason. Only one of the reasons she'd come to stay at Aunt Reva's for a while. This time, though, she had reason to feel anxious. These three buses held a total of ninety boisterous kindergartners, enough to strike fear into the stoutest of hearts.

Abby hadn't forgotten Reva's warning about the timing of her tenure as acting director of Bayside Barn. Two weeks remained of the school year, and those last two weeks were always the worst; not only did schools schedule more trips then, but the kids would be more excitable and the teachers' tempers would be more frayed.

Abby hurried to get Freddy, the scarlet macaw, from his aviary enclosure. "You can do this," she muttered to herself, remembering the Bayside Barn mission statement that Reva made all the volunteers memorize: *Bayside Barn will save the world, one happy ending at a time, by giving a home to abandoned animals whose unconditional love and understanding will teach people to value all creatures and the planet we share.*

If that wasn't a reason to get over herself and get on with it, nothing was.

Chapter 2

ABBY STROKED FREDDY'S FEATHERS ON THE WAY BACK TO THE parking lot, soothing herself as much as him. She *could* do this. She had helped Aunt Reva host school field trips several times. And five seasoned helpers were here, women who knew the drill from years of experience. The choking sense of anxiety drifted down and hung like a fog, somewhere around the region of her kneecaps.

With the huge parrot perched on her shoulder, Abby joined her helpers—two retirees and three student-teachers from the local college. Each wore jeans and rubber-soled barn boots; each wore a different-colored T-shirt with the Bayside Barn Buddies logo on the front.

The ladies had already directed the bus drivers to park in the gravel lot between the light-blue farmhouse and the bright-red barn. Ninety boisterous kindergartners spilled out of the buses, and the donkeys brayed a friendly greeting over the barn fence. Freddy clung to Abby's shoulder with his talons and hollered in her ear, "Welcome, Buddies!"

The teachers and parent chaperones in the first bus corralled their kindergartners into small groups. The hellions that had spewed from the other two buses yelled and chased each other around the roped-off gravel parking area. Feeling more relaxed now that the field trip experience was underway, Abby gave the kids a minute to get their wiggles out, then removed a gym whistle from her jeans pocket and blew three short, sharp blasts. Everybody froze.

"Listen up." She tried to channel Aunt Reva's stern schoolteacher voice. "Before we can begin, I need each of the teachers and parent chaperones to gather the kids in your group."

After a bit of shuffling, the crowd coalesced into small clusters of five-or-so kids surrounding each of the adults. A small swarm of kids milled around looking worried. Abby held up a hand. "Kids who aren't sure which group you belong to, please line up right here in front of me."

Within five minutes, every child had found the right group, and Abby's helpers handed out color-coded stickers, badges shaped like a sheriff's star surrounded by the words, *I'm a Bayside Barn Buddy*.

Abby blasted the whistle again. "Welcome to Bayside Barn. In a moment, you'll follow me to the pavilion where we'll watch a short video about the animals you will meet here today. Then, each group will go with the guide whose shirt matches your star. Together, you will learn and explore for the rest of the morning. We'll meet back at the pavilion at noon for lunch, and then you'll have another two hours of fun before you head back to school. Sound good?"

Abby allowed the chorus of excited talking to continue another minute. "Okay, everyone. Follow me to the pavilion."

She led the way with Freddy on her shoulder and Georgia walking alongside. A small hand crept into hers. A tiny, pigtailed girl with brown eyes as big as buckeyes skipped beside her. Abby swung the little girl's hand. "Hello there. What's your name?"

"Angelina. I like your bird. I ain't never seen a bird that big. Can I hold him on my shoulder like you're doin'?"

"I'm sorry, Angelina, but that wouldn't be safe. Freddy's a good bird, but if something startled him, he might bite."

"Where'd you get him?"

"All the animals at Bayside Barn came here because their families couldn't keep them."

Angelina stopped skipping and tugged Abby's hand. "My family couldn't keep me, either. Can I come live here, too?"

Abby's heart squeezed with the familiar breathlessness of

regret. Regret for promises she'd made to a child she had loved completely and yet failed to save.

A frazzled-looking woman grabbed Angelina's arm, mumbled an apology, and towed the child back to her group.

Abby kept her eyes on the pavilion and kept walking. The fresh scratches the kitten had made on her hands and belly stung with every movement. But her small pains were worth it, since the kitten was safe and secure in the darkened laundry room with a clean litter box, a soft blanket, and plenty of food and water.

Abandoned kittens could be saved.

Abandoned children, not so easy.

―――――

Quinn backed out from under the kitchen cupboard and shut off the shop vac. He sat back on his heels and listened. *What the hell...?*

He opened the sliding doors and looked across the pea-green pool water to the house next door. Over the tall hedges, he saw the tops of three school buses.

School buses, parked next door?

"Shit." That would account for the high-pitched screams and squeals. What kind of place had he moved next to?

Quinn clenched his jaw and pressed a thumb against his temple that throbbed as if someone had jabbed an ice pick into his head. His decision to sink every penny of his equity money into this place might have been a Very Bad Mistake.

After a lifetime of following his gut and making snap decisions that often had negative (okay, disastrous) consequences, Quinn had recently promised himself that from here on out, he'd write out the pros and cons of any major decision before making it. He'd done that before buying this estate.

Maybe the problem wasn't with his decision-making process. Maybe he was just good at finding gold and spinning it into straw.

He walked down the long gravel drive to the paved road and looked across the blacktop where a sea of yellow-flowering vines stretched to the distant horizon. It had seemed like such a grand idea to buy the crumbling estate across from all this wild extravagance. The invasive cat's-claw vine smothered trees and pulled down structures, creating a thriving and beautiful wasteland, the first of four selling points for the property he planned to flip:

1. Acres of yellow flowers across the street.

2. Bayside view at the back—with the potential for waterfront access.

3. Lonely country road on one side.

4. Only one neighboring property, well hidden behind an evergreen hedge.

He walked past that tall hedge to get a better look at the property next door. A double-panel iron gate stood open, flanking the entrance. A thick stone pillar surrounded an oversize mailbox. Under the mailbox, a brass plaque read:

BAYSIDE BARN

8305 WINDING WATER WAY

The ice pick jabbed into Quinn's skull again.

He remembered hearing about this place when Sean's class went here on a field trip in the third grade. Sean had come home sunburned, exhausted, and overexcited from a day at the barn and the hour-long bus ride to and from his elementary school in New Orleans. Sean had talked nonstop about the experience for the rest of the evening, then fallen asleep at the dinner table. For the rest of the month, he had galloped around the house every afternoon after school, waving a souvenir cowboy hat and yelling, "Go, Bayside Buddies, go!"

The place next door was a damn zoo.

―――――――

Reva stepped onto the horrifyingly long escalator to the ground transportation level, steadied herself as the step unfolded beneath her, then wrestled her too-big suitcase onto the step behind her as it, too, unfolded. She gripped the shuddering plastic handrail and held on, closing her eyes for a blessed moment.

God, she missed her husband.

Grayson had always taken charge of, well, everything. When they traveled, he was the one who made the arrangements, knew where to go and when to be there, and wrangled their luggage along the way.

What the hell was she doing here, so far out of her comfort zone that her heart hadn't stopped pounding since she left the house this morning? Did she even want to do this anymore? Without Grayson by her side, she felt untethered. Her parents were gone. Grayson's brother, Winston, and his wife—Abby's parents—had never warmed up to her. She and Grayson had made the decision not to have children, but to devote their lives to something larger, a mission to help animals. They'd built Bayside Barn together on the homestead he'd inherited from his grandparents.

This had been *their* dream. But was it still *hers*, if it meant doing it all without him? Grayson had been a force of nature, something between an exhilarating whirlwind and an unavoidable undertow. When the neighbors next door had moved into an assisted-living facility, Grayson convinced the city council to buy the land for an animal shelter, which she and Grayson would run. But then Grayson died, and the penny-pinching mayor vetoed the plan. He didn't see the upside of building an official animal shelter when the unofficial one at Bayside Barn worked well enough.

Without a doubt, Grayson's passion and vision would've convinced the mayor to go along. With his whiskey-colored eyes and lopsided grin, he could melt the hardest heart. God, she had loved that man. Still did, always would. He'd been gone almost two years, and Reva was still a little bit pissed off at the universe for letting Grayson's unwavering commitment to physical fitness lead to his own untimely death.

He had always teased her about her lack of interest in physical exercise and healthy eating. He'd poke her soft belly and claim that he would still love her when she got fat from lounging in the pool with a glass of wine while he swam laps. She slept in and rested her other side while he put on his running shoes and logged his five miles each day.

And then came the knock on the door that woke her from a sound sleep the morning that an inattentive driver—

"Hey!" A big hand gripped her arm and steadied her when the escalator steps leveled out and she stumbled over the ledge that devoured each step. Her eyes flew open and she grabbed onto a man's hard shoulder as he dragged her and her suitcase away from the steps that were being swallowed by the floor. "Lady, are you okay?"

She looked into the concerned green eyes of a very tall, very young black man. He still held onto her, and she still held onto him. In fact, she was afraid that if she let go, she might crumple down to the floor. Her ankles felt boneless; her knees felt like Jell-O. "I'm so sorry. I swear I only closed my eyes for a second. I didn't know it would move so fast."

"No worries, lady." His strong, reassuring grip didn't lessen. "You look a little shaky. You okay?"

She held onto his arm and took stock of herself. Steadier, she let go and stepped back. "I'm okay. Thanks for keeping me from falling on my face—or my backside."

"Lucky thing I was standing down here watching you." He

smiled. "Not being a creep or anything; I'm waiting for my girlfriend to come down on her way to baggage claim. I noticed you because your face looked so...peaceful, I guess...like you were thinking of something beautiful."

She felt an answering smile bloom, first in her heart, and then on her lips. "You're right. I was."

The young man moved off to embrace his girlfriend, and Reva headed for the ground transportation exit. For the first time since she'd left the house this morning, she felt like she was doing the right thing, and that Grayson's spirit would support her in fulfilling the dream they had shared. It was only right that Abby should come to Bayside Barn for healing and, in turn, give Reva the space she needed to find a way to move forward in her own life.

In a way, Abby was the child Grayson and Reva never had. Ever since Abby had been old enough to spend the night away from home, she had spent her summers at Bayside Barn. That old homestead was in her bones, and the animals that lived there were her childhood friends. Reva knew that Abby would take care of the farm and the animals as well as Reva could. And maybe the experience would deepen Abby's connection to the animals and allow her to practice her ability to communicate with them telepathically. Reva had shown her how, and though Abby's parents did their best to undo that teaching, Reva knew that Abby possessed the ability.

Abby hadn't embraced her gifts yet, but one day, she would. One day, Abby would receive a communication that couldn't be denied or passed off as her imagination. Reva wished she could do more to help Abby to recognize her abilities. But as Grayson had told her many times, "You can't push the river." She could only toss seeds upon the water and hope they would float to a fertile place that would support their growth.

Still feeling Grayson's presence beside her, Reva wheeled her suitcase out a set of double doors to a curbside pickup lane that smelled of car exhaust and stale cigarette smoke.

At the preappointed spot, a spindly, bored-looking man wearing camo pants and a plain green shirt leaned against a white-paneled van. Reva had expected a vehicle with a logo for the wildlife center on the side, but this looked more like a prison van. All her insecurities and doubts about the wisdom of leaving home for so long rose up to choke her, but she swallowed them down. "Hello?"

Immersed in his cell phone and his cigarette, the van guy seemed not to notice her. He took a slow drag from his cigarette, blew the smoke out sideways, then looked at her through one squinting eye. "Sorry. I'm a little hard of hearing. Come again?"

She spoke a little louder. "Is this the transport van to the wildlife refuge?"

"Yep, and you're the last to load up." He dropped his cigarette and ground it into the pavement with his boot. "You ready?"

She remembered the feeling of being protected and guided by Grayson, and she pulled that feeling around her like a blanket until she almost felt as if his hand rested at her waist. "I'm ready."

The driver hauled her suitcase into the back of the van, then waited while she dug into her purse and brought out a few dollars to plunk into his palm. He pocketed the money and grinned. "Get on in."

The row seats behind the driver were all filled with college-age students, many of whom had backpacks taking up the space beside them. Reva hovered in the van's open doorway. "Hello, everyone. I'm Reva. It's nice to meet y'all."

A chorus of unenthusiastic "hey" and "hi" and "hello" responses were even further diminished by the fact that only one of Reva's fellow passengers managed to look up from their cell phones. But from the middle seat, a pretty girl with purple-tipped dreadlocks waved and smiled. "Hey. I'm Dana. You can sit next to me."

Dana scooted closer to the window and stowed her backpack under the seat. Reva squeezed past the beefy guy with military-short blond hair on the end of the row to take the middle seat.

Startled, he looked up from his phone, then smiled. "Oh, hey." He took out one earbud and moved his long legs out of her way.

Reva got settled, then held out a hand and introduced herself to each of the kids on her row. As the van trundled out of the Miami International Airport complex, the kids in the two other rows looked up from their devices and started chatting with one another. A girl from the back put a hand on Reva's shoulder and introduced herself. A guy from the front turned around and said hi. Feeling more included, Reva relaxed. She reminded herself that kids these days used their phones as a way of coping with social anxiety the way she had once kept her nose buried in a book.

Once the van passed the brightly lit streets and began to bump along dark highways and back roads toward their final destination, everyone disappeared again into their electronic devices. She turned to her own cell phone for solace as well.

Hey, Abby, she typed. My flight landed safely and I'm on my way to the internship. Wish me luck! I hope everything's going well back at the farm. How was the school tour today? How is the new kitten? Did you get an appointment at the vet's office for tomorrow?

She hit Send, then tucked her cell phone into her purse's side pocket. Then she stared out the window at endless pine forests until the lumbering lurch of the van lulled her to sleep.

Quinn put on his headphones, turned up the volume on his playlist, and began the painstaking process of regrouting the vintage floor tiles in the pool-house bathroom.

First, he scraped out the top layer of the old grout with a grout saw—a small, handheld, inefficient tool that made his hands cramp.

The whole time he did it, he fumed.

How in the hell was he going to sell this place for a profit with a damn petting zoo next door? He might've just sunk a bunch of money—the last of his money, in fact—into a horrible mistake. Even after agonizing over all the potential pros and cons, he had failed to uncover a bigger con than his worst imaginings could have conceived of.

He scraped grout until his knees ached from inching along on the hard floor. Then he applied new grout, using a float to smash the gritty goop into the lines and smooth it level.

Why would Delia sell him this place without full disclosure of a deal-breaking drawback? Had she deliberately shown the property on a weekend knowing that weekdays sounded like schoolyard-playground mayhem all day long?

He pulled out one earbud to check if the mayhem was still ongoing.

Yes. The screaming went on all fucking day long.

"Time for a break." He would have to let the grout set for exactly thirty minutes before wiping off the hazy residue. His knees creaked when he stood with all the grace of an elderly monk rising from another round of useless prayers. When he reached out to steady himself on the doorframe, his fingers felt like sand-paper on the smooth painted surface. The grout had sucked all the moisture out of his skin. His hands felt—and looked—like the Sahara in dry season.

He had earned a beer by the nasty green pool. Yes indeed, his crepe-dry fingers assured him, he had.

But the beer he opened by the pool lacked the promise of respite, because any hope of relaxation was swamped by the happy shrieks of children running and playing next door. And, good God, was one of the little heathens climbing the hedge-covered chain-link fence between the two properties?

Quinn stood and stalked to the hedge, which some grimy-faced young boy had just managed to conquer. The kid's triumphant gap-toothed grin faltered a fraction when his eyes locked with Quinn's hostile gaze. "Hello, misther," the kid lisped as his spindly body draped over the hedge's bowing branches. "Don't be mad. I'm just playin' around."

"How 'bout you just play around on the other side of the fence where you're supposed to be? I'd hate to have to tattle to your teacher."

The kid looked over his shoulder and back again. "You don't know my teacher."

"Wanna bet?" Quinn pulled his cell phone from his back pocket and started punching in random numbers. "I know her well enough to know that she'll make you sit by yourself in the bus for the rest of the day while everyone else gets to have fun at the farm."

The boy's eyes opened wide. "Please, misther. Don't tell her. Don't..." He backpedaled and fell off the hedge with an "Oomph."

Quinn stepped onto a sturdy low-hanging branch and looked over the hedge to make sure the kid hadn't been hurt when he fell. Apparently not; all churning elbows and trailing shoelaces, he was sprinting back to the safety of the group.

Quinn hopped off the hedge, then chuckled and took a sip of his beer.

But his mirth was short-lived. If the current commotion next door was any indication, no matter how much money, time, and effort he sank into this place, the perfect buyer he had imagined would never materialize. He had thought that it would be a recently retired couple. His mind's eye conjured the visual of a stout man who enjoyed fishing and a plump woman who enjoyed gardening.

The man would launch his aluminum fishing boat from the adjacent dead-end street that ended in a cracked concrete boat ramp—or from their own private boat dock if Quinn managed to acquire the waterfront land. The woman would sit by the pool and read romance novels. She'd use a monogrammed shovel from Restoration Hardware to plant daylilies in the estate's rich, well-drained soil, an ideal mix of sand and silt washed up from the bay for the last hundred years.

Quinn was pretty sure that neither of those imagined retirees would be enthused about the idea of baby outlaws climbing the hedge, falling into the pool, and drowning so the kids' parents could sue them for everything they'd worked for all their lives.

He sat in the folding stadium chair and kept an eye on the empty hedge. Feeling antsy and unfulfilled, haunted by the image of the perfect retired couple and the futility of renovating a property they'd never decide to purchase, he made a quick decision. No time for making a list of pros and cons; something had to be done. It had to be done now, and it might require drastic measures.

Chapter 3

QUINN HAD INVESTED EVERYTHING IN THIS PLAN TO MOVE here and rebuild his reputation, his life, and his relationship with his son. He could have turned his back on the past, bought a condo in the Keys, and left all his regrets behind. But one thing—one person, his son, to be exact—held him back. If there was any small sliver of a chance that he could be a part of Sean's life, he had to take it.

He dialed the realty office, and some peon answered on the second ring, her voice way too chirpy for his taste. *Blah, blah, blah*—he held the phone away from his ear until she got to the important part: "How may I help you?"

He might have unloaded some of his frustration on the poor receptionist, but whatever. Anyway, within minutes he was speaking with the agent who'd sold him this piece-of-shit property.

"Delia," he roared. "Were you aware..." He went off on her about how he'd gambled everything on his plan to flip this property and make a sorely needed profit. She knew all this already, but it felt good to vent.

To her credit, she listened and said nothing but "Um-hmm, I hear you," until he'd worn himself out talking.

He needed a win. Goddammit, he'd been doing nothing but losing for so long, he needed—no, he deserved—a win. "Look," he finished. "I won't be able to flip this estate—and you won't be able to make the commission you'd been hoping for on the resale—unless we get rid of the petting zoo next door. What do you propose to do about this problem?"

She talked for a while about zoning and variances and grandfathered permissions to keep livestock on land that had been annexed into the city of Magnolia Bay.

"I don't care about any of that." He took another healthy swig of beer. "I just want you to fix the problem. Call City Hall. Circulate a petition. Do whatever you have to do. Just get that damn zoo gone. I have to be able to sell this place to a nice retired couple who can afford to buy it."

"Quinn, I've known you for almost a year." Had sex with him a few times, too. "And I know you don't really mean what you're saying right now. Can't you just talk to your neighbor and work it out?"

"You want me to go over there and say, 'Pretty please, stop making your living the way you have been for the last decade or so?' How well do you think that'll go over?"

Delia whined about the time and effort and red tape involved in rescinding grandfathered permissions to keep farm animals in the city limits.

"I don't care," he said again. "You showed me this place on a quiet Sunday afternoon, and I'll bet you scheduled the showing then for a reason."

"Aw, Quinn, come on. Stop being dramatic."

"Come on yourself, Delia. You never even answer your phone on the weekends. I should have known something was up when you couldn't meet me here during the week."

She declined to respond to that one. "I guess you need to vent, Quinn, so go ahead. I'll listen till you're done."

"Your lack of candor has caused me a big problem, and you need to fix it." If he couldn't sell this place, the money he had squirreled away for renovations wouldn't be worth a thin dime. "Tell you what. I'll pay you a ten-thousand-dollar bonus when you sell this estate for double what I paid for it. That's on top of your normal commission." He paused for a minute to let that sink in. "And remember that other little property you told me about." Quinn gazed out over the landscape where a hundred acres of marshland met the bay. "If and when it goes up for sale, we can both quadruple our profits. Now. Can you, or can you not, make the zoo next door go away?"

He heard her take a breath, then let it out.

"Well?" He took another pull at his beer, only to find that the bottle was empty.

"I'll do what I can," she said. "If I can."

"Fine. I'll trust you to handle it, for your benefit as well as mine."

"I will," Delia answered. "I'll handle it."

"Good. Keep me posted." Now that he had vented, he felt much more relaxed and easygoing than he had a half hour before. He strolled into the pool house, dumped the empty bottle in the kitchen's recycle bin, then went to wipe down the bathroom tiles.

He hummed and scrubbed, clinging to his pie-in-the-sky vision of the retired couple who would enjoy their happily-ever-after lives in the dream home he was determined to create here.

———

That evening, Abby dumped the day's trash bags into the can by the road, thinking about the *For Sale* sign the motorcycle dude had discarded in the weeds in front of the neighboring estate. She had completely forgotten to tell Aunt Reva, and maybe that was a good thing, because Reva deserved at least a few days of bliss before hearing that the animal shelter she'd been campaigning for would never happen. Abby slammed the trash-can lid. "Oh well."

Reva had begged the Magnolia Bay City Council to buy the abandoned estate next door and convert it into a much-needed animal shelter for the city. She had even offered to run the shelter as an extension of Bayside Barn, since all the strays got dumped there, anyway.

Abby looked down at Georgia. "Any bright ideas from the canine quarter?"

Georgia, as usual, was on it. She tunneled through the tall grass toward the downed sign. Her gray speckles and black spots disappeared in the vegetation, but her white-tipped tail waved above the tasseled grasses, setting dandelion seeds free in the warm Louisiana air. After a minute or two of consideration, she came back grinning as if a direct line to the powers that be assured her everything would be okay.

Abby wasn't so sanguine, but Reva's dog encouraged her to take the long view. "You think the city will buy the marshland behind here instead?" Not likely, since the bayside marshland behind the estates on this road wasn't for sale. In addition, the water-soaked bog filled with snakes and alligators was unsuitable for anything but a great view unless someone had a fortune to spend on fill dirt.

In other words, the land was unavailable, unsuitable, unattainable. Sort of like the men in Abby's life.

Bored with the ongoing conundrum, Georgia crossed the blacktop and sniffed at a tangle of smothering vines that edged the easement. While beautiful, cat's-claw could strangle every living thing for miles, and it had made a good start here.

Georgia growled and peered into the vine-covered forest with her hackles up.

"What's with the mean fur?" Abby imagined a pair of predatory gold eyes staring through the vines, watching. A chill poured through her. The fine hairs on her arms rose and she shivered. *Cat walking over her grave*, Reva would've said.

Abby scolded herself the way her mom always had. "Abby Curtis, your imagination is as wild as your hair. There are no cougars or wolves in Louisiana."

The eerie feeling of being watched wasn't just Abby's imagination, though. Georgia felt it, too. The little dog barked at whatever was hiding in the cat's-claw, threatening it with a don't-make-me-come-in-there-and-get-you tone.

"Come on, girl," Abby coaxed. "Let's go home."

Without warning, Georgia darted into the forest, sounding an alarm that would make most animals exit the scene immediately. But Georgia's barking came from a fixed location now. God only knew what poor creature cowered on the receiving end of her scolding. Not more kittens; Georgia never barked at cats. Probably a snake...

Abby's ever-present stream of worry escalated into a roaring river of panic. "Georgia!"

———

Wolf sat on his haunches under the canopy of vines. The little multicolored dog shot into the cat's-claw forest and charged at him. Hackles raised, she lowered her copper eyebrow spots into a fierce scowl and growled. "You don't belong here."

Wolf looked away, showing deference.

Georgia advanced. "What are you doing here? Go away."

Wolf hunkered down and crawled backward, retreating farther into the shadows. He refused to meet the challenge in her intelligent brown eyes, but he tried to use his body language to send a message of peace. "I won't hurt you."

"You aren't supposed to be here," she insisted. "Go home."

He eased back until his tail brushed the front wall of the half-roofed house hidden beneath the grasping vines. He'd been sheltering here ever since his human caretaker drove him far from home and shoved him off the back of the truck.

Discarded in disgrace.

He didn't understand why, even after days of hunger and thirst and thinking, thinking, thinking.

The woman's voice called out. "Georgia. Get back here, now." Beneath the command was fear, concern, love. His chest felt as heavy as the water-filled doormat he had once—in his exuberant puppyhood—dragged off the porch and torn up.

The dog named Georgia looked back but didn't retreat. "You don't belong here. Go home."

Wolf lowered his elbows to the ground and flattened himself in submission. He sent a silent message to Georgia. "I can't go home. I am being punished. My people left me here, and I think they will come back for me. I have to wait."

Georgia sat, panting. "What did you do wrong?"

Wolf didn't know. He waited for Georgia to ask a different question he might know the answer to.

"Georgia," the woman's voice called out, still high-pitched with anxiety but softer and sweeter than before. "Girlfriend, what are you doing in there?"

Her voiceless reply: "I am talking to the gold-eyed dog-thing."

So. She could tell he wasn't fully dog or fully wolf. She turned her fierce gaze on him, but the white tip of her thick brown tail flickered a greeting.

"Georgia." The woman's voice sounded sharp again, the tone veering between fear and love. "Get back here."

Georgia stood. "Abby is calling me. I do what I want, but it is time for me to go. You can stay." She turned tail and trotted back to the woman.

Wolf put his head on his paws and ignored the hungry rumbling of his belly.

———

With a last parting shot in the one-sided argument, Georgia bounded out of the cat's-claw, her gray speckled coat covered in damp yellow petals.

Abby's concern evaporated. "Did you tell 'em?"

Georgia sneezed, a gesture that looked like an emphatic *yes*.

"Good. Can we please go home now?" Abby waited for Georgia to trot past, then closed the wrought-iron gate and fastened the padlock. "What in the world were you barking at?"

Georgia danced around Abby's feet, whining and yipping as if she had important information to share.

Reva claimed that anyone could communicate with animals, and she'd given Abby a hundred-thousand short tutorials. But as Reva had often said, practice and trust were essential ingredients, and Abby had to admit that she hadn't provided either of them. So if Georgia was trying to say something, Abby didn't get it. She petted the good dog's silky head. "Whatever it was, I'm sure you took care of it."

But an image of watchful gold eyes made Abby's shoulders twitch. Georgia barked, tail wagging, reminding Abby that daylight was fading fast. "You're right. It's time to feed critters and toss the ball."

In the big barn with its hand-painted sign—*Welcome, Bayside Barn Buddies*—above the open double doors, Abby poured feed into various bowls and buckets, humming along with the faint melody coming from the new neighbor's stereo. It played loud enough for her to hear the tune, but not loud enough for her to recognize the words. After seeing him on that motorcycle, dressed in black leather, she might have expected him to be the sort to play abrasive music with abusive lyrics loud enough to rattle the windows.

Maybe he would be a good neighbor to Aunt Reva, who had never quite fit in here in Magnolia Bay. Though she had married a born-and-bred resident of the area, her hippie clothing and unusual talent of telepathic animal communication made most people around here act a little standoffish. When Reva's husband died two years ago, her chance of blending into the clannish community died, too. A good neighbor next door would be a blessing for Reva, and Abby should do whatever she could to facilitate that relationship.

She should bake a loaf of the secret-family-recipe pound cake and offer it to the new guy as a welcome to the neighborhood. It's what Reva would have done. Even though she wasn't really accepted around here, Reva remained unfailingly polite to everyone.

Removing her barn boots, Abby set them in the boot tray inside the back door, then padded into the old-fashioned farm kitchen and poured a glass of merlot.

Georgia sat, front paws in prayer position, a blue tennis ball in her mouth.

"You're right. It's ball time. But let's check on the kitten first." Abby went into the white-tiled laundry room with Georgia at her heels. The kitten growled and spat and hissed, all the purring and promise of yesterday forgotten.

"Baby," Abby chided. When she stuck her fingers through the bars, hoping to calm the kitten with a caress, it scrambled into the cardboard hideout, knocking over the food dish on the way. Georgia set the ball down long enough to eat the scattered kibble off the floor. Then she snatched up the ball and streaked through the dog door onto the pool patio.

"Right behind you," Abby promised. She set her wineglass on the dryer and stripped naked, then threw her clothes in the washer and turned it on. She took her swimsuit off the hook by the door—and had an epiphany. She was alone here! She could go naked if she wanted to. She hung the swimsuit back up and grabbed a towel. Feeling a slightly naughty sense of exhilaration at her secret indecency, she carried her wine outside and eased into the gently bubbling hot tub. Naked. Totally and completely naked.

It seemed like she was the only human in the universe.

So why couldn't she manage to relax? She ducked underwater to get her hair wet, then slid up onto the seat, tipped her head back, and willed her tense body to let go. Every muscle, every tendon, every molecule was clenched like a fist ready for battle.

Georgia dropped the ball and nosed it toward Abby's wineglass. Abby tossed the ball a few dozen times, then plunked it into the hot tub where Georgia wouldn't go. "No more playing."

Georgia settled on her haunches, elbows to the ground and feet pointing straight ahead in the classic cattle-dog pose. Eyeing the floating ball the way her ancestors had once eyed flocks of sheep, she waited patiently for Abby to make the next move.

Abby sipped her wine and surveyed her aunt's domain. Three—no, four—cats lounged within sight: Max, the big, gray tabby; Princess Grace, the elegant Siamese mix; Glenn, the black-and-white-spotted feral with a notched ear; and Jessie, another gray tabby with a notched ear. The others were all off doing cat things. Across the fence that separated the parking lot from the blue clapboard farmhouse, the petting-zoo animals rested in the big, red barn. Down the hill toward the bay, an owl hooted, answered by its mate a short distance away.

If Reva had been here, she would have told Abby what the owls were saying. "I'm here," probably. And "I'm here, too." Animals weren't always running off at the mouth like humans. Most often their calls back and forth were quick check-ins establishing location and well-being.

Family keeping up with family.

Something her parents had never seemed interested in. When Abby spent summers with Reva and Grayson, her parents hardly ever called. When Abby graduated from high school, they exchanged their three-bedroom house for a top-of-the-line home on wheels and offered to pay a year of storage fees for her stuff until she could "get the hang of adulting." When she graduated from college with a business degree, they didn't come; they'd been too busy avoiding the hot Louisiana summer by touring every campsite in Oregon.

When Abby cut herself adrift from her own life, she should've known to ask Reva for help first. Reva was a generous and forgiving Mother Earth, while Abby's father (Reva's brother-in-law) made Narcissus look like a philanthropist. Abby's mother, well, she was more like a ghost. Even when she was there, she wasn't really. Winston Curtis was the dense magnetic planet that kept his wife's dimming star from spinning off into oblivion. Whatever he said, she echoed, because she wasn't a whole person without him. Full of their customary thimbleful of compassion, they had advised Abby to tighten her bootstraps.

So when she found herself sitting in a leaking dinghy watching her bridges burn behind her, and her parents had given unhelpful advice but no actual help, Abby had asked her aunt Reva for a patch of uncharred earth on which to land. "Yes, of course," her aunt had replied without skipping a heartbeat. "You're welcome to stay for as long as you like."

Family taking care of family.

Abby thought of the little girl she'd met today—Angelina—and hoped that if the child couldn't be with her family, at least she lived with people who loved her. Everyone, human or animal, deserved a home in which they knew unconditional love and acceptance. Abby thought of the child she'd had to leave behind in order to save herself, and swallowed a mouthful of wine along with the worry and regret that never left her mind. That it wasn't *her* child didn't make it better.

With the comforting bulk of the house behind her, Abby leaned her head back and let her feet float up. A couple of early stars winked on in the deepening sky, and solar lights glittered off to the left, lighting a flagstone path to the aviary and the pavilion. Straight ahead and down the hill, a fenced pasture surrounded the swimming hole whose brown water glittered dimly as the sun's last ray disappeared beyond the horizon.

The granddaddy oak Abby remembered from every summer of her childhood stood guard over the wooden dock. Fifty feet up into its fern-covered branches, a tire swing's hefty rope was tied so older kids could swing far out over the pond before letting go.

Beyond, rolling pastureland led down to a wide strip of marshland that bordered the bay a few miles away. A boat's motor made a whining sound in the distance; someone night-fishing or checking trotlines.

Abby heard a munching sound and peered into the gathering shadows. At the property line between her aunt's farm and the new neighbor's estate, two long, curving horns bobbed in rhythm—a goat with his head buried in the privacy hedge. "Gregory." Out again, that bad, adventurous goat. "You could teach Houdini a thing or two."

Ignoring the goat—she could figure out how he'd gotten out of the pasture and into the yard tomorrow—Abby stood and set her empty wineglass next to her towel. The cooling night air tingled on her bare skin, raising goose bumps. She stepped onto the diving board, bounced a few times, and dove into the cool water.

Quinn sat by the pool in the gathering dusk. The frogs' mating song blended nicely with his new favorite song, "Any Man in America."

He felt kind of bad that tomorrow he would destroy the frogs' happy habitat with pool chemicals and a scrub broom. But maybe frogs also needed to learn about getting too comfortable and feeling too safe.

The Blue October song ended. Silence…then a strange rustling noise in the privacy hedge. Was crazy Old Ms. McDonald snooping on him? He eased to his feet and padded over, planning to surprise the old bat.

The hedge shook. He pulled apart a couple branches and met two blue eyes with strange-shaped pupils. He jumped back. *What the fork?*

He bent down and encountered a devil's face, complete with horns. "*Maaa*," the thing bellowed.

"I'll be damned." Quinn picked up a stick and poked it through the hedge-covered chain-link fence, right into the goat's nose.

"*Maaaaa…*" The goat bolted, leaving a perfect, goat-head-sized peephole into his new neighbor's backyard.

The sparkling-clean pool glowing blue, lit from within.

The kidney-shaped patio surrounded by globe lights.

His next-door neighbor's perfectly proportioned body diving naked into the swimming pool.

"Whoa." Quinn stumbled back, tripped over something, and fell on his ass.

He wouldn't be able to think of her as Old Ms. McDonald anymore.

Chapter 4

IT DIDN'T SURPRISE QUINN THAT HE HAD TROUBLE FALLING asleep that night, even though he had worked hard all day. Visions of his neighbor's slim, toned body and wavy brown hair followed him into fitful dreams.

In the first dream, she popped up from his frog-filled pool and wrapped her green-scaled mermaid arms around his neck. Pulling him into the murky depths, she showed him her magical cave of hidden delights. He knew she intended to keep him there forever, and he wanted to stay, until he realized with a shock that he couldn't breathe underwater.

Lungs convulsing, he broke free and kicked for the surface, but strong tendrils of seaweed dragged him down. He hacked at the seaweed, which turned into the dismembered arms and grasping fingers of all the other men she had lured under and destroyed.

He woke gasping for air, his legs tangled in the stiff, dye-smelling sheets on his new king-size bed. He got up and staggered to the kitchen, where he drank some water and shook off the lingering shreds of the dream's strange eroticism. When he went back to bed, sleep eluded him at first. He flipped and flopped like a gutted fish until the deep-throated burp of mating bullfrogs sang him back to sleep.

In the next dream, the woman next door wore the same yellow bathrobe and cowboy boots he'd seen her in this morning. She stood beside his bed, her hawklike eyes devouring him, but he didn't care. He knew she had some kind of mojo that was working on him, but he lacked the power to resist whatever magic she possessed.

Willing to die, he flung back the sheets.

She dropped the yellow robe and straddled him, her muddy boots digging into the new mattress. She rode him hard, waving a cowboy hat and yelling "Go, Bayside Buddy, go!"

Exhausted, he woke after dawn, disturbed by the strident wails of restless donkeys. He kicked free of the twisted sheets and sat on the edge of the bed.

Maybe he should admit defeat, sell this place for exactly what he'd paid, and go to work for another builder. Who cared about all the time and money spent getting his contractor's license? Who cared about crafting his own business as an independent contractor? Who cared about polishing up this old gem of an estate and reselling at a hefty profit?

Unfortunately, he cared.

Flipping this place and making a profit wasn't just about flipping this place and making a profit. It was about rebuilding his relationship with his son. It was about showing his ex-wife that she'd made an even bigger mistake than he had. It was about making a new life for himself in Magnolia Bay and establishing his construction company as a valued member of the business community.

He couldn't quit now. He couldn't quit ever. He had to make this thing work.

While the coffee perked, he ate a slice of cold, leftover pizza and slipped a granola bar into his back pocket for later. With a decent playlist drowning out the zoo sounds, he carried a strong cup of black coffee and a legal pad outside. He sat in a folding stadium chair by the murky green pool and made his to-do list.

1. Get the truck and empty out the crappy apartment.

2. Drop off the apartment key.

3. Unload the truck.

4. Buy pool chemicals, weed killer, telescoping loppers.

5. Buy mortar and sand to fill cracks in the brick facing.

With a plan in place and caffeine in his system, Quinn felt slightly less like killing himself. He battled through a tangle of trees and vines and weeds to the property's edge. The distant view of the bay reassured him that he hadn't made a horrible mistake. Despite the noisy neighbor, this place sparkled with possibility and had the potential to triple or even quadruple his investment.

As long as he could find a buyer who suffered from significant hearing loss.

———

Abby woke to the donkeys' loud, discontented braying. Disoriented, she sat up and glanced at the clock. "Shit." She rocketed out of bed like a pebble from a slingshot, dumping Georgia and Max the tabby onto the floor.

Nine a.m. already. The donkeys complained for good reason. Saturday morning coffee by the pool would have to wait. Her phone, plugged in by the bedside, displayed a slew of text messages, not that she had time to view or respond to them right now.

And wasn't there something else she was supposed to do today? She looked around the bedroom and chewed on a fingernail, waiting for her brain to kick in—and it did, sending a flood of adrenaline to her belly. *Shit!* She'd forgotten to call the vet's office yesterday. "Calm down," she said out loud. "It's not the end of the world."

The vet closed at noon on Saturdays, and that was their busiest day of the week. It would be too late to get an appointment now. Maybe that was just as well; it would take till noon to get the morning chores done. She promised herself that she'd make the call first thing Monday morning.

In the Daffy Duck boxer shorts and faded tank top she'd slept in, she put on barn boots and headed outside with Georgia and Max. When she walked into the barn, the hollering donkeys and ponies hollered even louder. A swarm of cats leaped onto the wide shelf above the food bins, yowling in anticipation.

Moving quickly, Abby scooped food from painted metal bins into matching color-coded buckets. (Aunt Reva had left nothing to chance.) Abby filled a green five-gallon bucket for the goats and sheep, a red one for the geese, chickens, ducks, and peacocks. Then, the single-buckets: blue for each of the ponies. A pink one for the bunnies' communal bowl. Purple for the mini zebu, and orange for the potbellied pig.

She fed the whining donkeys first. Outside in the chicken yard, she scattered chicken scratch and left the gate open so the chickens and ducks and peacocks could spend the day foraging. She fed the aviary birds and hosed down their concrete floors, then tossed flakes of hay into the pastures and let the barn animals out to graze.

Sweaty and tired, Abby decided shoveling poop could wait until after coffee. She set up the coffeepot and hit the button to perk. She had just removed her boots when a deep bellow of human rage galvanized Georgia, who sprinted across the yard and squeezed under the fence. A second later, her sharp barking joined the new neighbor's angry expletives. Abby ran barefoot along the hedgerow fence toward Georgia's hysterical barking.

A donkey's cry made her heart race. How had Elijah gotten into the neighbor's yard? Then she saw how. "Oh shit." She climbed over a section of crumpled wire fencing and burst through a thick tangle of vegetation into a scene of mayhem and hysteria.

The new neighbor charged toward Elijah and flung his hands in the donkey's face. "Shoo. Get out."

Elijah reared, eyes rolling, ears pinned back. Abby grabbed a stout stick and rushed to defend her aunt's traumatized donkey. "Stop! You're scaring him."

Bawling in terror, Elijah veered around the man's waving arms and leaped over the crumpled wire fence. Georgia—all thirty pounds of short, snarling protection—stood between Abby and the crazy neighbor.

This mean man would not be getting any of the secret-family-recipe pound cake.

Holding the stick out like a sword, Abby snatched Georgia up one-handed and held her close. While she and the dog both trembled with reaction, Abby glared at her aunt's new neighbor. "What is wrong with you? You scared that poor donkey half to death."

The stupid neanderthal crossed his muscled arms in front of his wide chest. "Me? You're asking what's wrong with me? That big moose knocked me down!"

"Moose? Elijah is just a baby! He would never—"

"He stole my granola bar!"

"He stole…what?"

The man glanced at her stick. Like a warrior calculating his advantage in an armed conflict, he advanced, his expression fierce and his blue eyes so wild she could see the whites all around. "Your baby—who is the size of a moose, by the way—came onto my property, knocked me down, bit me on the ass, and stole a granola bar from my back pocket."

Georgia trembled in Abby's arms and growled in promised retribution should the man come close enough for her to reach.

Abby clutched the dog tighter. "I'm sorry if he hurt you. But you didn't have to scare him."

"Your ass is fine. Mine's the one that's been wounded." He lunged forward and wrenched the stick from her hand, then tossed it aside, ignoring Georgia's escalating growl. "And yet you're planning to attack *me* with a stick?"

A hysterical giggle tickled the back of Abby's throat. She bit her lips and patted Georgia. Laughing in the face of an animal-hating psychopath—maybe not the best move. "Yes, you're right. I'm sorry. I hope your…" She smothered an irreverent snort. "I hope your ass will recover."

His lips twitched, a quickly stifled smile. "I guess it will, eventually." He let the smile have its way, and it transformed his face from surly to sexy. Straight white teeth and deep blue eyes contrasted with deeply tanned skin. His sun-bleached brown hair hadn't been combed this morning; he looked like a man who'd just tumbled out of bed and wouldn't mind getting right back in, given sufficient motivation.

Not that she was interested in providing any such motivation. Hadn't she learned her lesson? Hadn't losing everything—her job, her self-respect, and the child she'd come to love—hadn't that experience taught her anything?

It most certainly had. She was done with men. Done.

He crossed unfairly muscular arms over unfairly toned abs. "Enjoying the view?"

Her face heated. "Well enough." She couldn't deny that she'd been staring. But her appreciation of his well-developed form was purely academic.

"Only fair, I guess." He swept an appreciative glance from her bare feet to her heated cheeks. His blue eyes shining with humor, he trapped her gaze in his. "I bought this place for the view, but I didn't know until recently what a bargain I was getting."

"Oh?" She glanced down at her dirt-smeared attire, a getup not likely to inspire such a flattering comment. Had he seen her yesterday with her robe gaping open? Or worse… Had he seen her skinny-dipping last night?

Nah. It would be impossible to see through that thick hedge. As usual, Abby was letting her anxiety take over her mind and churn out scenarios of disaster. *Disasterizing*, Reva called Abby's newfound tendency to imagine the worst possible outcome and then dwell on it.

Georgia wiggled to get down, and Abby obliged. The dog

toddled over and sniffed the guy's boots, then the hem of his jeans. Tail wagging, she returned to Abby and sat.

"Oh." Georgia had introduced herself; Abby should do the same. Without Georgia in her arms, Abby became uncomfortably aware of her unbound breasts thinly covered by the sloppy tank top, but etiquette demanded that she step forward and offer her hand. "I'm Abby. This is my aunt's place, but I'm in charge for the summer while she attends a summer internship to—"

Abby cut herself off. She was babbling, giving too much information that he didn't care to hear. Another symptom of the overwhelming anxiety that had plagued her after one poor decision had derailed her entire life.

She tried again to act more like a normal person and less like a semihysterical nincompoop. "Welcome to the neighborhood."

He took her hand and smiled into her eyes. "I'm Quinn. Thanks for the welcome, unconventional as it was."

His touch ignited something inside her: a tiny flame she thought had been extinguished. A flame that needed to stay extinguished until she gained some control over her own life. She withdrew her hand. "I'd better get back."

She hobbled barefoot over the stick-covered ground toward the crumpled fence. Without the flood of adrenaline that had propelled her here, the skinned-up soles of her bare feet flinched at every step.

His hand at her elbow offered support. "Are you okay?"

She smiled up at him. "Yep, yep, yep. I always run around barefoot in briars. You should see the soles of my feet. Tough as shoe leather." Her mind cringed at her runaway mouth. *Shut up. Shut. Up.*

He escorted her to the fence and helped her step over. Georgia slipped through a gap underneath.

"I'm very sorry that Elijah trespassed onto your property and knocked you down. I owe you a granola bar."

He grinned. "Chocolate chip, please."

From their respective sides of the fence, Abby stretched the crumpled wire while Quinn straightened the bent metal posts. Working together, they reattached a few fence clips, but most had been lost to the dirt. "This should hold for now," she said. "I'll fix it for real later."

"I'll be happy to help. Just let me know when."

"Thanks. I will." All she wanted right now was to stagger inside, doctor her damaged feet, and sort out the swirl of emotions that had been stirred up by her aunt's sexy new neighbor.

Quinn trudged to the pool house, pressing a fist into the knotted muscles surrounding his lower spine. Much as he appreciated the appearance of his surprisingly attractive neighbor (or neighbor's niece…whatever), he could have done without the equine attack that prompted the meeting.

He chuckled at the memory of Abby's barefooted ferocity—ready to do battle in Daffy Duck boxers and a barely there tank top. With her hazel eyes flashing, her cheeks on fire, and a wild cloud of honey-brown hair tumbling over her shoulders, she tempted him to forget how much damn trouble women could be.

In the bathroom, he lowered his boxer-briefs, then twisted around in front of the mirror to assess the damage. Black-and-blue hoofprints marred his lower back. His left butt cheek sported burgundy-and-purple bite marks.

"Admiring your backside?"

At the snide tone of his ex-wife's voice, Quinn snatched up his jeans so quickly his underwear rolled into an uncomfortable wad around his hips. He met her dark eyes in the bathroom mirror. "Melissa, I don't recall inviting you in." And he had never *admired his backside*. Hers, yes. That was what had gotten him into this whole mess—the mess that was his life—in the first place.

He reached back and slammed the bathroom door in her face. She'd rejected him, not the other way around. But that didn't mean she could sashay back into his life whenever she took a notion. "What are you doing here," he yelled through the closed door.

"I can't have Sean coming here until I know it's safe."

Until she knows it's safe. Right. As if he'd do anything to endanger his own son, who at fifteen was nearly as tall as Quinn and could handle his own self in any case. Quinn readjusted his underwear and buttoned his jeans. Following his therapist's advice, he closed his eyes and counted ten cleansing breaths before he wrenched open the bathroom door.

Dressed to impress in a pin-striped girl-suit that impressed him more than he wished it did, Melissa stood with a smirk on her expertly painted face. "You look like hell."

Another deep breath allowed him to walk past his ex-wife into his small but clean kitchen. With determined civility, he poured water on the fireworks she seemed equally determined to ignite. He knew he had a lot to atone for, so as his therapist suggested, he let her snarky comments slide. They both had to work through their anger and resentment in whatever way worked for them.

For him, it was a determination to keep his mouth shut in the short term. In the long term, he planned to make a fortune he could flap in her face like a red flag.

For her, it was a determination to show him what he was missing in the short term. In the long term, she planned to get along better without him than she had with him.

She had the added secret weapon of snark, but he had to give her that advantage. He'd been absent when she needed him, so she'd learned to take care of herself, then kicked him to the curb when he lost everything. He understood her grievance and was willing to pay the price, but still, it stung. "Would you like a drink?"

Melissa kicked off her red-soled high heels and flung herself onto his new gray couch. "What've you got?"

He opened the refrigerator. "OJ, Coke, and V-8."

"I won't be here that long. I just wanted to see where Sean will be staying next weekend, if he decides to come."

If he decides to come. As if the kid would have any choice if his mother even pretended to uphold the court's visitation ruling. Quinn popped the top on a V-8 and sucked it down, then tossed the empty can into the trash. He knew better than to engage, but his ability to maintain detachment had its limits. "Feel free to look around."

"Already did that, thanks." She slipped into her shoes and stood. "Can't say I approve of all the prepackaged food in your cupboards, but I guess it won't kill him to eat junk a few days out of the month."

Quinn bit back a scathing comment. Proud he'd managed to keep his fool mouth shut, he followed her out and watched her wobble across the gravel in her high heels, then slide into a shiny, red BMW M6 convertible and drive away.

Wolf watched the man walk around the corner of the house and stand by the frog pool, his shoulders slumped, his energy deflated. Wolf hid under the hedge fence that enclosed the farm with its locked gate and all the tasty animal smells. The man glanced in his direction, and Wolf lowered himself to the ground, blending with the leaf clutter beneath the hedge's straggling branches.

The human didn't seem threatening now; not like he had earlier today when he yelled at the panicked donkey who had trespassed. Wolf had watched the commotion from a thicket of brush, ready to defend his new friend Georgia.

But he had made a terrible mistake before by protecting his family when his help wasn't welcome. He hoped his family would return for him, but he didn't deserve it yet. He had to reconcile the two halves of his nature and understand what his human family expected of him, even if it didn't make sense.

He didn't know exactly what he'd done wrong. The whole messy situation had become jumbled in his memory. But even though the details of the incident had blurred in his mind, the ultimate conclusion remained crystal clear.

Out of love, he had made a mistake.

That meant love was dangerous.

Birds flitted among the leaves above his head; a bright-red pair scolded him from the nest they were building. When the man went inside, Wolf would catch one of those birds and fill his shrinking belly. He made that promise to his growling stomach. Then he closed his eyes and brought his energy down low so the man wouldn't sense him lying in wait for a chance to drink, and maybe also to eat.

Every evening, Wolf drank from the green pool and caught frogs to eat. The bitter taste of frog skin turned his saliva to foam, but the meat and bones and entrails tasted no different than that of a rabbit or rat or mouse. Wolf hardly remembered the taste of the crunchy kibble he had eaten at home.

The wind shifted, a warm breeze blowing along the ground. Wolf lifted his nose and caught the scent of rabbits behind the fence. He had searched for a way in, but failed. He could have snagged a small goat this morning while the fence was down. But the people would have seen him, and humans had strange attitudes about which animals were okay to eat and which were off-limits.

Safety lay in hunting only at night when people hid behind solid walls and dark windows. Light windows meant people might still venture outside. Dark windows meant they would stay inside until morning. Wolf's hungry stomach made it hard to wait for safety, but he knew he must.

By the time the man went inside, the birds had flown into a tall tree. Wolf crawled low along the hedge, ran to the green pool to satisfy his thirst with a few quick laps, then streaked across the road to his hiding place in the cat's-claw forest. In the cool, green shade, he sprawled on his side, closed his eyes, and waited for sleep to silence his hunger. Tonight, when the sun slipped over the horizon, he would hunt.

Chapter 5

THAT EVENING, WITH CHORES DONE, REVA'S TEXT RESPONDED to, and a pound cake baked, Abby assembled her peace offerings in an old wicker basket that she'd found stashed among others above her aunt's kitchen cabinets. A bottle of sparkling cider paired with two cheap wineglasses from Dollar Tree; cheese, olives, and fancy crackers; the pound cake wrapped in a new dish towel and tied with twine; and as promised, a chocolate-chip granola bar.

Part of her hoped he wouldn't be home and she'd be able to leave the basket outside his door. She had included a handwritten note on Bayside Barn stationery that she found in her aunt's rolltop desk:

> To Quinn,
> Please accept my attempt at a more conventional welcome to the neighborhood than the one you received this morning.
>
> Abby Curtis
> P.S. Sorry about my ass biting yours.

The nagging, familiar voice of social anxiety whispered, reminding her of his cryptic comment about *the view* that made her suspect he'd seen more of her skin than he should have.

Instead of letting worry have its way, she went into the laundry room and tossed a scrap of twine into the crate for the new kitten to play with. This time, the kitten didn't flee for cover. Maybe it was beginning to realize that Abby was trying to help. She had doctored the road rash with Betadine and a thin film of Neosporin, and already it was healing up nicely.

In the kitchen, she gave Max the tabby a cat treat. "Please stay off the kitchen counter while I'm gone."

Sure thing, she imagined Max saying, though his slant-eyed smirk told her she shouldn't believe him. So much for all the things Reva had tried to teach her about animal communication. If all males were liars, why bother?

Abby glanced at her reflection in the sliding glass doors. Dressed in a leaf-print dress that brought out the green flecks in her hazel eyes, she looked well enough. But she hoped she hadn't overdone it by curling her hair and wearing mascara and clear lip gloss.

She wasn't interested in Quinn—she knew better by now than to be lured in by a pretty face and a rock-hard body—but she didn't want him to judge her unfavorably, either. She didn't want to look like a slob, but she also didn't want to look as if she'd tried too hard. Abby wished she could absorb a little of her aunt's complete disregard for what other people thought of her.

Abby had been that way herself once, but after trusting completely and then losing everything that mattered, she couldn't find her way back. Her recent tendency to worry about everything insisted that she doubt herself.

Georgia barked.

"Okay." Abby picked up the basket and a tiny wisp of courage. "I'm coming."

The setting sun glowed orange over the bay when she and Georgia walked along the hedge and through the iron gates of Bayside Barn. Abby propped one side of the gate open, then she and Georgia crossed the easement to the neighbor's property. The dilapidated house was dark, so they went around back, and Abby tapped on the sliding glass door of the pool house, where the glow of interior lighting indicated a human presence.

Charcoal-gray curtains had been pushed aside. The ceiling fan's globe light revealed brand-new furnishings. A gray couch and rug and overstuffed armchair, a distressed barn-wood coffee table and end tables, a flat-screen TV mounted on the wall across from the couch. No throw pillows, no lamps, no pictures on the walls.

Georgia whined and looked back toward the farm.

"No. We're doing this."

The new neighbor walked into the room shirtless, wearing jeans slung low on his hips and headphones in his ears. The headphones' yellow cord trailed down his toned chest and washboard abs, then twined around his waist and disappeared into his back pocket.

"Lord above, Georgia. Would you look at that?"

Unimpressed, Georgia whined and pawed Abby's leg.

"No, I said. No."

Realizing that he must not have heard the knock, Abby waved. But he kept going to the small kitchen and opened the fridge. She tapped on the glass door again. He took out a beer and turned, then saw her. His eyes opened wide. He set the beer aside, pulled out his headphones, and opened the sliding glass door. "Hey. Is there a goat in my pool or something?"

Georgia ran inside and leaped onto a chair.

"Georgia, no." Abby felt a blush spread up her neck and into her cheeks. "You weren't invited."

"It's fine." He stepped away from the door. "Come on in."

Abby handed over the basket. "This is a housewarming/apology basket." She couldn't help but notice the hoof-shaped bruises on his lower back. "I'm sorry Elijah hurt you. I'm sure he didn't mean to, but he can't resist sweet-tasting treats." Out of breath with anxiety, she powered through her prepared greeting. "I hope we can pretend this morning never happened and start over again."

He set the basket on the coffee table and held out a hand. "Quinn Lockhart."

She put her hand in his. "Abby Curtis, house-sitting for my aunt Reva. Welcome to the neighborhood."

"Thank you, Abby." His fingers wrapped around hers, his grip strong but gentle, his palm callused but warm. Up close, blue eyes the color of new denim smiled into hers. His touch and his smile melted the crusty outer layer of her anxiety.

He let go of her hand. "Have a seat while I put on a shirt."

Abby perched on the couch, crossed her legs, then uncrossed them. She inhaled and blew out a deep breath to release another layer of anxiety. The room smelled of fresh paint, newly dyed fabric, and recently milled wood.

Georgia's restless gaze tracked something outside the glass door. She whined, a worried furrow between her brows.

Abby leaned forward. "You see something out there?"

Quinn came into the room wearing a plain white T-shirt that wasn't too tight but still somehow clung to every muscle. He sat beside her on the couch and slid the basket closer. "Hmmm." He held up the bottle of cider. "This looks interesting."

Abby was more of a wine girl herself, but after twisting and turning over the decision of what to bring, she'd settled on cider, in case the new neighbor didn't drink anything containing alcohol. "I hope you like it."

He set the two glasses on the coffee table and opened the bottle. "Anything I share with you will be better than a lonely beer by myself."

Smooth talker. The sort she'd already fallen for once too often. "Please don't feel obligated to share. I meant it as a gift, not an intrusion." Her nervousness lifted her like an overfilled helium balloon. She half stood, then sat again.

Since she'd moved in with her aunt this spring, she had learned to handle hundreds of school kids along with their adult teachers and chaperones. But social situations requiring small talk still made her palms sweat. "I only came to welcome you to the neighborhood and apologize for Elijah's rude behavior this morning. I'm very sorry about the whole thing."

He poured cider into the two glasses and handed one to her. "Apology accepted, incident forgotten, starting over. Remember?"

———————

Quinn smiled into Abby's hazel eyes and tried to figure her out. Jumpy as a long-tailed cat in a room full of rocking chairs, Abby sat on the edge of the couch cushion. This morning, she'd been a stick-wielding force of nature. Tonight, she seemed sweet and genuine and endearingly nervous.

He lifted his glass. "To good neighbors."

She clinked her glass to his. "To good neighbors."

The cider was crisp and clean-tasting with a slight effervescent bite that lingered on his tongue.

"I hope you like the cider." She turned the bottle toward him. "I picked it for the pretty label. I liked the wolf and dove looking so comfortable together under the tree. They should be enemies, but they've made the choice not to."

"It's perfect. Thank you."

"You're welcome."

He lifted out the loaf wrapped in a dish towel. "What's this?" He held it to his nose and sniffed. Vanilla and cinnamon, reminding him of his mom's snickerdoodles. "It smells wonderful. Did you make it?"

"Yes. It's my grandmother's recipe, made with eggs from my aunt's hens, honey from her bees, and butter from her cow. It's great with coffee."

"I'll save it for the morning, then." He set the loaf aside and unpacked the rest of the basket's contents: several cheeses, a jar of olives, a box of fancy crackers. "I hadn't thought about dinner yet, but this will be perfect."

"You missed something." She dug into the basket and handed over one last item—a granola bar.

"Aww, you shouldn't have." Suppressing the odd compulsion to kiss her shiny pink lips, he went into the kitchen and gathered clean plates and silverware. He set everything out on the coffee table and handed her a plate.

While they filled their plates, a small silence expanded.

He sat back and put his glass on the side table. "You said the dog's name is Georgia, right?" The little mutt had been eyeing him, her expression intense and watchful. "What kind of dog is she?"

Abby sipped her cider. "I think she's a cattle dog/Jack Russell terrier mix."

"Maybe a little beagle, too." She looked it, with the copper and white markings and the brown patches around her eyes and ears. And even if he hadn't seen her, he'd heard enough of her piercing, yodel-like bark to make an informed opinion. "She's cute."

Georgia growled softly. Probably knew what he was really thinking.

"Aunt Reva says Georgia doesn't like to be called cute," Abby said. "She would prefer to be praised for her intelligence and athletic ability." Abby turned her attention to Georgia. "Wouldn't you, girl?"

Georgia wagged her white-tipped tail and grinned, her lips drawing back to show the top row of her teeth.

"See what I mean? She wants everyone to know she's more than just a pretty face."

"Is she your aunt's only dog? It sounds like you have a lot of pets over there."

"They're not pets." Abby sliced the smoked Gouda. "I know it sounds corny to most people, but to us, animals are family."

"Big family." He popped a chunk of aged Asiago into his mouth. "Good cheese. Don't tell me you bought all these for the pretty packages."

"No. I know about cheese."

He was percolating on a witty response—or at least one that

didn't sound idiotic—when she jumped in with a change of subject. "Are you new to Magnolia Bay?"

He gulped down his cider and poured another glass, wishing it were beer—or something stronger. He hadn't expected the Spanish Inquisition (because nobody expects the Spanish Inquisition). "I've visited Magnolia Bay before because it's my ex-wife's hometown, but I moved here to be closer to my son."

"Oh." Abby held out her glass for a refill. "That's...um, that's great."

He poured up. This conversation must be hard on her, too. "That's one way of looking at it."

"So, you've got a job here, I guess?"

"No, not yet." He didn't say the rest of it: *Because I lost my job and my reputation when I trusted my business partner and got sold down the river.* "I'm...between jobs right now. I was in the construction business in New Orleans with my best friend who's a building contractor, but it didn't work out. I'm hoping to start over here where I can be closer to my son."

"Oh. Well. That sounds..." She looked uncomfortable for a second, then perked up. "I'm sure you'll like the neighborhood. My aunt loves it here."

"So your aunt... Is she traveling or something?"

Abby swallowed. "Yes. She's doing a three-month internship at a wildlife refuge in south Florida. By the end of the summer, she'll be able to keep bobcats, owls, hawks, deer, and all sorts of injured wildlife at the farm."

"Great." Just great. How he managed to luck into finding such *great* neighbors, he'd never know. "Sounds like she's full up already. How many...um...animal family members do you have over there now? Aside from Georgia, I mean."

Abby set her glass down, stared at the ceiling, and counted on her fingers. "Twelve cats, eight bunnies, two donkeys, two ponies, three sheep, five goats, one mini-zebu cow, one potbellied pig—they're best friends. Two peacocks, five geese, six ducks, about eighteen chickens, one scarlet macaw, a pair of Amazons, six sun conures, a dozen parakeets, and a swarm of bees." She dropped her hands into her lap and smiled.

"And a partridge in a pear tree," he added.

"Not yet, but I wouldn't be surprised if one showed up." Her pink lips curled up at the edges, her hazel eyes crinkled at the corners. Her heart-shaped face and quiet features were pretty in an unvarnished way. She wore makeup, but it didn't look as if her eyelashes were in danger of crawling away by themselves.

"Magnolia Bay doesn't have an animal shelter," she explained, "so people who know about Bayside Barn dump animals off all the time. Dogs, cats, chickens, even the potbellied pig."

Again, just his luck to have an animal-hoarding neighbor with a hobo-friendly sign on the gate. "That must be—"

Georgia scrabbled at the sliding glass door and barked a high-pitched alarm.

Abby jumped to her feet, almost spilling her drink. "Something's wrong." She fumbled with the door latch. "Something's out there."

"Wait. I'll come with you." Quinn ran into the kitchen and grabbed a flashlight. The door screeched open, and Abby and Georgia rushed out.

"Fine," he said to the empty room. "Don't wait."

The flashlight's beam bounced as he ran, following the sounds of geese honking, chickens clucking, Georgia barking, and Abby yelling.

"Nooo." Abby's voice sounded anguished. "Bad dog. Drop it…"

The flashlight's beam caught Abby chasing an enormous gray canine who galloped across the yard with a flapping, squawking chicken in its jaws. She threw an empty bucket, but it bounced harmlessly on the ground. Out of breath, panting, Abby lagged behind.

Georgia kept going; low to the ground, bullet-fast, and closing in.

The big dog looked back, halted stride.

Within snapping distance of the larger dog's thick, plumy tail, Georgia stopped and sat.

The big dog turned and dropped the now-motionless chicken. Only paces apart, the two canines stared at each other.

The huge dog's eyes glowed yellow. Its large rounded head, pointed ears, long snout, and thick shaggy coat made it appear more wolf than dog.

Abby reached out, knuckles presented. "Hey, buddy. Where did you come from? Are you hungry?"

Quinn sprang forward. "Abby, no." If the thing lunged and bit, it could do serious damage.

The gray wolf dog broke into a scuttling run and streaked past, heading for the open gate.

Quinn grabbed Abby's arm. "Are you crazy?" His heart hadn't figured out that the danger was past; it hammered overtime, flooding him with adrenaline. "That big dog could have torn you apart."

"He wouldn't have. He was just hungry." Abby picked up the dead chicken and cradled it gently. "I'm sorry, Biddle."

Quinn shone the light on the chicken's limp form. "Is it dead?"

Dry-eyed, Abby nodded. "It's my fault. I left the gate open when I went to visit you. I should have closed the chicken coops, but some chickens were still out. I should have called them in and put them up."

Quinn turned off the flashlight and patted Abby's back in an awkward gesture of consolation. "Sometimes these things happen."

"No. Their coop is safe if I close the door. If I don't close the door, it's a predator buffet." Something stirred between them, and Abby gasped. "Turn on the flashlight."

He did. The not-quite-dead bird fluttered in Abby's arms.

"Biddle, you're okay." She stroked the bird's feathers.

"Amazing. She looked for sure dead."

"My aunt says that animals do that sometimes if they've

suffered a big shock. Their spirits fly away and don't come back until the danger has passed."

"Interesting concept." So Abby's aunt was straight-up crazy, and Abby had drunk the Kool-Aid.

Georgia stood up on her hind legs and whined.

Abby reached down to pet the dog's head. "Let's go inside and make sure Biddle doesn't have any injuries."

Abby walked across the neatly mown lawn, and though he walked behind, Quinn shone the light in front of her. "Do you mind if I come? I might be able to help." And he wanted to see inside the house next door. He told himself his curiosity was based purely on the resale value of his own property.

"Oh, thank you. I'd appreciate that."

Picture windows across the back of the house gleamed darkly, reflecting solar lights around the pool's patio. Abby opened the sliding glass door and flicked on the lights, and they stepped into a homey, country kitchen. The frosted-glass globe under a wide copper dome gave a warm honey color to butcher-block countertops and polished oak cabinets. Cabinet doors of opaque bubble-glass reflected copper-bottomed cookware hung above a central island.

Abby set the chicken down on the oak table and combed through its honey-brown feathers.

The damn chicken matched the damn kitchen.

An enormous gray tabby cat leaped onto the table to survey the proceedings. Georgia hopped onto one of the ladder-backed chairs and propped her chin on the table, watching.

Chickens, cats, and dogs, apparently all felt free to dance on the dining-room table. Quinn reminded himself never to eat over here without offering to wipe down the table beforehand.

"I don't see a scratch on her," Abby said. "Do you?"

"Not yet." He moved the flashlight, following Abby's gentle fingers as she turned the chicken on its side and lifted one of its wings, revealing sparsely feathered white skin. She repeated the process on the other side, then held the bird like a baby with its yellow claws in the air. The chicken struggled to break free, and Abby adjusted her grip. "Can you check her belly?"

Quinn held the light with one hand and sifted through the bird's feathers with the other. "Not a mark on her."

Abby sighed. "Thanks be. I'll go put her back in the coop."

Back outside, Quinn led the way to the chicken coop with the flashlight. Georgia jumped into an opening in the side of the coop, sniffed around, then hopped out again, tail wagging.

"Everybody there?" Abby checked on the other chickens and closed the coop door. "Yep, everybody's there."

She patted the closed door. "Sorry for the scare, everyone. I'll be more careful from now on."

Turning to Quinn, Abby wrapped her arms around his neck and gave him a totally unselfconscious hug. "Thank you for everything."

A zing of awareness flooded his body, reminding him how many months he'd been celibate—nine, exactly. But a brief period of postdivorce promiscuity had convinced him that he'd rather be alone than indulge in meaningless hookups that left him feeling even more unsatisfied.

Abby released him and stepped back, giving his arm an affectionate squeeze. "It means a lot to know that my aunt has a good neighbor she can count on."

He patted her shoulder. "Good neighbors," he repeated inanely. He could have corrected her assumption that he planned to live next door. But that would have been awkward, and anyway, what did he owe her? She wasn't his actual neighbor, in any case. Her aunt would figure out his plans to sell the estate next door when he put the new *For Sale* sign out front. He needed to keep a friendly distance from these new neighbors. Abby was sweet and attractive, sure. But her aunt's unconventional home-based business might stand between him and the high-dollar sale of the property on which he had gambled everything. And if that wasn't reason enough, he had Melissa to remind him of the dangers of falling for a pretty face.

———————

Wolf hid in the shadow of the frog-pool's house. Guilt and longing swirled with the burning acid in his empty belly. Algae-green water couldn't keep him alive, and neither could the frogs and bugs and worms he ate when the last three rabbits he chased outran him. Over the last few weeks, he had lost muscle, strength, and stamina.

Georgia, once she recognized him, let him have the chicken he had caught so easily. But the woman, Abby, said no, and her attitude about sharing sustenance with Wolf was clear in the way she secured all the animals behind locked doors and closed gates. Why didn't people want him to eat? Did he not deserve to live, too?

Head on his paws, he closed his eyes and ignored the clenching fist of hunger that squeezed a little harder each day.

He had hoped his people would come back. But he couldn't redeem himself if he didn't know what he'd done wrong. And because he couldn't redeem himself, his family wouldn't come.

No one would.

———————

That night, limp with exhaustion and relief, Abby settled under the covers and petted Georgia and the cats that hopped up and curled beside them. She checked her text messages and found another one from Reva:

Sorry I didn't call last night. We were told at orientation that we'll be way too busy to chat with folks back home. Plus, weak cell service, and only one old-fashioned landline phone on each floor of the dorm—with a curly cord attached to the receiver! We just got done for the day, and already there's a line of young people (I'm realizing that I'm OLD!) standing halfway down the hall waiting for the phone right now. I guess we'll be doing a lot of texting. How are things at the farm? Fine, I hope. If you need me for anything important, you will have to call the office here and leave a message at the desk. I'll send that contact info separately. (Photo of a tiny dorm room with two fold-down single beds.)

Abby replied: All is well here. (No reason to confess her lapse in not making the new kitten's appointment at the vet.) Nice digs. Seen any roaches yet?

She also decided not to tell Reva about the chicken incident or the new neighbor, including Elijah's kerfuffle with the guy. Biddle would be okay. Elijah hadn't seriously injured Quinn, who turned out to be nice, cute, and handy with a flashlight. If Abby hadn't sworn off men after barely escaping the last one, she might be tempted.

But she had, so she wasn't. Maybe Reva would; Reva was a young fiftysomething wise woman while Abby felt like a washed-up thirty-three-year-old failure. Reva seemed to have some supernatural knack for floating above life's traumas and dramas. Even when everything was going well, Abby found it difficult to drag herself out of bed each morning.

At least here at the farm, the animals kept Abby from burrowing under the covers and staying there until her body petrified. The farm, Abby decided, was a place of healing, not just for the animals who found their way here, but for people, as well.

Georgia stretched out with a groan and snuggled up close. Abby turned out the lamp and stared at the moon through the guest bedroom window's sheer curtain. The animals were all snug in their paddocks, stalls, coops, and cages, with full bellies and plenty of companionship.

Abby sighed, expecting the usual feeling of contentment that followed a full day of hard, satisfying work with the animals on the farm.

But instead, she felt sadness. Loneliness. Betrayal. Abandonment.

Sadness, yes of course. Abby was still learning to live with despair over the child she'd had to leave behind in order to save herself. When faced with the decision of being a whole person alone or a half person with someone else, Abby had looked to her parents' example and chosen to be whole, even though she'd had to cut her heart in half to do it. So now, she was walking around bleeding but whole, except for the part of her heart she'd had no choice but to leave behind.

Even though she knew that Emily wasn't in physical danger, Abby mourned the loss of a child she'd come to love as her own. Knowing Blair's self-centered tendencies, she feared for Emily's tender spirit. Abandoned first by her birth mother at the age of two, and then by Abby at the age of five, what chance did Emily have to form a concept of motherly love, of compassion, of belonging? Abby had struggled with those concepts herself, though her mother had never divorced her father or physically abandoned Abby.

Abby had hoped to do better by Emily but had fallen woefully short.

And because she had no legal claim on Emily, Abby had no recourse, no way of making things right. She had no choice but to let Emily go and hope—pray—for the best. The despair she felt over being banished from Emily's life would never leave her. As Aunt Reva said, that kind of sadness never goes away; it becomes a part of you that gets easier to bear over time. So when Abby explored the feeling of sadness the way the tongue explores an aching tooth, she had to conclude that the sadness she was feeling right now wasn't her own, but someone else's.

What about the feeling of loneliness? Did that feeling reflect her own emotion? No, not at all. Who could feel lonely surrounded by all these animals that asked for nothing and gave everything in return? Animals provided good company without infringing on Abby's need to retreat from entangled human relationships. Aunt Reva's gift was a place of solitude *and* connection, where Abby could heal and build a foundation of strength to launch a new beginning.

Betrayal? Well, yeah, but she'd put that pain behind her when she accepted responsibility for choosing an untrustworthy man with a charming smile.

Abandonment? She'd been the one to abandon Emily to her father's indifferent care, though only after two years of trying to make a relationship work when it had been wrong from the beginning.

So where were these feelings coming from?

An image flashed through her mind like a movie reel on fast-forward. An image of the big dog escaping without the chicken he had grabbed from its roost. He had run past Georgia, when he could have killed her with one bite on the scruff of her neck and one quick shake of his big, wolflike head. He had run past Abby, past Quinn, wanting not to harm, but only to flee.

Some predators, given the opportunity, would break into a chicken coop and kill for the sake of killing, leaving the carcasses and eating nothing. This dog had plucked one chicken off the roost without biting down hard enough to break the skin.

The dog hadn't taken Biddle out of meanness or mischief. Starving and alone, he killed only what he needed to survive. And now, somewhere in the dark, he waited for another chance to feed himself, a chance Abby had denied him.

She felt his hunger and loneliness as if it were her own.

Was this what it was like to communicate with animals? After all the summers that Reva had tried to teach Abby to trust herself, was she finally opening the door to her own telepathic abilities? Was she feeling the emotions of the big dog, or just imagining things?

Abby glanced at the digital clock's readout projected on the ceiling. Ten p.m. here meant it would be eleven in south Florida. Too late to text Reva—who'd surely gone to bed by now—but Abby knew what Reva would say: "Trust yourself. Trust your instincts. Your heart knows more than your head does."

Abby shivered and pulled the covers over her shoulders while her thoughts returned to the hungry dog she'd chased away. How many lost chances stood between a homeless dog and death?

Should she get up and take a bowl of Georgia's kibble out to the road? "No." Abby flopped to her other side and tried to relax. "Go to sleep, stupid." Getting out of a warm bed to traipse down the driveway in the dark would be the height of foolishness. She'd be eaten alive by mosquitoes for her trouble over a dog who had certainly run several miles from here by now.

But when Abby closed her eyes, an image of the cat's-claw forest bloomed in her mind, and she realized for the first time what Georgia had been barking at yesterday. The gold eyes, the feeling of being watched... Of course.

Why hadn't she figured it out before?

"Fine." She sat up. "Mosquitoes, here I come." If she didn't take food out to that stray dog right now, she wouldn't be able to sleep. She patted her aunt's good dog who snuggled on top of the quilt, warming Abby's legs. "Get up, Georgia. We have one more thing to do today."

Chapter 6

WOLF DRAGGED THE MANGLED POSSUM OFF THE ROAD WHEN the car's taillights disappeared in the distance. Dropping to his belly in the damp grass, he tore into the still-warm carcass and gulped down massive mouthfuls without chewing.

His eyes half-closed in bliss, he ate until his shrunken belly expanded like the hard, round ball the kids in his family had played with every evening. He remembered the tall boys bouncing the hard ball in the concrete drive, then tossing it into the air and whooping when it hit the round metal hoop.

Wolf had sat close by, watching his kids and making sure no harm came to them. The bad dogs who roamed the block knew not to come close. But the bad people whose energy leaked avarice or cunning were invited in by Wolf's human family. They showed up with sideways glances that didn't match their smiling faces. When Wolf growled, the alpha human beat him with a shovel.

Wolf stopped growling.

But he kept watch.

He watched the alpha's friends most closely. Especially the one who eyed the alpha's oldest girl and tried to catch her alone. The sneaky man only got close enough to corner her that one time, but Wolf stopped him with little effort. Before the girl recognized the danger, Wolf's well-placed bite changed everything.

Wolf knew his job: protect his family. He did his job. The screaming, the yelling, and the severe beating Wolf received afterward confused and humiliated him, but he learned his lesson. Humans, even those he thought of as family, could not be trusted.

A wavering, bouncing beam of light crossed the road. Gravel crunched; footsteps on the narrow drive where chickens and rabbits and other tasty animals slept behind wire mesh and locked doors. Wolf snatched up the possum's remains and ran into the forest. He dropped the dripping mass of shredded skin and bones onto a thick carpet of dry leaves.

Scraping metallic sounds announced the unlocking of the gate across the road; it swung open with a loud screech. He heard the light pattering noise of Georgia racing toward him, zigzagging over the trail he had taken with his dinner. He imagined her, nose to ground, tracking his location. When she burst out of the underbrush, Wolf backed up and sat, letting the carcass lie between them rather than guarding it, as was his right. "A gift," he offered.

Excited and happy, Georgia rolled in the carcass. "Thank you." Covered in the rich, oily scent of the possum's blood and fur, she shook herself and wagged her white-tipped tail. "I have a gift for you, too. Come see."

Wolf looked away from the flashlight's beam that pierced the draping vines of his hiding place.

"Puppy, puppy," Abby called. She placed a large metal pot on the grass and made the loud kissing sounds his girl used to make. "Come here, puppy, puppy. Come get some food."

Wolf hadn't been called *puppy* in a very long time. He whined at Georgia.

"Yes, she means you." Georgia trotted a few steps toward Abby, then turned back. "Come on. She's bringing you food."

Wolf dropped to his elbows. "Not hungry."

Georgia's tail drooped. "Come on, try some. It's good." She showed him an image of dry kibble, resurrecting his memory of the crunchy food he used to eat.

His mouth watered at the taste memory, but his stomach was full for the first time in days, and his heart felt strangely heavy at the memory of being loved and cared for. Wolf stood and followed Georgia to the edge of the forest. He hid beneath the overhanging vines, close enough to Abby to smell the animal dung clinging to the soles of her boots. Close enough to smell the dried-meat scent of her offering.

But humans, even the ones he thought of as family, couldn't be trusted. And this woman, who wasn't family, didn't deserve his trust. Besides, he wasn't hungry. Wolf sat.

"Come on, girl," Abby called to Georgia, who gave Wolf one last hopeful glance before obeying.

Abby turned the light away from Wolf's hiding place. "Maybe he'll eat it later. Let's go back to bed." Abby and Georgia crossed the road, then Abby closed and locked the gate. "Whew, Georgia. What is that smell? Please tell me you didn't roll in something dead."

Abby and Georgia disappeared behind the hedge, taking the light with them. Their sounds faded, first the crunching of gravel under Abby's boots, then Abby's voice growing fainter, sending up only snippets of her words on the night breeze. "...bath...sleep... food...puppy."

Puppy. Something Wolf hadn't been called in a long time, though Abby's voice made it clear she was referring to him. Longing for the sweetness she seemed to offer but unable to trust, Wolf waited in the darkness until the crickets and the night birds sang again. With his heart racing as if he were cowering from a mean man with a shovel, he crept toward the metal pot she'd left for him.

Cautiously, he sniffed the food. Dried meat, rice, carrots, berries... peas... He sniffed again. Just food, nothing else. Not the sweet chemical odor of the green slime that had killed Wolf's friends, the feral cats of his old neighborhood. Not the bitter smell of poison-laced meat the bad man had tried to feed him.

Just food. Only food.

Wolf grabbed the pot's metal handle in his teeth and tugged the bounty he'd been given across the slippery grass and into the forest.

The Sunday morning sounds next door woke Quinn hours earlier than he would have preferred. He rolled over and pulled a pillow over his head, but the screeches and brays and whinnies still managed to slice right through.

Oh well. He had work to do; might as well get up and do it. Tomorrow and for the rest of the week, he'd be in New Orleans every day, building custom shelves for a new indie bookstore on Magazine Street. He could paint Sean's room and assemble the furniture he'd bought in the evenings—the Big Easy was only an hour drive from Magnolia Bay—but today was his last full day to work on the estate. He'd use it to get the pool ready for Sean's visit next weekend.

Quinn rolled out of bed and padded into the kitchen, yawning and regretting his foolish decision to stay up late and watch a stupid movie he couldn't even remember.

With a fresh cup of coffee and a slice of the delicious cake brought by his delicious almost-neighbor, he sat in the canvas stadium chair by the pool. Exchanging his coffee cup for the legal pad he'd put on top of an overturned Home Depot bucket, he made a list.

1. Clean the pool filter.

2. Turn on the pump. (And hope to God it works.)

3. Shock the pool with chemicals.

4. Say bye-bye to the tadpoles and frogs.

5. Clean the filter again.

The shrubbery at the fence line shook. With steady determination, a large animal climbed up through the branches. Quinn set his legal pad aside and sipped his cooling, too-weak coffee. Yesterday's brew had been too strong. After a year of single life, he hadn't mastered the fine art of coffee making.

A cat's head popped up from the foliage, followed by the rest of its body. The hedge trembled as the cat scrabbled for balance on the topmost branches. The thing was huge. With its buff-colored long hair and tail-less backside, the cat looked more like a miniature polar bear than a feline. It spied Quinn and leaped down onto the leaf clutter on Quinn's side of the fence. It landed with a loud *murf*, and sauntered over. Purring like Quinn's Harley, the enormous cat rubbed against Quinn's jeans leg.

"Hey, cat." He stroked the cat's big head. Its fluffy, cashmere-soft fur didn't feel like regular cat hair. "Are you some fancy breed, or what?"

The cat hopped up onto Quinn's lap. "*Murf.*"

"Nice to meet you, Murf."

The cat sniffed Quinn's coffee mug, then stuck its nose right in and tried a couple of laps.

"Fine, go ahead." The strange-looking feline could have the tepid brew. "I'm done anyway."

Given permission, the overly puffy feline changed its mind. It hopped down to crouch at the pool's edge and lap at the green water. When Quinn opened his toolbox and took the cover off the pool pump, the cat inspected everything—the toolbox, its contents, the upturned pump cover, the pleated filter. "You haven't heard that line about curiosity killing the cat?"

Purring loudly, it climbed into the toolbox and sniffed around. Apparently finding everything satisfactory, the cat sat in the box. Perched on the jumble of hard-edged hammers, wood-cutting tools, screwdrivers and other tools, it stopped purring and stared at Quinn with unblinking gold eyes.

"That can't be a comfortable place to sit." But Quinn didn't mind the company. He dragged the hose over and cleaned the filter, spraying water into the accordion pleats. A few droplets hit the cat; it hissed and leaped out of the box.

Quinn chuckled. "Sorry about that."

The cat gave a disgruntled *murf* and moved to the splash-free zone of Quinn's stadium chair. Quinn put the filter back in, fastened the lid, made sure the switches were all set correctly, then turned the pump on.

Nothing.

He went into the pool house and rechecked the breakers.

No problem there.

Hands on hips, Quinn studied the situation. "Guess I'll have to take the motor apart." Kneeling, he reached into his tool box for a socket wrench—

A dripping-wet socket wrench.

A dripping-wet socket wrench that smelled of cat piss.

Quinn rose up with a roar and lobbed the wrench in the cat's general direction. As Quinn had expected, the wrench landed a good five feet away from the cat. But the clatter of metal bouncing on concrete scared the feline, who shot straight up into the air, then hit the ground running.

Straight into the pool with a mighty splash.

Eyes wide, lips pulled back in a grimace of fear, the cat struggled to the pool's edge and scrabbled at the algae-slick tiles. It yowled a bone-chilling feline scream, then fell back into the pool and went under.

"Griff?" Abby called from the other side of the hedge. "Griffin? Where are you? Here, kitty, kitty."

The cat came up sputtering, splashing, and moaning in fear before it sank again.

"Griffin?" Abby's voice sounded panicked. "Kitty, kitty?"

"Dammit," Quinn muttered. He grabbed the pool net and

chased the cat along the pool's edge. "Your damn cat's over here," he yelled. "It fell in the pool."

Finally he managed to get the pool net underneath the cat, but when he lifted it out of the water, the long handle bowed under the cat's weight. The damn thing had to weigh forty pounds, at least. Moaning, the cat splayed its big feet out to the far sides of the net and tried to stand. The net wobbled and tilted. The cat screamed and clawed, spinning the net upside down, where the stupid pisser hung by its claws. "Be still, stupid cat!"

Quinn maneuvered the quivering net with its shivering, yowling, hanging-upside-down cargo out of the pool.

Abby ran around the corner of the house when the net's pole bent completely in half, bouncing the cat's noggin on the concrete while it clung to the pool net. Panting, Abby skidded to a stop, her barn boots scattering clods of who-knew-what on the patio. "Oh, no… Oh my God… What happened? Is he okay?"

"I'd guess not," Quinn said with some sarcasm. "Damn thing has a death wish, looks like."

With his claws tangled in the damaged pool net, the bedraggled cat whirled and moaned until the netting tore, setting him free. Like a rock from a slingshot, he ran to the chain-link fence and tried to push through the unyielding metal mesh to the other side.

"Come here, baby." Abby followed in a crouching run, unsuccessfully grabbing for the panicked cat who bounced off the chain-link fence time after time in an effort to push through. Cutoff shorts showed off Abby's long shapely legs, but Quinn tried not to notice. "Griff, stop," Abby whined. "You'll hurt yourself. Here, kitty, kitty…"

"*You* stop." Quinn followed along behind Abby and grabbed her arm, hauling her back. "Chasing him isn't helping. The damn cat'll be fine once he calms down."

Sure enough, as Quinn held Abby still with her back against his chest, her backside against his front side, the cat climbed up through the hedge and leaped over the fence to safety. Although tempted to hold her against him long enough to get her attention, Quinn knew better. He didn't have room or time in his life to start something real, and he didn't want anything less. He ran a hand down Abby's arm, then released her. "See?"

Abby put a hand on her heart and turned toward him. He could practically see her heart beating, a hectic flutter of pulse in her delicate neck. "How in the world...? I mean, how did Griff fall into your pool? My aunt has a pool; none of the cats have ever fallen in. They're all very pool-savvy." She took a breath. "I can't imagine why on earth Griff would fall into your pool. Did you see it happen?"

Quinn waited for Abby's nervous prattle to subside, then shrugged. He deliberately avoided glancing toward the pissed-on wrench that lay somewhere between the pool pump and his stadium chair, looking instead into Abby's trusting hazel eyes. "I have no idea."

———

Abby's restful weekend wasn't fated to last long; a child's birthday party was scheduled for the afternoon. Then, after another week of nonstop school field trips, she should be done hosting events at Bayside Barn for the rest of the summer. Though a group of scouts or homeschoolers might book an outing, or a family might book a birthday party, the summer months, at least on paper, looked to be blessedly free of commitments.

If Abby could just get through the next week, she'd be home free, with nothing to do but care for the animals, lie by the pool, fill out online job applications and send out résumés. Office manager jobs were few and far between—especially when she couldn't get a reference from her cheating ex, Blair—but she had three whole months to find something. Reva had offered Abby a full-time job helping around the farm, but Abby knew that Reva couldn't really afford it, even if she kept half to cover room and board. Nope; Abby couldn't rely on Reva forever. She had to find a real job.

First things first, though. She had a birthday party to get through. She planned to give the farm tour and let the kids pet the animals, then leave the group on their own for a couple of hours to have their party in the pavilion and swim in the pool, or even the pond. The party participants had all signed waivers of liability and were free to swim as long as the party organizers provided supervision.

She moved the benches to the edges of the pavilion and set up several picnic tables. Then, with an hour to spare before the group arrived, she decided to go for a swim herself.

Or maybe just a float.

She set her phone's alarm so she wouldn't accidentally fall asleep, then stretched out on a pool float and closed her eyes. The goats and sheep bleated softly from their pasture, happy sounds of contentment and communication with one another. Abby made a mental note to chop some carrots for the birthday-party kids to feed them.

Celery too. The stalks she had in the fridge were beginning to go soft. And goats with limp celery fronds hanging from their mouths would make great photo ops for the partygoers.

As Abby floated, her mind floated, too.

She thought of Reva, who must be busy because she still hadn't called, though they'd been texting a lot.

She thought of the wolf dog, who had dragged two of Reva's cooking pots into the forest. Great that he was eating the food Abby put out, but she'd have to figure out another, less-expensive container to use. As she thought of the poor stray, she realized he must be thirsty, too. Then she thought of the neighbor's pool. Green and slimy it may be, but at least it was wet. The dog probably drank there; the warped and battered gate to that property was permanently rusted open.

She thought of the good-looking neighbor, who—

A phone rang, and Abby nearly turned the float over reaching for hers before she realized the sound came from next door.

"Hey, Sean!" Quinn answered. He sounded delighted, and also desperate. Like whoever had called was a loved one who had spurned his advances and was now doling out phone calls the way a prison guard might hand out moldy bread to a starving prisoner.

"That's…that's wonderful, son. I'm glad to hear it."

Son. Oh, right. Abby remembered him saying he had a kid. After that heartbreak with Blair, Abby had promised herself that she would never again get involved with a man who had children.

Never, never again.

"I can't wait for you to see this place," Abby heard Quinn say. "I have your room ready, and the bathroom renovation is almost done…" His voice trailed away; he had been interrupted and was listening now. "Yeah, only one bathroom, but…"

Interrupted again. His son must be a little jerk. She wondered how old he was. Probably a teenager. By the sound if it, she'd have no chance of falling in love with Quinn's bratty kid, as she'd done with Blair's daughter. Cranky teenage son put Quinn back in the running. It also took him out. No way did she want to be a stepmother to a terrible teenager.

Abby sighed. She needed to get over her tendency to see a cute guy from a hundred yards away and start planning a life with him. That's what had gotten her into trouble in the first place. All the other women who worked in the dentist office knew to stay away from their charming asshole boss, Dr. Blair White, a.k.a. Dr. Blaring-White Teeth.

And yes, his teeth were as beautiful as the rest of him.

Abby was the only one in the office who had to learn firsthand that while the dentist was gorgeous on the outside, on the inside he was as rotten as a cavity-riddled tooth.

Abby had started out as the office manager and carried on as the dashing dentist's live-in lover and surrogate mother for his precious daughter who, to hear him tell it, had been abandoned by her drug-addicted mother. Abby had learned only after she'd lost her job, her home, her self-respect, and the child she'd come to love that the story had been nothing more than a compelling fabrication. Emily's mother had been forced out, made to believe that she would never be able to compete with Blair's ability to provide for their daughter. Too afraid to stand up for herself and her daughter, Emily's mother had drifted away instead.

Nope. No matter how cute Quinn was, Abby would have to give him a pass.

Her phone's alarm hadn't buzzed yet, but Abby realized that when it did, Quinn would hear it and realize that she could also hear his conversation with his son. She quietly swam to the pool's edge, used the towel to dry her hands, then turned off the alarm. Reva had left a text message, so she clicked to open it.

Having so much fun! (Photo of Reva holding an old, repurposed messenger bag full of baby possums.)

Abby replied: Sweet!

"Make sure you bring your swimsuit when you come next weekend," she heard Quinn say. "I fixed the pool pump today, and I'm at this very minute pouring in chemicals to clear the water."

Chemicals. Oh, well. Abby would remember to take a bucket of water out to the stray tonight when she took his food. A five-gallon horse bucket of water should be too heavy for him to move or tip over. Meanwhile, Abby hoped the stray wolf dog would be smart enough to avoid the chemical-tainted water next door.

Wolf sat on his haunches next to the frog pool, but it wasn't a frog pool anymore. A strong chemical smell rose from the clear water, and a thick layer of brown gunk floated near the pool's bottom. A few bloated toads bobbed belly up on the surface.

Thirsty enough to try the water, at least, Wolf stuck the tip of his tongue in, but changed his mind before lapping some up. It hadn't done those toads any good; it wouldn't be good for him, either.

A new swarm of screaming young humans had invaded the farm next door, ruling out the possibility of finding water there today, even though the gate by the road had been left open. Lifting his face to the wind, he sniffed. The ditches around here had all dried up. The only clean water he could access would be down the hill in the bay, or in one of the marshy inlets that fed it.

He trotted through a tangle of overgrown weeds and shrubs, then encountered a stretch of open land that someone had recently mowed. Feeling exposed, he ran until he reached the tall marsh grasses between the hills and the water.

As he stood among the upright blades of tough grasses and plants that cloaked him in their concealing shadow, cool mud sank beneath the pads of his feet. The scent of water beckoned now. The smell clung to the roof of his mouth, and he knew that the water would taste rich with nutrients imparted by sand, soil, and plants.

The mud got deeper, softer. His paws sank farther down with each step, tearing through tender root systems before plunging into a bottomless slurry of mud mixed with water. Half walking, half swimming, he surged leap by leap through the shoulder-high muck toward the sandy beach he had seen from the hills above.

A low growl filtered through the leaves, seeming to come from all sides at once. It sounded like a dog's growl, but Wolf knew it wasn't. This deep, bellowing growl came from the throat of something much bigger than any dog Wolf had ever seen.

And whatever it was, it was growling at him. His hackles rose at the unseen threat.

The growl moved closer, and Wolf could tell now that it was

coming from behind him, accompanied by the silky, swishing sound of something big slithering through the mud, somehow staying on top of it instead of being swallowed by it.

Panting, floundering in the ever-deepening mud that sucked at his feet with every swimming step, Wolf struggled toward the smell of the clear water beyond the marsh. His front paws struck something hard and slick, something hidden deep under the muddy surface that the reeds seemed to grow on top of rather than sending roots down. Wolf scrabbled to get all four paws on the shifting platform, then pushed off and leaped forward...only to land in an even deeper pool of mud.

No bottom. No bottom. He went down, down, down. The mud closed over his head.

Eyes closed, mouth closed, knowing better than to inhale the muck that clogged his nostrils, Wolf swam, all four legs moving in unison but getting him nowhere. Was he going up, toward the surface, or farther down to an unknown bottom from which he would never escape? He couldn't tell.

Whimpers rose in his throat; he could hear them, pitiful sounds that reminded him of puppyhood, of being taken from his mother with no explanation, no chance of turning back or saying goodbye.

Something slammed into him, shoving him up out of the mud. He rolled, his eyes too covered in mud to blink, his nose too clogged to inhale. He gasped, shook his head, and opened his eyes just enough to see past the dripping mud that covered his face.

The thing roared and its log-shaped body lunged forward, its huge mouth open wide. The soft pink abyss of flesh was surrounded by enough teeth to fill the mouths of a dozen dogs.

All but blinded by the gritty mud that dripped into his eyes, Wolf leaped away, but his back legs collapsed under him. The thing's teeth sank into his side, snagging fur and skin. It held on to him, slinging him back and forth the way he'd once played with the squeaky toys of his youth.

He scratched and bit, but the thing's flesh wasn't flesh at all; it was as hard as wood or bone. Wolf's teeth couldn't penetrate it.

A small toy in this monster's mouth, Wolf went limp. The thing slung him sideways, his skin ripped, and he tumbled into the bay.

He swam, feeling clumps of mud fall away in the dark water, knowing that the monster would be right behind him, its big mouth opening wide for a bigger bite, a better grip. With a desperate surge of energy, Wolf veered back to the sandy beach, looking for a safe path to high ground.

But there was only the water, this small strip of sand, and the deep, muddy bog that had swallowed him whole. He was trapped.

Chapter 7

THE BIRTHDAY PARTY FOLKS HAD A FINE TIME. ABBY WAS GLAD to see them arrive, glad to show them around, and glad to see them go. The whole time, she'd been strangely distracted by thoughts of the stray dog. She'd planned to take a bucket of water across the street later this evening, but worried that she should've done it already.

What if he got so thirsty that he decided to go out in search of water and got hit by a car?

What if he'd been without water for too long already and was suffering from heat exhaustion?

What if he died?

All day, flashes of imagination haunted her. Visions of the stray popped into her head whenever she let herself relax between tasks. She saw him struggling through grassy weeds in search of water that remained out of reach.

What if he got hurt because she hadn't helped him?

When the last car drove away, Abby wasted no time in filling a five-gallon bucket of water and carrying it across the street. The bucket was almost too heavy for her to carry, and water sloshed all over her boots. But she knew the stray would turn over the bucket if he tried to drag it into the shadowed forest. She hoped to avoid that by filling it so full that it would be bottom-heavy, and by setting it just inside the sheltering overhang of the draping vines.

Georgia sniffed the bucket, then ventured into the forest and came back unsatisfied. She whined at Abby and looked past the old estate to the intersection, where Winding Water Way crossed the potholed track that led down to the landing.

"I know," Abby said, though she hadn't clearly understood what Georgia wanted. "I hope he'll come back, too."

Georgia lifted her face and sniffed the air, then whined again. She trotted toward the intersection, then turned around and came back, her earnest brown eyes imploring Abby to understand.

But she didn't.

"I'm sorry, girl. I don't know what you want."

Georgia sat in her ball-playing cattle-dog position, down on all fours, front feet pointing forward. She whined again, then looked toward the intersection.

"You want us to go there?"

Georgia leaped to her feet, her expression one of excitement and approval. She must feel like she was playing charades with a very dim-witted person. But at least she didn't lose hope that given enough clues, Abby would eventually catch on.

"Okay, fine." Abby walked back to close the gate and dummy-lock it, then clapped her hands. "Lead the way."

Georgia leaped up a couple of times, doing a good imitation of the Snoopy dance. Then she ran out in front of Abby, her tail a happy curl of triumph over her back. Abby had to jog to keep up. At the intersection, Georgia paused a second to make sure Abby knew they were turning toward the bay.

"Yes, Georgia. I'm right behind you."

Abby wondered if Georgia was leading the way to Wolf, or simply bored with staying at the farm. Reva often took Georgia for walks; maybe Abby should, too.

The unnamed dead-end road to the old landing bordered the new neighbor's land, and Abby wondered what Quinn was doing. Maybe she should…? No. Scratch that thought. She should not invite him for a walk, or anything else, for that matter.

The jungle of overgrown plants and vines that covered most of Quinn's estate transitioned to reedy marshland close to the water. All the estates on this road were the same: fertile high ground tapering down to a wide strip of swampland on the way to the bay.

Reva's husband, Grayson, had tried to purchase the acreage behind them in order to preserve the lovely view of the bay and the valuable feeling of seclusion and privacy that the wide strip of marshland provided. But the bank declined to offer a loan for land that was prone to flooding, and the owners declined to allow Grayson to pay in installments.

Abby stood near the boat ramp while Georgia noodled along the overgrown bank. Abby couldn't imagine anyone wanting to build anything out here in the boondocks. Who would drive all the way out here when there were much nicer recreation areas closer to town?

Although there was a shiny, jacked-up crew-cab pickup truck with oversize tires parked on the grassy verge, along with a big boat trailer hooked to the tow bar and secured with a padlock. So maybe there was some lure to these backcountry places.

The ratty, cracked-concrete launch was tucked into a shallow slough that hid the view of all but the opposite bank. With dead trees fallen into the water and vegetation draping low, it looked pretty fishy around here. And snaky. Probably alligatory, too. She looked back at Georgia—who had disappeared.

Abby panicked. "Georgia!"

The little dog gave a yodeling *barroooo* from the depths of the marsh grasses. Abby could just imagine an alligator snapping her up. And then, good God, she heard the bellow of an alligator from farther down the bank. Way farther down—the sound carried a long way—but still. Where there was one alligator, there were probably five more. "Georgia…?"

No way was she going in there after the fool dog. "Come back here, now!"

The bad critter emerged looking like a black-stockinged cancan dancer, her legs covered with mud. She also smelled like dead fish, even from ten feet away.

"Great. Now I have to give you a bath." Abby turned toward home. "See if I take you walking again, you bad girl."

━━━━━━━━━━

Quinn slowed his truck at the intersection—he rarely came to a complete stop. But he did stop when he saw Abby and that little dog walking up from the boat ramp. He rolled down his window. "Hey. How's your waterlogged cat doing?"

She came closer. Her honey-brown hair glowed with golden highlights in the afternoon sun. Her skin glowed with a golden tan. Her eyes... *Shut up*, he told himself. *Stop looking at her.*

"Griff?" She shrugged. "Fine, I guess. I haven't seen him since he went swimming in your pool. He's probably hiding out somewhere." She narrowed her eyes at him, and Quinn wondered if she suspected him of having something to do with the cat's impromptu swimming lesson. Then she put a hand up to shade her eyes from the sun. "What are you doing out and about? I thought you'd be working on your pool all day today."

"Hardware-store run. Needed more chemicals. Got the pump running, though."

"That's good." She nodded. "Hey, have you seen that stray dog lately?"

"Nope. Sorry."

"Hey—" they both said at once. He was about to say *Hey, I've got to go*, but he'd been taught to be a gentleman, so he motioned for her to speak first.

"You want to come for dinner tonight?"

Terrible, bad idea. He should say no. Keep his distance. "Sure." Being a friendly neighbor was one thing; getting to know the neighbor was another thing entirely. He could still come up with an excuse. "I'd love to come. What time?"

Wolf paced the water's edge, then the fringes of the tall grass. Afraid to go either way, he whimpered. His side burned with every breath, but he couldn't stop panting in fear.

Where had the creature gone? Wolf had tumbled into the water, and by the time he'd climbed out, the creature had abandoned his pursuit and disappeared. Was it waiting for him in the water, or hiding in the marsh? Trembling with indecision, Wolf let out an involuntary howl.

The thing growled again.

It was in the marsh. Hiding, but not from Wolf. Hiding from something bigger and more terrifying than itself. A loud roar echoed across the water, even louder than the creature's bellow. The loud roar became a high-pitched vibrating whine that hurt Wolf's sensitive ears. He yelped, turning in confusion. Which direction was safe?

The roaring whine flew toward him over the water like a bullet. Like a car. Like a truck. But it floated on top of the surface, then skimmed over the sand, landing halfway on the bank and halfway in the water. He knew he should hide, so he backed up to the tall grass where the creature hid, but he didn't step into it.

The people in the bullet water-car made whooping sounds like the bad kids he'd heard at the farm earlier today. He watched the people who might hurt him, but he listened for the sound of the creature who had tried to eat him.

"Whoa!" one of the men yelled. "Look over there! It's a wolf!"

Afraid to move in either direction, Wolf cowered.

Another man leaped into the water and splashed onto the shore, moving toward Wolf with purpose. "It's not a wolf; it's a dog. He's hurt."

One of the women squealed. "Get back in the boat, you idiot. Do you want to get bitten?"

"Probably belongs to somebody," someone else said.

But the man kept coming. Bending low, he held out a hand and talked in a soothing voice. "Come here, puppy."

The name *Puppy* sounded different when this man said it than when Abby had. Abby's voice had been soft with compassion. This man's voice held a different vibration; he genuinely wanted to help, but also had an ulterior motive.

Wolf shivered with indecision.

But a rustling sound in the reeds behind him made up his mind. He stood on shaky legs, the wound in his side flaming.

The man looked back at the—what had the woman said?—boat. "Somebody bring me a rope or something."

Wolf didn't understand all of the man's words. He had learned some of the sound patterns that humans used, along with their meanings. That knowledge, combined with his ability to understand human thoughts and intentions, gave Wolf a more complete understanding of the nuances of human language.

He understood that this man's intention was to get Wolf into the boat. Whether the man's motivations proved to be good or evil, Wolf's best option was to go with him, away from the certain death that awaited in the marsh or the uncertain potential of escape into the choppy brown water.

Decision made, he leaned briefly against the man's side, then walked toward the boat. At the bank he hesitated, but the man picked him up and carried him, then dumped him inside. Wolf fell, landing hard on his injured side. He scrambled to get upright and quickly found a place to hide under an empty seat. People sat in all the others, talking above the loud music that seemed to be coming from everywhere. They all seemed content to drink beer and ignore Wolf.

All except one.

"Dude!" The biggest man—the alpha—swatted a towel at Wolf. "He's getting mud all over my boat. And blood, too! Ugh."

"Fuck you," Dude said. The word was ugly, but he said it in a bored, disinterested tone. He pushed the boat away from the bank, then hopped inside and sat in the seat under which Wolf hid. "I'll wash your damn boat. This dog's a wolf hybrid. He's probably worth a lot of money."

Wolf understood only three words of that exchange. *Fuck* meant "I don't like you." *Wash* meant "bath," a horrible punishment he'd only received once. *Boat*, he had just learned, was the rocking vehicle he sat in now. But he knew something more important than the words he understood. He knew, without knowing how he knew, that the man who had saved him from the creature with the wooden skin was a bad man.

As soon as he could, Wolf had to get away.

The boat rumbled and roared, rocketing backward then forward with frightening speed. Wolf closed his eyes—and tried to close his ears, too—until the boat came to a rocking halt in the churned-up waves.

The driver maneuvered the boat close to a rippled concrete bank, and someone else hopped out and sloshed through the water to the shore. The man sitting above Wolf held onto him by the scruff. Wolf sat still and submissive; he could break the man's hold, unless they decided to put a rope around his neck.

Another motor rumbled, and a truck backed almost into the water. Then the driver drove the boat onto a wheeled frame that pulled it onto dry land. People stood up inside the boat, gathering items and chattering.

Dude stood, releasing Wolf just long enough to bend down and pick him up. Wolf lunged away and shot through the tangle of bare legs to the side of the boat. Amid all the screaming and yelling, he leaped out.

Abby dressed for dinner in a soft jersey sundress with a flowery print and a flirty skirt that swirled around her thighs when she moved. Her damp hair would probably frizz, and her cheeks would be too shiny, so hopefully the cute dress would provide a distraction from the total picture.

Because when faced with the realization that she had time to either clean the house or dry her hair and put on makeup, she'd opted for the house. While she zipped around barefoot with the vacuum, while she cleaned the kitchen and dusted the furniture and wiped down the butcher-block countertops, she told herself she'd made the right choice.

Quinn had seen her without makeup, so that cat was out of the bag. The cat still inside its bag was the one that could've spilled the secret that Abby wasn't exactly a neat freak. After three days of not picking up after herself, she had to admit that Reva's house was beginning to look a little grim.

She'd just put away the vacuum and lit a few good-smelling candles on the table when Quinn tapped on the glass door.

Dressed in oh-Mama-fitting jeans and a Lord-help-me-fitting T-shirt, Quinn also had a charming grin on his face and a bottle of red wine in his hand.

She might have fallen just a little bit in love before she even opened the door. "Hey, you're right on time." She grabbed ahold of one of his bare, superfine biceps and dragged him over the threshold. She couldn't seem to help herself; anxiety had fluttered up from nowhere and urged her to get the greetings over with.

"Come on in." She released his yummy, warm arm and stepped back to close the door. "So glad you could come. Hope you like… um…" For a second, she forgot what she'd already prepared and put into the preheated oven. Then Georgia reached up with her front paws and propped them on Quinn's thighs, saving Abby from her anxious downhill spiral. She took a calming breath, and her brain came back online. "Hope you like baked salmon and asparagus with roasted potatoes."

"That sounds wonderful." He bent down and petted Georgia's head with one hand and gave Abby the bottle of wine with the other.

She took the bottle into the kitchen and hunted for the corkscrew. "Thanks for the wine." She pulled out another drawer. "I don't know where…"

Quinn straightened and stepped into the kitchen. "Can I help you with anything?"

Georgia followed, staying close to invite handouts or hugs, should anyone offer.

"Nope, nope, it's all done. I just can't find… Oh, wait." She yanked open the door of the still-running dishwasher and waited for the cloud of hot steam to clear. Then she reached in and grabbed the hot metal implement that had eluded her. "Corkscrew's in the dishwasher." She closed the door and fiddled with the control buttons. A sudden attack of nerves made her clumsy. "How do you restart…?"

"Um… Abby?" Quinn leaned against the opposite counter, his hands in his pockets. "I'll figure out the dishwasher in a second. But first, can you come over here?"

She laid the corkscrew aside and turned to Quinn. His blue eyes were just as steamy as the foggy mushroom cloud that had just escaped the dishwasher. "I'm sorry… What?"

He took one hand out of his pocket and crooked a come-here finger. "I'll help you with the dishwasher. I want to help you with something else first, though."

"Um…" She licked her lips and stepped closer. "Like what?"

"You seem a little nervous," he said, still motioning with that come here finger. "Let me see if I can help with that."

While Abby stood there distracted by his beckoning finger, Quinn wrapped his other arm around her waist and pulled her close. "You don't need to be nervous with me," he whispered, his mouth just inches from hers. He trailed that finger from her chin, down her neck, along her collarbone. He gently pushed aside the thin braided strap of her sundress to bare her shoulder. Goose bumps erupted along her arms as he explored her skin with that one questing finger. "Nice dress. And I especially approve of your choice of footwear."

She leaned in to him, her lips a breath away from touching his. "I'm barefooted," she managed to say.

He chuckled. "My point exactly." His breath smelled like mint and his smooth skin smelled like cheap bar soap, almost aggressively clean. His warm lips closed over hers...

And he was right. All the jagged energy of anxiety that had been zipping around inside her melted away like warm candle wax.

Then Georgia barked outside, and Abby jumped. "I'd better go check what's going on out there."

With a satisfied smirk of a grin, Quinn slowly slid the strap of Abby's sundress back up onto her shoulder. "Yes, ma'am. I'll restart the dishwasher."

Wolf woke in complete darkness. The smell of his friend Georgia lingered in the leaves beside his nose. The wound in his side stung as if he was being attacked by a nest-full of angry, stinging hornets. His mouth, even his body, felt hot and dry. He needed water.

He staggered to his feet and stumbled toward the road's edge; maybe some dew had collected on the grass.

He spotted a flash of red in the cloud-dimmed moonlight; a bucket of water next to a pie pan full of dog food in the place where Abby had been feeding him. Wolf gratefully lapped up as much water as he could hold, then scarfed down the food. Replete but still in pain, he thought of Georgia's insistence that he should come to the farm and ask for help—or had that been a fever dream?

No. It had been real. She'd said the gate to the farm would be left open, and it was, the black-painted metal gleaming dully in the dark. Wolf wanted help. He needed help. But something held him back. He wanted to deserve help, not just to ask for it without giving anything back. He limped across the darkened street and looked down the drive toward the farmhouse.

What could he do to help Abby so maybe she would want to help him, too, even more than she already had? He'd been taught tricks that made his family happy. He knew sit, stay, bark, and no bark. He knew shake, leave it, and no, stop! He knew bang-bang, which always came with a hand signal that mimicked a shooting gun, something the alpha's friends liked to do in the field behind the house.

When the alpha gave the bang-bang command, Wolf would fling himself to the ground and roll to his back, paws in the air. Then he'd close his eyes and let his tongue loll, and lie very still while the alpha's friends laughed and laughed.

But he couldn't do bang-bang for Abby if she didn't give him the signal, and she wouldn't know about that. It was something only the alpha and his friends knew about. None of Wolf's tricks would work unless Abby asked him to do them first.

The moon floated out from behind the shredded clouds, and Wolf noticed something lying in the driveway: a dew-wet roll of paper, the same kind he'd been taught to bring to the alpha's wife every morning. She liked to cut the paper into little squares that she kept inside a leather bag. She took the bag with the paper squares inside it everywhere she went, so Wolf knew that the work he did in bringing the paper was important and appreciated.

This paper had been run over and smashed flat many times. The alpha's wife liked her papers to be smooth and dry, with leafy sheets that crinkled. This mass of waterlogged paper had fused into a wet lump. But who knew why people liked the things they liked, and whether Abby would prefer her paper dry, the way the alpha's wife had, or whether she liked a soggy and soft roll like this one.

Wolf, himself, preferred the soggy and soft kind; they felt squishy and bubbly in his mouth, while the dry kind had a sharp taste that made his tongue prickle. Wolf picked up the roll of paper, holding it gently so it wouldn't fall apart. He limped down the driveway, taking short steps so the wound in his side didn't hurt so much.

The windows in the front of the house were dark, but the ones that faced the pool all radiated light. He crept onto the back patio, worried that Abby would see him in the circle of lights that illuminated the salty pool's blue waters. But she didn't notice him; she and the sad man were standing in the kitchen, so close together that they looked like they were trying to become one big person.

Wolf padded as close to the entryway as he dared, close enough to smell the comings and goings of many feet, and laid the long lump of paper there. In the morning when Abby found the paper, maybe then she'd be happy, and maybe then she would decide that Wolf was worthy to receive more than the generous offerings of food and water she had already given him.

He didn't hope to belong, or to be part of the family, as Georgia was. But he did hope that at least the next time Abby saw him, she wouldn't chase him away.

Wolf wondered where Georgia was, and as if his thoughts had called to hers, she ran through a small, flap-covered opening in one of the doors. She gave a happy *barroo* and danced on her back legs, licking at Wolf's mouth.

He backed up. "Shhh. Don't warn the humans that I'm here."

But it was too late. At Georgia's happy yodel, the humans sprang apart and looked out the big windows that filled an entire wall from the floor almost to the ceiling.

Wolf ran into the safety of darkness.

Chapter 8

FIRST THING MONDAY MORNING, ABBY OPENED THE SLIDING glass door and stepped outside—onto a wet, smashed wad of newsprint that squelched under her bare foot. "What on earth?"

Georgia sniffed the paper with great interest.

"Did you do this?" Abby asked the dog.

Georgia continued to sniff the paper. Then, making some sort of decision, she threw herself shoulder down onto the squishy mass and rolled, just once, before hopping up and shaking herself.

"Little dog," Abby said, "why you do the things you do is a mystery."

You're a mystery to me, too. The words popped into Abby's head. She looked down at Georgia, who was giving Abby an intense stare.

Abby laughed and reached down to pet Georgia. "You're right, I'm sure. Sometimes, I'm a mystery to myself."

Of course, Abby knew that the words she'd thought of were just as likely to be her imagination as any message Georgia was trying to relay, but whatever. It was fun to play the game of pretend that she might know what Georgia was thinking. Reva would be proud. After all the years she'd spent encouraging Abby to at least consider the possibility that she could communicate telepathically with animals, she might finally be getting the hang of it. "Just play with it," Reva had said. "Don't make everything so bloody serious."

Even as a child, Abby hadn't really known how to play, when everything in her life at home *was* bloody serious. No wonder she'd always been plagued by anxiety. Like a cloud, it had always hovered just above her head, and even when it drifted away a bit, it remained close enough for her to see in her peripheral vision.

When she left Blair, it became debilitating, paralyzing. She second-guessed everything she did, every decision she made.

Yesterday evening, when she was with Quinn, the cloud had disappeared completely the moment his lips met hers. But she had no business using a man as self-medication for a disorder she should learn to manage for herself. Her mother had done that and lost her identity.

Abby had vowed not to make the same mistake. She had pinned her hopes on Blair and the ready-made family he promised, but he turned out to be as self-centered, self-involved, and self-indulgent as Abby's father. She had felt like such a loser, asking her parents to take her in when her entire world imploded, demolished by her own hand in a weak moment of wine-fueled anger.

Drinking box wine while scrubbing lipstick stains from her live-in lover's boxer shorts had proven to be as effective for burning bridges as a lit torch. Forgetting for the moment that she had no legal claim on Blair's daughter, she had thrown the damp, stain-treated shorts in her lover's face. And with that one, satisfying splat, she had literally thrown the baby out with the bathwater.

Because Blair had never let her see Emily after that.

Abby knew she'd made the right decision in leaving, but her heart twisted at the thought of Emily going through rounds and rounds and rounds of well-meaning stepmothers who always left in the end.

"Animals are better than people." They didn't lie or obfuscate or use their children as bait to attract the next unwary victim. "I'll stick with animals from now on." Abby tossed the flattened newspaper into the recycle bin and took the phone out onto the patio to call the vet's office and make an afternoon appointment for the new kitten. The kitten hadn't suffered from a few days' wait. In fact, she had become more settled and trusting, so the upcoming ordeal would be less stressful.

Then, Abby prepared for her own upcoming ordeal—the

group of fifth graders set to arrive at 10:00 a.m.—by rushing through the morning's chores in order to make time to swim a few laps before her tour-guide helpers were set to arrive.

She swam hard enough to banish her regrets, at least for now. Then she turned to her back and floated, letting her mind drift back to Quinn's kiss...

Could she let herself imagine a future with him?

Her phone's alarm shrilled at the poolside; time to get ready for the next challenge. She had just stepped into the shower when the sounds of Georgia barking, horns honking, and kids shrieking filled her heart with terror. The buses were here a half hour early, before any of Abby's helpers had arrived. She pulled clothes on over still-damp skin, then grabbed the key to the gate's padlock and ran outside, untied shoelaces flapping. She unlocked the gate and picked up Georgia while the buses barreled past. Kids hung out of the buses' open windows, whooping and hollering.

Thank God she'd seen Quinn leave early for a carpentry job in New Orleans, and he wouldn't be back till dark. The noise of this unruly crowd would certainly have made his head explode.

Abby ran to catch up with the buses, holding Georgia close until all four of the buses stopped moving. Then she put Georgia down, and the smart little dog ran under the farmhouse's front porch and hid.

Abby wished she could hide, too.

Freddy, denied his usual job of sitting on someone's shoulder and greeting new arrivals, screamed from his aviary.

The bus doors opened and the Hordes of Hell burst free, screaming into the parking lot and beyond. Teachers and chaperones trickled out more slowly, already defeated by the prospect of corralling this bunch of hellions.

"Welcome to Bayside Barn," Abby said to the first adult who made eye contact. "Aren't all you Bayside Barn Buddies a tad early?"

The tired-looking woman with frazzled blond hair and an already sweat-stained school T-shirt shook her head. "I know. I'm sorry. The kids on the lead teacher's bus were acting up, so she decided they didn't deserve the pit stop we had planned to make on the way." The woman shrugged. "Sorry. Where are your bathrooms?"

Abby pointed toward the pavilion's bathrooms while her skin prickled with adrenaline. Every one of these kids was an accident waiting to happen, and they were running in all directions while the adults stood around helplessly, though a few of them had begun to corral the better-behaved kids who weren't running fast enough to get away.

A bunch of gangly boys chased the chickens around the chicken yard. The pig squealed hysterically from inside the barn; God only knew what some kid was doing in there. Abby patted her jeans pocket, but she hadn't picked up her whistle in the rush outside. She clapped her hands and yelled instead. "Everybody! Everybody, please listen!"

Nobody did.

Freddy clung to his aviary wire and screamed, then shouted. "Welcome, welcome! Shut up! Bad bird! Bad bird!" A tall boy had found a stick and was poking it through the wire, laughing when Freddy tried to bite the stick. "Bad bird," Freddy yelled. "No bites! No bites!"

Abby ran into the house, snagged the whistle off the key rack, and hurried back out, blowing the whistle as loudly as she could.

Other whistles joined in—at least one helper had arrived, thank God—and slowly the crowd simmered down. Some of the kids drifted toward the sound of the multiple whistles. Abby wilted in relief. Two more of her helpers had arrived, and another car pulled in a moment later.

Thank God. Abby realized she was shaking all over, trembling with fear that one of the animals would be harmed before she could get the situation under control.

Edna Fitzgerald, the oldest volunteer and a retired school-teacher, put a hand on Abby's shoulder and squeezed. "Do you want me to take over for a bit?"

Abby blinked back sudden tears of relief. "Yes, please."

Edna blew her whistle again. "Everybody FREEZE!" She pointed her whistle at the boys who had climbed the fence into the goat pen and apparently thought they were invisible. "Yes, I mean you. Get back here."

The boys slunk back over the fence into the yard.

"In a minute," Edna said, "I'm going to blow this whistle again. When I do, I want every human who arrived here on a bus to be standing in front of me. Got it?"

A few kids nodded, and others mumbled or said something affirmative-sounding. That wasn't good enough for Edna. "Signal you heard me by shouting, 'Yes, ma'am, Miss Edna!'" (Amazing, wonderful Edna.)

She glared at some kids who were still fidgeting, and incredibly, they stopped moving. "Now, for those of you who might not have heard, I will repeat myself only this once. When I blow this whistle, you will immediately make haste to stand silently in front of me and await further instruction. Do you understand?"

A chorus of voices answered, "Yes, ma'am, Miss Edna!"

Abby was overwhelmed by a rush of pure love, admiration, and respect for Edna, who had cast a magic spell over these horrible hellions and their ineffective adult chaperones.

Edna nodded approval, then blew the whistle.

As the children ran toward Edna, Abby felt a weak sense of optimism begin to flow through her. She—and the animal ambassadors of Bayside Barn—might make it through this day after all.

Quinn threw his phone onto the passenger seat and lowered the visor to block out the late-afternoon sun. Driving west into the sunset wasn't as annoying as the fact that every time he called Sean, the kid's phone went straight to voicemail. Either Sean was deliberately avoiding him, or he'd let his battery die.

Quinn hoped it was the battery.

He swung by Home Depot and picked up more sandpaper and another bucket of varnish for the bookstore shelving project he would complete by the end of this week. The shelving unit and the sliding ladder he'd constructed to reach its top shelves were a thing of beauty. With a fine sanding and another coat of high-gloss varnish, they'd be breathtaking.

And the final payment he would receive at the end of this week would allow him to breathe freely for the first time in months. The child-support check he'd written to Melissa last month had barely squeaked through his depleted checking account. Without this infusion of cash, the next check would hit bottom with a big clunk. The very thought of what would ensue if *that* happened gave him heartburn.

But all would be well once—

His cell rang with Sean's ringtone. Quinn took his eyes off the road just long enough to grab it and answer. "Hey, Sean!" His voice sounded too hearty, too happy to hear his son's voice. He cleared his throat and toned down his next words. "How's everything going?"

"Fine. Mom said you've been blowing up my phone. I was outside mowing the grass. I'm earning money so I'll have plenty to spend this weekend."

A trickle of foreboding made Quinn clench the steering wheel. "You won't need any money when you're with me, dude! You know that. I've got your room all ready, and I'm planning for us to—"

"Dad, my friends and me—"

"Excuse me? Your friends and who?"

"My friends and I"—Sean corrected himself with a huff of annoyance—"have been invited to go to a game in New Orleans this weekend. We'll get to stay in a fancy hotel and eat out and everything. It's all paid for except for whatever souvenirs we want to buy. Mom said she didn't think you'd mind if we swap out for the weekend after this."

Quinn gritted his teeth. They'd already swapped out so many weekends that Quinn only saw Sean about half the time he was supposed to. "That sounds like fun, but I have a lot of fun things planned for us, too, and I haven't seen you in—"

"So now you're guilt-tripping me, Dad? Really? You think that's going to make me want to come and see you more than I do already? All my friends are going. If you say no, I'll be the only one who doesn't get to go."

Quinn could just see Sean's reaction if forced to spend the weekend with him. He'd simmer and fume and isolate himself, playing solo video games and texting woe-is-me texts to his friends who were out having fun. "Fine," he capitulated. "Go ahead and have fun with your friends this weekend. Just please save next weekend for me, okay?"

He hated the pitiful sound of rejection he heard in his own voice, so he tried to lighten the tone of both his voice and the conversation. "How was school today? It's final exam week, yeah?" The second the words left his mouth, he realized his change of topic would be an epic disaster.

"I'm not failing, if that's what you mean."

"No, Son. I just want to know what's going on in your life. If I can't see you in person, I'd at least like to talk to you on the phone."

"Yeah, Dad." Sarcasm dripped from Sean's words. "Sure."

"I picked a bad subject, I guess. What would you like to talk about? How's your girlfriend... What's her name? Jenny?"

"We're not dating anymore, and her name is Jenea, not Jenny."

Strike three—or was it strike four? Quinn had lost count. But damned if he'd stop trying. "I've been building a huge set of book-shelves for an indie bookstore in NOLA. Did I tell you?"

"You texted a bunch of pictures."

"Oh, yeah. I'd forgotten that." Sean hadn't responded, so Quinn had wondered if the text had gone through. But he knew better to bring that up. Sean would take it as a criticism and become even more defensive than he already was.

"Look, Dad. I need to go. I've got exams to study for."

"Oh, okay. Sure. Talk to you later."

Sean didn't even say goodbye; he just ended the call.

Defeated, Quinn tossed his phone back into the passenger seat. The battered old truck's radio wasn't worth listening to, and road noise drowned out his cell phone's speakers. If his ex-wife hadn't kept all their friends in the divorce, he'd call a friend to make the drive back to the pool house seem shorter.

But she had, so that left him with few options.

His mom was off on another cruise with her husband, so he couldn't call her. His dad was going deaf but refused to get a hearing aid, so phone conversations with him were almost as frustrating as talking to Sean.

Quinn even thought about calling Abby, but what would he say? They weren't friends, just friendly neighbors. They'd both been lucky that the little dog's barking had distracted them last night before they made a big mistake they'd both regret. That first kiss had been hot enough to burn, so he'd made sure the one he gave her at the end of the evening was no more than a lukewarm gesture of thanks. He shouldn't have kissed her at all, but hell. How could he resist?

He could blame it on the wine, or on her excellent cooking, or on all of the atoms and molecules that combined to make her exactly who she was. He could blame it on his loneliness, or on her fluttery nervousness that he seemed to know instinctively how to diffuse. No matter what he blamed it on, he knew that following up on that steamy kiss with a phone call would have unavoidable repercussions. If he called her today, right after that lucky near-miss, he'd be making a conscious decision to take that relationship in a direction he didn't have the time or energy or money to travel.

But when he thought of Abby's sweet, guileless face and her luscious body that looked just as good in boxer shorts and a tank top as it did naked, he wished he did have the time and energy and money to make that call and find out whether they could be more to each other than friendly neighbors.

―――――――――

When the last bus pulled out of the barn's parking lot, it was all Abby could do not to fall to her knees in relief. Edna patted her back. "You did just fine today. None of the animals or kids got hurt, and you taught those hellions why it's important to respect animals. You've changed some minds, and maybe even the trajectory of a few lives today; probably even saved one or two of them from ending up in jail. Your aunt would be proud of you."

"Thank you, Edna. I appreciate you more than I can say. If you hadn't arrived this morning when you did—"

"You'd have handled it. I probably shouldn't have stepped in the way I did."

Abby hugged the older woman. "If you hadn't, you would have had one more screaming person on your hands. I'm very glad you offered to take over."

"Well, honey, I was glad to help. This place changes people for the better. It's an honor to be a part of it."

The other volunteers had zoomed out of there the moment the buses were loaded, and Abby didn't blame them one bit. Edna always waited to see if there was anything more she could do to help. This afternoon was no different, but Abby let her off the hook. "I have to take a kitten to the vet this afternoon, so I'll do all the chores when I get back. Thanks for the offer, though."

When Edna left, Abby glanced at the clock. She'd have to hurry to get there on time. Quickly, she put the kitten in a travel crate and drove Reva's car to the vet's office, arriving exactly on time for the scheduled appointment.

She had worried that this late in the afternoon the office would be packed, but she was in luck; the gravel lot was empty. She parked under a big oak tree whose thick branches were covered in resurrection fern. An old-fashioned wooden sign with green lettering hung from a post on the shaded lawn:

MAGNOLIA BAY ANIMAL HOSPITAL

MACK MCNEIL, DVM

She took the crate off the passenger seat and shushed the kitten who meowed plaintively and stuck her little paws out of the crate's slots. "Shush, baby." She kept the crate level and walked up to the vet's office, a cute clapboard building that had once been someone's house. A wide front porch with a white rail was bordered by hanging ferns, the colors echoed by a row of white rocking chairs with green cushions. The building itself was a subdued shade of butter yellow with white trim.

Abby tried to open the door to the office, but it was stuck. Or, wait…. Was it locked? She set the crate down and peered through the door's ornate, leaded-glass window. Seen in a kaleidoscope of rainbow images, the empty waiting room looked like something out of a 1940s movie, a mix-up of mismatched antique furniture that looked just right in the room.

But the only light came through the half-closed plantation blinds on the porch windows; the lights in the office were out. Why was the office closed when Abby had an appointment? She knocked on the door, but no one answered.

Never mind, whatever, the office was closed. "Well, hell." She picked up the crate and headed back to the car. She was crossing the parking lot when her phone dinged with an incoming text. She checked the screen and unlocked the car door. When she saw that it was Quinn, her heart gave a little skip of excitement.

Her skipping heart calmed down when she read his message: Fence down again, crumpled beyond repair. Goats wreaking havoc, eating everything not nailed down. Please come ASAP. Bring 50' wrapped-wire fencing, 9 posts, small bag fence clips.

Her heart skipped again at his last, romantic words: I'll help.

Chapter 9

AS ABBY STOOD IN THE PARKING LOT OF MAGNOLIA BAY Animal Clinic, a battered Ford pickup sailed into the lot and rocked to a stop beside her. The vet himself, Mack McNeil, stepped out. At fiftysomething, Mack still had the sort of muscles that came from a lifetime of wrestling headstrong horses, cantankerous cows, ornery sheep, and who-knew-what-else. Today, his jeans and shirt were liberally covered with red dirt, and his short dark hair stuck straight up, not with hair gel, but with a good coating of dirt and sweat.

"Hey, Abby." He smiled, crow's-feet crinkling at the corners of his amber eyes.

"Hey, Mack." She'd known him since she... Well, since before she could remember. She'd spent just about every summer at Aunt Reva's farm, and Mack had been good friends with Reva's husband. "You look like you've been having fun."

"Just delivered a foal." He grinned in delight; clearly, Mack loved his job. "Cutest thing ever." He slammed the truck door and leaned on the bed's side rail. "You coming or going?"

"Going. I had an appointment, but you didn't show."

"Awww, I'm sorry. New kitten appointment, right?" He gave a puzzled look around the parking lot, then at the dim, lights-out office. "I don't know why Patricia isn't here. But at least I caught you before you left. Come on in."

She shook her head. "Sorry, but I've got to run back to the farm and mend a fence, and I've got to stop for supplies first."

"Aww, please. I'll feel really bad if you leave now. Come on in and let's tend to that kitten. I promise I'll get you out of here in five minutes or less." He reached out for the crate, and as she handed it over, he glanced around the parking lot with an irritated scowl on his face. "I'll give you my cell number so you can reach me directly if this ever happens again."

"Thanks, Mack."

Abby followed Mack back to the office and—not quite as promised but still pretty darn good—he gave the kitten an exam, wormer, and shots in ten minutes, and gave Abby a tube of anti-biotic for the road rash. When Abby asked about payment, Mack waved her away. "Nah. I don't know anything about billing, and I don't want to learn. If Patricia wanted to charge you, she should have been here to do it."

As Abby was driving home, Reva called. "Hey, I'm sorry I haven't been able to call before now. How's that new kitten doing?"

"Fine," Abby said. "She's had her shots, and her road rash is much better. I've named her Stella."

"That's perfect," Reva said. "How's everything at the farm going?"

"Welp, the goats and donkeys keep knocking down the fence between us and the new neighbor. I'm on my way to the hardware store right now for supplies."

"New neighbor? What new neighbor? Somebody bought the place next door?" Disappointment rang in Reva's voice. As long as the place remained on the market, there had been a chance—a slim one—that the city might still buy it to convert into an animal shelter. "Well, hell. I guess that's that, then."

"I know," Abby said. "But I think you'll like him. He's pretty nice. He's going to help me repair the fence."

"That's good," Reva said, but her voice still sounded subdued. "What else is going on? I have to admit that I've been too exhausted to check in with the animals like I promised. Georgia keeps pinging me, though. Something about a new dog? I'm too tired to really connect in and get a clear picture. They're working us from dawn till dark at this place. I'm surprised I'm paying them instead of the other way 'round."

"Aw." Maybe that was a good thing; the animals wouldn't be telling on Abby. "Yep, there's a stray dog hanging out across the street. I've been feeding him, but he won't come close. I've only actually seen him once." She didn't add that it was when he tried to kill a chicken. "How are the classes?"

"Amazing. I'm learning a lot that isn't in the manual. I'm glad I decided to learn hands-on instead of just studying the manual and taking the test."

Abby pulled into the local hardware store's parking lot. "Hey, well, I'm here at the hardware store," she said.

"Oh, okay. I'll let you go, then. You're using the Bayside Barn credit card for all that stuff, right?"

"Yes, ma'am, I am."

"And you're paying the bills as soon as they come in, right?"

So far, she'd just been piling the mail in a stack, but she planned to catch up on that tomorrow. "Yes, ma'am. But hey, let me let you go so Quinn and I can get this fence repair done before dark."

"Quinn, hmmm?" The speculative tone in Reva's voice sounded like her psychic powers might be kicking in. "Is he cute?"

Time to get off the phone. "I'll tell you all about him later. I'm hanging up now. Bye, Aunt Reva."

———

Quinn sacrificed a new bag of generic-brand Fruity Loops that he'd bought for Sean. Shaking the bag as bait, he led the goats into an empty barn stall, tossed in the bag, then locked them in before they knew they'd been fooled. The unhappy *baaa*'s didn't begin until after he'd lured the donkeys into another stall with a granola bar.

The damn goats had skinned the hedge down to its toughest branches, eaten the top three cardboard boxes of laminate flooring he'd left stacked in the bed of his truck—just the boxes, not the flooring, thank God—and scattered the contents of his tool belt to kingdom come.

He used a big magnet to find nails and screws and an assortment of tools in the tall grass beyond the pool. By the time Abby pulled up next door, he had set up a heavy-duty stand of work lights, removed the damaged section of wire fencing, and pulled up the bent metal posts. With the late-afternoon sunlight slanting through the straggly trees on his side of the fence, the lights weren't needed yet. Whether they'd need them at all depended on how helpful Abby could be.

He wasn't holding out much hope. Women, in his experience, only got in the way when there was real work to be done. If she decided to wander off and make lemonade, he hoped she put a liberal amount of vodka in it.

Abby backed Reva's car up to the gap and got out pulling on a new-looking pair of work gloves. "The smallest roll they had was a hundred feet. I was on my knees praying that the guys at the store would be able to fit it in the trunk. It's gonna be a bitch to lift; we'll have to do it together."

"Ya think?" Unable to resist showing off, he lifted the roll out easily and carried it to the wooden corner post where they would begin the run. The wooden posts were concreted into the ground every sixteen feet and interspersed with two cheaper metal posts between each wooden one. The old metal posts were bent and rusted; he had tossed them on top of the tangled pile of wire in the fenced pasture beyond.

He went back to the truck for the new metal posts and dumped the whole bunch on the ground near the work area. "I rolled up what's left of the old fencing and tied it with baling string. It's in a pile over there"—he nodded in the general direction—"along with all the old posts. I'll take it all to the metal-recycling place on my way to work tomorrow."

"Thank you." She put a hand on his arm and leaned toward

him. He thought she might kiss him, but she didn't. "I really appreciate all your help."

Georgia appeared from somewhere to supervise the operation, sniffing the tools and fencing material, then toddling off to eat grass, or poop, or do whatever it was dogs did when they had nothing to do.

Abby and Quinn worked together well. He jabbed the prong end of a metal post into the ground, then she held it while he used the post driver to hammer it deeply into the ground. She held the fence roll against a wooden post while he nailed the wire to the post with U-shaped nails. He used the come-along to pull out the slack in the wire, and they both worked together to fasten the wire to the metal posts with specially shaped fencing clips. He snipped the wire at the end of the run while she held the roll taut to keep the raw edges from snapping back.

No lemonade-making miss, he thought appreciatively. Knowing that he was in danger of doing more appreciating than he should, he said the first thing he could come up with that had nothing to do with Abby's sweet smile, her glowing cheeks, or her curvaceous body. "You really should replace the rest of this fence line. The part that runs through the hedge is pretty much rusted out."

"I don't know if Reva wants us to do that," Abby said, sounding worried. "Wouldn't we have to cut down the hedge first?"

"We'd have to trim it back pretty drastically," he agreed. "But the goats have already gone some distance toward completing that project. I didn't notice that they were in my yard until they'd already had a grand old time unloading my truck and chomping on the hedges."

"I'm glad they stayed in your yard. If they'd gone as far as the cat's-claw forest, we might never have seen them again."

"Damn. I didn't think of that." He grinned at her and started gathering tools. "I locked them and the donkeys up in the barn instead of shooing them across the road. Too bad."

"You don't mean that," Abby chided. It was clear she thought he was too nice to chase her aunt's wandering goats away, when in fact he just hadn't thought of it.

"Don't fool yourself; I may not be as nice as you think I am." He unplugged the work lights and rolled up the extension cord. It hadn't gotten dark enough for the lights to be useful, but Quinn hadn't known how long the fence-mending would take. Abby had been much more helpful than he'd anticipated, and the work had gone smoothly.

Once they'd cleared away all the tools and stashed the unused wire in the barn's storage room, Abby invited Quinn to dinner. But they'd done that yesterday, and look how that had almost turned out. He'd better go back to being the friendly neighbor on the other side of the fence. "Thanks, but I've got a lot of work to do next door. I'm installing new flooring in the master bedroom."

Since Sean wasn't coming after all this weekend, Quinn had decided to sleep in Sean's room this week—the only room he'd finished—and complete the renovations in the rest of the pool house. If he worked every evening this week, he could have the whole place done—except regrouting the vintage floor tiles in the kitchen. Those bitches would take forever.

"I understand you're busy," Abby said. "But would you at least let me fix you a plate? I'll bring it over so you can eat while you work."

There wasn't any way he could decline a hand-delivered dinner without seeming rude, and even though he wasn't interested in a relationship, he wanted Abby to like him. "Sure, that'll be great. Thanks."

When she delivered a foil-covered plate an hour or so later, he set the plate on the coffee table and invited her in for a glass of wine, but she stood in the open doorway and shook her head. "Nope. I won't keep you from your work. But I do have one quick question: You haven't, by any chance, been tossing newspapers over the fence onto my back patio, have you?"

"No." He turned toward her and laughed. "Should I be?"

She laughed, too. "No. I was just wondering. This morning, I stepped on a soggy newspaper someone had left on my doorstep, and when I came home this afternoon, there was another one. Dry and readable this time, though. I might clip some coupons later."

"Whoa. You're living the good life over there on your side of the fence." He stepped close, close enough to see the threadlike gold rim around the pupil of her hazel eyes and the pale brown tips of her black lashes.

She smiled the shy smile that had captivated him from the beginning. "I wouldn't say I'm living high on the hog, but life on the other side of the fence isn't all that bad, either."

She put a hand on his arm and leaned in. And this time, she did kiss him. "Thanks for everything."

Her kiss had been a chaste peck, her closed lips soft on his. "You're welcome," he responded, looking into her eyes. He debated with himself for a moment, but decided he couldn't allow that chaste little kiss to stand. He wrapped an arm around her and drew her body up against his, hip to hip, stomach to stomach, heart to heart. He could feel hers hammering, or maybe that was his. Her mouth had dropped open, an O of surprise.

He couldn't stop himself from taking advantage of that surprised little O.

When he finally pulled away, her eyes were dazed, her cheeks were flushed, and her wavy hair stuck out where he'd run his fingers through the thick, soft strands. "That's better."

She nodded, and her hand drifted up to touch her lips. "Um… Okay. Well…good…um… Good night."

"Good night, Abby. Sleep well." The word *sweetheart* came up from somewhere inside him, but he had the good sense not to say it. She wasn't his sweetheart. He didn't have the time or the money or even the inclination for a sweetheart. And yet, when she left and he closed the sliding glass door behind her, he felt disappointed that he hadn't taken her up on her dinner offer.

———

Every day for the rest of the week, Abby stepped out the door to find a new, crisp newspaper folded on her doorstep. Every day, Georgia sniffed the paper with intense interest, then looked up at Abby with a "Do something" demand in her imploring brown eyes.

This morning was no exception. "I don't know what you want me to do," Abby wailed. Disgusted, Georgia turned away, tail low. She hardly even ate her breakfast, just picked at it before walking away.

As always, after completing the morning feed and cleanup routine, Abby tended to the stray dog across the street by dumping and refilling the water bucket and putting out a new (disposable) food dish, which the dog invariably carried off into his vine-covered lair. As always, Georgia followed, attending to her supervisory duties and clearly judging Abby's work to be inferior. When Abby began to head back across the street, Georgia sat and yipped, looking from Abby to the forest and back again.

"I can't go in there," Abby said. "He's going to have to come out."

Georgia wagged her tail and barked again.

Abby put her hands on her hips. "Puppy, puppy," she called, knowing it wouldn't work because it hadn't worked yet, and she'd been doing it every morning. She made kissing noises. Again, no response. "Puppy, puppy, come on out. We won't hurt you."

Apparently satisfied that Abby had at least tried, Georgia stood and headed back down the driveway, tail waving like a banner.

Abby poured a glass of iced tea and sat in a chaise on the patio to check her text messages. The night before, Reva had texted Dog-tired after shoveling shit all day; I could have stayed home to do this. The text had been followed by a photo of a wheelbarrow full of animal poop with a close-up of Reva's blistered hands in the foreground.

Abby had replied: Should I mail a pair of gloves?

Reva's reply had come through later that night, after Abby had gone to bed. No, don't need gloves; I was wearing gloves when I got those blisters. They keep us so busy! Hardly had a chance to relax all day. Even lunchtimes are used for instruction; we eat while watching PowerPoint presentations. It's 11:00 p.m. already, and we have to get up at 6:00 a.m. Hope all is going well at the farm. Please text and send pics so I can communicate with the animals when I get a break. (You know it's easier if you can see their eyes.) Especially Georgia. She keeps pinging me as I'm falling asleep; she says you need to be talking to that stray dog that's been hanging around. How did the fence-repair project go with the new neighbor? How are the chickens?

This message had come along with a photo of a cafeteria with a blurry projector screen at the front of the room and a bunch of college-age kids photo-bombing the picture.

Abby took a sip of her iced tea and replied: Who's the cute blond guy with the buzz cut?

The distress call of a donkey rose up from behind the barn, loud, insistent, and terrifying. Elijah sounded hurt, and his cries of fear and pain rose in volume and intensity. Abby dropped her phone on the chaise and ran toward the sound.

"Abby," Quinn yelled over the fence. "Everything okay?"

"No," Abby huffed as she ran. "I don't know."

"I'm coming to help," Quinn yelled. "Hang on."

Abby ran around the side of the barn to see Elijah in the field, tangled in the roll of used fence wire she and Quinn had left out. "Damn!" Abby had completely forgotten about that old wire. The poor donkey had tried to step over it to get to some tasty over-hanging leaves, and ended up with the wire tangled around his legs. Elijah bellowed in fear, his eyes rolling, his nostrils distended.

He tried to rear, but the wire around his legs hobbled him. Miriam, the other donkey, stood nearby, wailing in sympathy.

Abby approached Elijah, one hand out. "Shhh," she soothed. "Be still, baby."

Quinn rushed up, breathing hard. "Don't try to help him yet, Abby. You'll both end up getting hurt."

"Well, I don't know what you expect me to do," she hissed without sparing Quinn a glance. She rubbed Elijah's nose. "I'm not going to walk away and leave him like this."

"Do. Not. Move. I'll be back in a minute."

Why hadn't Abby paid more attention to where Quinn left the old bent-up wire and posts? Because he'd promised to take them to the recycling place the next morning, and he hadn't done it, that's why.

Quinn came back with a halter and lead rope in one hand, and a pair of stout bolt-cutters in the other. He handed over the halter. "Here. Put this on him and hold him still."

She buckled the halter—it didn't fit but was better than nothing—and gathered the lead rope into short loops so she could hold it close to Elijah's chin and keep him from rearing. She hoped. "Why didn't you take that wire away like you promised?"

"My bad." Quinn started clipping the wire strands that held Elijah captive. "I forgot. I'm sorry."

"Elijah better not get hurt because of this." Abby knew that her accusing tone wasn't fair; she'd been as responsible as Quinn for this trap they'd set. She should have paid more attention when he told her where he'd left the wire. She should have reminded him to take it away. She shouldn't have released the donkeys—and the goats, for that matter—into a field that wasn't safe.

"I said I'm sorry." Quinn clipped more strands and separated the wires that wound around Elijah's left back leg. "I take complete responsibility, and I'm doing my best to fix the problem." Quinn pulled away a wadded section of wire, releasing Elijah's leg, which he promptly used to kick out at Quinn. "Would you hold him still, please, before he kills me?"

Abby knew that a well-placed donkey kick could be lethal, and Quinn had no choice but to bend over, putting his skull in too-close proximity to Elijah's flashing hooves. "I'm trying," she griped. "Maybe you should get his front legs free first, so he can't kick out."

"Eventually, I'll have to free all of his legs," Quinn reasoned. "I'd like it if you'd just keep him still so he can't decide to kick my damn teeth in."

"I'm doing my best." She jerked down on the lead rope. Elijah rolled his eyes and plunged up and down on his front feet. "Be still, you bad donkey. We're trying to help."

"For God's sake, don't rile him up more," Quinn fussed. "Pet his nose or something."

"I can't pet his nose or something," she retorted with irritation. "I need both hands to hold on to this lead rope so he doesn't kick your thick head in."

Quinn moved around to free Elijah's front legs, doing what Abby had suggested by leaving the remaining back leg for last. He didn't, of course, give her credit for a good idea—it might not end up being a good idea anyway. The test would come when the last leg came free.

Georgia, who'd been who-knows-where for the last few minutes, came in close to sniff out the problem. She inspected the tangled wire, and then sniffed Elijah's newly freed back leg. "Georgia," Abby hissed. "Go away."

Quinn flicked the bolt cutters in her direction. "Move, dog. You're not helping." He pulled free another section of fence. "Two legs down, two to go."

Miriam came close to sniff a section of fence that Quinn had cut away and tossed aside. Quinn half stood and flapped a hand at the curious donkey. "Shoo."

Abby heard the bleat of goats in the distance, followed by the unmistakable sound of the entire herd coming this way at a fast clip. "Hurry up, Quinn." Abby imagined the hullabaloo that would occur with a dozen animals milling around this operation. The goats' heads and horns bobbed up over the hill's horizon line, then the whole herd galloped into sight. "Shit. Here they all come."

Quinn pulled aside another section of wire, and with another couple of quick clips, he had entirely freed the donkey's front legs. "One left." He moved around to the still-ensnared back leg. "Pull him forward so he doesn't have room to kick out. Then hold him still."

Goats had begun to nibble at the discarded wire. Gregory chewed at Abby's shoelaces, and Esmeralda bit at Quinn's jeans. "Georgia," Abby said, "aren't you supposed to be a herding dog?"

Georgia looked up at Abby, then immediately chased the goats away, nipping at heels and expertly keeping stragglers from turning back. When the goats had all disappeared behind the hill, Georgia came back and sat, panting. Abby's stress level dropped, and she relaxed her hold on the lead rope.

"Okay," Quinn said. "This is it." He clipped the last wire holding Elijah's leg and pulled the chunk of wire away.

Elijah brayed with joy and plunged forward as if Abby wasn't standing right in front of him. She landed on her butt. Cradling her rope-burned palms, Abby watched Elijah run over the hill with the lead rope flapping out behind him. "You're welcome," she snarked at the ungrateful equine's backside.

"You okay?" Quinn put out a hand. When she hesitated to put her still-burning hand in his, he grabbed her wrists and tugged to help her stand.

She stood, keeping most of her weight on her right leg. When she shifted, her left ankle buckled, and a sharp, knife-edged pain shot from the sole of her foot to her knee. She sat abruptly. "Owww."

Quinn knelt down beside her and took her booted foot in his hand. "Owww," she complained. "Don't."

"Shit. That damn donkey has broken your fucking foot."

"Broken? No. It can't be." It hurt like holy hell, though.

He looked her in the eye, his blue-jean-blue eyes serious. "You want to stand up and prove it to me?"

The very thought of standing on that foot made adrenaline flare like a gas stove meeting a lit match.

Chapter 10

Quinn scooped Abby up and stood, holding her against his chest. "Please tell me you don't have a field trip scheduled for today."

She wrapped her arms around his neck. "I don't." The hot breeze blew her hair across his face; the wavy strands smelled like flowers.

"Good. I don't have work, either, so we both get to spend the day in the ER." He carried her toward the closed field gate, which they had both climbed over when the hysteria began.

"Wait," she said. "You've got to clean up all the wire first."

He held her tighter. "And leave you sitting in the dirt? I don't think so."

"But…"

He unlatched the gate. "Shush. First things first." He carried her into the barn and put her on the UTV's passenger seat. Georgia hopped in, too, then Quinn drove back into the field and loaded up the damaged wire. "Can you take that boot off? You probably should, in case your foot starts to swell."

She started working on the laces. "Ow, ow, ow… We should have done this in the first place."

"Done what?" He tossed the fence posts on top of the wire. "Broken your foot? Taken off your boot?"

"No. I'm saying that we should have put all the discarded wire in the UTV before any of this happened." A nice way of blaming him, he thought—saying *we* when she really meant *him*.

"Live and learn." As he recalled, he'd been too busy noticing her cute backside and can-do attitude to be thinking very hard about equine safety concerns. He climbed over the closed half-door of the UTV and wrestled the stick shift into reverse. "I've made an mistake I won't repeat."

"I'm not blaming you," she blurted out. "If anyone's to blame, it's me."

He ground the gears and the UTV shot forward. "Of course."

"No, really," she insisted. "Aunt Reva told me to check the grazing field for hazards on a regular basis. I didn't do it at all, or I'd have—"

The UTV's brakes squealed and gravel scattered when Quinn stomped on the brake, parking next to the farm truck. "Truck keys?"

"In the ignition."

He picked up Georgia, who growled at him. "You can't go," he told her. "Where do I put this dog so she'll stay put while we're gone?"

"You know, I really think this isn't as bad as you think. Probably I just need to rest it."

Yeah, not really. He was pretty sure he'd heard a snap when that donkey ran over her. He lowered his eyebrows at her and looked down at the dog he held.

"Close the doggy door in the laundry room and leave her in the house. And grab my purse from the... From wherever it is. It's pink leather. Might be hanging on those hooks by the door. Or maybe..."

He didn't hear the rest of what she said because he'd gone inside and closed the door. He got the dog situated and found the purse, kicking himself the whole time. Who was gonna feed all these hollering animals when she was hobbling around on crutches?

As if the universe delighted in answering his question, he caught a glimpse of himself in the mirror by the back door on his way out.

Quinn was such a gentleman! He carried her into the waiting room of the local ER, deposited her into one of the wheelchairs by the door, and then wheeled her to the sign-in desk. He hadn't been very chatty; in fact, he'd been a little broody. He was probably worried about her.

Within minutes, the efficient medical staff had taken over, passing her from a nurse who typed up the intake info to a fourteen-year-old X-ray technician to the elderly orthopedic doctor. He slapped a big sheet of film up on the light box on the wall. "Good thing you've got somebody to wait on you for the next few weeks." He pointed out two clearly broken bones on the arched foot in the blurry image. "You're gonna need it."

Abby's heart sank low. Yes, her foot hurt like hell, but she'd been hoping for a mild sprain. "For how long?"

"Six to eight weeks, I'd say. But you can tell your man anything you want. If you want to milk it for more than a cool two months, I won't tell."

He put a cast on Abby's foot that went all the way up to her knee. "In my opinion," he said, "a cast is better than a boot."

"I feel all better, then," Abby said, softening the snark with a smile. While the fiberglass cast dried and hardened, she chewed her fingernails and worried about what she'd tell Aunt Reva—and about *when* she'd tell Aunt Reva. Maybe she should call right now and 'fess up to the wire they'd left lying around, and the danger she'd put the donkeys in.

Or maybe Abby shouldn't tell Reva at all, because she knew her aunt would drop the internship and come back home. At only two weeks into her sabbatical, Reva might take Abby's accident as a sign from the universe that she should abandon the idea and come back home. (Reva took pretty much everything as a sign from the universe.)

As Abby pondered the wisdom of calling (or not calling) Reva, her phone pinged with an incoming text from her aunt. Is everything okay at the farm? For some reason, I can't get you off my mind today.

Abby made a few false starts, typing and then deleting what she'd written. She finally settled on an evasive truth. Everything's fine at the farm! Don't worry about us!

Because Abby and her broken foot weren't at the farm at the moment, so technically, everything at the farm *was* fine. She followed that text with another; a smiley-face emoji and Hope you're having a good day.

Better than good. A dream come true day! This was followed by a photo of Reva bottle-feeding a bobcat cub. Her aunt was grinning like a teenager at the prom, and the cute studly guy from the cafeteria picture—the one with the buzz cut—had one arm around her while he held the phone out with the other, selfie-style. Blond guy is my lab partner. He's about your age. Should I inquire?

Seeing how much fun her aunt was having made Abby glad she had decided not to tell Reva after all. No need to worry her. Abby would manage. She responded to Reva's text with a horrified-face emoji, and NO! Not interested in blond guy. You can keep him. Cute bobcat, though. Maybe you can bring him home.

Abby knew she'd have to tell Reva about her broken foot sometime, just not right now. She could probably hobble around just fine and do all the chores. The next time Reva called, Abby could report that she had broken her foot, but everything was fine, and she was managing quite well. At the thought of putting off the inevitable, Abby's stress level dropped significantly.

Maybe sometimes, letting the bull wander off into the field was better than trying to take it by the horns.

Quinn took Abby to the pharmacy and the medical supply store. He picked up fast food so she could take her pain medication on a full stomach. He held her elbow while she maneuvered on crutches and made it inside the house. He unfolded the knee scooter and set it by the back door.

While he did all these things, he surrendered to the fact that he was about to pay, and pay dearly, for his stupid decision to help with the fence-building project and then leave a roll of fence wire lying in the neighbor's grazing field. His father had always said, "No good deed ever goes unpunished." Quinn was beginning to see the wisdom in that viewpoint.

"Thanks for taking such good care of me." Abby leaned against the doorframe, balancing uneasily on the new crutches she had already managed to drop or trip over at least a dozen times.

Georgia came out of the bedroom and shot out the open door into the darkness, barking at nothing. The donkeys brayed, the goats baaed, and a general sense of unrest settled like a smelly old blanket over the farm. "What can I do to shut these hollering animals up?" he asked. "I know they're expecting to be fed, and there must be chores...?"

Abby shook her head. "I couldn't possibly ask you to do my chores. We'll be fine. I'm just gonna use the scooter and—"

"You're *just* going to sit on that couch with your foot elevated, while I do what needs to be done around here." She'd better not be a reluctant patient; he didn't have time to do all her work and argue about it, too.

"But you won't know what to do unless I show you." She leaned the crutches against the wall and held on to the doorframe, hopping on one foot to make tiny, incremental progress through the doorway toward the knee scooter.

"What are you doing?" He grabbed her arm. She stumbled over the threshold, and he held her up. "You trying to kill yourself?"

"I'm going to feed critters." She grabbed the handlebars of the scooter and put her knee on the cushion, then pushed the scooter forward and hopped behind it. "You can come, too, if you want."

"Where are you going?" He put a hand on her back; she didn't look too steady, and she was hopping in the exact opposite direction from the barn. "You're going to fall and break your other foot if you're not careful."

"I'm trying to get to the barn."

"Oh, really? Well, you're going the wrong way."

"I know that." Hopping sideways, she wrestled the handlebars and almost tipped the damn thing over. "How does this thing turn around?"

"You have to make a wide circle, I think. Push it forward and then circle back."

She shoved the scooter out in front of her and hopped to keep up with it. "Damn fucker," she mumbled when the wheels stuck. Then she looked over her shoulder at Quinn. "Push it forward," she mimicked. "Circle back around. That's exactly what I was doing when you yelled at me."

"I didn't yell," he yelled. "I never yell."

She snorted, then laughed. "Thanks for letting me know what a pussycat I'm dealing with. I had no idea."

Together, they struggled toward the barn, step by hopping step. Scooters and flagstone pavers across a grassy lawn didn't mix well. But Abby had proved herself to be even more incompetent on crutches.

Georgia tried to urge Abby on at first, dancing around and yapping at the wheels of the scooter. Finally, she gave up and hopped onto the padded seat next to Abby's knee. She looked forward, ears up, eyes bright, tongue hanging out. In the barn, she hopped down and rushed to the first food bin, doing her own version of Vanna White. Her wagging tail was just as expressive as Vanna's graceful wrist flick. If Georgia could speak, she'd be saying, "This one's first; that one's next."

Quinn felt like he'd landed back in kindergarten when he encountered the color-coded buckets and bins and scoops arranged in a line below the color-coded instructions written in wide-tipped Vis-à-Vis markers on the big whiteboard.

"First, you put the buckets on the floor next to the same-colored bins," Abby instructed. "Then, you use the same-colored scoops to dish up the food."

"No shit. How ingenious." Because yes, Reva's instructions had left nothing to chance, unless the person doing the work was color-blind.

"Yeah, I know, right?" Abby chirped. "My aunt Reva is really good at breaking things down into small, doable chunks."

"Color-coding makes everything better." Lord God, he thought. Just let him finish this, throw down these color-coded buckets, and get out of here. He wanted nothing more right now than to be sitting in front of the TV in his pool house, drinking a beer and watching a WWE match. Spurting blood and the smell of hops might soothe his battered spirit right about now. "Brilliance must run in your family."

Abby scooted closer to the bins and held one open for him. "Reva is definitely smarter than the average bear. I'm not so sure about myself."

I'm not so sure about you, either, he thought, until she leaned forward to hand him the next feed scoop, and he got a clear view down the front of her tank top. At that point, his brain stopped working altogether, and he wasn't sure about anything.

Abby's foot throbbed. She looked out the bedroom window at the lights blazing in Quinn's pool house. He had offered to spend the night on the couch in case she needed help. Of course, she had declined. She could have fed the critters this evening; the knee scooter allowed her that much freedom. But unfortunately, she wouldn't have been able to shovel poop or empty and refill water buckets.

But she had managed to get ready for bed by herself without incident. Quinn had insisted on waiting in Reva's living room in case she ran into trouble, but she hadn't.

Now that she was in bed, she realized that the pain meds didn't dull the pain; they just made her head so fuzzy that she didn't care how bad her foot hurt. Hoping the meds would kick in with a little more oomph soon, Abby checked her phone and found a text message from Reva.

Someone brought in an injured mama deer today. She had been hit by a car. Her injuries will mend, but I know that she had babies who are waiting for her to return. She told me where she'd hidden them, but no one with access to a vehicle would help me look for them. Everybody thinks I'm crazy. I can't stop crying right now. Maybe I should just come home.

Abby didn't know how to reply. She settled for a sad-face emoji.

She tried to think of something more eloquent or helpful to write, but couldn't. With a sigh, she plugged the phone into the charger and set it facedown on the bedside table, then turned out the lamp.

Georgia stretched out against Abby's good leg and groaned. Abby tried to relax, but something still left undone niggled at the edges of her consciousness.

Quinn had done everything; she could relax.

She tried a progressive-relaxation technique, going from toes to ankles to knees, then moving upward, on and on to the top of her head, systematically relaxing each part and parcel of her body, bit by bit. She got as far as the heart chakra when she remembered.

She hadn't given fresh food and water to the stray wolf dog across the street. She sat up in bed. "Georgia, why didn't you remind me?"

Georgia wagged her tail and lowered her chin. *I tried, but you weren't listening.*

Abby imagined the words of Georgia's response and knew

that even though she couldn't communicate with animals as well as her aunt did, her impression in this instant must be the truth. Georgia had formed a bond with that stray dog. She would have chosen to feed him, and lacking that ability, she would have tried to get someone else—Abby—to do it. The fact that it hadn't been done meant that Georgia *had* tried to tell Abby, but Abby hadn't listened. Maybe it was time for her to really start trying instead of doubting herself all the time.

"I don't think I should chance us going outside right now," Abby said.

Georgia whined and looked toward the bedroom door. *Are you sure? He's hungry, and that water bucket is almost empty.*

"I can put a pan of food and a bowl of water on the back patio," Abby promised. "But you'll have to tell him to come."

Georgia leaped down from the bed and ran into the kitchen as if to acknowledge the pact they'd just made. Maybe there was something to this animal communication thing after all.

Abby dished up a bowl of dog kibble and set it on the back porch, then filled a stockpot with water and put it out, too. The whole operation should've taken less than five minutes. But now that she had to push herself around with the scooter, the task took a half hour and left the kitchen floor splattered with splashes of water. Thank God she'd gotten the knee scooter with the handy basket between the handlebars.

Back in bed, Abby felt better, more complete. She'd done what was most important to do today. She imagined the stray wolf dog cowering in the forest across the street, and tried to send welcoming vibes to lure him in. Then, while her foot throbbed and the pain medication made her head float several feet above the bed, she dropped into a deep sleep, the descent marked only by a jerking-awake sensation that pulled her up for an instant before she fell even deeper into the abyss.

She dreamed of a wolf dog who swam in the pool out back,

retrieving rolled-up newspapers that floated on the surface, then setting them on the edge of the pool. The newspapers held some significance Abby couldn't quite grasp, and she wondered if there was a message she could read inside them. She picked up each roll and tried to open it, but every time she tried, the papers snapped back as if they were made of plastic. The words she sought were inside, but she wasn't given access to them.

In the dream, she stacked the papers by the doorway, and the wolf dog sat guard over the growing pile. "What is the message inside these papers," she asked him.

"The message isn't inside the papers." He spoke to her in a human voice that reminded her of Quinn's. "The papers *are* the message."

The beer and TV therapy Quinn had been looking forward to didn't have the desired effect. He couldn't relax. He kept glancing over at the place next door, wondering how Abby was doing. He'd stayed till she got ready for bed, then made her promise to call him if she needed any help after he left.

He kept looking out his sliding glass door toward her bedroom window, which he could see now that the goats had cleared out that section of hedge. The light had been turned out a while ago...

But wait! Light bloomed behind the gauzy curtain, and a second later, his phone buzzed. He muted the TV. "Abby?"

"It's JP." Quinn's high-school buddy and sketchy ex-business partner.

Shit. "What do you want, JP?"

Quinn heard a faint whispering sound: JP rubbing his palms together, a nervous tic that meant he wasn't being entirely honest. "I heard that you just bought a reno property. I'm guessing that after your divorce, you're about skinned, and I thought I'd offer an olive branch. I might be willing to take that old estate off your hands for the right price. You'd still make a hefty profit, mind you. Save you some time and trouble in getting it, though."

Quinn ended the call.

His phone buzzed again. He ended the call.

The third time, he picked up. "I have no interest in anything you have to offer, JP." And yet, he'd picked up the phone because he couldn't blame the guy entirely. Though JP was guilty of using substandard materials and untrained work crews while charging a premium for top-grade materials and licensed workers, he wouldn't have gotten away with it if Quinn had been paying attention. "I'm only hearing you out because I'm not blameless. I shouldn't have let you do the ordering and billing when that was my job."

"I can tell that you're still pissed, and I guess you have a right to be. I'm sorry I wasn't more up-front with you." JP gave a nervous-sounding laugh. "I know I made a mistake, and I want to officially apologize and try to make it right if I can."

I guess? One mistake? "You made quite a few mistakes, JP. You made a whole barge-full of mistakes that drove our business over the dam while I wasn't looking." He hadn't been looking, because he had confessed to JP that his marriage was in trouble and he needed to spend more time at home. JP had clapped him on the shoulder and given him a bro hug, then told him to take all the time he needed. JP would handle the business end of the business till Quinn got his personal life sorted out. *After all,* JP had said, *what are friends for?*

All Quinn had to do was show up from eight to four at the dried-in job sites and work his magic on the baseboards and the fancy crown-molding and the custom carpentry projects. Meanwhile, behind his back, JP was swindling the clients Quinn had hoped would be the foundation of their growing reputation as premier contractors for high-end construction projects.

Quinn took another swig of his beer; it tasted like spit. "Yeah, you brought us both down." Ruined Quinn's life, in fact. "And I was the stupid fuck who didn't see it coming." Sure, he'd already been standing at the precipice of a bottomless pit, but JP's unexpected kick in the rear had pushed him in. "I was too busy focusing on my family to see that the business my family depended on was going under."

"Melissa would've left you anyway, so I hope you're not blaming me for that, too."

Quinn rubbed the back of his neck. "No, JP, I'm not blaming you for that, too." Though going bankrupt sure hadn't helped to bring any spark back to Melissa's dark, damning eyes. "What do you want, JP? Absolution? Forgiveness?" They had been friends since high school, after all. "Fine, you've got both. Are we done?"

"I hope not," JP said. "I screwed up. I screwed up royally. I'm admitting it and apologizing from the bottom of my heart. I want to make it up to you, if you'll let me."

Quinn looked out the sliding glass doors at Abby's bedroom window; the light was still on.

"We've been friends forever," JP reminded him. "I know I don't deserve a second chance, but damn, man, I've got something new going—totally legit and aboveboard—and I hope you'll let me make it up to you by bringing you in on the team. I've scoped out the land, and I already have investors ready to bankroll the whole thing. We're talking millions of dollars plus investment dividends—and you wouldn't have to invest your own money; I'd pay for us both to have a continued interest in the profits going forward."

Quinn couldn't help but laugh. JP was always full of grandiose ideas that never panned out. "Yeah, sure."

"No, for real," JP assured him. And this time, Quinn couldn't hear the telltale sound of JP rubbing his palms together. "For a couple years' work, you'd be set for a lifetime. Melissa would be begging you to take her back."

Quinn scoffed. "Thanks for the vote of confidence, but that ship has sailed." He was surprised JP hadn't made a move on Melissa by now, and he realized with a shock that he wouldn't care if that happened.

"You could be in charge of the building project—head carpenter, HMFIC, whatever—and you can examine the books anytime you want. I want you to be comfortable with this deal, if you decide to make it."

Quinn did have to admit that the lure of selling as-is for a quick profit had its allure. "I'll take all that under advisement, JP. I'll think about it and get back to you, but right now, I've gotta go."

He had to get up early and feed Abby's damn farm animals, then spend the rest of the day doing his own work of laying the new flooring in the master bedroom of the pool house. He should quit looking at Abby's window and go to bed; she had probably started reading a book and had fallen asleep with the light on.

"Sure thing, dude. You have a couple months to think about selling that land. I've got some other deals in the making, so that can stay back-burner for now."

Abby's light went out, leaving the farmhouse next door a dark silhouette in the moonlight. "Bye now, JP. Thanks for calling."

"I won't ask anyone else about that job, either, until I hear back from you. You're the best carpenter I know, and I want you on our team when this thing gets going."

Quinn just wanted to get off the phone. "I'll think about it and get back to you." Or not.

He ended the call and turned off the TV.

A distant, mournful howl made goose bumps erupt on the back of his neck. That wolf dog had been howling for the last few nights, the sound of loss and despair, maybe even of pain. Quinn went outside onto the patio. The pool pump made soft humming noises, and the automatic pool cleaner made chug-chugging sounds as it ate its way along the pool bottom.

Abby had said something about feeding the wolf dog. She'd forgotten to do that today. He'd do it, then. The stray was probably hungry. She'd been taking water to it, too, so Quinn took an almost-empty milk carton from the fridge, poured out the suspicious-smelling dregs, then rinsed it and refilled it with water. He'd pour the water into the bucket she'd left out there. "Okay. What next?"

Food wouldn't be as easy. Quinn didn't have dog food here, or any kind of processed pet food. He opened the fridge door again and peered inside.

Beer... No.

Raw eggs? Because he wasn't going to cook for the damn dog... No.

He had just enough lunch meat and cheese to throw together a sandwich for himself tomorrow morning. "Nope, not gonna sacrifice that."

He didn't even think about the steak he knew was in the meat drawer. That steak was *his*. He planned to throw it on the grill for dinner tomorrow night.

He closed the refrigerator door and checked the pantry.

Peanut butter... He could make the dog a sandwich. He took out the remnants of a loaf of bread, but only enough slices remained for his own breakfast and lunch.

Canned soup... No.

Brownie mix? He'd bought it for Sean's visit. And though Sean wasn't coming this weekend, the mix would last, and again, not cooking for a damn dog.

The freezer yielded the only possible food item he could take to the still-howling wolf dog. A frozen pepperoni pizza. He wasn't cooking for the dog, but hey, if it was hungry enough, it'd eat whatever was offered, frozen or not.

Right?

Right, he told himself.

He took the gallon of water and the frozen pizza out to the roadside, lighting his way with his phone's flashlight. Hearing something walking beside him—after he damn near shit himself with surprise—he swung his light toward the sound.

"Georgia. What are you doing here?" His first panicked thought of whether Abby was okay slipped away when Georgia wagged her tail and leaped up to sniff the pizza. He didn't think the dog would be this interested in pizza if she'd come to him for help. He hadn't thought before this moment that Georgia probably went outside at night on a regular basis. She had her doggy door to the outside, and even if Abby hadn't decided to start leaving the gate open, Georgia was small enough squiggle under it. God only knew what rich sort of night life this little dog got up to when everyone else was sleeping.

Quinn emptied the water into the bucket. Then, while Georgia sat up in an admirable begging sit with her front paws in prayer position, he flung the boxed frozen pizza, Frisbee-style, out into the cat's-claw forest.

Chapter 11

WOLF AND GEORGIA SAT TOGETHER IN THE CAT'S-CLAW FOREST, looking up.

"Why do you suppose he did that?" Georgia asked.

Wolf stood on his hind legs, his front feet up on the big tree's slanted trunk. "Maybe it's a test. Maybe if I climb the tree and rescue the food, they'll let me stay."

Georgia climbed partway up the trunk, but stopped where it grew straight up. She sniffed the air; the thawing pizza's scent leaked from the closed box. "I think he doesn't know how to throw pizza. He brought you water; maybe this pizza was supposed to be for you, too."

Wolf sniffed the air, too. "It might rain. Maybe the box will get knocked down if it rains." His stomach growled. "Are you sure it's not a test?"

Georgia hopped down from the tree trunk. "Who knows? People don't know what they're doing half the time. I think he just can't throw."

Wolf put his head on his paws and groaned. "I was hungry."

Georgia licked his face. "There's kibble and fresh water on the back porch. Abby just put it out for you."

Wolf sat up. "Really?"

Georgia sniffed the wound in his side. "This smells bad. Are you keeping it clean?"

Wolf turned to demonstrate his inability to turn around far enough to reach the tear in his flesh. "Can't reach."

Georgia came close and tenderly licked the wound, using her teeth to pull out bits of matted hair, dead skin, leaves, and twigs that had stuck to the raw, oozing gash. Wolf eased to his elbows on the leaf-cluttered ground, then stretched out to allow Georgia better access.

The wound stung and itched with every swipe of her gentle tongue, but Wolf lay quietly, aside from a few twitches he couldn't help. Finally, she finished, and moved up to his face, licking his eyes, his ears, and his mouth. Showing love and deference. Granting him the privilege of being her alpha.

———

Abby woke the next morning to Reva's text: Sorry for the sad text yesterday. I have to learn that we can't save everyone. Mama deer looks okay this morning; still sad, but okay. Next came a picture of Reva sitting on the floor of a stall, petting the deer.

Later that morning, Abby waited outside the aviary complex while Quinn unlatched the door to the lockout and went inside. The door, with its compressed-air spring, clapped shut behind him. After a moment of silence, Abby called out. "Can you tell who's supposed to get which food?"

"I'm not color-blind," Quinn called back. She heard one of the metal cupboard doors slam shut. "And I did graduate from kindergarten, in case you're wondering."

"Just checking." For lack of anything better to do, she checked her phone and found another text from Reva. Mama deer looks okay and everyone says to give her time, but she isn't doing well. Though her injuries are minor—cuts and scrapes and bruises— she won't eat or drink. She misses her babies and knows they will die without her, if they haven't already been killed by predators overnight. I'm calling an Uber and going to find those babies. Wish me luck. I may get kicked out of the program for doing this, but I have to.

Abby replied to Reva: Be careful!

Then she sat back and told herself to be patient about her

inability to help Quinn with her farm chores. Waiting for Quinn to do the work was worse than doing the work herself. She hadn't bothered to tell him that she usually prepared a bird salad for the morning feed. She figured she'd probably sneak back and feed them their salad in the afternoon, once Quinn left—and maybe after she'd had a nap.

The aviaries consisted of four separate octagonal structures on a raised concrete foundation. The wire-covered enclosures were connected by a common lockout entrance in the center, a safe zone designed to keep birds from escaping. While each aviary had a walk-through door for humans, feeding could be done through smaller access doors to the food bowls and water bottles. Running water, an industrial sink, and a heavy-duty hose with an adjustable spray nozzle made cleaning the aviary complex one of the easiest farm jobs. Inside the safe zone, each wire enclosure was fronted by a tall metal storage cupboard (color-coded, of course) for food and other supplies.

She realized that the birds' sounds changed when Quinn fed them. The parakeets' chirps went from frenzied excitement to contented chirps. The sun conures started talking in their high-pitched voices. Sun conures weren't known for their ability to talk, but at least some of these six were able to produce a few words. "Hello, good morning," a couple of them said in their automated-sounding voices. Another screeched, followed by a pretty-good rendering of "Are you hungry?"

"Dammit!" Quinn yelled.

One of the Amazons laughed and said in a surprisingly human-sounding voice, "Oops! So sorry!"

A metal door slammed shut inside the lockout. "You fucking little fucker!"

Without getting up, Abby moved the scooter forward to get a better view through the aviary wire. "Are you okay?"

Quinn had wrapped a cleaning towel around his right hand.

He peeled the towel back for a quick look, then pressed it to the wound again. "Damn bird's got a beak like a can opener."

"Band-Aids are in the light blue cupboard with the cleaning products."

"Fuck you, too," he said, his tone surprisingly light given that he might be missing part of a finger. "Band-Aids might not be enough to put my finger back together again, but I appreciate your helpfulness."

"Fuck you!" Freddy, the big macaw, yelled cheerfully. "Fuck all y'all!"

Aunt Reva would kill her if Freddy started cursing again. A cursing parrot didn't make a good steward for school field trips, and it had taken Reva more than a year after Grayson's death to cure Freddy of that habit. "Please don't curse around the parrots," Abby chided. "They'll pick it up and start repeating it, especially when they shouldn't."

Quinn peeled back the towel again, then opened the blue cupboard and rustled around.

"I think the first-aid kit is on the second-to-top shelf," she said. "Do you need help finding it?" She walked the scooter forward with her heels.

"Don't. Move."

The warning tone in his voice didn't deter her, but the three stair steps that led up to the aviary did. "Okay. I'll stay out here, if you say so. Just let me know what I can do to help."

"Try not to hurt yourself." His voice sounded growly and just a little bit sexy. "That'll do fine."

"If you want to wait till later to hose out the enclosures," she called, "that'll be okay."

He came outside and rammed the bolt home on the aviary's door. "I'll do it this evening. Isn't it time for you to take a pill or something?"

Actually, it was past time for her morning pain medicine, but she hadn't wanted to take it until she and Quinn had finished the chores, because it made her sleepy. "Let me look at your hand."

He took the handlebars of her scooter and pushed her toward the house, wheelchair-style. "I'll let you look at my hand if you'll promise to stay inside the house and let me finish the chores in peace."

The paved walkway ended at a series of concrete stepping-stones surrounded by a sprawling ground-cover plant with deep-green leaves and purple flowers. With a huff of irritation, Quinn left the scooter behind and swept Abby up into his arms, then carried her the rest of the way to the farmhouse. Abby couldn't resist the urge to lay her cheek against his shoulder and breathe in his scent. Though he'd been working all morning, his warm, damp skin still smelled of soap, and his silky hair smelled of cheap but fragrant shampoo—green apple and coconut; strange combo but nice enough.

So yeah, he smelled good. And he'd looked mighty fine—from his tight butt to his bulging biceps to his wide shoulders—when she had watched him shovel stalls. But what made her tingle all over was the feel of his muscled arms cradling her against his hard chest as if she weighed nothing. Heady stuff that challenged her determination to get her own life together before she considered a relationship with anyone.

Inside the farmhouse, he hitched her up a little higher against his chest. "Bed, or couch?"

"Couch," she answered with conviction. If he put her on the bed, she'd have a hard time resisting the urge to pull him down with her. The devil on her shoulder whispered naughty suggestions in her ear: What harm would a little summer fling do?

She was determined *not* to find out.

He deposited her on the couch next to Georgia, who had already curled into a ball on top of her special red blanket. "Can I get you anything?"

"First-aid kit's in the laundry room, second cupboard on your left."

"I've put a Band-Aid on it. It'll be fine."

"Not good enough. Wash your hands with the bar of Dial soap on the mop sink, then bring the kit in here. Don't make Dr. Abby come hobbling after you."

"Fine." He sighed, then complied, coming back with the kit in his freshly washed hands.

"Light, please."

He turned on the lamp, pulled up a footstool, and sat in front of her. Reluctantly, it seemed, he held out his injured hand.

"Ow!" Abby commiserated. That bird had taken a chunk out of Quinn's pointer finger, just below the middle knuckle. "You need stitches."

"I've fixed worse cuts than this with duct tape." He dug through the kit and handed over a tube of Neosporin. "Just get on with it."

"How did he get you so bad?" As gently as she could, she smeared the antibiotic cream over the open gash.

"Made the mistake of leaning my hand on the aviary wire when I poured the food into his bowl." He handed over a fresh Band-Aid. "I won't do that again."

"I'm sorry. I hate that you're having to do all this for me." She wrapped the Band-Aid around his finger and smoothed down the adhesive edges.

"My fault, remember?" He replaced the bandages and Neosporin and snapped the lid shut. "Can you please stop apologizing?"

"I'm sorry."

He tucked a strand of hair behind her ear. "How does your foot feel?"

The throbbing pain from earlier this morning now burned with the heat of a thousand suns. "Not too bad. I should probably take something, though, to keep it from getting worse."

She told him where to find the medicine, and he brought back a couple of tablets and a glass of filtered water from the fridge door. She took the pills and set the glass on the side table. "You want one of my pain pills for your bird finger?"

"No, thanks." He turned off the lamp. "Lie back."

She obeyed, and he tucked pillows under her foot, then covered her with an ugly crocheted throw that draped over the back of the couch. "Think you can manage to rest with your foot up for a couple hours? I'll get some work done next door, then come back and check on you when I'm done."

"Thank you."

He put his hands on his hips and scowled down at her. "I wish you'd stop thanking me, too."

"I'll try, but I really am grateful for all you're doing."

He knelt down next to her, his blue eyes serious. "You are driving me crazy, you know that?"

"Am I? I'm sorry."

He ran a hand along her arm, a light touch that made her shiver. Then he leaned in close, so close…his mouth inches from hers. "Stop apologizing."

Then he kissed her. His lips were warm, firm, gentle, exploring. He teased her lips with his tongue, encouraging her to open her mouth. She did, and he slipped his tongue inside, just a little. With light flicks of his tongue on hers, he teased her to respond. She explored the tastes and textures of the inside of his mouth; his tongue soft-rough and sweet, his teeth shiny-slick and tasting of peppermint. And while their mouths were getting acquainted, the rest of her body tightened and tingled, everything in her reaching out toward him.

He stood and brushed his feathery hair back with both hands. "Get some rest. I'll check on you later."

When the streetlight came on and a pair of hummingbird moths' tiny wings roared quietly among the yellow cat's-claw flowers, Georgia came to see Wolf. Again, she tenderly cleaned his wound. When she finished, she sat, tail wagging. "It's better. Smells clean now."

Wolf licked her face in gratitude.

She looked toward the farmhouse. "Abby can't come all the way out here anymore. You have to come to the farmhouse to eat. She put out fresh kibble on the patio."

Wolf looked up to the darkening sky where tiny lights winked through the cat's-claw canopy. "Not dark enough yet."

Georgia stood and trotted to the edge of the forest. "You have to let her see you sometime. She won't hurt you."

Wolf averted his eyes. "She'll chase me away."

"She won't." Georgia wagged, her tail making a rhythmic whapping noise against the overhanging vines. "Unless you eat the chickens."

Wolf believed Georgia's sincerity, but the memory of being chased away still stung. He wasn't ready to risk that humiliation again. "I'll come at night."

"You'd better hurry, or the raccoons will get it."

"I'll come when the house lights go out."

Georgia sneezed. "She'll leave the gate open for you."

When Georgia left, Wolf stretched out on his soft bed of fallen leaves and tried to sleep. Maybe he did sleep a little, but not the deep healing sleep he needed. A tantalizing smell woke him fully; not the smell of food, but the scent of a female dog in heat. The sort of scent an intact male wolf dog such as himself could not ignore. Though his side ached and his stomach growled and his spirit ached for the kind of rest only a dog with a home could afford, he got to his feet and followed the elusive scent through the cat's-claw forest and beyond.

Quinn's *Law & Order* rerun seemed to have some random, high-pitched noises in the soundtrack. Or was it…? He muted the TV.

"Shit." He leaped to his feet. Georgia was outside in Abby's backyard, barking hysterically. He stepped into his shoes, grabbed the flashlight, and ran.

All the way down his drive, all the way down hers, his mind spun with panic-induced scenarios. Abby had fallen on the hard tile floor. Or in the pool's deep end. Or in the donkey stall where she'd be trampled to death.

Cats fighting.

He heard the sound and slacked off on his headlong sprint to save Abby. It was just a cat fight.

Catching his breath, he rounded the corner of the house. A dozen cats rolled and fought each other on the patio, then broke apart when his movement triggered the motion-sensor safety light at the corner of the house. Blinded for a split second, he moved so the light's glare wasn't coming straight at him and swung the flashlight's beam toward the melee.

Not cats.

Raccoons.

Raccoons and cats. A screaming, yowling, chattering heap of raccoons and cats fought each other. He'd seen some pretty intense bar brawls in his lifetime, but nothing to rival this. The fighting animals attacked, defended, rolled, and sprang apart, all the while hissing, screaming, yowling and moaning. Georgia barked with high drama, darting in now and then to snap at a raccoon's backside whenever the opportunity presented itself.

With thoughts of rabies shots spinning through his mind, Quinn charged at the unruly group. "Shoo! Stop it! Break it up!"

The fight calmed, and most of the animals, raccoons and cats alike, fled for the safety of the shadows. But the biggest raccoon turned and hissed at him, teeth bared.

Quinn took two steps back. The thing was huge. The grand-daddy of all raccoons stood on his hind legs, just about tall enough to reach Quinn's crotch.

With those long, sharp teeth.

With those long, sharp, possibly rabies-infected teeth.

Quinn swung the flashlight at the creature, whose mouth, Quinn was sure, dripped with blood. "Shoo! Get out of here!"

The raccoon dropped back down to all fours and glared at Quinn. Its eyes shone gold in the porch light. Georgia lunged at it, snapping and barking.

"No, Georgia," Quinn commanded. That granddaddy raccoon was bigger and meaner than Georgia ever thought about being. "Let him go on his way."

But still the raccoon lingered, eyeing the metal pan of dog kibble Abby had left on the back porch for that damn stray dog. Tonight would be the last night she did that, if Quinn had any-thing to say about it.

And, he decided, he did. He did have something to say, and by God, whether she wanted to or not, she'd listen.

Quinn flung the metal pan toward the raccoon Frisbee-style, sending the few remaining morsels of kibble flying. The pan wob-bled in a wide arc, completely missing the raccoon, but he got the message. With one last aggrieved glance, he trundled off.

Quinn knelt down and snapped his fingers at Georgia. "Come here, girl."

She crept close, her head down, her tail tucked, her demeanor submissive.

"I'm not gonna hurt you." He set the flashlight down. "I just want to see if you're okay."

He skimmed his hands along her face and head, then down her sides and back. "You okay?" He didn't feel the dampness of blood, and she didn't flinch at his examination. "You're lucky they didn't get you."

A low, moaning meow came from the shrubs between the house and the aviary.

"Griff?" Quinn stood and shone the flashlight at the base of the shrubbery. A pair of yellow eyes blinked. "Come here, buddy."

The cat growled, a low, whining sound.

Georgia went to the cat and sniffed cautiously, then sat back, whining.

"Dammit." Quinn laid his flashlight on the ground so the beam illuminated the cat, then dropped to his knees and crawled under the shrubs. Griffin's eyes flashed, and he hissed. "I'm sorry, dude." Though Quinn felt sure that he was about to be flayed alive by the cat's claws, and that spiders and ticks were at this moment skittering down his shirt like teenage groupies slipping past the bouncer into a New Orleans bar at midnight, he bent lower and reached farther. "I've gotta bring you out of there."

Griff growled and hissed again. Quinn grabbed the cat's scruff and dragged it out of the bushes. Miraculously, the cat hung limp and didn't bite or scratch. Quinn cradled the battered feline and got to his feet. "You're really hurt, aren't you?" The cat's fur felt matted and lumpy, and Quinn felt the stickiness of blood seeping through his shirt.

And now, Quinn wondered for the first time, where was Abby? Either drugged enough to have slept through all this or, as he'd worried before, passed out on the tile floor inside the house, trampled to death by donkeys, or dead at the bottom of the pool?

The farm next door wasn't just loud; it was exhausting. He was too old for this shit.

He glanced into the pool. No floaters at the surface, nor dead bodies being sucked down to the bottom by the drain. Dismissing the donkey scenario as the ramblings of a sleep-deprived brain, he knocked at the sliding glass door. When Abby didn't answer, he tested the door, and it slid effortlessly open.

Now, he could add a new worst-case scenario for Abby: the

victim of a violent criminal who stalked the neighborhood at night, looking for unlocked doors.

Quinn was not a worrier; never had been. He had only recently trained himself to ponder decisions before making them because of the disastrous outcome of some of his more spontaneous choices. He had always flung himself headlong into whatever he wanted to do without fear or doubt.

He had never worried about Melissa or Sean. Melissa, with her high-heeled shoes and manicured nails, was tougher than the most seasoned cage fighter. He pitied anyone, armed or not, who tried to cross her, and if anyone messed with Sean, Melissa's mama bear came out with a fury. Her vicious and public dressing-down of the vice principal when he had unfairly accused Sean of cheating was the stuff of Audubon Elementary School legend.

Abby's vulnerability brought out something unexpected and tender inside him, and it scared Quinn to death. He hadn't been able to give Melissa the support she'd needed, and she was one of the most self-sufficient people he'd ever met. Abby came with an entire multispecies crowd of needy creatures, including the battered cat he held in his arms.

He paused in the bedroom's open doorway. He could see Abby bundled up under the covers despite the muggy warmth of the Louisiana night. "Abby. Wake up."

She didn't move. Her deep breaths were audible, just shy of actually snoring.

"Abby!" He didn't want to alarm her, but hell, maybe he did. This was a veterinary emergency, after all. Griffin, the hefty toolbox pisser, was way too limp and passive in his arms. "Wake up. We have a problem."

Abby stirred, rolled over, and made a quiet huffing sound before settling down again.

"Abby." Quinn made sure his voice was as deep and booming as he could make it. "Wake the fuck up."

"Huh?" Abby sat up, and, no doubt seeing his shadow looming in the bedroom doorway, screamed.

"It's me, Quinn." He flicked on the bedroom light. "Get up. We have a problem."

Chapter 12

ABBY FLUNG THE COVERS BACK. THE SUDDEN FLARE OF THE bedroom light half blinded her. "What's wrong?"

"You just slept through a damn poolside turf war."

"What?" She sat on the edge of the bed and pushed the hair out of her eyes. She'd been sleeping so deeply that her whole body buzzed with the shock of waking up. "I slept through what?"

"Look," Quinn commanded.

She did, and… "Oh, my God, Griffie! What happened?" She grabbed the scooter's handlebars and hurried toward Quinn. The cat was lying limp in Quinn's arms, torn and bleeding, eyes half-closed, tongue hanging out. "What happened," she screeched, one-hundred-percent awake now. She reached out to stroke Griff's head, but couldn't find a spot to touch that wasn't bleeding.

"He was fighting a bunch of raccoons on the patio. I heard Georgia barking."

"Oh, no. Why would—" She stopped. She knew why. The raccoons had come to eat the dog food she'd left out for the stray, and Griffin had been defending his territory.

"Some of the other cats were involved, too, but he's the only one I saw. Hopefully, everyone else is okay." Quinn paused. "Or okay enough."

"Shit." This was all her fault, and with her damn self tied to a damn scooter, there was just about nothing she could do about it. "He's in shock, and hurt too badly for Band-Aids and Neosporin to do any good."

She sat on the scooter's seat and called Mack's cell phone. He answered, sounding groggy. She explained the situation, and he agreed to meet them at the vet's office in fifteen minutes. "Okay," she said to Quinn. "Give him to me. You'll have to get a crate from the laundry room and line it with towels."

Twenty minutes later, they pulled up in front of the vet's office. The lights were on, and the front door stood open a crack. Quinn grabbed the carrier and rushed up the steps, then looked back at Abby—he'd forgotten her handicap.

"Go," she ordered. "I'll use the wheelchair ramp and catch up with you." When she came in, the bell that hung from the doorknob jangled, and Mack called out. "Lock that door, then come on back."

Though the waiting area had been dusty the last time Abby was in the clinic, the surgical room gleamed with shiny silver everything and smelled faintly of Clorox. Mack wore jeans and a wrinkled green scrub top, and his dark-brown hair stood up on one side. He had clearly rolled out of bed and come straight to the office, but he already wore a pair of surgical gloves and had assembled a tray of sharp objects and other frightening veterinary paraphernalia.

Griffin lay on a big, silver operating table, his mangled body illuminated by a bright adjustable lamp above the table.

"Y'all want to stay and help?"

"Um." Abby looked down at the cat's bloody gashes, and a spotty haze started to close in on her. She gulped. "I think I might wait outside, if that's okay."

Mack shrugged. "I don't want to be picking you up off the floor, so yes, it's fine."

Quinn wrapped his arms around her and held her close. "Are you okay? Do you need me to take you out to the car? Or take you home? Tell me what you need."

She burrowed into his warmth. Wrapped her arms around his waist. Held on to his solid strength. "I'm okay."

He squeezed her tight. "Can you make it back to the waiting room?"

She made herself pull away. "Yes." She scrubbed her face with her shaking hands, though there were no tears to wipe away. "I'm fine. I'll be fine. If you can stay, I'll wait."

He stepped closer and tucked a wild strand of hair behind her ear. "You sure?"

Not at all sure but determined not to be a wimp, she nodded and stepped back, gripping the handlebars of the scooter. "I'm sure. I'll go to the waiting room and text Reva." She turned and left the room, glad for Mack and Quinn's ironclad stomachs and compassionate resolve.

"I'll stay," she heard Quinn volunteer.

"Great, thanks," Mack said. "They sure got him good, didn't they?"

She didn't hear Quinn's response; she had already scootered halfway down the hall, headed for the dusty waiting room. She almost fell off the scooter when her cell phone buzzed in her back pocket. For a split second, she imagined that a big, hairy raccoon had come up behind her and taken a swipe at her butt. She stopped near the receptionist's desk, pulled the phone from her pocket, and looked at the screen. Aunt Reva, of course. Calling after midnight—no doubt because she'd had a disturbing dream about raccoons.

"Hey, Aunt Reva."

"What's going on? I was dead asleep and woke up thinking I heard cats fighting. I think it was just a dream, but I can't shake the feeling that something bad has happened. I called the house phone, and…well, as you know, you didn't answer. What's happening? Who's hurt? Are *you* okay?"

"Griffin had an altercation with a raccoon." No way was Abby going to tell Reva about her broken foot in the same phone call as this horrible news. "We're at the vet's office now."

Reva took a breath, then went quiet. After a second, she spoke. "Griffie says that it looks bad, and it feels bad, but he'll be okay, so don't worry. Just stop telling the raccoons they're invited to dine on his patio."

"I know." An unexpected prickle of tears tickled Abby's sinuses. She sniffed the tears back into submission and got hold of herself. Falling apart wouldn't help anyone, least of all Griffin. "I'm sorry. I put food out for the stray dog. I shouldn't have done that."

"Why didn't you put the food across the street? Isn't that what you've been doing up until now? I'm getting a strange feeling that you're not telling me everything. Not that I don't trust you—of course I do. But are you okay? You're not sick, are you? You don't sound sick."

"No, I'm not sick." Luckily, Reva asked a hundred questions at a time instead of just one, so Abby could pick the ones she wanted to answer and ignore the rest. "I wanted to lure him closer to the house." True, even if it wasn't the actual reason she'd put the food on the patio.

"Good instinct," Reva praised. "But he wants to earn his place. He won't come to the patio until he knows you'll welcome his presence." Reva paused, and Abby heard her take a breath. "Aww. He's been bringing you presents?"

Holy shit. The newspapers. The realization had come to her in a barely remembered dream: The newspapers didn't contain a message; they *were* the message. "He's been bringing me newspapers. I've been leaving the gate open, and he's been putting them on the patio by the back door. Should I close the gate, though? I mean, because of the raccoons?"

"No. Gates don't keep raccoons out. They can climb anything. Hang on a second."

Abby took the opportunity to lay the phone on the scooter's seat and push the contraption to the dark waiting room, where she sat on one of the dusty Victorian velvet sofas. She picked the phone up again and put it on speaker. "Reva, you still there?"

"Hang on," Reva said, sounding a little irritated.

While she waited, Abby switched over to her texts and saw one she'd missed from Reva. Couldn't find the mama deer's babies, but met a nice farmer who sold me a runty baby goat that he was bottle-feeding. I didn't get in trouble—my roommate (who is usually a pain) covered for me. Now everyone is wondering where the baby goat came from. And look! Abby scrolled down to see the photo of a spotted baby goat nursing from the mama deer.

She hit the !! button.

"Okay," Reva said. "I talked to the wolf dog."

Abby switched back to the phone-call screen, though it didn't really make any difference; she could hear and respond either way. "And?"

"He wants to be useful. He wants to know the rules, because human rules don't make sense to him, and even when he thinks he knows what people want, the rules keep changing."

"Okay. So what am I supposed to do with that information?"

"He wants to know where he belongs. He is afraid you'll chase him away again."

"I won't."

"Well, he doesn't know that."

Frustration crawled up Abby's throat and came out as a growl. "How am I supposed to let him know I won't chase him away?"

"Tell him!"

Abby closed her eyes. "Okay, fine. Tell me how to do that."

Reva's huff of irritation sounded the same as Abby's had. "How many times have I explained this to you?"

Starting when Abby was five years old? Maybe eleventy-million times by now. "Not enough, I guess."

"Pay attention this time."

"Fine." Abby sighed. She had paid attention all those other times, too, but it didn't make her any better at communicating with animals. Truth was, she didn't trust herself. Reva had done her best to teach Abby to trust, but then she'd go back home and have that trust shamed out of her. What felt right at the farm felt silly everywhere else. "I will."

"All right. Both feet on the floor, relax your body and let your breath flow through you, as if you're an empty straw." Reva took a slow, deep breath and let it out with an audible whoosh.

Abby did the same.

"Breathe up through the soles of your feet, then down through the top of your head," Reva instructed. "Release anything that isn't yours. Release your worries to the heavens, release your baggage to the earth. Clear yourself, clear the channel of communication." Together, they did a few cycles of deep breathing over the phone.

"Ready?" Reva asked.

"Ready," Abby responded. Her body felt energized with a pleasant buzz, oxygenated by the deep breaths she rarely took in her day-to-day life.

"See the wolf dog walk up and stand in front of you."

With her eyes closed, Abby imagined what it would look like if Wolf came up to her, sniffed her hand, and sat, giving her his full attention. "His name is Wolf."

"Good!" The approval in Reva's voice stroked Abby's ego, giving her a burst of confidence. "He's giving you information you haven't even asked for. Now you know you're in. Tell him you won't chase him away again. Tell him he is welcome to live at the farm. Ask him to come."

In Abby's imagination, Wolf turned away from her and looked down a hillside toward something she couldn't see.

"He's looking at something else."

"Yes, he is. Ask him what he's looking at."

"Dogs. Lots of dogs. They're everywhere, scattered all over the hillside, and none of them have people to belong to. They're all separate, but they want to come together. They need a tribe to belong to."

"Yes. But that's not a literal image, right?"

Abby didn't know how to tell the difference. "I don't know."

"Ask!"

She didn't have to ask; suddenly, she knew. "He just wants to belong somewhere. He doesn't care if it's with a pack of strays or a human family."

"Really?"

The scene of all the disconnected dogs scattered across the countryside changed, coalescing into a line of dogs, following the leader like sheep, all heading to Bayside Barn. "No, you're right. They want a family, a home, and a safe place to live."

"Anything else?"

"They want to love and to be loved."

"Yes. And what does Wolf want? What does he want from you, in particular?"

In her imagination, Abby apologized to Wolf for chasing him away. She told him that she understood, now, that he had only caught the chicken because he was hungry. She asked him to please come to live at the farm, so she could stop worrying about him being on his own in the cat's-claw forest.

"He's listening," Reva said. "But he wants to be useful, too. He wants you to give him a job."

Abby laughed. "I don't read the newspaper."

"What else can he do," Reva prompted. "What can he do to prove his worth and do his part as a family member at the farm?"

In Abby's imagination, she saw Wolf turn toward her, his golden eyes shining. She asked him what sort of job he thought he'd be best at and enjoy doing. The word *protector* blossomed in her mind. "He can protect the farm's cats from wild animals."

"Get more specific. Birds are wild animals; blue jays don't hurt the farm animals, but hawks will kill the chickens. You're telling him what you want him to do. What do you want him to do?"

Abby felt like her body was floating, not quite connected to the earth anymore. "Protect us from animals who want to do harm."

"Yes." Reva's voice was rich with approval. "Yes. Now, tell Wolf what you want. He needs a gold-plated invitation and a job to do, or he won't come."

Abby heard a door close, and Quinn and Mack talking to each other as they moved closer. She suddenly felt silly—talking to a dog or, worse yet, pretending to. The pleasant floating sensation evaporated, and Abby became aware that her foot ached. She snatched up the phone and turned off the speaker function just as the men walked into the room. "Just a minute, Aunt Reva."

Quinn frowned at Abby and reached down to prop her foot on the scooter's seat. "Elevation, remember?"

Without even asking, Mack took the phone from Abby's hand. "Hey, Reva. How's your class coming?" He walked out of the room.

"How's Griffin?" Abby asked Quinn.

"If he makes it through the night, he'll probably be okay. Mack is keeping him here for a few days so he can get IV fluids and antibiotics." He sat next to her and put a hand on her thigh, lightly massaging. "You ready to go?"

"Welp, I'll need to get my phone back first."

Mack's deep voice and low laugh drifted from the reception area.

"Sounds like they know each other pretty well," Quinn commented.

"Yeah, they do. Mack and Reva's husband, Grayson, were buddies from way back. Also, with all Reva's animals, she's one of Mack's best customers."

"Yeah, she is," Mack confirmed, walking back from the reception area. He handed Abby her phone. "She single-handedly paid for my truck. Don't tell her I said that, though, because then she'll want to ride in it, and my wife won't like that."

"Probably not." Abby would bet money that Patricia McNeil wouldn't want Reva riding in Mack's truck. Though Mack's wife was pretty enough, she couldn't hold a candle to Reva's lit-from-within beauty; the kind that didn't fade with age.

Quinn helped Abby to her feet. "Let's get out of here so Mack can go home and get some rest."

"Thanks for everything, Mack," Abby said. "Meeting us here after midnight... That's above-and-beyond territory."

Mack chuckled. "Nah, not really, since I'll be sending Reva the bill for my time."

On the way back home, Quinn rested a hand on Abby's thigh. "How are you doing? How's your foot?"

"Fine. I'm fine. My foot's fine." Actually, she felt like death warmed over and her foot felt even worse than that. "I'm sorry you're going to all this trouble for us." Us being the multispecies collective at Bayside Barn. "I don't know how we'll be able to make it up to you."

"You don't owe me a thing." He rubbed her thigh; she could tell that meant he was thinking. "But I do have a favor to ask. My son, Sean, is coming to visit next weekend. I really appreciate all the meals you cook for me when I'm at the farm doing chores, and it would be great if Sean could come, too, when he's around. It's not all that often." Quinn sighed, and his hand on her thigh felt heavy. "Unfortunately."

Quinn's sadness and regret over the damaged relationship with his son ignited Abby's despair over the daughter she would never see again. At least Quinn had a chance with Sean. Could Abby deny him whatever help she could provide? Offering to help didn't mean she had to embroil herself in their relationship. She could cook a few meals and still remain uninvolved.

"Of course, Sean is welcome to come to the farm whenever you're there." She definitely didn't want to form a personal relationship with the boy herself, but if Quinn and Sean could bond over her dinner table, what harm would there be in that? "I'll be happy to cook all your meals, especially since you're helping me so much."

They had just pulled into the driveway at Bayside Barn when

Abby's phone pinged with a text message from Reva: Don't forget to finish the conversation with Wolf. Also, why is Georgia telling me that you're always riding a bicycle, even in the house?

———————

Wolf heard Abby talking in his head. He had always been able to hear some of what the people near him were thinking, or understand some of what they were saying. But this was different. This time, he knew Abby wasn't anywhere near him, but he heard her voice in his head. And she was talking *to* him, as if she wanted to have a conversation with him the way people talked to each other.

He'd been following his own scent back to the cat's-claw forest, but he couldn't talk to Abby and pay attention to his nose at the same time, so he flopped down exactly where he was: in a strange, man-made field with alternating rows of raw dirt and small bushy plants. To be sure he was safe, he took stock of the area by sniffing the air.

He smelled wild rabbits close by—different than the ones at the farm—and the oily, rubbery odor left in the dirt by farm equipment. He could still get a whiff of the female dog he had followed and coupled with. After he fulfilled her request, she had no further use for him and trotted away, unconcerned. He had hoped she would come back with him and help him to start a pack so he'd have a place to belong. But she made it clear that she already had a home, and he wasn't invited to share it.

Georgia had invited him to live at the farm, but Abby had chased him away. He wished all the dogs who didn't have homes could somehow find their way to the same place so they could be together. There would be safety and security if they all banded together.

He could tell that on some level, he was telegraphing his thoughts to Abby in the same way people often did without being aware of it. But he knew what he was doing, and so did Abby. He calmed his thoughts to make room for hers.

"I'm sorry," he heard Abby say in his head. "I was afraid for the chicken you caught, and I didn't understand that you were hungry. If you will come to the farm, I won't chase you away, and you'll have plenty of food to eat."

Wolf could tell that someone else—another human—was listening in on the conversation. It felt like she was helping Wolf and Abby to hear each other better. He tried to show them how his fear and reluctance to trust held him back. He tried to show them that he needed to feel useful and have a job to do.

Then, the connection broke. Abby dropped out of the conversation. The other person tried to keep Wolf engaged, but he had to get back to the forest. It was unsafe to sleep in an unfamiliar place, and his body craved rest now.

But more than that, he had a bad feeling that he had somehow let Georgia down when he followed the other dog's tantalizing scent. He would have to explain to her that he couldn't help losing himself in these overwhelming urges that took over his rational brain and compelled him to do whatever it took to satisfy the biological imperative.

Then he thought of Georgia's sweet face, her soft brown eyes, her healing presence; and he realized that he wouldn't have to explain anything. She knew him, she understood him, and she accepted him, just as he was. That knowledge made him more determined than ever to truly deserve everything she gave him freely without demanding anything in return. Even though it scared him more than any terror he had faced before, he vowed to try to fit into Georgia's life. Maybe he could do it without having to get too close to the humans.

He knew without asking that she wouldn't leave her people to go with him. But if he could find a close-by place to dig a den for them to share, he might be able to convince her that he could be her home, too.

Wolf made it back to the forest when the sky at the horizon turned orange and pink. The hum of a small motorbike and the soft thunk of a rolled-up paper hitting the ground lured him out of the forest before he had the chance to lie down and rest. He picked up the paper—this one still sharp with the smell and taste of fresh ink—and carried it down the farmhouse road, then dropped it by the see-through door. Inside the house, the lights were off. He pressed his nose to the cool, damp glass. A small, dark kitten curled up on a soft pillow that was raised off the ground on polished blocks of wood.

He remembered pillows.

He missed pillows.

Chapter 13

OVER THE NEXT WEEK, QUINN'S LIFE SETTLED INTO A REGULAR rhythm. Not an easy rhythm, just a regular rhythm. He woke early and walked to the farm, where he brought in the roll of advertising flyers that miraculously appeared at the back door every morning. (Abby blamed the elusive wolf dog; Quinn figured it was Georgia.)

Then he did the morning chores. Abby had stopped following him around outside, which made things go faster. When he finished feeding the animals and cleaning stalls and enclosures, he went to the farmhouse where Abby always had a hearty—and sometimes elaborate—breakfast ready for him. Fresh eggs he had gathered the day before, prepared a dozen different ways. Cheese grits or hash browns or a vegetable-and-potato concoction blended with scrambled eggs and coated with melted cheese. Biscuits and honey, or pancakes and syrup. Fresh berries or fruit—most of it from Reva's garden; he had harvested the berries just this morning.

Today, he tucked into a plate piled high with fresh crepes, blackberries, and whipped cream drizzled with honey, along with three strips of bacon on the side. Also, fresh-ground coffee blended with a spoonful of coconut oil, half-and-half, and butter—yes, butter! Sounded strange, but tasted magnificent, like an ultra-rich cappuccino. And, everything tasted all that much better because he had worked up an appetite.

Abby put a glass of fresh-squeezed orange juice by his plate. Feeling appreciated in the best way, he reached out and snagged the waistband of her shorts. "Thank you," he said with his mouth full. When she tried to slip away, he wrapped a finger around the stretchy elastic and pulled her back. Swallowing, he tilted his face up to hers, inviting a kiss. God, he really wanted a kiss; he could feel it already—her warm, full lips smashed against his.

But she must not have felt the same way, because she slipped away from his questing hand, then patted his shoulder and moved away, humming.

So she wasn't thinking of climbing into his bed the way he was hoping to climb into her shorts. He was okay, for now, with the kind of appreciation that filled his belly if not his heart, that satisfied his hunger if not his libido. He could get used to this. He hadn't realized that this sort of food even existed outside of fancy restaurants. (Melissa's idea of breakfast-making had consisted of putting slabs of frozen bread products into the toaster and keeping them there until the edges were charred. He hadn't minded; she made excellent coffee, and McDonald's was on his way to work.)

After breakfast, Quinn planned to head back to the estate, where for the past few days, he had been clearing out the undergrowth with the help of Reva's tractor and bush-hog attachment. The pool house was completely renovated now; late nights sitting up looking out at Abby's bedroom window—not being creepy… for real, just making sure she didn't need help—had given him plenty of time to finish the tile-and-grout work in the kitchen. The pool water was looking good, but the water level concerned him. It seemed to lose water much more quickly than the pool at Bayside Barn. Something he'd have to keep an eye on.

"Did you ever find out whether your pool is leaking?" Abby asked, apparently reading his mind.

"I think it might have an issue where the steps meet the side of the pool. I'm keeping an eye on it."

"So what's next on your renovation agenda?" Abby took his empty plate to the sink and started running water.

"Gonna start on the old house today." He thought—for a millisecond—about telling her his plans to flip the estate once he'd completed renovations. After all, she hadn't made any secret of the fact that she was looking online for office-manager jobs. He thought about confessing, but couldn't quite bring himself to do it. Instead, he got up and took his cup and glass to the sink, where she was washing dishes by hand. Coming up behind her, he put his arms around her waist. Her hair smelled like lemons or limes or something citrusy. He breathed in, getting a little whiff of bacon, too. "Mmmm. What's for dinner?"

She laughed. "You only just now finished breakfast, and you're thinking about dinner?"

He moved her hair aside and nuzzled her neck. It smelled good, too, soapy and clean. He kissed her neck, openmouthed so he could taste. Salty and sweet. "Mmmm." Maybe he could have her for dinner.

But no. He knew she wouldn't allow that, and he didn't dare voice his thought out loud. They hadn't done more than kiss so far; she had set some pretty firm boundaries. Not with words, but with actions. Every time he tried to corral her for more than a kiss, she squirmed away. Even now, with her knee propped on a scooter and her hands buried in dishwater, she managed to maneuver herself out of his reach.

Strangely, her reluctance fueled his desire to push for more, even though he had decided months ago that sex without love or commitment was inherently unsatisfying. Now, he was learning that these homey little interludes with Abby were much more dangerous to his peace of mind than outright lovemaking. Everything about her, even the boundaries she set between them, made him want more.

He moved around to her other side and dropped a kiss on her bare shoulder. The fact that her skin tasted like honey didn't help.

"What do you think Sean would like for dinner tonight?" Abby asked. "Hamburgers? Pizza? I want to make a good first impression."

Abby had filled the refrigerator and the cabinets in advance of

Sean's first weekend visit with Quinn. Though Quinn and Sean would be sleeping at the pool house, when Quinn mentioned Sean's upcoming visit, Abby had reminded him that she planned to cook all their meals. "Anything you make will be a step up from what he's used to, believe me."

Abby pushed her butt back against his hips in a teasing way. Because of the scooter under her injured leg, her aim wasn't quite square, but maybe that was a good thing. "I was thinking of twice-boiled broccoli and blanched parsnips with a side of spinach. Maybe some slow-cooked beef liver for protein."

He slid his arms around her waist and settled his hands on her belly. He barely resisted the urge to let his fingers glide upward—accidentally, of course—to caress her breasts. "Whatever you just said—sorry, I wasn't listening—sounds amazing. I'm sure he'll love it."

Abby must've read his mind, because she scooted away and swatted him with a damp dish towel. "Get out of here. You've got work to do at your place, and I'm sorry to tell you this, but you smell kind of sweaty."

"Okay, fine." He took a step back. "He'll be here this afternoon around three. I thought I'd give him a quick tour of my place, then bring him over here to help out at feeding time."

She rinsed and stacked the last utensil in the drain rack, then turned off the water. "Don't make him work his first day of visitation. Why don't you let him try out your pool instead? I'll still cook dinner for y'all."

"I think he'll enjoy feeding the animals." Quinn had learned to enjoy his work at the farm. In fact, sometimes, in his most wild imaginings, he wished he could figure out a way to keep the estate himself, and maybe get a horse or something. Crazy thought, though. Flipping the estate was the first step in his business plan. Without it, he couldn't build the construction business he dreamed of, the one he needed to support himself and his son.

Though Sean lived with Melissa, Quinn wanted to pay his child support and then some. He didn't want Sean to lack for anything, or for Melissa to lack for anything because she was raising his son. "I'll give Sean the option and let him decide."

"Either way, you need to get going," Abby reminded him. "That tractor can't run itself."

Feeling good in spite of the fact that he'd just been kicked out, Quinn ambled up her drive and down his, then spent a few hours on the tractor, running the bush hog that impressively chewed up weeds and brush and even small trees, covering the ground with a pulpy mass of vegetative debris. When he had decimated about a half acre of overgrown underbrush, he lowered the tractor's bucket and shut off the engine.

He used a chainsaw and hedge clippers to denude the trees of clinging vines and skin off any branches that dared to grow lower than he could reach. He stacked all the branches that were large enough to be used as firewood into a pile between two of the larger trees. Smaller branches and vines went into the tractor's bucket, to be deposited onto a burn pile that he and Sean would set on fire Sunday afternoon.

He put his hands on his hips and admired his handiwork. Man, oh man, this property would be beautiful when he was done with it. And if he could somehow afford to buy the bayside property behind the estate and turn it into a private beach for the residences on this road, this place would be worth a million or more, and he'd make even more selling off each parcel behind the estates.

A tiny seedling of a dream—that maybe he'd stay—sprouted in his imagination, but he ruthlessly snatched it up by the roots and tossed it aside. Keeping this old house and turning it into a home for himself and his son was a luxury he couldn't afford.

He didn't have the expendable income to build a small office annex off the living room where he could bring his clients. He needed an office in downtown Magnolia Bay, not out here on this back road. His thought of showing off the estate as proof of his carpentry and building skills, and taking on only two or three custom-cabinet or home-building projects at a time was just plain silly and self-indulgent. Just because he'd have enough money to eke by with a few custom cabinetry jobs over the summer didn't mean he could make an actual living at it, let alone make a name for himself, a name and a trade that Sean would be proud to inherit.

Besides, the dream of building a life on this estate was an idyllic illusion; at the summer's end, all the school buses would come back, and so would Abby's aunt Reva. And Abby would probably take a job somewhere else, which was all well and good. She needed to prove herself to herself, not ride on her aunt's coattails and forever doubt her own potential.

He parked the tractor in a dilapidated pole barn behind the pool house and went inside to get cleaned up. Sean would be here in less than an hour, and Quinn wanted to be ready to give his son a quick tour of the estate before heading over to Abby's. She had texted him while he was in the shower: Shrimp scampi, broccoli—yes, broccoli—doused in cheese sauce, Alfredo noodles, buttermilk-and-cheese biscuits drizzled with honey, side salad topped with bacon crumbles, and blueberry pie with ice cream for dessert?

The old adage of the route to a man's heart being through his stomach took on a depth of meaning he'd never before considered. Plus, he couldn't wait to get his hands on the parts of Abby that she hadn't yet let him touch.

He texted back: I know you're trying to kill me, but somehow, I don't care.

She responded: I'll let you make up your own mind about my motives. ;-) Everything is ready to pop in the oven; just waiting for you and Sean to arrive. Can't wait to meet him.

Sean texted that he was on the way, and Quinn met him at the curb. As Melissa said goodbye to Sean, Quinn took the mail from Bayside Barn's big mailbox. Idly, while he pretended not to notice Sean leaning across the console to hug Melissa's neck, he leafed through the neighbor's mail.

Electric bill.

Water-sewer-trash bill.

Some bulk-mail junk destined for the trash.

Sean climbed out of the passenger seat and hitched his backpack over his shoulder. "Hey, Dad."

Waiting for Melissa to drive away, Quinn glanced down at the last envelope in his hand. The first line of the return address made his stomach clench: *Magnolia Bay Municipal Court.* The bright-red stamped banner that partially obscured the barn's mailing address made his heart skip a beat—and not in a good way: *Important Correspondence! Time-Sensitive: Open Immediately.*

Had Delia actually *done* something in response to his letting-off-steam phone call about rescinding Reva's permission to keep farm animals?

God, he hoped not.

Melissa leaned out the car window and flapped her manicured hand to get his attention. "I'll be back to pick him up Sunday afternoon at five. Make sure he's ready."

Quinn slipped the frighteningly official-looking envelope to the back of the pile. "Of course."

Sean wrapped his arms around Quinn's shoulders. The kid's heavy backpack slung around and slugged him like a fist to the kidneys. "It's great to see you, Dad. I'm sorry I haven't come before."

Quinn hugged his son, holding tight. His throat felt full with everything he wished he could say. "I'm glad you're here now."

With the back wall of his brain on fire from the Municipal Court envelope, Quinn forgot all about his intention to give Sean a tour of the estate. He clapped his son on the shoulder and led him down the graveled drive to meet Abby. He hardly knew her, but already she felt like a lifeline to him. He stuck the thick sheaf of envelopes into his hip pocket and resolved not to think about the letter until he had time to find out what it was about. Maybe it was nothing.

"We'll be having dinner with my next-door neighbor," he told Sean. "I can't wait for you to meet her. She can cook like nobody's business."

———————

Sean looked like a darker version of his father. Quinn's hair was a sun-streaked light brown; Sean's was dark chocolate with milk chocolate highlights. Quinn's eyes were a smiling blue-jean blue; Sean's were a deep, serious indigo. Quinn's skin was dark-golden tan; Sean's was Mediterranean olive.

"Man," Sean said, just before he shoveled in another massive forkful of twirled-up noodles with a fat shrimp on the end. He chewed with gusto and swallowed, then smiled at Abby. "This tastes just like restaurant food. Even the broccoli is good, and I usually hate broccoli. I was planning to take a few bites and feed the rest to the dog, but I'm gonna eat it myself." He reached down to pet Georgia, who sat between Sean's chair and Quinn's. "Sorry, girl."

Abby had set the table with the three place settings at one end. Abby and Sean sat across from each other, with Quinn between them on the end. Georgia sat with her chin on Sean's knee, having rightly determined which side of the table offered her the best chance of getting a handout.

Abby smiled at Sean. "I'm glad you like it." She took a sip of wine and glanced at Quinn, who was surreptitiously texting, his phone held under the table. "Quinn, is everything okay? You seem a little distracted."

Quinn glanced up, looking guilty. "Sorry. Work stuff." He set his phone facedown on the table. "I'll stop."

Sean poked Quinn's shoulder. "You always fuss at me for texting during dinner, Dad. Shame on you for not setting a good example."

Quinn pushed his phone farther out of reach, as if even now, its evil lure tempted him to stray. "You're right. Completely right. I apologize."

Abby felt guilty herself; she had been keeping Quinn away from his own work while he tended to hers. "You know, Quinn, my foot is feeling much better. I think I can take over the chores from now on so you can get back to your own work."

Quinn ate another shrimp and pointed his fork at her. "You heard the doctor, Abby. Two full weeks off that foot before you even think of resuming normal activities."

"Yes, but—"

"You know what?" Quinn's face lit up. "Maybe I could hire Sean to help out around here."

A bright idea she figured he'd thought of long before now; having his son working next door would give Quinn the excuse to spend more time with Sean. "Maybe we should let him decide for himself after he helps with the evening feed."

Sean shrugged. "I could definitely use the money. Mom doesn't pay me for the yard work anymore. She says I ought to do it anyway, just to pitch in."

"I agree with your mom," Abby said. "Kids should help out around the house, because that's what families do. Wouldn't it be silly if your mom made you pay her for cooking your dinner or picking you up after school? What would you say if she did that?"

Sean grinned around a mouthful of cheesy broccoli. "I'd tell her it's a sin to charge money for the crap she cooks."

"Sean," Quinn said in a warning tone. "You don't get to disrespect your mother that way."

Sean swallowed, and his olive cheeks turned a dusky rose. "Sorry, Dad."

"Your mother and I may have our differences, but she deserves your respect—and mine, too. It's not easy being someone's mother, and it's even harder now, because she has to do a lot more of the parenting by herself."

"Sorry," Sean said again. Shamefaced, he met Abby's eyes. "I apologize for being rude at your table, Miss Abby. I wasn't thinking."

Abby's heart melted. Quinn and his ex-wife had obviously raised a respectful teen, and the fact that Quinn hadn't allowed Sean to bad-mouth his mother made Abby's estimation of him rise another notch. "Apology accepted." Abby pushed back her scooter and stood, leaning on the handlebars. "Now, who wants dessert?"

Not that Quinn's gallant defense of his ex-wife meant that Abby would let him get past her panties anytime soon. Though she was sorely tempted to say yes to a summer fling, she knew her still-aching heart wasn't up for it. Quinn had just now proven himself to have a measure of decency Abby's ex had never claimed nor aspired to. But as Abby told herself on a regular basis, she had no business falling in love with any man who had a child she wouldn't be able to keep in her life if things went wrong between her and the child's father.

Abby had fully expected Sean to be a terrible teen, someone whose prickly exterior would easily repel any motherly feelings she might be inclined to experience. But no, Sean wasn't a terrible teen; in fact, he seemed to be just the opposite. Knowing that, she had to be even more on guard against developing any deep romantic feelings for Quinn.

After dinner, Quinn topped up Abby's wine, then he and Sean cleaned the kitchen. Griffin, shaved down and stitched up, came in from the bedroom, looking for a handout.

"Oh, wow." Sean swiped some cheese from the casserole dish and let the cat lick a spot of cheese off the tip of his finger. "What happened to him?"

"Raccoon fight," Quinn supplied. "It was gnarly."

"'Gnarly' isn't a word anymore, Dad." Sean sat on the kitchen floor and petted Griff's head. "But, how did you know it was a raccoon? Did you see the fight?"

"Yep." He told the story—embellished somewhat, Abby hoped—while she sipped her wine and brainstormed with herself on ways to feed Wolf closer to the house. Quinn had taken over the task of putting food out by the road every night on the way back to his place. Abby didn't want a repeat of what had happened before, but she wanted to lure Wolf closer to the house so he could join the Bayside Barn family.

But no matter how she twisted it, she couldn't come up with a solution. The only kibble that stayed out overnight was the cats' food in the barn. The raccoons didn't bother those bowls, because the barn cats' food shelf and all the food bins were near the donkeys' stall window, and donkeys were fiercely protective of their space. According to the donkeys, cats were allowed; raccoons were not.

"Dad?" Sean's voice sounded tentative. "Now that you've got your own house with a yard and everything, can we have a cat? Or a dog?"

When Sean asked whether they could have a cat or a dog, Quinn's heart soared and then just as quickly plummeted back to the ground. He turned off the faucet, and the kitchen went quiet. "Maybe."

His heart had soared with happiness that Sean would want to stay with him enough to have a pet. And, a relationship with a beloved animal would be another reason for Sean to visit as often as possible. But then his heart plummeted because he hadn't told Sean, either, that he planned to flip the estate. He hadn't told anyone but Delia, his real estate agent. Why he was keeping his plans so quiet, he wasn't quite sure; maybe because he didn't want to be seen as a failure if his plans didn't succeed. "I'll think about it."

On the way to the barn with Sean, Quinn stuck his phone in his back pocket and shoved the potential problem he may have set in motion out of his mind. The text he'd sent to Delia earlier hadn't been answered yet. But it was the weekend already, and Realtors had lives, too. If she had taken him seriously and instituted some sort of complaint to the city, he would go to the city clerk's office Monday morning and pull the plug.

Simple. Easy. Practically done already.

Quinn put his arm around his son's shoulders. "How did you like dinner?"

"You were right when you said that Abby can cook like nobody's business." Sean swung a Ziploc bag of sliced apples Abby had prepared against his leg. "I even liked the broccoli." He let out a long, manly burp of satisfaction. "She ought to open a restaurant."

"You should tell her that."

"She's a nice lady," Sean continued. "And pretty, too. Maybe you should date her or something."

Quinn just about choked. "Or something?"

Sean broke away from Quinn at the barn's open door. "Whoa!" He ran to the first stall, where the two ponies stuck their heads over the open half-door. "Horses!"

Ponies, horses, short horses, whatever. Quinn couldn't help but smile at Sean's enthusiasm.

"Here, give me the bag." Quinn took the bag of apples from Sean and handed over one slice. "Hold it in your palm with your hand flat, like this." He demonstrated the way to present the apple and press it up into the horse's (pony's, whatever) mouth so it couldn't bite his fingers. "See?"

When one of the ponies nibbled up the apple slice from Sean's palm, he giggled like a girl. Quinn loved seeing his kid so happy. "Cool, huh?"

"Yeah!" Sean dug into the bag for another slice and presented it to the other pony. "What are their names?"

Quinn pointed to the wipe-off whiteboard next to the stall. "Sunshine and Midnight."

Sean scoffed. "Lame."

"Abby says most of the animals here are rescues; they usually keep the names they came here with."

Sean stroked the white blaze that streaked up the middle of Sunshine's butter-colored face. "Usually?"

"Abby says that sometimes the animals want to keep their old names, and sometimes they want a new name to mark a new phase of their lives." Sounded like twaddle to him, but Sean would probably think it was cool that the animals had a choice in their names. Or maybe he'd think it was twaddle.

Sometimes, Quinn felt like he knew nothing about his son.

Sean nodded. "Cool." He petted the white blaze on Midnight's predictably black forehead, then moved down the line to the donkeys.

Quinn handed over another apple slice. "Elijah is the bigger one. Miriam is his mother."

"Did they choose their names?" Sean asked.

"I don't know."

Sean scratched Elijah's head. "I think they did."

By the time they had passed out apple slices to all the animals and done the evening feed for the barn animals, full dark had fallen, and the cicadas and tree frogs and crickets roared in the tall live oaks outside the barn. Sean had been brimming with excitement even before Quinn turned on the aviary light. They went inside the lockout and Quinn closed the door behind him. "Don't rest your hand on the wire," he cautioned his son before introducing the parrots.

"Can I hold one?" Sean asked.

"Not only no," Quinn replied, "but hell no."

"I do want to work here," Sean said. "Especially if that means I get to eat here, too." Quinn hadn't heard this much enthusiasm in his son's voice since—well, since he couldn't remember. "Do you think Mom will let me? Maybe she could drop me off in the mornings on her way to work and pick me up on her way home?"

"All we can do is ask," Quinn replied. His heart soared with hope at the thought of spending so much time with his son, but reality swooped in like a big flyswatter and smacked it down. Melissa was extremely unlikely to allow Sean to spend that much time here, even when it meant he'd otherwise be sitting home alone while she worked at the exclusive boutique she'd bought with her half of the equity money.

"Do you think she'd let me come on weekends, too? And could I bring some friends along to hang out while I work?"

"We would have to ask Abby about having friends along. And maybe we should do a trial run during our scheduled visitation days this summer before asking your mom for more. You don't want to hurt her feelings." Because Melissa with hurt feelings was about as dangerous as a wild boar with an arrow stuck in its side. Quinn clapped Sean on the shoulder and changed the subject. "You brought swim trunks, right? I thought we might go for a quick swim after we head over to our side of the fence."

"Yeah!" Sean leaped up and punched the air. "I love it here!" Then he ran for the farmhouse, leaving Quinn standing by himself.

Chapter 14

EARLY THE NEXT MORNING JUST AS THE SUN WAS BEGINNING to shine through the bedroom curtains, Georgia growled, then sat up in bed and barked. Her ears pricked forward, her gaze locked on the bedroom doorway.

Abby sat up and glanced at the clock; just after 7:00 a.m., about a half hour too early for Quinn's arrival.

Someone tapped at the glass door. Georgia growled, but her tail wagged, too. She hopped off the bed and ran out of the bedroom. A second later, Abby heard the dog door bump. Georgia's happy *barroo!* let Abby know this was a friend. Sean must have woken Quinn early.

Abby put her knee on the scooter she'd parked next to the bed and hopped into the kitchen. She slid the glass door open to see Sean kneeling on the patio and caressing Georgia's ears. Quinn wasn't there.

"Hey, Sean. Good morning. Where's your dad?"

Sean looked up and grimaced. "Still sleeping." He handed over Wolf's daily delivery of newsprint. "And I'm bored. Can I help with the chores?"

"Let's get some breakfast going first, okay?" Quinn always did the chores before breakfast, and Abby wasn't about to let Sean do the chores without supervision. "Come on in."

She hit the button on the coffee maker, then leaned down awkwardly over the scooter's handlebars to open the narrow drawer beside the oven.

"Let me." Sean opened the drawer for her, revealing vertical dividers where the sheet pans were stored. "What do you want?"

"I need the big, flat cookie sheet on the left and the smaller one on the far right."

She turned on the oven, then cut parchment paper to fit each of the sheet pans. Sean parceled out frozen biscuits on the smaller pan. (Yes, frozen biscuits. Guilty as charged. She hoped he wouldn't snitch.) She arranged bacon strips across the larger pan, then covered it with aluminum foil.

Quinn tapped on the door, then came on in. "I see you've kidnapped my son."

"Yes." Abby started breaking eggs into a bowl. "My evil master plan is already a success. Do you want to know the next step I have planned for world domination?"

"Not really." Quinn peeked in the oven.

Abby swatted him with the dish towel—at least, she tried to. The damn scooter wasn't as agile as she'd prefer. "You have a half hour to do the chores before breakfast. Y'all better get busy unless you want to eat cold eggs."

"Awww," Sean pouted. "I wanted to help you cook."

"Come on, dude." Quinn herded Sean out the door, with Georgia right behind them. "You're on the clock."

Abby sliced a red bell pepper—western omelets and skillet potatoes today, she decided—while Stella, the new kitten, twined at her ankles and purred, hoping for a handout.

The days with Quinn had settled into a homey domestic routine of morning chores and breakfast—sometimes by the pool—followed by several hours of alone time while Quinn worked on his property. When Quinn wasn't around, Abby did housework or sent out résumés through the job-search sites she'd been using to find an office-manager position. (So far, no bites, even after she'd widened her search radius.)

Every day while he did the evening feed, she cooked dinner, and they'd usually sit by the pool with wine afterward. They'd have been *in* the pool every evening if not for her stupid cast, and Abby knew she should be thankful for that situation, because if they were in the pool together, the eventual outcome would be drifting together followed by kisses, followed by…

Abby shut the door on that thought.

Just as well Sean was here for the weekend, because even with the added level of difficulty presented by the cast on her foot, she had come dangerously close to letting Quinn venture into below-the-waist territory. Once that happened, she knew it would all be over but the shoutin'. They'd sleep together, and she'd fall in love. Bad, bad idea.

She had no business falling in love. A summer fling might have been possible if Quinn had been less charming or intelligent or helpful around here. But unfortunately, he possessed all the qualities she'd be looking for in a man, if she were looking. Well, except for the fact that he had a kid. A nice kid that she'd also be in danger of caring way too much about.

A heady and horrible combination she should stay well away from if she wanted to keep her peace of mind. Sure, Abby still hoped to be a mother one of these days, even though she knew that loving another child wouldn't banish the ache of losing Emily. But now wasn't the time. She needed to heal, and she had to do that on her own. "Moving forward," she said out loud. "Take care of yourself before you take on anyone else."

Besides, it was becoming clear that any suitable job she might find was likely to be far from here. She chopped a yellow onion with more gusto than necessary, filling the air with a sharp, biting scent that made her eyes water.

The house phone rang, and she quickly washed her hands before scooting to Reva's office area—a converted coat closet—and picking up.

"Hey," Reva said. "I have a short break between classes and wanted to check in."

Abby stuck the phone between her shoulder and her ear and scooted back toward the kitchen. "Everything's fine."

"Did you ever talk to that wolf dog again?"

Shit, no. Abby started setting the table. "I haven't seen him. I know he's eating the food Quinn—I mean, the food I've been putting out by the side of the road."

Silence. Judgment. Abby shouldn't have changed her story midsentence.

"I'm sorry I haven't made time to connect in—or try to—but I promise I'll do it this afternoon."

"Ask him where he's been sleeping at night. The answer might surprise you."

"Why don't you just tell me?"

Reva laughed. "Nope. You have to learn to trust yourself, and you won't do that if I keep holding your hand. Hey, I've gotta go. Talk to you later."

After breakfast, Abby shooed Quinn and Sean out and cleaned the kitchen by herself. The scooter forced her to do everything more slowly, so she let the whole kitchen-cleaning exercise become a contemplative experience. She even washed the dishes by hand instead of using the dishwasher.

With her hands in the warm soapy water, Abby's thoughts drifted back to her childhood summers with Aunt Reva, when she'd stood on a stepstool and helped Reva wash dishes. Abby's parents had been so completely wrapped up in their own lives that shipping her off for a whole summer each year hadn't caused a blip on their parental radar screen. They had hardly ever called, and Abby hadn't missed them. She had loved pretending that she was Reva's daughter and not just her niece.

Reva had tried, even then, to teach Abby how to communicate with animals. And Abby had pretended that she could. Sometimes it had felt so right, as if she really was communicating. But now, seeing it from a grown-up perspective, Abby wondered if she been so hungry for Reva's mothering that she had convinced herself in order to please Reva. Abby did believe it was possible to communicate telepathically with animals; she'd seen Reva do it too many times to doubt. But she wasn't sure of her own ability.

Reva had always said it was okay to let it be what it was, either real or pretend, and not to worry about it. Reva said that one day, Abby would have a communication experience that couldn't be explained away, and when that happened, she would understand and accept her abilities.

That day hadn't come yet, though Abby had experienced glimpses of clarity that felt real. But it seemed that whenever she noticed the door of communication opening, it quickly slammed shut. Maybe she was the one doing the slamming, without meaning to. Maybe she was so afraid of being wrong that she hadn't allowed herself to really try.

Something about the slow, solitary work of cleaning the kitchen—moving meditation, Reva called it—made Abby feel relaxed and receptive, sort of the same way she'd felt when Reva talked her through the conversation with Wolf the other night when she was waiting at the vet. Maybe now would be a good time to have that conversation, or at least try to.

Abby took the scooter to the sofa and sat with her foot up on the scooter's seat. Her phone, which she'd been keeping in the scooter's basket, buzzed. A text from Reva, Abby knew before she checked the message.

Scan his health, see if you notice any aches or pains, and if so, where it hurts.

Ask him where he's been sleeping at night.

Ask him where he'd like to be fed.

Ask him to show himself.

The tractor started up next door. Abby leaned back against the couch cushions and did the relaxation thing of breathing and imagining her body as an empty straw through which communication would flow. She imagined Wolf coming to sit in front of her. She tried the body-scanning thing Reva had taught her long ago, imagining that her body was Wolf's body, as if she could slip her hands and feet into his paws, zip her body up into his skin, and become him. Then, she took another deep breath and let it out, and allowed her attention to go where it wanted.

Her right side tingled; a tickling, tightening feeling, her skin itching, crawling, almost burning. She scratched the spot, and the burning sensation intensified, so she lifted up her shirt to make sure an insect wasn't in there biting her. Nothing.

Okay, so maybe he had fleas. Or maybe, she did.

She took another breath and tried again. She tried to imagine what it would feel like to have paws instead of hands. She tried to imagine what it would feel like to have furry ears that stuck up, and a fluffy tail to wag. She imagined a beam of light scanning from her furry ears to her fluffy tail, and waited to see where her attention wanted to stick.

Except for the spot that itched and burned, it didn't.

She blew out a breath and stood. "This is stupid."

She grabbed the handlebars of the scooter, put her knee on the seat, and tried to see how fast she could make it to the refrigerator. "World record, yay."

She wasn't hungry this soon after breakfast, but her body required something to conquer the antsy feeling that had come over her. The chicken salad she'd made yesterday, no. Chicken salad on a bed of green salad, no, and no.

A few spoonsful of Ben & Jerry's Strawberry Cheesecake later, she went back to the couch and tried again.

Stella, the bad little calico who'd pretty much decided that her only use for humans was as a source of food and water, hopped into her lap and started purring. "Well, that's a new attitude." She petted Stella's silky head. At Abby's gentle touch, Stella hissed and jumped down, tail twitching with irritation. "Okay, then." Maybe not such a new attitude after all. "Never mind."

Abby put the bad little cat out of her mind and refocused on her conversation with Wolf. She closed her eyes and imagined Wolf coming to sit in front of her, but he was already there, giving her a slit-eyed look. *You left*, she imagined him saying. *I've been waiting.*

"Sorry. I'm here now." She felt a stab of irritation, and let it go. "Where have you been sleeping?"

Nothing. Reva always said that when you get nothing, it can mean you've asked the wrong... Wait. "Where have you been sleeping at night?"

She saw an image of him curled up on her back patio. She saw his ears flicking when bugs bothered him; she'd been leaving the patio light on, hoping to discourage the raccoons, but the light attracted bugs, too.

"Okay, I'll leave the light off if you're sleeping on the patio. Is that what you're doing?"

Same image.

"Okay, got it. Where would you like to be fed?"

He showed an image of him eating from a bowl on the patio.

She imagined a band of raccoons coming to eat the food and fighting the cats.

He showed the image of him curled up on the patio. *I won't let them come. I will protect everyone from harm.* In her imagination, he lowered himself to his elbows and put his head on his paws. *I won't harm anyone, not even the chickens or the rabbits. I won't need to eat them if you are feeding me.*

"Will you show yourself, so I can see you?"

And just like that, his image in her imagination melted away.

Wolf slept hard that night. The bug-attracting light had been turned off, so he was able to rest without insects buzzing in his ears. The first few nights of his vigil, he'd slept lightly, waking often to chase away the masked intruders that seemed so humanlike with their little five-fingered hands and their ability to stand, and even walk, on their hind legs.

He allowed the armadillos and possums to stay. They assured

him that their only interest was in eating any bugs and grubs they could find in the short grass. Georgia came to visit him after the lights went out inside the house. She cleaned his wound, which didn't hurt much anymore but itched and burned as new skin grew from the edges inward, coming together to cover the scabbed-over patch. When she finished, she curled up in front of him. They lay like that for a long time, like one leaf curled around another.

Maybe her presence was the reason he'd slept so deeply. He'd been alone for so long, he had nearly forgotten how it felt to relax into the safety of companionship. Georgia went back inside the house just before dawn, and Wolf stretched out on the cool cement patio to doze till morning. He would leave before the dew was absorbed into the grass or suspended in the air. He knew that Quinn—and the young Quinn he'd seen from a distance—would come then, and he didn't want to scare them.

More than that, he didn't want to be chased away.

And though Abby had promised not to chase him, Quinn hadn't promised him anything. A few of the cats came close to sniff him cautiously, and he remained still so they could explore him without fear.

Stillness lured him back to sleep, and he dreamed of rabbits and ground squirrels sleeping with each other the way he and Georgia had: one leaf curled around another. He dreamed that the yard was filled with pillows on top of wood blocks, like the one in the house where the cat slept. He and Georgia shared the biggest pillow, a fluffy, soft one that puffed up around them like a nest.

He didn't hear the Quinns arrive until they were right on top of him. He barely had time to run around the corner of the house.

"Whoa, did you see that?" He heard the young Quinn say.

"No, what?" The first Quinn knocked on the glass door.

"Nothing, I guess."

Wolf hid in the den he had dug in the red dirt under the front porch. He hoped it would show Georgia that he could be her home just as much as her people now were. But it also gave him a place to hide in case someone closed the gate and blocked his escape route into the forest. It hadn't happened, but at least he had options. He wouldn't stay hidden in the den for long this time, just until he heard the sounds of the two Quinns feeding the barn animals. Then, he would run back to the isolation of the forest.

Chapter 15

QUINN KEPT SEAN BUSY AFTER CHORES ON SUNDAY WITH pool time in the morning followed by lunch with Abby followed by an afternoon paddleboard excursion, just the two of them.

They carried the boards all the way down the driveway, all the way to the corner, and all the way down the dead-end road next to the estate. Quinn figured Sean would complain about the trudge, but instead, he complained that paddleboards weren't as cool as kayaks.

"I think you'll like it once you try it," Quinn said. "Paddleboards are more versatile; you can stand or sit, or even lie flat if you want. In a kayak, all you can do is sit, and after a while, your butt goes numb."

Sean grinned. "Your butt, maybe."

They put the boards in at the crumbling old boat launch. Sean stood in the knee-deep brown water and held his board steady while Quinn secured a life jacket and water bottle in the net on Sean's board, then put the small cooler of snacks Abby had packed for them on his.

"Are you sure this bayou even goes to the bay?" Sean's voice wobbled uncertainly.

"You're standing in the bay right now." Quinn pushed his own board out a little deeper, straddled it, then sat cross-legged and put the paddle across his lap. "All these little bayous around here are part of it."

Quinn let his board drift while Sean struggled to climb onto his own board without tipping the edges into the water. "Just sit, Son," he instructed. "You're gonna get wet regardless, so go ahead and sit."

Looking as if he'd rather be anywhere else on God's green earth, Sean sat. "Even if these little backwaters are technically part of the bay, we could still get lost in them, couldn't we?"

"We won't get lost, I promise," Quinn said.

Sean made a frustrated grumbling sound; his attempt to paddle away from the launch was turning him in circles, and he was about to end up in the weeds. "Aaaagh, shoot!"

Quinn knew he'd get the hang of it soon enough, and he didn't want to start out by giving orders, but Sean held the paddle backwards and was sitting too far back on his board for the thing to be stable. "Scoot up to the middle of your board and turn your paddle so the logo is facing the other way." Huffing with annoyance, Sean managed to comply.

"Now paddle over here, nice and easy. Don't dig the oar so deep into the water; that's it... Let me show you where we are on my phone, and then you'll see why we can't get lost." On a map of Louisiana, Magnolia Bay looked like a small slice of blue water with a smooth and definite coastline. But in reality, the bay's edges consisted of a multitude of small, interconnected waterways that snaked around acres of marshland interspersed with sandbars and cypress tree islands. The GPS map showed exactly where they were among all the nooks and crannies, bayous and byways.

"See?" Quinn held his phone out to Sean, who gingerly paddled closer to take a look. He leaned over—by about two inches—and glanced at the phone without really looking. "Okay, fine. I just hope you know where we're going."

"I do." Quinn tucked his phone (protected by an OtterBox and secured to his board by a lanyard) back into the bungee net. "I know how to get back, too. Are you ready?"

"As I'll ever be." They'd barely started paddling down the narrow, marsh-lined channel when Sean freaked out. "Dad! Holy shit! There's a big fucking alligator on the bank next to us!" Sean started paddling faster, nearly tipping his board over in the process.

Quinn looked back at a huge alligator sunning himself on a small spit of sandy bank just a few hundred yards from the landing where they had put the boards into the water. It looked so much like a fallen log that he probably wouldn't have noticed it. He hurried to catch up with Sean and reached out to steady his board. "Calm down. He doesn't care about us."

"Jesus, Dad." Sean was a breath away from hyperventilating, his dark eyes so wide Quinn could see the whites all around the iris. "Let's go back before we get eaten." He tried to turn the board around by digging the paddle deep into the water, but only succeeded in making the board dip dangerously to one side.

"Sean." Quinn wrenched the paddle from Sean's anxious grip. "Look at me."

Sean's breathing quieted—just slightly—and he pinned his gaze on Quinn's, his eyelids flickering with panic. "Shit, Dad," he whispered, his entire body shaking. "Shit."

Their boards drifted along with a current that gently guided them farther away from the gator. Quinn had to admit—to himself only—that if the huge-ass alligator had launched himself into the water, Quinn would've probably crapped his pants in fear. But the bloated-looking armor-plated creature continued to doze placidly in the afternoon sun.

"Look at him." He pointed back at the twelve-foot-long alligator who hadn't so much as twitched. "You see that he's busy napping in the sun, and that he is completely unconcerned with us?"

Sean turned to look back, his movements jerky with fear. "I guess."

"Alligators mainly eat big fish and small animals. They don't go after people, unless those people are flailing around in the water so much that they seem like wounded prey. Alligators are lazy opportunists." Like some people Quinn could think of. "About the biggest thing they'll go after is a dog."

"Can we go back now?" Sean whined. "This isn't fun. It's scary."

Quinn hardened his heart and his voice. "No, we're not going back. We're going to paddle to the end of this little bayou, at least. Come here, let me show you." He held out his phone and showed Sean the map, this time making sure Sean really looked. "When we get here," he pointed to a small cypress island, "we'll paddle around the island, then come back to the landing from the other side."

Sean's shoulders lifted toward his ears, and he looked back toward the landing with a yearning expression on his face.

"Think of it like this." Quinn forced a happy note into his voice. "We'll be going around the long way, but we won't have to paddle past old Goliath again."

"Unless he moves upstream," Sean replied in a tone of doom. "But okay. I don't want to give him a chance to change his mind about eating us."

Quinn handed over the paddle he'd confiscated. "Good deal."

Assisted by a gentle current, they paddled away from old Goliath, but Sean kept glancing over his shoulder. Quinn pointed out turtles and birds. They stilled their paddles to listen to a heavy rustling sound in the dense underbrush of the swampy island bog between them and the bay's main channel.

"You think it's a deer?" Sean asked.

"Or a wild hog rooting around," Quinn answered. "They're both pretty nocturnal, but out on these little islands where people don't go, they feel safe, so you can sometimes spot them during the day."

They never saw whatever it was making noise beyond the trees, so they paddled on. Eventually, Sean's shoulders relaxed and he started to engage with the natural environment around them. "Look, Dad! Is that a hawk?"

Quinn looked up at the large, majestic bird gazing out from the top of a dead-looking cypress tree dripping with Spanish moss. "Red-tailed hawk, yes."

The paddle around the island took a couple hours; they weren't in any hurry. When they'd made it to the tree-lined shade of the bayou that led back to the launch, Quinn unzipped the soft-sided cooler. "Hungry?"

Sean clutched his stomach. "'Bout to die."

Quinn handed Sean a sandwich and a bag of chips, and they let their boards drift down the bayou. Quinn took a bite of his pickle-laden chicken sandwich, and it was so good he just about groaned. Pickle juice dripped down his chin, and he wiped it away with his wrist. How had she managed to keep the bread from getting soggy? Must be some kind of culinary magic.

"Dad?" Sean asked.

"Huh?" He took another bite; damn, Abby knew how to make food taste good.

"How come you know about all this nature stuff, even though you grew up in New Orleans?"

The sour taste of regret filled Quinn's mouth, ruining the taste of the gourmet sandwich. He swallowed, wishing he'd spent more time out in nature with his son when he'd had the chance. "My best friend's dad had a fishing boat. We spent hours on the bayous outside the city. Even spent the night on the boat a bunch of times."

"You mean JP?"

"Yep." JP, his once-best friend and business partner, who'd forgotten all about morality in the pursuit of greed. Quinn tossed a chunk of his sandwich into the water for the fish, then put the rest back in its fancy beeswax-and-cloth wrapping. Then he hoisted his paddle and dug it deep into the tea-brown water. "Sun's skimming the treetops; we'd best get back now, or the bugs'll get us."

Back at the pool house, they hosed down the boards and life jackets, then left them by the pool to dry while they lit the burn pile of branches that had accumulated from Quinn's land clearing. Before Sean left that day, he hugged Quinn; a real hug, not one of those sideways bro hugs. "I had fun, Dad."

From way up by the mailbox, Melissa honked the car's horn again; she had texted Sean that she didn't want to drive her new car down Quinn's rutted driveway. Fair enough. Quinn didn't necessarily want her all up in his business anyway. He patted his son's back, feeling a rush of love, not only for the child Sean had been, but for the man he was becoming. Quinn might have a lot of problems with Melissa, but the way she'd raised Sean wasn't one of them.

"I'll talk to Mom about working here sometimes," Sean said.

"That would be great," Quinn answered. "I'd love to see more of you."

"Me too, Dad." Sean bumped shoulders with Quinn, an awkward show of affection after years of anger and resentment. A lot of the strife between him and his son had been planted and fertilized by Melissa, but he had to admit, he'd doled out some of the same bullshit fertilizer himself. Hurt feelings on both sides had led each of them to react with hostility rather than to act with love. Quinn walked with his son down the long driveway and vowed to himself that he would make up to Sean—and to Melissa, if she'd let him—for the fact that he'd been an absentee dad too much of the time.

He had worked long hours from the beginning; at first so he could establish a solid financial foundation for his new family. But slowly, so slowly that Quinn couldn't remember when and how it happened, the reasons for his workaholic tendencies had shifted.

Melissa and Sean had become their own little universe, from which Quinn often felt squeezed out. At the same time, Melissa had started getting snarky about him not helping out enough—but when he tried, nothing he did pleased her. After a while, the only time she asked for his help was when Sean needed more discipline than she could provide. So Quinn became the bad cop Sean dreaded to see coming home some days. Maybe now that Quinn and Melissa were officially divorced and living separate lives, he and Sean could start fresh building a new father-son relationship, unencumbered by the past. This weekend gave him hope that they'd already made a good start.

"Next time you come, we'll go paddleboarding again." It occurred to Quinn that he could build a storage shed at the far end of the yard and install a gate so launching the paddleboards or other water toys from the public launch would be easier. "We'll explore around here some more."

In a way, Abby's broken foot had helped Quinn to make more time for Sean this summer. So that he could stay nearby and help with the farm chores, he had taken on a custom cabinet-building job that he could work on in the estate's garage. All he'd had to do on-site was measure the people's kitchen, and once he'd built the cabinets to fit, he would deliver and install them.

"I'd like that," Sean responded. When they reached Melissa's car, Sean turned toward Quinn. "Dad?" With his back to Melissa's car, he spoke so quietly, Quinn had to lean in to hear. "Thanks for making my room so nice and everything, and for buying the Xbox and stuff."

Quinn clapped Sean on the shoulder. "You're welcome, Son. I've missed you, and I want you to know that you can come here whenever you want, as long as your mom doesn't object."

Sean nodded. "I do know that, Dad." He swallowed, and his Adam's apple bobbed in his throat. He almost looked choked up. Then he turned away, and the moment evaporated. "See you Wednesday," Sean called over his shoulder as he got in the car.

"Bye." Quinn lifted a hand to wave, but the tires on Melissa's car peeled out so fast and loud that Sean could've neither seen nor heard Quinn's goodbye. Quinn turned toward the pool house, though Abby's presence next door pulled at him like a strong undertow.

Three days ago, he'd have thought that undertow was possibly a dangerous one. But after spending this weekend with Sean and

Abby together much of that time, he was beginning to wonder if he should rethink his options. Why couldn't he renovate this property and just stay? Why couldn't he see what sort of relationship might be possible with Abby, a beautiful, gentle, sweet woman whom his son obviously liked, and who seemed to like his son? Maybe he didn't need to flip this estate after all.

———————

Abby wasn't snooping. She had just happened to decide to sit on the wraparound front porch that afternoon instead of the concrete patio out back. She had only recently discovered that while the patio was great if you could get in the pool, when you were reduced to pushing a scooter everywhere or hobbling around with crutches, the shaded front porch was the place to be.

Without chores to do, she had poured an early glass of wine (five o'clock somewhere, right?) and settled into one of the wicker chairs on the front porch with her foot propped on a pillow-topped ottoman and Griff on her lap.

From her comfy chair, Abby could see one small sliver of the road in front of the house: the bit that included the end of Reva's driveway, the end of Quinn's driveway, and his rusted-out mailbox. A fancy red convertible zoomed past both driveways, slammed on brakes with an audible squealing of tires, then backed into Reva's drive for a three-point turn that narrowly missed Quinn's already-bent mailbox pole. The car stopped with the driver's door roughly even with the mailbox.

The top was down, so it was easy to see—in fact, impossible not to see—the driver, a beautiful (from behind, anyway) woman with long, dark hair and olive skin. Sean's mother, Melissa, of course. She appeared to be texting, her head tilted down as she focused on the phone in her lap. Then, her chin came up and she glanced around idly, first at the cat's-claw forest, then toward

Quinn's battered mailbox. Looking back over her shoulder and then into the rearview mirror, she opened the mailbox and peeked inside, then slammed it shut.

"Nothing in there," Abby muttered to herself. It was Sunday, after all. "Miss Snoopy Pants."

Stella, the new kitten, hopped onto the porch rail and stared down at Georgia, who had decided it was more fun to toddle around in the shrubbery and snoop under the porch than to sit with Abby. With the front half of the old farmhouse on pier-and-beams and the back addition on a raised concrete slab, there was a lot of naked space under the old part of the house.

"You'd better not be digging under there," Abby warned. Georgia gave a happy *barroo!* from an under-the-porch spot directly under Abby's chair, and Griff stiffened in her lap.

Abby stroked his shaved head. "Poor buddy." A week after the attack, he still looked like a battered prizefighter, with one eye half-closed (scratched cornea) and multiple stitched cuts on his neck, back, chest, and face, plus one really long laceration on his fat, hanging-down belly. Mack had shaved down all of Griffie's long, luxurious fur to make sure he didn't miss any hidden lacerations. The stitches would come out in three days, and the fur was beginning to grow in, a downy-soft covering of peach fuzz on the cat's porcelain-pink skin.

Quinn and Sean came into view, walking up Quinn's drive toward Melissa's parked car. Sean turned to his dad and said something, and Quinn clapped him on the shoulder. The second he got in the car, Melissa drove off like she'd just robbed a bank and needed to make a quick getaway. Quinn raised his hand to wave goodbye, but there was no way Sean could've seen it.

"Bitch." Abby took another sip of wine. "She could've waited for them to say goodbye."

Quinn stood there for a minute, looking sad and lost.

"Poor guy."

Georgia barreled around the corner of the porch, her little feet on the wood planking sounding like horse's hooves. She leaped onto Abby's lap, carelessly shoving Griffin aside and spilling Abby's wine.

"Rude!" Abby swiped at the splat of wine that had landed on her bare thigh. "And covered in dirt!" Georgia's face, feet, and belly were a dark, orange red. "Where have you been digging?"

Georgia gave a triumphant *barroo!* and wagged her tail, clearly satisfied with herself and the world in general.

"Get down." Abby set her now-empty glass aside and shooed Georgia onto the porch. "You bad girl. You're gonna get a bath."

Abby had cleaned the floors earlier—not an easy feat pushing a vacuum cleaner while also depending on the knee-scooter for balance. No way was she letting Georgia walk across her clean floors on those feet. "Hope you enjoy getting a cold water-hose bath, 'cause that's what it's gonna be." She stood. "Let's go to the barn."

Bathing Georgia was usually a quick half-hour task, including brushing and drying her. This, Abby knew, would take a good hour or more. "But it's gotta be did," she said to herself. (Like cursing, deliberately incorrect grammar usage often made her feel better about the unfairness of life.)

She got down the steps by sitting and scooting down one step at a time while easing the folded scooter along with her, step by step. At the bottom, she used the porch rail for balance, stood on her good foot and opened the scooter. With trepidation in her heart, she mounted her unruly steed and began the long and dangerous trek across the front yard, down the drive, and over the flagstone path to the barn.

The damn scooter—she really ought to give it a name; a horrible, terrible name, something like Hannibal—tried to kill her at least a dozen times a day. It instilled a false sense of security by gliding like an ice skater across the manicured grass, but on the gravel drive, it dug ruts and threatened to tip sideways whenever it encountered a rock that didn't slide merrily out of its way. And the flagstone walkway, forget about it. If it wasn't the flagstone's uneven surface tripping her up, it was the deep and treacherous pit of pea gravel sucking her down.

But she made it to the barn, finally, and said a prayer of thanks for smooth concrete flooring. Georgia, who'd been right beside her all the way, hung back when Abby scootered into the horse-washing stall, clearly suspicious of its heavy-duty coiled-up hose and top-of-the-line multifunction spray nozzle.

Georgia eyed Abby for a second, then turned and trotted to the barn's open door. *Not doing this*, the dog's demeanor declared.

"Yes, you will, too," Abby said, her voice hard. "Get over here."

Abby took bottles of horse shampoo and conditioner off the shelf and set them down on the rubber-mat flooring next to the drain, which emptied into a buried 55-gallon drum with holes in the bottom. (Abby knew this because she'd been staying here the summer the barn was built. Grayson had called the drain system a cheap man's septic tank.) Abby turned on the spigot and uncoiled the hose.

Georgia sat by the door and looked contrite, her tail thumping ever so slightly.

"Yeah, I know you're sorry. But you still have to get a bath."

The tail thumped some more, and Georgia whined softly, looking out toward the yard. She'd been trained to obey, to come when called, and not to run free unless she'd been given permission.

"That's right. You'd better come here. Don't make me come and get you."

Georgia wouldn't run, but she wasn't going to make this easy, either. Abby took a lead rope off the wall and scooted toward Georgia, who leaned into the corner and looked toward a freedom she knew better than to take.

"I don't know why you do this to yourself." Abby clipped the lead rope to Georgia's collar. "You know it always ends up this way."

But to be fair, Abby usually bathed Georgia in the bathtub with warm water, which she didn't seem to mind all that much. But enduring the cold water that spewed from the outdoor hose with punishing force obviously wasn't on Georgia's list of favorite things to do.

But you know, Abby felt put-out enough at Georgia's misbehavior that she didn't much care whether the bad little dog enjoyed her bath or had to suffer through it. This whole exercise had interrupted Abby's happy hour, completely obliterating the relaxing effect of the wine. Now, once Georgia was clean, Abby would have to start relaxing all over again, but she'd already be 140 calories in the hole.

She tugged the unwilling dog into the washing stall and picked up the dripping hose. Georgia pulled against the restraining lead rope, and Abby jerked back, then tied the rope to the handlebars of the scooter. "It'll be over before you know it," she promised. Relenting a bit at the sight of the dog's trembling flanks and desperate eyes, Abby turned the nozzle to the gentlest setting. "Come on. It won't be that bad."

She wrapped her fingers around Georgia's collar and hit the nozzle's spray button. Next thing she knew, Abby was on her butt, the scooter was halfway across the barn, and Georgia was gone.

Chapter 16

QUINN STOOD IN THE LIVING ROOM OF THE SPRAWLING, Craftsman-style estate house, taking stock. He'd been running the AC, so a little of the musty smell had begun to dissipate. A good deep-cleaning might remove the rest of the odor, and a few coats of paint and varnish would bring out the timeless beauty of this old place. Even the tile in the kitchen and bathrooms didn't look too bad to regrout and refinish. The place was starting to look good, but that didn't mean he should fall in love with it, or with the idea of staying once he'd completed the renovation. He needed to remain committed to his goals.

He knew the idea of putting down roots here was pie-in-the-sky thinking brought on by a better-than-imagined weekend with Sean, the first time they'd really connected in years. Quinn tried to stop his imagination from spinning out impossible scenarios, but they kept coming back, so he let himself dream a little dream that could never come true—not if he planned to make any money. Maybe if he won the lottery...

He didn't mind the animal noises and the school field trips quite as much as he had at first.

No, scratch that. He couldn't fool himself about the field trips. But at least those subsided during the summer months, and if he decided to stay and live at the estate, he'd be out working during the weekdays anyway. And after spending a significant amount of time with the animals, their braying and honking and crowing and barking and clucking and meowing didn't bother him anymore. Worn out from staying busy all day, he even slept right through the rooster's early-morning alarms.

So yeah, if he won the lottery, he could see himself staying here and building a bayside paradise, not for an imaginary retired couple, but for himself, for Sean, and maybe even for Abby, if that worked out. He and Abby and Sean could plan and renovate the estate house together, then they'd all live there, happily ever after. Abby would be next door to her aunt Reva, so they'd each have a built-in support network right next door.

And Reva would probably retire sometime, right? So the field trips would be a thing of the past one of these days. Meanwhile, Sean could have a cool part-time job that would keep him close to Quinn. During the summer months—to supplement his lottery winnings—Quinn could take more cabinetry jobs that would allow him to work at home, make his own hours, and spend even more time with his son.

The more he thought about it, the more possible it all seemed. (Well, except for the lottery part. For that, he'd have to buy a ticket, though he knew that would only just barely improve his chances of winning.)

Tomorrow, he'd be back down to earth. But today, he let himself believe. The weekend he'd just spent with Abby and Sean made him think that anything was possible. And maybe it was, as long as his real estate agent hadn't acted on his suggestion—okay, mea culpa, insistence—that she do something to get rid of the farm next door. At the time, he'd been pissed off and freaking out that his only hope of a bright future was about to be sabotaged, and he hadn't cared what the neighbors thought, because he planned not to know them.

He didn't want to think about the drama it would cause between him and Abby if Delia had set something nasty in motion. He hoped to God that Delia had ignored him and done nothing, but he had no way of knowing because she still hadn't answered his text.

He'd told her once that he admired her ability to separate work and real life by setting regular hours and not being a slave to her phone during the time she'd chosen to block out for living her life. At the time, he'd meant it. They'd been dating then, and he'd been glad she wasn't always available—to her clients or to him—because he didn't plan to be all that available, either.

Now, he wished she wasn't quite so disciplined.

He checked his phone, just in case, but no. Nothing. He tried to call her again, but got the same message he remembered from before: *Sorry I missed your call. I'm out of the office until Monday. Please hang up and leave a text message.*

He'd have to wait until tomorrow to do anything, so he might as well put it out of his mind until then. Fortunately, Quinn was good at sticking his head in the sand; he'd done it for at least a decade of his marriage. He popped the cap off a Stella Artois and turned on the TV, planning to zone out until time to go next door and feed the animals.

———————

Wolf was taking an afternoon nap on a newly built and not-quite-soft bed of leaves. Recent rains had taken his old bed from soft to soggy, and the scant supply of new-fallen leaves was only just now dry enough to make a bed. Not quite asleep, less than awake, he drifted in between, wishing he felt safe enough to stay in his soft dirt den under the farmhouse porch.

He missed pillows.

Ever since he'd seen the kitten curled up on a pillow inside Abby's house, resting in the secure knowledge that she could sleep deeply without worry, he'd been dreaming of pillows. Big pillows, little pillows. Fluffy pillows, flat pillows. Pillows in sunlight and pillows in shade. Pillows on the ground and pillows elevated off the ground by wooden blocks. When he saw himself floating in the air on a pillow that turned out to be a cloud, he had a thought: *Now, I'm falling asleep. Now, I'm dreaming.*

His soft cloud-pillow bumped into another one. He looked up, surprised to see his mother, whom he hadn't seen since the alpha took him away from her. At first, he'd been proud to be chosen and had hardly looked back at his mother, who was busy sniffing at the round, rubbery-smelling feet of the big metal thing—which he later learned was a truck—that the alpha had dumped him into before driving away. That was when Wolf realized that his mother wasn't coming with him, and that he would never see her again.

In the dream, his mother sat upright and howled, her nose tilted upward to an evening sky that was streaked with orange and purple and many other colors he didn't have names for. Silhouetted against the setting sun, she looked so beautiful, her gray fur tipped with black, her golden eyes half-closed, her ears tilted back as she gave herself to the end of another day. Then, she turned and leaped onto his cloud, scratching at his side. "Wake up," she moaned, scratching him again. "Hurry. Please wake up. I need your help."

Mother had never asked for his help before. She had always been the one to help him and his siblings. He tried to wake, to rouse himself, to come to her aid, but he couldn't. She scratched at him again, and the cloud she'd been sitting on floated away. Suddenly, she wasn't beside him anymore, but sitting by herself on a cloud that drifted farther and farther away from him on the uncaring breath of the wind. "Mama!" he whined, trying to call back her comforting scent of milk and dirt.

She scratched him again…even from so far away? She scratched him…and he woke.

Georgia, her eyes pleading, whined and worried and pawed at his side. "Help. I did a bad thing, and I think I hurt Abby. Can you help?"

He sat up. "What happened?"

She sent her thoughts and fears at him so quickly he couldn't keep up. All he got was a sense of panic. He stood and shook himself. "Show me."

She scurried through the forest, streaked across the road, and bolted down the driveway. "Hurry, hurry!" Her tail waved like a flag, not in happiness, but in anxiety and warning. On the way, she kept trying to explain what happened, but with his own emotions churning, he didn't understand.

He followed, his nose on her tail. He followed, ready to defend her and her loved ones from anything, even if it meant he had to give his life to do it.

She led him to the opening of the barn, where Abby sat on the floor next to a bent hunk of metal. He saw that Abby wasn't hurt, and his adrenaline rush subsided. Finally, Georgia's explanation sank into his consciousness. "I got scared and I pulled and I ran away. I made her fall, and she needs help."

When Abby noticed them, she inched toward them in an awkward, scrambling movement like an upside-down spider. "Georgia!"

Georgia turned and ran, leaving Wolf alone with Abby, who didn't seem to be hurt—but it didn't look like she could stand up, either. He sat, panting with anxiety. *I don't know what to do.*

"Get help."

Wolf didn't understand the words, but he knew what she meant. He ran down the drive, turned the corner, and ran to the frog pool that had killed all the frogs. Sounds came from behind the hard see-through door that was covered by a dark cloth. He scratched at the door, but nothing happened. Georgia crept up to sit beside him. "I've tried that already."

Wolf scratched again, pawed at the see-through door with as much strength as he could muster, and Georgia helped.

But she was right; it wasn't working. The hard surface resisted his claws, no matter how much he tried to break through it. He stopped pawing at the door and sat. Turning his nose up to the sky the way he had dreamed of his mother doing, he howled.

Georgia joined in, and Wolf thought how beautifully her voice blended with his. His howl was low and mournful for all he'd lost and all he didn't understand. Hers was high-pitched and beautiful with the blended sounds of love and worry and contrition. In the melodious tones of her howl, he heard her joys and her sorrows, her hopes and her dreams of the future. Her howl contained everything he already knew and loved about her, and everything he hoped he'd one day have the chance to learn. Every note was so beautiful it made his heart ache.

The see-through door slid open with a screech worse than a barn owl's, and Quinn—the first one, not the other—ran out and passed Wolf without even looking. He didn't say anything, but just kept running like he knew where to go, and it turned out that he did. Wolf followed at a loping run, with Georgia hustling right behind him as fast as her little legs could go.

At the barn's opening, Quinn yelled, "Dammit, Abby. What the hell?"

"I'm sorry," she whined. "I..." Wolf didn't hear anything after that except a melody of human whining sounds (Abby's) and human angry sounds (Quinn's) that made no sense to him.

Georgia had already absconded, and Wolf didn't see any benefit in staying, either, so he followed her scent to the den he'd dug under the front porch.

"What's wrong?" Wolf asked Georgia. "I think she's okay. Are you okay?"

Georgia shivered and hid at the back of the den. "I knew I shouldn't run. I knew I shouldn't pull. But I was scared and I couldn't help it. I pulled, and she fell over. I've hurt her."

"I think she's okay," he repeated. He curled himself around his friend from behind and tried to absorb her shivering.

"I did wrong." Georgia backed up against him. "I know I did wrong."

He knew how that felt. "It's okay. I'll take care of you. If we have to, we can run away together. I'll take care of you."

"I don't want to leave." Georgia showed Wolf how much she loved her home, and how much she loved Reva, whom she felt she'd betrayed. "I hurt Abby, but I didn't mean to." Georgia's shivering came in short, violent bursts. "I was supposed to take care of her. I didn't mean to hurt her."

Wolf didn't have any good advice to help Georgia with her regrets, her fears, or her worries. If he had, he wouldn't have been exiled from his family and banished to the forest. All he could do was curl himself around her and try to comfort her until her shivering subsided and she finally fell asleep.

———————

Abby sat next to the folded-up scooter in the middle of the barn aisle. She held a rolled-up lead rope in her hand.

Quinn knelt beside her. "What happened? What the hell are you doing out here by yourself? Why didn't you wait for me?" He realized he was yelling, and not giving Abby a chance to respond. He took a breath and let it out. "Are you okay?"

The corners of her truly luscious lips tilted upward. "I'm butt-hurt, but other than that, I'm fine."

Quinn opened the scooter and set the safety latch, then rolled it back and forth. "Good as new." He helped her up and put her and the scooter in an out-of-the-way spot next to the hose connector. He took the lead rope from her and hung it with the others. Georgia's collar—still fastened—hung from the lead rope's snaffle. He unclipped it and tossed it in her lap. "Why is Georgia's collar attached to a lead rope?"

She turned off the spigot. "I was trying to bathe her. And you know what? The wolf dog came out here. He looked at me and then ran off."

Hands on hips, Quinn gave her a pointed look for trying to change the subject. "And how'd the scooter end up halfway across the barn if you were bathing her in the wash stall?"

"My stupidity." Abby blushed. "Like I said, I was trying to bathe Georgia, and she was trying to avoid getting a bath. So I stupidly clipped the lead rope to her collar and tied the rope to the scooter's handlebars. She got away from me, taking the scooter with her."

He shook his head. "You." He pointed at her. "You need a keeper. Do you think you can manage to sit right here"—he pointed at the floor under the scooter—"in this spot, without moving, while I feed the animals?"

"Yes, sir." The expression on her pretty, heart-shaped face seemed sincere and contrite.

But he didn't like her placating tone, nor the fact that she'd tacked on the word *sir*, which made it seem like he was being unreasonable, which he was *not*. He shoveled the animals' food into buckets. What if he'd been away from his house? What if this had happened after feeding time when he'd already gone back to the pool house? What if she'd been really hurt? She might have lain here for hours, in pain, without any way of getting help. "Did you even bring your cell phone out here with you? Not that it works under this metal roof anyway."

"Yes, I did. My phone is in my back pocket. If I'd been hurt, I would have called you for help."

He scoffed. "Unless you'd been knocked unconscious when your hard head hit the concrete."

"Are you saying I'm hardheaded?"

"That's exactly what I'm saying." She didn't have a comeback for that, so he finished setting up the stalls with food and water in silence. He glanced over at her once. She was scrolling through her phone, pretending disinterest. Fine.

"I'm going to bring the equines in now. Stay put."

"Yes, sir." She didn't look up from her phone.

Bringing in the equines was easy; Quinn left their stall doors open, then opened the gate to their pasture. They all knew where to go, no problem.

The problem was Abby's hardheaded insistence on doing stupid things—her words, not his—by herself when she should know better than to put herself in danger. Maybe he should just move over here for the duration—at least until she got free of that damn scooter, which was a danger in itself. He'd seen it come close to tipping over a half-dozen times when he'd been nearby to grab the handlebars and steady the damn thing. What if it happened when he wasn't here?

He followed behind the line of trotting beasts and closed each of the stall doors. It really seemed like he had no choice but to stay with Abby and save her from her own foolhardy attempts to do things for herself. "Bathing the dog," he muttered.

She looked up from her phone. "What?"

"Nothing. I'm done here. You coming?"

She turned around and put her knee on the scooter, then hopped down the barn's aisle. "Spaghetti for dinner," she said over her shoulder. "I hope that's okay. I wasted a bunch of cooking time on that bad little dog."

Up until Abby broke her foot, he'd been having beer and chips for dinner most nights. "Whatever you want to cook will be fine."

He held onto one of the scooter's handlebars while she navigated the flagstone and pea-gravel walkway. She was doing better at navigating rough ground with the scooter, but he wasn't about to tell her that, given her predisposition toward biting off more than she could chew. "Speaking of a bad little dog, where'd she go? She scratched at my door and howled to get my attention, but I haven't seen her since."

"Hiding under the front porch, probably. That's why she got in trouble in the first place, for digging and getting herself dirty. Did you see the wolf dog? It almost seemed like she went to him for help."

"Nope, didn't notice. Just heard the howling and scratching and knew something had to be wrong over here. I came running and didn't look back."

"How'd you know I was in the barn and not the house?"

He shrugged. "I don't know. Just had a feeling, I guess."

When they went inside, he poured a glass of wine for Abby, then opened a beer for himself. Abby browned a pound of organic beef, sauteed all sorts of chopped vegetables, and sprinkled on all sorts of spices before she even opened the jar of sauce. He hovered behind her, helping when she let him, but mostly sipping his beer and watching to make sure she didn't hurt herself.

Okay, to be honest, he was watching the way she moved so gracefully, as if cooking was an intricate dance she did with herself. Watching the way her cropped top rode up when she bent over, exposing the tantalizing dip and curve of her spine. Watching the way her wavy, sun-streaked brown hair fell forward unless she tucked it behind her ear.

"Hey, I need a cookie sheet from the cabinet next to the oven." She moved aside and pointed to the cabinet where vertical dividers kept an assortment of flat pans upright and separated from each other.

He lifted out the pan and set it on the counter. "We're having cookies?"

"Buttered garlic bread." She lined the pan with parchment paper and turned on the oven. "You get to do the honors; there's a loaf of French bread thawing in the fridge. Slice it lengthwise and butter both sides with the garlic butter—it's in that blue bowl."

While he did that, she made a salad to go with: not just lettuce, but lettuce and tomatoes and cucumbers and sliced olives and feta crumbles. While her back was turned, he tasted the sauce and just about moaned in pleasure. Abby's version of spaghetti beat any restaurant's spaghetti he'd ever had.

If he did decide to stay here—and if she decided to let

him—he would have to make a point of exercising every day so he didn't gain too much weight because of her excellent cooking. Then again, shoveling stalls qualified as exercise. And he had earmarked tomorrow morning for yard work; the grass needed mowing and edging, another thing Abby couldn't do because of his stupidity.

Thinking of stupidity, he resolved not to fuss at Abby about her little mishap today. Instead, he would offer to stay and look after her. Because really, he had to, right? He owed her that much for leaving that roll of wire in the pasture—because he knew better. He had just forgotten to pick it up the next morning as promised.

"Abby?" He was about to make the offer to move in, but when she turned and looked at him, he changed his mind. Maybe he would wait till after dinner. Top up her wine and get her settled all cozy on the couch while he cleaned the kitchen, then propose—no, nix that word—suggest that it would be best for her safety and his peace of mind if he were to move in temporarily and take care of her while her foot mended.

"Yes?" Her wide hazel eyes were so pretty, gold around the pupils surrounded by a starburst of turquoise that melted into a deep, mossy green outlined in brown.

"Um…" He swigged the last sip of his beer. "I think I'll switch to wine for dinner. Will you scoot over so I can reach the glasses?"

An hour later, Abby topped up Quinn's wineglass, emptying the bottle they'd shared during dinner. He leaned back in his chair. "Dinner was amazing, as usual. Thank you for cooking."

Abby sipped her water. "You're welcome. Thank you for taking care of the farm."

"I'm gonna mow the yard tomorrow."

"Aw, you don't have to—"

"You wanna get snakebit, too, on top of everything else? You think I've got time to take you to the emergency room?"

She laughed. "You're right. I'm sorry. I have a hard time accepting help, as you may have noticed."

"You need help," he said. "I didn't realize how much until today. You're lucky you didn't get hurt."

She set her glass on the table and spread her arms. "As you can see, I'm fine."

"Yeah, and it could just as easily have gone the other way."

What was she supposed to say about that? I'm sorry? I should have known better? Yes, she'd been stupid, but what good did it do for him to beat her over the head about it? "Well, I guess I'm just lucky."

He stood and started gathering up plates and silverware. "I'm not sure I want to trust your luck to hold out any further."

"And I'm not sure what you're getting at." She crossed her arms and leaned back against the scooter's backrest. "I promise that I'll try not to do anything stupid again, but I can't promise not to be human. What do you want me to do?"

He took the stack he'd accumulated to the kitchen and set the dishes in the sink. "I want... No, I need..." His voice trailed off and he turned the faucet on. "I think you need more help here than you have right now."

Abby turned around on the scooter. "I'm not going to tell my aunt to come back home." She hopped into the kitchen and maneuvered the scooter between Quinn and the dishwasher. "This course she's taking is very important to her. It's something she has always wanted to do but put off for years. I won't take that from her." She held her hand out for the skillet he was scrubbing. "Give me that."

He rinsed the skillet and handed it to her, and she stacked it in the dishwasher.

"I'm not suggesting that you ask your aunt to come back home." He rinsed the sink and wiped it clean.

She dropped a pod into the dishwasher. "Well, what, then?" She held her breath for his answer; whatever it would be, it felt like something *big*.

He took a few haphazard swipes at the butcher-block counter with the dishrag, then turned to her. "I think I need to stay here— within shouting distance, at least—and take care of you until you get that cast off your foot."

"Oh." What was she supposed to think about that? "I'm not sure what to say." Or even what to think. Abby had been sleeping in the guest room. He could stay in Reva's room, but was that really necessary?

And more important, was it a good idea for her and Quinn to be that close? They would probably wind up in bed together if they started living in a pseudo-marriage situation. Alarm bells in her rational brain clanged, but the joyful peals of anticipation in her erogenous zones did their best to drown out any warning. "What sort of arrangement are you suggesting?"

Chapter 17

QUINN SQUEEZED OUT THE DISHRAG AND SPREAD IT TO DRY over the central divide of the massive farm sink. (Melissa would have gone crazy over this huge antique cast-iron-and-porcelain sink; it was probably worth a couple thousand dollars.) He met Abby's eyes and set aside a niggling sense that no matter what story he told himself about his desire to move in with Abby—temporarily of course—he might have some ulterior motive, such as getting her into bed with him. "I don't want to come here one day and find that you've had some sort of accident and needed help I wasn't here to give."

"So," she repeated, "what are you suggesting?" She closed the dishwasher door and got it running. The low hum of circulating water filled the empty space between them.

"I'm thinking I should move in here, with you. In case you need me." He held his breath, partly hoping she'd say no, but mostly hoping she'd say yes.

"What about Sean? What about when he comes on weekends?"

"His next overnight stay won't be for two weeks." Quinn cleared his throat. He hadn't actually thought that far ahead. Abby could stay at the pool house with him just as easily as he could stay at the farm. But Melissa would pitch a fit if Quinn had a woman staying over during Sean's overnight visitation. Melissa didn't want Quinn, but she didn't want anyone else having him, either. "Two weeks is a long time. Your foot may be much better by then."

Abby nodded, and Quinn noticed that a blush had spread over her cheeks. "Okay," she said. "You can stay in Reva's room. Go get your stuff."

That was easier than he'd thought. "All right. What are you gonna do while I'm gone?"

"I'm going to go out on the front porch and call Georgia. It's not like her to stay away so long, especially when there's food involved."

At the pool house, Quinn quickly assembled what he would need for the night. He could get more tomorrow. As he shoved his shaving kit down on top of everything else in his battered duffel, he wondered what the hell he was getting himself into. But he had already been spending a lot of time with Abby. Staying overnight, sleeping at opposite ends of the same house, wouldn't make that much of a difference, would it? The more he thought about it, the more he figured that not much would change, really.

Two hours later, when Abby came out into her aunt's living room with her dewy skin and her just-washed hair and her cropped pajama top and lace-edged tap pants, he knew that everything would change. He shifted position on the couch to cover his body's strong involuntary reaction to her presence.

"Has Georgia not come in yet?" she asked. Her voice wobbled with worry, because it was clear that the little dog hadn't made an appearance.

"Nope." He muted the TV and patted the couch beside him, inviting her to sit. "Sorry. I tried to call her, too. Maybe she went across the street with the wolf dog."

Abby sat beside him and took her cell phone from the scooter's basket. "I have to ask Aunt Reva."

Abby sent a text, and a few minutes later, the phone rang. He watched and listened while Abby told her aunt that Georgia had run off after a failed attempt to bathe her, and she hadn't been seen since. She left out the part about Georgia causing her to fall. Then, leaning back and closing her eyes, she listened. It almost looked like she was falling asleep, but he knew she wasn't, because she held the phone to her ear. After what seemed like forever, she said, "You think?" Then she got quiet for a minute before speaking again. "Okay, yes, I can see it, but I don't trust myself. Are you sure?"

This was the strangest phone conversation he'd ever witnessed.

"Okay, okay." Abby sat up, eyes open, acting more like a normal person having a normal phone conversation. "I will. Thank you, Aunt Reva. I love you. Yeah, okay. Bye."

She ended the call and put the phone back in the basket. Then she looked over at him and noticed his reaction. "I guess that phone call may have seemed a little strange."

He couldn't help but grin at her understatement. "A little."

"Aunt Reva says that Georgia is hiding out, either under something or in something, like a cave or a den. And Wolf is with her. We think they might have dug a hiding place under the front porch."

Quinn chuckled. "And you've determined all this how?"

"Telepathy." Abby sat up and gave him a challenging look. "If you must know."

He grinned. What a bunch of horseshit.

Abby scowled. "Don't laugh. I'm serious. And it would make sense, because Georgia's feet were dirty today. It's why I wanted to give her a bath."

"Okay, Ms. Pet Detective." He made a straight face, though an indulgent grin kept wanting to break through. Her obvious irritation at his teasing was kind of cute. He held up the first three fingers of his right hand. "Scout's honor, I won't laugh."

"You already did laugh, but okay. I know you don't get it."

"You're right. I don't get it, so please explain it to me. Your aunt knows all this from five hundred miles away how?"

She took a breath and let it out. "My Aunt Reva is a telepathic animal communicator. She can connect with animals and know what they're thinking."

He couldn't help himself; a snort of disbelief escaped him before he knew it was coming. "Okaaay."

"Shut. Up." Abby really looked mad now. She bolted to her feet and wrestled the handlebars of the scooter around, obviously prepared to flounce away, only too bad for her, flouncing wasn't easily done when she had only one foot on the ground and had to hop behind a scooter.

The very thought of her trying to make a huffy exit behind that scooter made him chuckle. "I'm sorry." But his funny bone had been tickled, and now he couldn't stop laughing.

"Don't you dare make fun of this just because you don't understand it." She stormed out of the room, hopping as fast as that stupid scooter would go. Boy, she really was mad.

"I'm sorry!" He went after her, laughing even harder. If she knew how silly she looked right now, she'd know he wasn't laughing at her aunt's crazy ways, or even her own. He was simply laughing because she was so damn cute. He should've made her mad long before now, because watching her hop around in a fury was so entertaining. He bit his lip and tried to sober up. At her side now, he refrained from touching her. He was pretty sure that if he reached out a hand, he'd draw back a nub. "Where are you going?"

"I'm going to get a flashlight, you…" She looked over at him, so pissed that she couldn't think of a word bad enough to call him. "You asshat."

Shit. He had to laugh again. "So now I'm an asshat. I'm wounded that you would call me such a terrible name."

She wrenched open a kitchen drawer and took out a foot-long metal flashlight. "Shut the fuck up." She turned on him with such a daggered glare that he backed up a step in case she was thinking of beaning him over the head. "Get out of my way."

He held up both hands. "Yes, ma'am. I'm sorry. Where are you going?"

She took a deep breath and puffed up with dignity. "I'm going to look under the porch and see if Georgia and Wolf are there." Her eyes looked suspiciously bright, as if she might cry.

His sense of hilarity died a quick death. He really hadn't meant to hurt her feelings. "Let me."

She hesitated at first, but then handed over the flashlight. "I'm coming with you."

"As far as the porch," he specified. He walked behind her onto the porch, hoping she was realizing right this minute that she definitely needed his help. "Wait here."

"Fine." She didn't much sound like she was appreciating his presence, but maybe she'd think about that later, when she wasn't so worried about the dog. He went down the stairs and walked around the porch, looking for a break in the dense azaleas that surrounded the house. He wanted to point out that if he hadn't been here, she'd be hobbling around outside in the dark all by herself. But maybe he should wait until he found the dogs to do that.

Around the far side of the porch, he found a scraggly, puny azalea that had been partially dug up by the gutter's rain spout. He turned on the flashlight and got to his hands and knees, pushing forward in the less-dense spot until the bushes parted enough to allow him to see under the porch. Sure enough, a freshly dug mound of dirt loomed before him, the area around it patterned with dog footprints, some big and others small. "I'll be damned."

He couldn't see the entrance to the den, so he crawled around where the porch overhang met the backside of the shrubs, brushing cobwebs out of the way with the flashlight. "Georgia?"

Unlikely visions of badgers and coyotes flashed into his already weirded-out brain, and he was pretty sure something was crawling in his hair. But he pressed on until he could see the edge of an opening in the den that seemed to go under the foundation of the house. Smart construction; it would be out of the wind and sheltered from rain not only by the roofed porch but by the foundation itself, and the dirt mound formed a wall that would keep the opening hidden from predators. "Georgia," he called. "Come here, puppy."

"Do you see her?" Abby asked, sounding excited.

"No, but you're right. There's a den under here." He shone the light's beam at the big mound of dirt, marveling again at the ingenuity of the dog—or whatever—that had built it. "She's not coming out, though, and I can't see into the den. What do you want me to do?" He wasn't eager to crawl all the way under the porch and confront whatever might be living in that den. Even if it was, in fact, Georgia and the wolf dog, he didn't want to risk getting his face ripped off by the bigger dog.

"Come on out." Abby sighed. "Reva said Georgia will come out on her own when she's done pouting."

He crawled back around the porch to the thin spot where he had entered the shrubs and pushed through. Abby leaned over the rail. "What do you have to say about animal communication now, smarty-pants?"

"Pretty incredible, I guess." When he'd first seen the den, he *had* felt a thrill of revelation, as if maybe Reva and Abby did have some direct line to the consciousness of those two dogs. But between that moment and this one, his brain had been busy rationalizing.

The existence of a den might have seemed to be some sort of validation at first, but after further reflection, he wasn't convinced. Abby could have deduced that the dogs might have dug something under the porch because she'd observed Georgia's dirty feet earlier. He didn't know how Reva would have known that, but he didn't hear Reva's side of the conversation.

For all he knew, that den could've been there for years, and Reva probably knew that Georgia liked to hide out there when she was in trouble. The fact that some fresh dirt had been deposited there recently didn't mean anything. But he wasn't about to say any of that now, knowing that it would shatter Abby's satisfied smile, and then she'd probably kick him out.

After stomping the mud off his boots, Quinn came up the porch stairs and handed over the flashlight. "Unless you need me to crawl around in the shrubbery some more," he said, realizing too late that his wording sounded a tad ungracious, "I want to grab a shower before all the spiders in my shirt decide to bite me."

Abby's lips tightened, but she didn't say anything. She just dumped the flashlight into the basket, grabbed the scooter's handlebars, and hopped ahead of him into the house.

"Um…" He closed the front door behind them and locked it, then hurried to catch up. "I didn't mean that like it sounded. I mean, if it sounded any type of way."

"You're in a hole," she tossed over her shoulder. "Might be smart to stop digging. I'm going to bed."

―――――――――――

Abby woke just after 3:00 a.m. when Georgia jumped onto the bed. Abby reached down to pet her, then brushed the dirt from her gritty fingers on the thin, summer-weight quilt. "Great, Georgia. Thanks a bunch."

Georgia licked Abby's fingers. It felt like an apology. "I'm sorry, too, girl. I shouldn't have insisted on bathing you when I knew you were scared."

Georgia licked Abby's fingers again, then stretched out along Abby's leg and settled down to sleep. Abby petted Georgia's sandy head and went back to sleep herself. She was right in the middle of an excellent dream when the house phone—the landline in Reva's office—started ringing. It rang five times before voicemail picked up. Abby rolled over and burrowed under the covers. She had just about fallen asleep when it started ringing again.

Who would be calling here this early? Not Reva; she would text first, even in an emergency. Eventually, the phone's ringing was bound to wake Quinn, though he was sleeping in Reva's room at the opposite end of the house. With her eyes still blurry from sleep and her limbs feeling heavy and uncoordinated from the pain meds that had put her so far under, Abby slung back the covers. Georgia rolled over and groaned, sending Abby a look of annoyance before closing her eyes again. "Don't let me disturb you," Abby groused.

The answering machine picked up, but in no time, the damn phone started another round of ringing. No way would she get there in time to pick up before the machine kicked in. But by now, she knew that the asshole on the other end of the line would try again. "I'll try not to wake you when I come back to bed in five minutes." Abby set her knee on the scooter and hopped into the living room, where a weak hint of sunlight was just beginning to lighten the walls. She made it to Reva's desk when round four began. She snatched up the receiver and yelled into it. "What!"

"Please tell me I didn't wake you, Reva," a querulous old-lady voice said. "I wouldn't be up myself if your big, black cat wasn't yowling at my window."

"And who is this?" Abby asked, not bothering to correct the old woman about the multitude of facts—okay, maybe just two—that she'd gotten wrong.

"It's Mildred, your next-door neighbor?" This said in a tone that suggested Reva might have recently lost her mind. "And the only neighbor who is on your side in your recent troubles, apparently, though I'm rethinking that position."

Recent troubles? On Reva's side? Was the old lady suffering from some sort of psychosis that made her imagine things? "Miss Mildred, this is Abby, not Reva. She's out of town and I'm house-sitting. Reva has a lot of cats, but none of them are black." Though if there was a feral tomcat in the area, Abby had no doubt that he'd end up here sooner or later. "Do you need to borrow Aunt Reva's live trap?"

"Abby? Who's Abby?"

"Reva's niece. I spent every summer here when I was a kid."

"Oh, yes," Mildred gushed, finally sounding happy. "I remember you. Long-legged skinny thing with a wild mane of wavy hair. Lord knows, I tried to tell Reva to try coconut oil on that hair. I know she wrestled with it something fierce whenever you'd come in from a day of climbing trees and whatnot. Yes. I remember you."

"That's great, Ms. Mildred. Do you need me to send someone over with a live trap for that cat? He's not ours, but if you can catch him, we'll take care of getting him fixed up and adopted out." Unless no one wanted him, in which case, he'd stay and live here like all the others.

"Well, honey, I don't know how to set up that contraption. And as you may remember, Wilbur isn't mechanically inclined, bless his heart. But if you want to come and set up that trap, I'd appreciate it."

"I can't come myself, but I'll send someone else this afternoon." She'd ask Quinn to do it.

"That'll be fine, honey. Just call first, because we might be napping."

"I know we all value our sleep," Abby agreed with some lightly veiled sarcasm.

"See?" Mildred chortled, in high spirits now. "I told those people that you were good neighbors."

"What people?" Abby asked.

"I don't remember their names right off," Mildred said, beginning to sound confused. "But Wilbur sent them packing before they'd set foot inside the house. He's not like me, you know. He doesn't believe in inviting folks in from off the street. But you know; I like those Jehovah's Witness boys, so well dressed and polite, coming around on their bicycles trying to spread the word of the Lord. I always invite them in for a nice chat and a glass of sweet tea. You know how hot it gets out here, and how easily even healthy folks can get heatstroke. Why, you know, when—"

"Ms. Mildred," Abby interrupted. "I think somebody's knocking at my door." Not likely at the butt crack of dawn, but Abby was determined to go back to bed and sleep until eight thirty, at least. "I'll call you this afternoon about that live trap. Okay?"

Abby slipped back into bed without waking Georgia, then managed to take up dreaming where she'd left off. In the dream, she'd found a new job on a tropical island, where she managed an open-air office on a white-sand beach. She was still trying to figure out what sort of office it was when the smell of coffee brewing and bacon cooking coaxed her gently awake. Abby sat up and stretched. Sun streamed through the thin curtains, brightening the pale-yellow walls to a deep buttery tone. Georgia had already followed her nose to the kitchen.

Abby dressed in shorts and a Bayside Barn Buddies tee, then hopped into the kitchen.

Quinn's too-long brown hair stuck up on one side, but aside from that one minor imperfection, he looked like a movie star standing in her aunt's old-fashioned kitchen. Barefoot and shirtless in low-slung jeans, he used tongs to turn the bacon in the heavy cast-iron frying pan. When it splattered, he jumped back and rubbed his chest. "Shit fire," he muttered, turning the heat down.

She opened a cupboard and took out a splatter guard, setting it on top of the frying pan. Then she adjusted the gas burner, turning it down a couple notches. "Good morning."

He turned those blue-jean-blue eyes on her. "Good morning." He looked at her lips, and for a second, she thought he might be about to kiss her, but the second passed by without incident. "I'm cooking an apology breakfast."

"Oh, okay." She took a mug from the cabinet and yawned. "You have coffee already?"

"Not yet. But I'd love some, if you're pouring."

She poured coffee into the blender and added all the ingredients that made it bullet-proof, then filled two mugs with the rich, frothy concoction. He turned off the heat on the bacon, then took her mug and motioned for her to go ahead of him. "I thought you might like to sit by the pool with your coffee while I cook. I'll bring breakfast out when it's ready."

She sat in one of the lounge chairs and took the mug he handed her. "I like the way you apologize."

He winked. "I can apologize in more delicious ways than this, but we don't know each other that well yet."

"Sexual harassment!" She held up a hand as if flagging down a taxi. "Somebody help!" As if in answer, Georgia hopped into Abby's lap, her feet and coat dyed orange by the den's dark red-orange dirt.

"I'm not sure who's harassing whom here," he said, giving Abby the stink eye along with a mischievous grin that quirked up one corner of his mouth. "But we can figure that out later."

With his wide shoulders, bare chest, tight abs and just-out-of-bed hair, he was too handsome for anyone's good. He bent forward in an obsequious butler's bow. "I've gotta finish cooking breakfast for milady. And, by the way, I've already fed Georgia and the inside cats. I'll do the rest once I've delivered your breakfast to the patio."

"Fine." She waved him off and took a sip of her coffee. "While you cook, I'll decide whether I want to forgive you for being such an asshat last night."

"Would it help if I whipped up a mimosa to go with your coffee?"

"No, thank you. Coffee is enough." She had already forgiven him. Some of her angst yesterday evening had been due to her own insecurity. Reva had always been good at claiming her ability of animal communication without regard to what anyone else thought. But Abby *did* care what other people thought, no matter how much Reva preached about the dangers of becoming an approval whore. Reva said that knowing you were fulfilling the mission you'd been born to accomplish was all that mattered. What anyone else thought of you was none of your business.

A flash of gray, a flicker of movement at the edge of her vision, caught Abby's attention. Barely seen and gone already, it had to have been Wolf. Georgia's ears pricked up, and she whined. Abby sat forward and turned around on the chaise to look toward the corner of the house. "Come here, buddy," she called, knowing Wolf was near enough to hear. "Come on, we won't hurt you."

Tail wagging with anticipation, Georgia quivered and stared at the spot where Wolf had been. Abby had the impression that Georgia was communicating with Wolf, inviting him to show himself.

"Puppy, puppy," Abby called. She whistled low. "Come on out."

The azaleas shivered, then Wolf appeared. Nose first, low to the ground, he commando-crawled onto the open lawn. "Hey, Wolf, you're okay." Abby held her hand out, knuckles first. "Come on."

He crawled forward a bit more, then dropped back down to his haunches, sending anxious glances toward the house.

Georgia hopped down and ran across the lawn toward him, jubilant and encouraging. She stopped in front of him and rolled to her back, licking his mouth in welcome.

Then Quinn opened the door, and Wolf disappeared into the azaleas like a ghost. The moment was lost.

———————————

"You should've seen it," Abby gushed. "He came closer than ever this time."

Quinn kicked back in the recliner and muted the TV, because he didn't need the sports commentary to know what was happening on the field. "I'm sorry I missed it."

She had told him this story about a dozen times. He didn't mind hearing it again, though, because her pretty face was so animated, beaming with happiness about such a simple thing. Wolf had shown himself a few times, but only when Abby was outside alone, and only for a few minutes. He'd been coming closer each time, but never close enough for Abby to touch.

"Wolf was so scared, I could see him trembling. But he wanted to come to me. I could tell. And Georgia was so sweet to him." She reached down to stroke Georgia's thick fur. "It's like they're in love, isn't it, girl?"

Abby sat on the couch with a book in her hand, her foot propped up on the ottoman. Georgia stretched out next to her on one side, Max the tabby lay on the other side, and Griffie sat like a half-chewed loaf of bread in her lap. "I wish he'd just come to me," Abby said. "I know that big scab on his side needs vet care. It looks like something tore a big chunk out of his skin."

"Maybe the next time you see him, he'll let you touch him."

Sharing the recliner with Quinn, the new kitten, Stella, kept stretching up to nuzzle his chin. He had given up pushing her away. Abby said Stella hadn't had any use for her since the day Abby had grabbed her from the culvert, but the kitten seemed to have decided that Quinn was okay. He stroked her soft fur and decided that he liked her, too.

"I know I'm probably trying too hard," Abby said. "It's enough right now to know that he's getting fed."

"Yep." Quinn put a bowl of dog kibble out on the patio every night and went back to pick up the empty bowl an hour later, so they knew Wolf ate his food as soon as Quinn went inside. "There's no harm in letting Wolf take his time deciding that this is a safe place." Especially since they knew he *was* safe in his den under the porch.

"I just worry that he hasn't had his shots, and he might need antibiotics for that wound in his side."

Quinn knew that Abby wanted to get Wolf the veterinary care he needed and to get him neutered (a concept that made Quinn squirm whenever he thought about it). But first, they had to earn his trust. "All we can do is all we can do, though, right?" Quinn stopped petting Stella, and she settled down in his lap. He was almost getting used to being surrounded by animals, and it wasn't all that bad. In fact, he enjoyed having a cat or two purring next to him in bed at night.

"Hey," he said to Abby. She looked up from the book she was reading. "That pile of mail I've been putting on your aunt's desk is getting pretty thick."

"I know. I'll handle it tomorrow. Promise." She closed her book and sighed. "I think I'm about done for. I'm going to bed."

He wished he had the courage to follow her in there. He had long since stopped torturing himself by denying their mutual attraction. He'd been keeping his distance, though, because that's what she seemed to want. Since he had moved in, they had fallen into a routine that felt as intimate as an old married couple's life together. Like Abby's emerging relationship with Wolf, they were close, but not close enough to touch.

After the morning chores and a big breakfast, Quinn and Abby went to separate ends of the house to get cleaned up for a grocery run in preparation for Sean's Wednesday evening visit. In the guest bathroom, Abby plugged the tub and turned on the taps. When the tub was full of perfect-temperature water, she performed the yoga-like ritual of stepping into the tub with her good leg, then lowering herself carefully into the water while leaving her cast hanging over the edge.

Reversing the process was a little trickier; she had to lift herself out of the water while keeping the cast outside the tub, then get her knee on the scooter's seat while holding the handlebars for balance—

The scooter sailed out from under her and crashed against the wall while her butt skidded off the tub's edge and hit the floor. "Ow, dammit!"

Georgia yapped outside the closed bathroom door, and Quinn came in without knocking. "What happened? Oh, shit. Dammit, Abby."

As if she'd decided to fall on purpose. "Don't yell." Her tailbone hurt all the way up to her molars, and the inside of her left thigh burned like fire. "It's not like I planned to do this for fun."

He scooped her up, seemingly oblivious to the fact that she was buck naked. Next thing she knew, she was on the bed and he was touching her just about everywhere, feeling for broken bones, she guessed, because he wasn't being the least bit romantic about it. "Stop it." She batted his hands away. "I'm fine. Please go get a towel."

"Oh." He sat on the edge of the bed and ran a shaky hand through his hair. He gave her a surprised once-over, as if he'd only just now realized that she was soaking wet and naked. He bolted into the bathroom and came back with a huge folded bath towel, which he whipped out and draped over her like a tablecloth. The thing covered her from the knees up, including half of her face. "I'm sorry." He dragged the towel down a bit so she could breathe.

He patted her awkwardly—trying to pat her dry? His tanned cheeks flushed a dusky rose color. So now that he'd seen her naked, even carried her naked self from the bathroom to the bed, his primary emotion was embarrassment.

How sweet.

And infuriating. She scowled at the back of his head while he gently patted her legs dry. Did he not find her attractive at all? And here she'd been arguing with herself for two whole weeks over whether or not she should let him get into her panties, while he seemed to consider her to be a responsibility, nothing more. She sat up awkwardly and grabbed his hands, not caring whether the oversize towel slipped. "Quinn. Stop."

"Shit." His gaze dropped to her breasts, then zoomed back up to her face. "I'm sorry."

Some kind of devil made her do it; she leaned toward him and wrapped her arms around his neck. "Stop apologizing." Then, she kissed him.

His tongue slipped into her mouth, tentatively at first, then with a bold exploration that ignited nerve endings from her teeth to her toes. With one hand at her back and the other behind her head, he laid her back on the bed and stretched out on top of her. Her knees fell open, and her hips formed a cradle that his hips fit into quite nicely. It was just getting good when he stopped kissing and looked down on her with a worried frown. "Is your foot okay? You want me to put a pillow under it?"

"Forget about my foot." She wrapped an arm around his neck and pulled him down. "Kiss me." With his tongue stroking hers, her broken foot was the last thing on her mind, and she hoped it was the last thing on his.

Even through the damp towel wadded between them, she felt his erection hard against her. She gave the towel a tug, trying to drag it out from between them, but he wrapped his hand around hers, stopping her. His blue eyes were serious, his jaw tight, his face flushed—but this time not with embarrassment. "Don't move that towel unless you mean it."

She looked into his eyes and tugged at the towel again. He lifted his hips, taking his weight off her, and she slipped the damp terry cloth out from between them.

He stared back at her as his shoes hit the floor, one by one.

Thunk. Thunk... The sound of the invisible walls they had each erected between them falling to the ground.

Hungry for the heat of his body against hers, she pulled his T-shirt up over his head and unbuttoned his jeans. Then, oh, glory, the rest of his clothes fell to the floor with a soft, tumbling sound, and his naked body skimmed against hers. Rough and smooth, warm and hard, he felt every bit as good as she had imagined.

He rolled her to her side, and they lay facing each other on the lumpy old quilt some long-dead ancestor had so painstakingly stitched. He skimmed his fingers down her arm, a butterfly touch. "You know what this will mean, right?" he asked.

She reached out to touch his face, feeling the warmth of his taut skin, the barely there stubble of beard on his jaw. "No, what will this mean?"

"Everything." He cupped her breast, lightly rubbing her nipple until it pearled up under his palm. "Are you ready for that? Because I won't do this lightly. I'm fucking tired of cheap hookups, and I'm fucking tired of being alone." His voice was deep and quiet, and just a little raspy. He swallowed audibly and looked away from her face, instead watching his fingers move over her breasts. "If we do this, it'll be the start of something."

Goose bumps broke out over Abby's skin, a thrill of excitement—and of foreboding. Ever since she'd met Quinn, she had toyed with the idea of having a fuck buddy she could take or leave—or take and then leave. It wasn't her style, never had been, but her last failed relationship still stung, so she'd been hoping for a fulfilling relationship that came with an easy way out. Despite her fears and insecurities, she said the only thing her heart wanted her to say, even though the words came with a stomach-dropping lurch that felt like stepping off the edge of a cliff. "I'm ready."

Chapter 18

QUINN WONDERED IF THOSE TWO WORDS ABBY HAD JUST said, *I'm ready*, felt as heady and exhilarating and frightening to her as they did to him. "You sure?"

"Yes. Now stop talking." She reached down, wrapped her fingers around him, and leaned in for a kiss. If her tongue hadn't been in his mouth, he'd have gasped at the gentle pressure of her hand squeezing, then releasing, squeezing, then releasing, as if she had all the time in the world to make him come and didn't mind spending it.

If only she knew how long it had been, how close he was to exploding just by seeing her luscious naked body, just by touching her beautiful breasts and feeling her responsive nipples draw up into hard little beads.

Time to take charge. But first... He moved her hand away from him. "Hold that thought." Thank God he had stashed a few condoms in his shaving kit, just in case. "I'll be right back."

He made it back in zero-point-two to find her burrowed under the quilt, with only her face sticking out at the top and her broken foot with the cast sticking out at the bottom. "You cold?"

"Maybe." But she was blushing.

He climbed onto the bed and knelt over her, pinning her under the covers. "I'll warm you up." She squirmed, tried to bring her arms up, but he bent forward and put his weight on his elbows. "I think I like holding you captive like this."

She relaxed under him and her eyelids drifted shut. She lifted her mouth for a kiss, and he obliged, but on his terms. Slowly, slowly, he licked the seam of her lips with just the tip of his tongue. When her mouth dropped open, inviting more, he moved to kiss the upturned corners of her full lips, then her eyelids, her cheeks, her chin. He sucked lightly at the little dip between her jawline and her neck, where a rapid pulse fluttered. Not enough to leave a mark; he was careful to treat her tender skin gently.

Also careful to avoid her cast, he sat up and straddled her hips, then began to roll down the old-fashioned quilt she'd covered herself with out of modesty.

He vowed to himself that she'd have no modesty left after he was done with her. Exposing her delicate collarbones, he traced them with his fingertips, then followed with his lips. He brought the quilt down below her breasts and cupped the two perfect handfuls of soft, yielding flesh in his palms. The barest touch of his thumbs across her nipples made them contract in response. Lord, she was beautiful.

She feathered her fingertips across his chest and pinched his nipples lightly. His stiff cock lurched at the current of sensation that seemed to connect those three seemingly unconnected body parts. His balls contracted, too, a warning sign that he needed to go slowly. He backed up out of her reach. "Nope, sorry. My turn first."

He folded the quilt aside and kissed his way down her flat abdomen, then explored her body more intimately. The just-bathed skin of her soft mound and even softer pubic hair smelled of rose-scented soap. The silky, damp skin below filled his mouth with the slight tang of salt and the elusive, compelling scent of a woman—not just any woman, but *this* woman.

She grabbed his shoulders and made some token protest, some suggestion that he stop what he was doing and come inside her. He heard her voice, but he felt her body, and he knew which one to listen to just now. He learned the touches that made her tense and those that helped her relax. He learned what made her tremble and what made her inner muscles clench and pulse with reaction. With his hands and his mouth, he brought her almost to climax, just about there, then kissed his way up her belly.

"Don't stop," she moaned, her fists clenching the bedsheets.

"Not stopping," he promised. "Just getting started." He sat back and put on the condom one-handed while he stroked her with the other hand. The truth was, he was so turned on by the eroticism of hearing her pleasure and feeling her approach orgasm that he was about to come himself, and when he did come, he wanted to be inside her.

He already knew that she was wet, slick, ready for him. But he still wanted to hear it from her. He kissed the outside of her ear, then whispered, "What do you want?"

He hovered over her, weight on his elbows and knees, waiting for her answer.

She made a low, growling sound, reached between their bodies, and guided him inside. Raising her head off the pillow, she bit the edge of his ear—not lightly, either. She bit down hard enough to hurt. Then she blew a hot breath into his ear that made him shiver. "This," she whispered back. Clutching his butt with both hands, she lifted her hips and drove him inside even farther. "This is what I want."

His body inside hers was an epiphany. *This.*

This.

He'd made her say it out loud, made her admit it to herself and to him. *This* was what she wanted. This was the start of something neither of them had expected, like finding a diamond winking from a fissure in a cracked sidewalk. Now that they'd found this unexpected gift, they could never go back to the way things were, no matter what.

This was, as he'd promised it would be, *everything*.

He had made the offer, then made sure it was her decision; and with that decision, she had grabbed his firm butt and driven him home inside her.

He filled her; he more than filled her. Not just her body, but her mind, her spirit, her soul. All her fears and all her failures dissolved in that moment, replaced by the knowledge that from now on, she'd be his home, and he'd be hers. "Tell me what you want," she whispered in his ear.

He pulled out and then slid in again. "This."

He set up a slow, deep rhythm that brought her right to the edge of orgasm again.

"And this." In and out again.

"And this." Slow, easy, deep.

"And this…" He kissed her neck, caressed her breasts, and battered her down below with an intensity that hurt even as it healed.

"Yes." She clenched Quinn's shoulders and looked up at the sunlit ceiling where the fan circled lazily above the bed. Something inside her spiraled up and up toward that circling fan, and she experienced a sensation she had only felt once before, just before fainting. The edges of her vision dimmed, then sparkled, like stars in the night sky gathering toward the Milky Way while she watched from somewhere outside herself.

"Oh…" She spoke to something inside herself that she'd never met but knew intimately all the same. "Yes." She spoke to the sky, to the stars, to the coming together of a million separate elements she couldn't even imagine. "Yes, please."

"God, yes," she heard Quinn moan as he buried his face in her neck and slammed his body into hers again and again and again.

Then neither of them could talk as their minds emptied and their bodies moved together in a mindless, wordless communion that knew more than what either of them wanted, or even what they needed. It knew…*everything*.

"Burgers and fries for dinner," Abby decided after studying the contents of the fridge and glancing at the clock. "That's all we have." Because they had spent the day making love, then napping, then making love again instead of going to the store. "It's also all I have time to cook, because Sean will be here any minute." His visit was only for the evening, but for Quinn's sake, Abby wanted to make it special.

"Stop worrying." Quinn kissed the back of her neck and pulled her away from the refrigerator, closing the door. "Whatever you have the time and inclination to cook will be perfect. Or I can take y'all out after Sean and I feed the animals."

He held Abby against him, his front to her back, and pushed his hips into her backside, as if they hadn't already made love until she was sore. "You have no idea how low the bar is when it comes to Sean's expectations about food. Leftover pizza, flat cola, and a handful of stuck-together gummy bears for dessert would thrill him."

"Don't talk ugly about your ex," she chided, pulling away on the pretext of reaching for a big bowl on the cupboard's top shelf. Her ex-boyfriend, Blair, had vilified his ex-wife constantly for abandoning him and their daughter. Abby had bought into his story, only to realize later that he'd been feeding her a plate of bullshit piled as high as he could manage. He'd probably said the same thing about her, when he'd so ruthlessly cut her out of Emily's life. The only difference between Abby and Blair's wife was that he hadn't had to drag Abby through court and accuse her of being an unfit mother, because he'd held all the power in their relationship. "You wouldn't say that in front of Sean, so please don't say it in front of me."

"I'm sorry." Quinn took down the bowl she was reaching for and set it on the counter. "You're absolutely right. Melissa is no Martha Stewart, but she is a good mother. She deserves my respect for that, and she's got it."

"I know." Abby set an onion and a green bell pepper on the chopping block. "I appreciated the way you took up for her when

Sean was here before. It means a lot to me to know that you're raising your son to have respect for his mother. Aunt Reva always said that a boy who is raised to respect his mother will respect his wife when he's an adult."

Abby had once seen her ex spew ugly expletives at his mother, and she'd thought then, *I hope he never treats me that way*. Then she'd learned—too late—that Reva was absolutely correct when she said that a man who will disrespect his mother will disrespect any woman in his life. She had tried to influence Blair in a positive way, tried to help him become a better man, especially when it came to treating his daughter with the love and respect any child deserves. But he had invited her to "keep her big butt out of *his* relationship with *his* daughter." Though Blair had used Emily to lure Abby deeper into his life, he never missed an opportunity to point out that the child she took such joy in mothering wasn't *her* child.

With a huff of annoyance at the rabbit hole her thinking had gone down, Abby attacked the bell pepper with a sharp paring knife. As she cored the pepper and sliced away the ribs, she reminded herself that her spectacularly poor judgment in choosing Blair was no reflection on Quinn, who was honest and decent and kind.

Quinn started chopping the onion. "How fine do you want it?"

Helping with the cooking without being asked? Her kind of man. "As fine as you can get it. I'm gonna mix the onion and some minced garlic"—she plopped an entire head of garlic on the block—"with the ground beef and some spices before making the patties."

Quinn broke apart the head of garlic and had just started smashing each of the cloves with the flat edge of the knife when his phone buzzed. "Guess that means Sean's here. Can you grab it?" He turned his back to her. "Back pocket."

She dug into his back pocket and took out his phone, which

was still buzzing. She hit Answer and held the phone to his ear. "Yeah, hey. Come on over to—" He paused. "Yeah? Okay, sure. We'll come out." He moved to the sink and rinsed his hands. Abby ended the call and handed over the phone; he dried his hands and took it. "Sean's about halfway down the driveway, but there's a big shaggy dog standing there who won't let him come any farther."

"Wolf!" Abby felt a bloom of excitement at the thought of maybe getting Wolf to come to her this time. She turned the scooter and hurried after Quinn. "Hang on. Wait for me. Don't scare him."

Quinn waited for Abby to catch up, but impatience oozed from every pore and surrounded him like a cloud. "It's not the dog being scared that I'm worried about." He grabbed the scooter's handlebars in one hand and wrapped the other around Abby's waist, hustling her over the flagstones. He set her and the scooter down on the gravel drive.

Sean stood halfway down the driveway, backpack in hand. Wolf sat about ten feet away from him. "Hey, Dad," Sean called. "Watch what he does."

As Sean took steps toward the right side of the driveway, Wolf moved to the right and crouched, elbows to the ground and butt in the air. When Sean went to the left, Wolf did the same. When Sean walked toward Wolf, he backed up, always keeping the same distance between them.

"What's he doing?" Quinn asked. "Is he guarding the house? Keeping Sean from coming closer?"

"No," Abby said. "He's just playing. See how he puts his elbows down and his backside up? It's called a play bow."

"I don't care what you call it; it looks like a challenge to me."

Abby had to admit that the dog was sending mixed signals. "Wolf," she called, making kissing noises. "Come here, puppy."

"Wolf!" Quinn commanded, striding forward and clapping his hands. "Move, dog!"

Wolf didn't move.

Georgia ran up to Sean and jumped at his legs. He picked her up, and she licked his face. Under the spell of Georgia's calming presence, Wolf's body language changed from playful yet intimidating to a calmer vibe. His plume of a tail swayed side to side, and he walked up to Sean and sat in front of him. Tongue hanging out in a doggy smile, he waited for Sean to bend down and pet him.

"Sean, no." Quinn's long strides had brought him nearly even with Sean, but too late to keep the boy from kneeling and putting his hand on Wolf's neck. Georgia hopped out of his arms, circling the boy and the bigger dog with excitement.

"Quinn, it's fine," Abby called out. The last thing Wolf needed was for Quinn to scare him away at this critical moment when he willingly solicited human touch. She pushed the scooter over the gravel, but the uneven surface was more uncooperative than it had ever been. "Let them be."

Quinn glanced at Abby and stopped moving. It was clear that he was ready to spring forward if need be, but at least he was giving her opinion the benefit of the doubt—kind of a big deal considering the situation. Wolf's plumy tail swayed back and forth as Sean stroked his fur. Then the big dog gave Sean's face a big, wet swipe of his long tongue. Sean fell back onto his butt, laughing. "Quit it!"

Wolf didn't quit; he walked right over the boy's prone form and licked him even more, with Georgia joining in. Sean wrapped his arms around Wolf's neck and rolled. Then both dogs and Sean were wrestling on the dusty gravel driveway, with Sean giggling like a girl and both dogs' tails wagging with glee.

Quinn stood over them, hands on hips. "Well, I'll be damned."

Abby caught up with the crowd and linked arms with Quinn. "After all the hours I've spent courting that elusive dog, he does this." Her feelings were a little hurt, but at the same time, a warmed-honey flood of gratitude and happiness overflowed her heart and flooded her entire body.

Quinn shrugged. "I guess he likes kids best."

A cloud of dust rose up from the driveway where the happy trio played together. Sean's dark hair was turning gray from the dust, and so were his jeans. "I'll have to wash his clothes while we're eating dinner. I don't want his mother to get mad at us for ruining his clothes. Do you have something he can change into?"

Quinn snaked an arm around her waist. "Yeah, I'll find something."

Sean sat up and hugged Wolf, who laid his chin on Sean's shoulder and looked for all the world as if he was hugging back. Satisfied with her good work of successfully introducing Sean and Wolf, Georgia came back to Abby and hopped onto the scooter's seat. Abby moved her knee to the very edge of the seat to make room and fondled Georgia's ears. "You always know just what to do, don't you, girl?"

Georgia looked up and grinned. Abby heard in her mind, clear as a bell, *Yes, I do.*

———————

After Sean left that evening in the small, loud car without a top, Wolf lazed in the dappled sunlight that filtered through the cat's-claw vines. He sighed with repletion, not from a full belly, but from a full heart. He had missed playing with his kids, even more than he'd realized until he had the chance to do it again with the little Quinn whose name he later learned was Sean.

When he saw the boy get out of the car, he had slunk behind him at first, but then Sean noticed him and clapped a hand on his thigh to call Wolf to him. Not trusting, Wolf hadn't come at first. But when the boy started to walk on, Wolf found that he couldn't let him go. He realized in that moment that he *needed* to play. He needed to connect with a human who was still young enough to play, but more important, someone who wouldn't try to trap him. He didn't know how he knew that about Sean, but he did. The boy's energy wasn't as tight or controlling as either Quinn's or Abby's.

So instead of letting the boy walk away, Wolf had run around in front of him and done a play bow to show what he wanted. And he did want to play! But then when the boy came closer, Wolf got scared and backed off. They did that dance for a while, the dance of coming close and then backing away, until Georgia came outside and helped everyone to relax—even Quinn and Abby, who had rushed outside, too, determined to interfere. But Georgia hadn't let them. She had, as usual, taken charge of the situation. She had given Wolf a great gift, one of many.

Then the grown-ups got tired of watching Sean play with Wolf and Georgia, and they both said some words that made Sean stand up and follow them inside. The boy invited Wolf to come, too, and Georgia hopped around with excitement, licking Wolf's lips and wagging her tail to encourage him.

But he couldn't accept that kind of closeness with humans. Not yet. Maybe not ever.

———

Early that Friday morning, Abby turned the faucet, but nothing happened. She set her toothbrush on the edge of the sink and turned the faucet again—off, then on, then off. Nothing.

Quinn's reminder to check the mail rang in her ears, along with Reva's reminder of the water company's tendency to cut the water off first and ask questions later. "Shit."

Knowing already that she'd done this to herself, she maneuvered the scooter into the living room toward the alcove that had once been a closet but now served as Reva's office space. Abby had been avoiding the accumulated stack of mail on the rolltop desk. Ever since her life with Blair had gone to hell, opening the mail made Abby nervous, as if each envelope might contain bad news or a bill she couldn't pay.

At the beginning of their live-in relationship, she had thought it sweet that he paid all the bills so she could concentrate on taking care of him and Emily. But over time, his insistence on handling anything involving money evolved into hypervigilance over every penny Abby spent, then every minute she spent away from home. As her autonomy seeped away, her relationship with Emily grew even more precious, and for a very long time, she told herself that the good times outweighed the bad. But all his subtle reminders that she wouldn't be able to survive financially without him had deep tentacles that hadn't yet released her.

Life just didn't seem safe anymore.

"Look at this," she muttered to herself. Her hands were shaking as she leafed through the stack of envelopes. "Stupid." She tossed bulk-mail advertisements into the recycle bin and set anything official-looking aside. Water bill; a bright-pink slip shining through the cellophane window. "Shit."

She ripped the envelope open. Cutoff date...she glanced at the calendar that hung above the desk...today.

Quinn came in from the patio, scratching his head. "Abby? The water in the barn isn't—"

"Yes." She flapped a hand at him. "I know. I forgot to pay the water bill."

He smirked. "I seem to remember telling you to check that stack of mail several days ago." Standing there with his dirt-smeared hands on his hips, he shouldn't have been smirking, but he did have a point. "How long since you've paid the water bill?"

She huffed at him and flapped a hand again. She wasn't about to tell him that the answer to that question was *never*. "We can use the water at your place until I get this sorted out."

"That's fine for the animals, but I can't see you loving a hose bath any better than Georgia does."

She scowled at him.

"Come on," he coaxed with a grin. "That was supposed to be funny. This isn't the end of the world."

She ignored him. "They won't let you pay online."

"And they don't take credit cards, either," he added, "because I tried to set up auto-pay from my credit card account, and they don't do that." His grubby fingers took the bill from her, and he looked it over, reading the fine print. "We'll have to drive into town. You have to pay in person before they'll turn it back on. It doesn't say whether they'll take a check or cash. But knowing them, it'll only be one, not the other."

"Well, hell." Abby needed to get over her idiotic avoidance of going through mail. It would've been so much easier to pay the bill before it came due. It wasn't like she didn't have access to Aunt Reva's account, which could easily afford the water bill, a mere $32.98. Reva had taken Abby to the bank and given her signatory privileges so she could write any checks she needed to. She even knew the PIN of the account, for which Reva had given her a debit card. "Let's just go now and get it done. I'll take a shower and brush my teeth later, when they've turned the water back on."

Quinn set the bill aside. "I'm not done with the morning chores yet. I've at least got to feed all the animals their breakfast, and I can run a hose through the fence from my place to yours to give everyone fresh water. Meanwhile, please go through the rest of this stack and see if anything else needs to be dealt with sooner rather than later."

Abby felt like a chided child, and she knew she deserved it. She moved the desk chair out of the way and sat on the scooter instead. "Okay."

While Quinn finished the chores, she turned the stack of mail upside down and worked from oldest to newest. She wrote out checks to all the utility departments—the electric bill was overdue, too, and would also have to be paid in person—and opened an official-looking envelope from the city courthouse.

Cordial invitation to present your case at a town hall meeting…

"Present your case?" Abby scanned through a bunch of legalese and blah, blah, blah.

…to determine whether it is in the best interest of the city of Magnolia Bay to extend your establishment's permission to keep farm animals within the city limits.

Abby's mouth went dry, and her heart tried to explode out of her chest. "What?" She scanned the letter again. Her fingers were really shaking now. This was bad.

Quinn came inside. "What?"

"I don't know." Abby held out the letter and shook it at him. "I don't know what's going on. This seems serious." He took the letter, and she wrung her hands while he read through it. His face flushed a dull red, and his hand started to shake, too. *Shit. Shit.* She should have gone through the mail every single day, instead of leaving it all till now. "I've fucked up, haven't I?"

Adrenaline prickled her skin and stung her sinuses. She wanted to cry, to sob, to scream. God, she'd fucked up everything so badly, the way she always did. Sticking her head in the sand, leaving everything until past the last minute, so afraid of making a mistake that she failed to do anything at all. "I should have told Reva about this. I should have read it a long time ago. When does it say…?"

He continued to scan the letter. His face was flushed, his jaw clenched, his hands gripping the pages as if their contents affected him, too.

"I'm so glad you're here. I'd be freaking out even more if I'd been here all by myself right now." Knowing that she wasn't in this alone gave her strength and courage. She clutched his arm. "When is it? What time?"

He shook out the front page and put it behind the others. "It's today. This afternoon at the Magnolia Bay Municipal Courthouse. It's a town hall meeting about whether Bayside Barn should be able to keep farm animals in the city limits."

She'd already read that part—twice—but when she heard Quinn say it out loud, another shock of fear coursed through her. "Bayside Barn won't be able to exist without the animals. This place is all about the animals, about teaching people how important they are to us." She looked up at him, begging for reassurance she knew he couldn't give. "Why would they do this? Was it something I did? Something I did wrong?"

"I doubt it." His reply sounded offhand and meaningless; he couldn't know any more than she did until he finished reading the letter.

She tried to be quiet and let him absorb the message, but couldn't stop herself from wailing, "Why is this happening?"

"It looks like there's been a petition going around, and a bunch of people have signed it."

Abby's skin crawled. Mildred had said something about *those people* coming to their door and being turned away.

"Our neighbor on the other side called to complain about our cat." And shit, Abby had forgotten to ask Quinn to go over there with a live trap. "But she ended up being really nice once I explained that it wasn't Reva's cat that was bothering her." Abby felt as if she were drowning, going under in a tidal wave of trouble over which she had no control. "I just don't know who would've done this."

Her whole body felt ice-cold, encased in a fear so dense and impenetrable that it stopped her breath. He took her in his arms, making her feel so safe and protected. "Shhh," he said, his voice a soft shushing sound, a lullaby of comfort. "Shhh. Don't worry. Whatever it is, we'll take care of it."

"How?" she wailed. "Do you think I should call Reva?"

"I don't think there's anything she can do right now. But maybe you should call some of the volunteers that help out on field trips. See if any of them can meet us at the town hall. It'll look better if we have a crowd on our side."

"We could have had a crowd if I'd opened the mail sooner."

His arms tightened around her. "Let's not worry about what's over and done with. Let's think about what to do now."

She nodded. "I'll call Edna." Just the thought of having the kind woman's stalwart support calmed Abby, though she still felt like a panicked swimmer whose chin kept dipping below the waterline. "Just hold me first."

He rocked her in his arms, and though her leg fell asleep from its position on the scooter, and a pins-and-needles feeling from lack of circulation coursed from her toes to her hips, she clung to his steady strength and let him hold her until she could breathe again.

Chapter 19

WHILE ABBY SHOWERED AT QUINN'S PLACE WITH HER CAST wrapped in a plastic trash bag, he tried for the umpteenth time to call Delia and find out what the hell was going on. But of course, true to form, she wasn't answering. Not his phone calls, and not his texts.

Maybe this whole thing wasn't his fault. When Delia had failed to respond to his messages, he told himself that she hadn't done what he asked and was therefore ignoring him.

Part of him hoped that the neighbors on the other side of Bayside Barn had complained and started the petition, but another part knew better. Unless they had complained to the city long before they complained to Abby—which didn't make sense— there wouldn't have been enough time for them to circulate a petition and set up a town hall.

"Quinn?" Abby called out from the bathroom. "Help."

"Coming." He nudged the door open and went inside, where Abby fought with the scooter's handlebars, which were jackknifed between the wall and the bathroom cabinet.

"Everything's all cattywampus." She hopped backward and held on to the towel bar, giving him better access to the scooter.

"Wow, you're really stuck." He wrestled the scooter into a forward-facing position, all the while ignoring the fact that only two tiny scraps of thin, see-through fabric hid her most interesting parts from view. And those two scraps—thong panties and a barely there bra—were more of a distraction than an actual cover-up. "Okay. Here you go."

Instead of climbing onto the scooter, Abby wrapped her arms around his neck. She leaned against him, all warm and willing and smelling of soap and shampoo and mint toothpaste. "I don't know what I'd do without you right now. I'm so lucky that you moved next door to my aunt when you did."

She kissed him, roaming her hands up and down his back in a way that made him wish they had more than a half hour to get out of this house and on the way to the courthouse. Her fingers tunneled through his hair, and she grabbed hold, tilting his head for a deeper kiss.

He obliged by kissing her as deeply as she was kissing him, but at the same time, he felt his face fire up with shame and embarrassment. He might not be the cause of this problem they were about to face, but then again, he might. Would the answer be revealed at the town hall meeting?

Whether or not it was, and whether or not he was actually to blame, he knew that he didn't deserve Abby's gratitude or approval. He cupped her face in his hands and studied the beautiful colors in her eyes. "We've got to go."

She blushed and looked down at the tile floor. "You're right. I'm procrastinating."

He moved aside and let her pass. "The rest of your stuff is in my bedroom. I'm gonna take a shower while you get dressed."

"Okay, thanks." She touched his arm. "You have no idea how much this means to me—all your help, everything you're doing."

"It's nothing." Less than nothing if she ever found out that he might have been responsible for this mess. He changed the subject to get some sense of control over the situation. "We've got to leave here in half an hour, at the latest, so we can pay the bills and get to the courthouse on time. Make sure you're ready."

She leaned forward and kissed him gently, caressing his cheek as she turned away. "I'll be ready. And I know you don't like to be thanked, but I want you to know that I won't forget this. I owe you one."

He returned her kiss, hoping this wasn't the last time she'd let him touch her. Whether this situation was his fault or not, he knew he had to make it right. Reva might benefit from having to move if the price was right, but if it happened against her will because of him, this budding relationship with Abby would wither and die. And he realized—not too late, he hoped—that his relationship with Abby meant more to him than he could've ever dreamed.

The courtroom was packed when Abby and Quinn walked in and settled at one end of a row of the church-style bench seats, leaving Abby's folded scooter beside their pew. They sat on the hard, uncomfortable bench holding hands, their fingers intertwined and both their palms sweating with anxiety.

They had arrived a half hour early because Abby had hoped to get some information by speaking informally with some of the city council members—one of whom was the town's veterinarian, Mack McNeil. She had sent him a text earlier but hadn't heard back.

But apparently, the town hall meeting and the day's court docket were scheduled with little time to spare between the two, so Abby's plan to mingle before the event wasn't going to happen. A few well-dressed people came in quietly and sat in the rows of padded chairs that would normally be reserved for a trial jury. Probably they were city council members; she knew that for sure when Mack came in and sat in that partitioned-off area. He looked down surreptitiously at his cell phone and didn't seem to notice that Abby and Quinn were sitting there. She started to text him again, when a text from Reva popped up onto the screen.

Abby texted back but didn't share any of the drama. Hopefully, it would be over soon and she could avoid mentioning it at all.

The day's docket wound down, and one by one, the ne'er-do-wells of Magnolia Bay shuffled up to the judge and repented their sins so the judge could pass judgment on them. Most walked away with a plan for supervised personal improvement; some were led through the back door of the courtroom on their way to incarceration.

Finally, the judge and the lawyers and their clients left the room. After that, a thin stream of townspeople who'd been waiting outside trickled in and started filling the church-pew seating. Quinn stiffened beside her, and she looked at him in surprise. "What?" she mouthed.

He shook his head and whispered back. "Nothing."

Though the courtroom wasn't the setting of an official court proceeding any longer, the place exuded a feeling of sanctity in which normal tones weren't welcome except from the chosen few who stood behind the podium.

Her phone buzzed with an incoming text. It was from Mack:

> Just saw your text. Does Reva know about this?

> *No, and I hope she never has to find out, so please don't tell her. I don't know what's going on or why. Do you?*

> Just found out when I got here and saw the agenda. Don't know any details.

Abby couldn't tell whether Mack knew she was in the courtroom or not. He still hadn't looked up.

A tall black woman wearing a beige dress and a multicolored silk scarf with matching earrings stepped up to the podium. She opened a leather-bound folder on the podium, adjusted the microphone, and leaned forward to speak into it.

"Good evening," she began in a strong, confident voice. She introduced herself as Tammy Goodson, the president of the city council, before reading the agenda for the meeting. The controversy over Bayside Barn would be dead last on the agenda.

Plenty of time to work up a hefty case of extreme anxiety.

Abby barely heard most of what went on; people got up and talked, then sat down again. About an hour into the proceedings, she was biting her nails and halfway listening when a plastic-looking Ken-doll sort of guy in a *Miami Vice* suit with a collarless shirt got up and stood at the podium. He gave a speech about the city's desperate need to bring in tourism dollars by developing unused marshland along the bay. Which of course, as a big-shot New Orleans contractor, he could oversee if the city would buy the land and then bankroll his operation. A snort of derision escaped Abby's throat before she knew she had formed an opinion.

Someone from a hardwood seat in front of them stood and agreed with *Miami Vice* Ken-doll about the lucrative potential of bayside restaurants and bars and marinas.

Someone else got up and preached about the impact of water-front development on the marshland ecosystem. A few people clapped, and Abby joined in.

Tammy took the podium and gave an eloquent speech about the history of Bayside Barn and its place in the community. She waved a sheaf of stapled-together papers and said that more than fifty people—fifty? Really?—had signed a petition to rescind the farm's permission to keep farm animals within the Magnolia Bay city limits.

"For those of you who don't know our procedure," President Tammy said, "the petitioners have gathered more than the required minimum number of names to bring this matter before the city council for consideration. We won't make a decision today. We will set that for next month's meeting, or possibly the month after that, depending on how long it takes each of the concerned parties to present their case. In the interim, the notes from today's meeting will be published online at MagnoliaBayCityCouncil.com, as well as in the Magnolia Bay news flyer that y'all all get. I would urge anyone who has an interest in this matter to spread the word and to gather any information you'd like the council to consider at the next meeting before we make our decision."

Tammy handed the petition to the secretary and asked him to enter it into the meeting notes. Then, she asked whether anyone present here this afternoon wanted to comment on the subject.

Quinn grabbed Abby's hand and squeezed, but before she could stand, *Miami Vice* Ken hopped up again and hogged the podium. When he said that that the presence of farm animals, with their offensive smells and sounds and potential health hazards, might keep investors from recognizing the lucrative potential of the adjacent waterfront property, she gasped. Maybe she'd been stupid, or just plain too riddled with anxiety to be listening effectively, but she'd only just now figured out that the land the guy was talking about was behind Bayside Barn.

He went on to say that he had heard from a reliable authority that the waterfront acreage would soon be up for sale. She felt Quinn stiffen beside her. Maybe he had just figured it out, too.

But the guy had to be crazy. Abby didn't imagine that soggy wasteland would be a viable place to build anything. Still, *Miami Vice* Ken continued to expound on the financial merits of a potential bayside development and urged the city council to get behind the idea with their existing capital and fund-raising capabilities. Finally, after not just one but two turns at the podium, the guy wound down and went back to his seat.

Abby started inching out of the pew to make her statement, but someone brushed past her from behind and gently pushed her back down with a hand on her shoulder. Abby recognized the tightly curled gray hair and rotund build of her favorite Bayside Barn volunteer. Edna!

Edna, the retired schoolteacher who volunteered at the farm, got behind the podium. She set a bright-orange clipboard on the podium and set a battered shoebox on top of it. Wearing a conservative blue jacket over a plain white blouse and a sensible, trim-fitting skirt, she unleashed her schoolteacher voice and her schoolteacher stare and her schoolteacher pointer finger.

She aimed her stare and her finger at the *Miami Vice* guy, shooting darts of angry energy that made him shrink back into his seat in the front row. "You must not be aware, sir, that Bayside Barn has nurtured and educated schoolchildren on the importance of animals and our relationships with them for the past twenty years!"

She shuffled through the shoebox and took out a stack of photographs. Walking up to the jury box, she gave Tammy a photo. "Here's a picture of you, Tammy, in the eighth grade, hugging a goat." She marched up to each of the city council members and handed out photographs, one by one, to the individuals in the photos. She had at least one photo for each person sitting in the padded chairs. "You're too old to have visited the barn on a school field trip," she said to one of the ladies. Abby winced at Edna's blunt statement, but the lady didn't seem to mind. In fact, her wrinkled old face softened when Edna added, "But this is a photo of your grandchild, isn't it?"

The woman nodded. "Can I get a copy of this?"

"You keep it. In fact, all of y'all can keep any pictures of yourselves or someone you love. And when you look at them later, I hope you'll remember how much these animals mean to the community." After Edna had given a photo to each of the city council members, she turned to the crowd and handed out dozens more of kids interacting with the animals at the barn. "Look at this one." She waved a yellowed Polaroid at a guy on the front row, and he took it from her.

"Look at that kid's face," Edna said, her voice loud and passionate. "Look at the joy in that smile." The man passed the picture on while Edna kept talking. "You think with his torn shirt and dirty overalls he had everything he needed in life?"

"I knew this kid," someone said.

"I can tell you that I knew that child, too, because I taught him. And I can tell you that he did not have what he needed. His daddy beat him, and his mama stayed drunk most of the time. He spent his school years in and out of foster care. When he lived with his parents, he came to school dirty and hungry every single day, and the other kids teased him about it."

Tammy wiped a manicured fingertip under her eyes, and she wasn't the only one affected by Edna's speech. Plenty of people in the crowd were either sniffing back tears or smiling with reminiscence.

"To those animals at Bayside Barn, that poor, unloved kid was just as good as every other kid in his class. All he had to do to get love and acceptance in that place was to hang on to a pony's neck and absorb the loving energy it had to give. And that little bit of love meant a whole lot to a kid who had nothing."

She gave another photo to the guy on the front row. "Here he is, holding a baby pig." That photo began to make the rounds. "And here he's holding a bunny in his lap."

"You know what that kid is doing now?" She put her knuckles on her hips, though she still held a fistful of photos in each hand. "He runs the veterinary medicine department at a major university. I called him this afternoon, and you know what he credits for his success?" She paused and looked over each and every person in the audience, letting her gaze linger on the real estate developer for a heartbeat before moving on.

"He says he learned respect for others—both animals and humans—by visiting Bayside Barn every year. Two of his older siblings who came up through school before we started the field trips to the barn are in prison now. He says he'd probably be there himself if it weren't for the unconditional love those animals gave him every time his school class went to Bayside Barn."

Edna paused for effect, smiling at the crowd, making eye

contact with several people. "He still has a collection of the plastic Bayside Barn Buddies sheriff's stars that they were giving out back then. He said he'll be happy to write a letter or sign whatever he needs to sign, but I only found out about this thing earlier today when…" She nodded at Tammy, who nodded back. "Well, when I found out."

So Edna had known even before Abby called. That made sense; Edna had only said, "Of course I'll be there, honey. Don't you worry."

Edna gave a stack of photos to the folks in the front row of the hard-seat gallery. "Pass those around. Look at the joy on those children's faces. Some of those kids didn't ever get hugged at home, but they damn sure got hugged by the animals at the barn."

She moved on to the second row and handed out more photos. "Some of those kids got everything they ever wanted given to them on a silver platter, but they never learned how to treat animals. Some of those kids had loving parents who taught them respect for other beings, but they weren't accepted by their peers. All those kids, each and every one, needed what the animals at Bayside Barn gave them freely without asking for anything in return."

She gave the remaining photos to the last two rows. "That's what animals do for us. And most of the time, we need them more than they need us."

Some of the photos had made the rounds, and Edna started gathering them up. Others were still being passed up and down the rows. The person next to Abby handed her a yellowed Polaroid of a kid's beaming, gap-toothed smile while he sat on a shaggy pony that Reva's husband Grayson held by a lead rope. Abby felt an unexpected rise of tears, and her throat clogged with emotion. She slipped the photo into her purse to give to Reva when she came back home.

Edna went to the podium with the tap of her sensible low heels. "This time," she said, sending her schoolteacher gaze around the room, "this time, the animals at Bayside Barn need us. They need us to stand up for them, even in the face of people who would offer us the moon to turn our backs on the lowly creatures of this world so they can tear up the environment and make money." She nodded at the crowd, then let her gaze linger on *Miami Vice* Ken while her mouth drew up in a parsimonious frown. "Those developer folks have their petition, and we all know what they're after."

She gave the orange clipboard to the first person in the front row. A Bic pen dangled from a thick loop of braided embroidery thread. "I'm starting a petition right now to support the animals of Bayside Barn. This time, I hope we'll have the courage to do what's right."

A hush fell over the room as people started passing around the petition. Most people signed, but some passed it along without looking.

Edna went back to her seat, winking at Abby as she walked past.

Tammy took over the podium. "If no one else has anything to say, we'll adjourn this meeting."

Abby sent a panicked look to Quinn. Should she try to follow Edna in speaking on behalf of Bayside Barn? Edna had done such a good job; maybe they should quit while they were ahead.

He gave a slight negative headshake.

And anyway, it was too late. While Abby sat there paralyzed with fear and indecision, President Tammy adjourned the meeting.

After the meeting, Quinn took Abby and Edna out to the town's only Mexican restaurant to celebrate Edna's moving presentation.

Quinn knew that Edna and Abby thought the first battle in this war had been won. But Quinn had seen his smarmy ex-business partner in action before. Jefferson Pearson didn't care what anyone thought of him, and he didn't play fair.

"Who was that guy who looked like a throwback from *Miami Vice*?" Abby asked.

Quinn didn't answer her, but when he'd seen JP walk into the courtroom, he'd struggled with a knee-jerk feeling that he should run for cover and hide. Even though Quinn hadn't known that JP had been padding costs and fudging estimates to get more money from their clients, he should've known. And some would say that as JP's business partner, Quinn was just as guilty—he certainly felt that way. In any case, though no one ever pressed charges, word had gotten around well enough that the fledgling business had failed. Quinn was just lucky that JP had been the "face" of the business while Quinn had led the work crews. Lucky for him, he'd been forgettable enough that JP's stink hadn't stuck to him.

"He's some real-estate developer from New Orleans," Edna said. Quinn held his breath at first, half-fearing that Edna knew that he and JP had been business partners for a brief time.

Edna leaned closer to Abby. "I've heard that he inflates the prices of supplies, he doesn't pay his workers, and he cheats his clients by invoicing for materials he uses elsewhere. He's bad news. I hope the folks on city council know that, and if they don't, I won't mind educating them."

Abby looked over at Quinn, and he could see the wheels turning in her mind. He wondered whether she remembered what he'd said when they first met, about his construction business partnership with a friend not working out.

"Edna," Quinn said, "let me see what I can find out about his plans before we go off half-cocked. You're right that he's unethical, but he's also very persuasive."

"Wait." Abby sat forward, her face lit with excitement and curiosity. "You know him?"

"We worked together for a brief time. But I really don't want to get into it until I know more about what he's up to." He knew he'd have to find a way to tell Abby the truth about his business relationship with JP, but not right here, not right now. "I hope you'll both calm down a notch and let me look into this before you start blabbing to the city council about things you don't understand."

Abby drew herself up. "I don't blab."

Edna took another sip of her margarita and giggled under her breath. "I do."

"Please don't," Quinn reiterated. "Not until I can get some concrete information to act on."

And, he didn't want JP to know that anyone with more than a bleeding-heart objection to the destruction of an old barn and a bayside marshland ecosystem was against him. JP would do anything on this or that side of the law to get his way. "I can ask around, maybe find out what he's up to. We'll do better if we don't say anything until we know everything. So please, let's focus on something we can do, like getting an avalanche of signatures and letters sent to the city council in favor of Bayside Barn." At least it would keep Edna and Abby busy while he figured out what to do.

"Hear, hear!" Edna held her glass up for a toast. Flushed with the success of her speech—and her second frozen margarita—she fanned herself with the orange clipboard and laid out her battle plan. "We'll get fifty signatures in no time." She took another sip of her frosty top-shelf drink. "We'll get a hundred. Two hundred! I'll print up extra pages and we'll all go 'round asking for signatures till we've asked everyone in Magnolia Bay."

True, they were well on the way to getting fifty signatures. By the time everyone had filtered out of the courthouse, the petition on Edna's orange clipboard held almost thirty, and she'd given out blank pages for people to take home to their relatives, friends, and neighbors, along with preaddressed, prestamped envelopes to mail the pages to the city council.

"And you know what else?" Edna added. "We should host an

open house at the barn! Make it a big, citywide event. It'd be good PR for Bayside Barn, and we could get even more signatures that way."

If Quinn ever had to go to war about anything, he wanted Edna to be the general leading the charge. But this particular war might be unwinnable. Both Abby and Edna held starry-eyed views about right winning out over wrong. They were both too innocent to realize that they could get all the signatures in the world and still lose.

Abby held up a hand and she and Edna did a high five. "Hosting an open house is a great idea, Edna. I'll pick a date and start planning."

Edna stirred her margarita and took another sip. "I'll call up all my old students and get them to write letters about what the animals at Bayside Barn meant to them. The folks on the city council will need wheelbarrows to hold all the mail they'll get between now and next month."

Abby clinked her glass to Edna's. "I'm glad you're on our side, Edna."

Quinn clinked his glass to theirs, hoping they didn't notice his lack of enthusiasm. The waiter brought their food, and Quinn dug into his steak fajita dinner, hoping that Abby and Edna would eat quickly so they could get out of here. He knew that Abby planned to call Reva once they got home. Knowing that she'd be sitting all comfy and staying off her foot till he got back, Quinn would go to the pool house and call Delia. And this time, if she didn't answer, he'd have to make some excuse and go to her house so she'd have to talk to him.

He sipped his drink—just one, knowing he'd be driving Edna and Abby home after dinner—and hoped to God that his complaint to Delia hadn't alerted JP to an opportunity he wouldn't have known about otherwise. If JP had gotten a whiff of it, it must have come from Delia, and she only knew about JP because of

Quinn's pillow talk about his failed construction business back in NOLA.

The top-shelf tequila burned in his stomach, because he had a bad feeling that he had set this downward spiral into motion.

Chapter 20

AFTER QUINN DROPPED OFF EDNA AT HER HOUSE, ABBY relaxed in the passenger seat of Reva's car and indulged in a tequila-induced rose-colored-glasses glow. She knew she'd probably wake up at 2:00 a.m. and lie there till dawn worrying, but for now, everything was fine. Tomorrow, she'd get busy planning the open house. Quinn would dig into *Miami Vice* Ken's motives, and Edna would gather enough signatures and solicit enough letters to bury the city council in an avalanche of public opinion.

At this moment, with her body sinking into the soft leather seat and her face and lips tingly and numb from one more margarita than was strictly necessary, Abby knew everything would turn out all right.

"You okay over there?" Quinn asked.

"Mmmm." Better than okay, but she didn't want to make her mouth work too hard to form those words just now. She closed her eyes and floated, obligingly wrapping her arms around Quinn's neck when he carried her into the house, undressed her, and tucked her into bed. She'd planned to call Reva, but decided tomorrow would be soon enough.

"I've got some stuff to do next door," Quinn's voice said from high above her in the darkened bedroom. "Your scooter is next to the bed, and your cell phone is plugged in on the bedside table."

"Mmmm." She rolled over and pulled the covers up to her chin. "Mmm-kay." The bed was so comfy, the sheets so cool and soft on her bare skin, the summer-weight quilt so perfect. "Mmmmm."

"You know," Quinn's voice said, interrupting her blissful sinking down into sleep, "I've changed my mind. You and that scooter might not be the best combination right now, so I'll stay close by in case you need anything."

"Mmmm-kay," she answered, resisting the call of the pleasant swimmy-headed feeling that lured her into waking dreams of her and Quinn, their hot, damp bodies tangled together in the cool sheets.

Quinn sighed, and Abby felt him kiss her forehead. "Call out if you need me."

I need you, she thought, but the lure of sleep pulled her in before she could say the words out loud.

Quinn tucked Abby into bed with Georgia—who'd been quick to snuggle down next to her—then stepped outside onto the dark patio, leaving the back door cracked open so he could hear if Abby called out.

Gardenia blossoms scented the air with their thick, sweet vanilla scent. A shooting star arced across the night sky, and a warm, muggy breeze embraced him as he sat in a lounge chair and took out his cell to call Delia.

He'd expected that she wouldn't answer, but the message he'd been prepared to leave died in his throat when she picked up. "What now, Quinn?" she snapped. "I do have a life, you know. And yet, somehow you always manage to call me outside of office hours."

"Two things, and then I'll let you go." He took a breath and let it out. "I want the name of the person you took my complaint to, and the names of anyone you told about the bay parcel."

She heaved a martyred sigh. "Okay, fine. I took your complaint to Jefferson Pearson. I told him about the bayfront land and put a bug in his ear about how valuable that property could be if it didn't have a rinky-dink wannabe zoo in its backyard. I knew from what you told me about him that he and his incredible greed would handle everything. Are you happy now?"

Quinn's mouth went dry, and a triple shot of hot liquid regret poured through his veins. "Shit." This whole thing was his fault.

Which meant he had to fix it, starting with making sure JP didn't get his hands on the bayside marshland. "That acreage is an integral part of my plan," he reminded her. "We can't let it slip away."

"When it goes on the market," Delia insisted, "you'll be the first to know, because I'll tell you. You can make an offer before the sign goes up, so whether or not JP knows anything will be a moot point."

"Yeah, right," he scoffed. "We'll be in a bidding war before the listing goes up on Zillow."

"Not if you make an offer before then, which I'll give you the opportunity to do. So I'm not sure what you're going on about. JP will be the bad guy, and you'll get exactly what you wanted."

"How can you be sure I'll have time to make an offer before anyone else gets wind of it?" His imagination tried to come online with visions of staying and living at the estate himself, but he turned out the light on that glowing image. He couldn't buy the marshland if he didn't sell the estate. It was a simple math equation.

"Don't worry. I haven't forgotten the bonus you promised me. It's in my interest as well as yours. We're in this together."

Something brushed against his hand, and Griff jumped into his lap. He stroked the cat's soft fur and felt his ire seeping away. "Fine. I guess it doesn't matter that JP knows about the bayfront property."

Visions of him and Abby living next door to her aunt Reva kept intruding, and he knew it was because his new relationship with Abby had shifted his priorities. Maybe if he didn't sell the estate, he could still advise all the homeowners on the street to get together and buy the bayfront parcel, just to keep a big development from ruining their view. Though if he didn't flip the estate, he couldn't afford that, either… "But here's the thing, Delia. I've rethought my objections to the farm. I don't want to have anything to do with this campaign to ruin Bayside Barn."

"Well then, don't," Delia snapped. "In fact, if you want to come out in opposition to it, come on out. It's too late to stop this snowball from rolling downhill, but you can protest all you want. It won't make any difference."

It better make a difference, or Abby's aunt Reva would lose her livelihood, and the animals at Bayside Barn would lose their home. "But Delia, don't you think that with enough community involvement—"

"No," she interrupted. "I don't. Community sentiment whispers. Money talks. And the potential of making even more money hollers out loud. Now, I've gotta let you go. And as a friendly reminder, my office hours are Monday through Friday, 10:00 a.m. to 5:00 p.m. Feel free to call me anytime during those hours. Unless you are ready to buy or sell a property. In that case, call me anytime."

"Wait. Does anybody—"

The line went dead, cutting off the question he'd been about to ask: Does anybody know that he was the one who'd asked her to get rid of Bayside Barn? If she hadn't told JP or anyone else that Quinn's complaint to her had started this whole ugly mess, then no one need ever know that he was to blame.

He wished that thought were as comforting as it should be.

He petted Griff and looked out over the moon-silvered landscape. "You're not such a bad cat, are you?" he asked the purring feline, who dug sharp claws into Quinn's thighs and lifted his face for more attention. Then, without warning, Griff stiffened and stared into the darkness. With a deep-throated hiss, the cat dug in his claws and leaped off Quinn's legs—giving a new meaning to the word *catapult*. "Okay, yes, you are bad." Quinn rubbed his stinging thighs; that cat's claws had penetrated his jeans and latched into skin.

The dog door bumped; the spooked cat skedaddling into the house. Quinn narrowed his eyes and tried to see into the shadows. More raccoons?

He heard the faint *scrip-scrip* sound of a dog's nails on concrete as Wolf crept toward him from the corner of the house. Quinn moved slowly, reaching his knuckles out toward the big dog who crouched uncertainly just inside the glow of the patio's solar lighting.

"Come here, buddy," Quinn called softly. The dog's quick acceptance of Sean had not extended to Quinn, nor even to Abby, who had tried so hard to win the skittish dog's trust. And even that acceptance had melted away the second Sean tried to get Wolf to follow him to the house. The dog had backed away, looking indecisive, then slunk off to hide in the bushes across the street. Sean had wanted to follow, but Quinn wouldn't allow it. The dog seemed half-wild, with two feet in the wolf's world while the other two feet yearned for the safety and security of a domestic dog's life. Quinn didn't quite trust the side of Wolf that didn't trust humans.

"Come on." Quinn snapped his fingers and made kissy noises. "I won't hurt you."

Wolf belly-crawled closer. Just out of reach of Quinn's reaching fingers, the dog rolled to his back, tail thumping in submission. At the same time, the dog's lips curled back in a menacing snarl, revealing astonishingly long, sharp teeth that gleamed in the reflected glow of the landscape lighting. Without touching, Quinn pulled his hand back. "I won't hurt you, but I don't want you to hurt me, either."

Wolf rolled to his belly and crawled closer, whining softly. Quinn realized that the lip curl must have been something like Georgia's strange little grin, another sign of submission along with a touch of nervousness and anxiety. "I won't hurt you," he said again, his voice low and soft. He held his knuckles out. "Promise."

Wolf sniffed Quinn's hand. Apparently satisfied by his scent that Quinn was trustworthy, Wolf stood and turned, presenting his back for Quinn to stroke. The dog's fur didn't feel at all like Quinn had expected. Rather than the rough coat of a German shepherd, Wolf's coat was thick and soft as rabbit fur, just like Griff's. Like a wolf, this dog had fur, not hair.

Quinn raked his fingers through Wolf's thick, soft fur. Expecting to find matted fur, or ticks, he instead found a thick circular scab or scar on the dog's right side, about the size of Quinn's palm, where the fur didn't grow. When his questing fingers touched the center of the scab where the flesh was still raw, the dog flinched but didn't move away or offer to bite. "Poor buddy," Quinn said. He moved his hand and went back to stroking the dog's back. "Whatever happened to you must've hurt pretty bad."

Wolf turned again, this time to sniff Quinn's face. Quinn sat very still, his hand resting on the dog's back as he allowed it to explore his scent. Wolf licked his cheek once, as if in thanks, then backed away and melted into the shadows.

Quinn sat for a few more minutes, listening to the crickets' chirping and the sound of an owl calling to its mate. A warm breeze sighed through the trees with a soft shushing sound as millions of leaves brushed against each other in a quiet symphony.

Tomorrow, the fight for the animals of Bayside Barn would begin. Quinn had no illusions about his chances of winning against JP. But he had opened this can of worms, so it was on him to stuff those night crawlers back into the tin and close the lid.

Tonight, before the battle, it was enough to sit in the quiet darkness and absorb this moment's peace. Quinn imagined that Wolf had probably bedded down for the night, curled up in his den under the porch. The dog would wake at dawn and fetch the rolled-up newspaper and leave it by the back door. After the chores were done, Quinn would take the petition Edna had crafted to each house in the area she had assigned him and solicit signatures from the homeowners.

It seemed to Quinn that Wolf and he were both struggling to find how—or if—they fit into the microcosm of this farm. Each of them needed to be of service; Wolf in order to earn a place here, and Quinn in order to make up for his mistake in not seeing the beauty of this place that existed only to educate and serve the community.

Edna had said that Bayside Barn changed people for the better. Quinn realized that was true, because it had changed him. He had moved into the estate next door feeling desperate to prove himself, and he'd thought that the only way to do that would be to make a ton of money as quickly as possible.

As he leaned back in the chaise, he wondered if he could entertain the two opposing visions for the estate—flipping it for a profit or finding a way to keep it and put down roots—without pushing either option away. Could it be possible, in some future universe he hadn't yet considered, that he could keep the estate and still buy the marshland? The only thing he knew for certain was that Abby's aunt Reva must be allowed to continue the legacy of Bayside Barn, and it was on him to figure out how to make that happen.

His brain started to spin out scenarios and plans of attack, ruining the peace of the starlit patio. At the same time, the mosquitoes found him. He slapped at a particularly noisy one that insisted on whining in his ear, then stood. "Time to go in, anyway."

He showered and brushed his teeth, then padded quietly into the bedroom where Abby slept. The soft sound of her breathing assured him that she was sleeping, so he turned to go.

"Hey." Her sleepy voice snagged him, made him turn back. "Where you goin'?"

"Thought I'd sleep in the other room tonight. Just checking on you first. Didn't mean to wake you."

She pulled the covers back, inviting. "Come to bed."

He climbed in, and she scooted to make room. After a quick kiss, he turned his back to her, planning to sleep and to let her do the same. She spooned behind him, then snaked her arm around his waist. She caressed his chest, then trailed her fingers down his abs to the waistband of his boxers. "What's this?" she asked. "Weren't you planning to take advantage of my drunken state?"

He chuckled. "Nope, I wasn't."

"Shame, shame." She slipped her hand lower, caressing lightly. "That's a waste of good tequila."

He rolled to his back, careful not to bump her cast. "What did you have in mind?"

Abby pushed the covers down and knelt over him to remove his boxers and toss them aside.

Georgia hopped down in disgust and left the room in a huff. "Sorry, Georgia," Abby said, a laugh in her voice. "You can come back later."

The dog door in the laundry room bumped open and shut; Georgia going outside.

Abby leaned over Quinn, her wavy hair brushing his belly as her lips closed over his erection.

Her mouth, still warm from sleep, drew him in while her soft hands cradled his balls, and Quinn forgot all about the dog.

———

Early the next morning, Abby heard a text come through, a soft buzz on her silenced phone. She eased out of bed, dragging the damned cast across the sheets as quietly as possible. Quinn was sleeping so well, she didn't want to disturb him just yet. Maybe she'd wake him up later, but first she knew she needed to talk to Reva. Hopefully, Reva wouldn't be too busy to talk this early on a Saturday morning.

Cursing the scooter's squeaky wheels on the wooden floor, Abby wheeled as quietly as possible out of the bedroom, then eased the door closed behind her. In the kitchen, she turned on the coffeepot and viewed Reva's message, which wasn't a message at all, but a photo of a tiny baby skunk curled up in Reva's palm.

While the pulsating dots on the screen showed that Reva was typing something, Abby sent Awww, sweet! And then, Do you have time to talk? I need to tell you something.

Reva's message came through: I got to take a baby skunk into my dorm room last night! He's so tiny! I had to give him electrolyte water every two hours because we couldn't feed him until he was fully hydrated. Now he's in the infirmary with a few raccoons that are about his size.

Now, Abby felt bad about bursting Reva's balloon with a worrying phone conversation, but it was too late, because Reva texted, Calling the house phone now.

Abby bolted to grab the landline before it could ring and wake Quinn. (Not easy to bolt with a knee scooter, but she managed to grab the phone before it made more than a short chirp.)

"Hey," Reva said, sounding breathless. "Your timing is impeccable. Someone just got off the dorm's phone, and I snagged it before anyone else realized it was free."

"Yay, Aunt Reva," Abby said quietly. She held the phone between her chin and her shoulder and headed to the patio so she could talk louder.

"What's up? Why are you whispering?"

Abby realized she hadn't quite thought through the mechanics of her early-morning phone call with Reva. "Well…"

"Oh!" Reva laughed. "Oh my God! Did the new neighbor sleep over? Oh my God!"

"Um…" Abby closed the sliding glass door and sat on a chaise by the pool. "Well…"

"He did!" Reva tittered. "I wanted you to be neighborly, but I didn't expect you to go quite that far."

"Well, okay, yes. You are correct." Abby cleared her throat. "But that's not what I wanted to tell you."

"Uh-oh. What else?"

Forget about the broken foot; she'd delayed telling that news long enough that it wasn't news anymore. They were supposed to take the cast off in another week. "There was a disturbing letter in the mail that I need to tell you about."

"Okay." Reva took an audible, steadying breath. "Tell."

"Apparently, someone has complained to the city about Bayside Barn. They've circulated a petition, and they're going to try to rescind your permission to keep farm animals."

"Oh." After that one word, Reva went very quiet. Abby knew that this news hurt Reva's feelings. Her aunt had always felt like an outsider, and this drove that feeling home like a knife through the heart. "Well, it's not like they haven't tried that before."

"Edna and Quinn and I are fighting it. All the barn volunteers are, too. We're circulating our own petition to allow Bayside Barn to stay, and I'm planning an open house to get the community even more involved."

"I guess..." Reva sounded lost, bewildered by what certainly felt like an attack. "I guess I'll have to come home early. Who..." Her voice broke, and she cleared her throat. "Who complained? Was it Mildred, do you think?"

"Aunt Reva, I really don't think it was any of the neighbors. I think it's something bigger than that. I think it's someone who wants to develop the property behind you."

"But..." Reva sputtered, "But Bayside Barn isn't the only estate that's adjacent to that land. Why... I mean—"

"I guess it's because once Bayside Barn goes, the others will be easy to pick off, one by one. Quinn is going to talk to some of his contacts in the building business and see what he can find out, so try not to worry."

"I should... I think I should come home and deal with this myself."

Quinn came out onto the patio and handed Abby a cup of coffee before sitting on the end of the chaise. He held out a hand for the phone. "Let me talk to her." Abby gladly gave up the phone. She hadn't known what to say anyway. Georgia hopped into her lap, and she stroked the little dog's fur.

"Hey, Reva," he said. "It's Quinn Lockhart, your new neighbor." He immediately stood and started pacing while he listened to Reva and then responded. "No, I don't think so. The next meeting isn't for another month. Why don't you hold off at least until then? We'll keep in touch and let you know of any new developments...." He paced to the other side of the pool. "No, I don't think they'll make any decisions at that meeting. Maybe you should ask Mack, though..."

As Quinn talked with Reva, Abby closed her eyes and soaked up the sunlight, letting his voice wrap around her while his words drifted from her consciousness. Something soft brushed her arm, and she felt Georgia wiggle with excitement. She opened her eyes, and there stood Wolf! Slowly, Abby reached out, and though Wolf panted with anxiety, he finally let her touch him. "Thank you," she whispered.

Then he backed away and sat, just out of reach.

Out of reach again, but at least this time he didn't disappear.

Chapter 21

To celebrate the removal of Abby's cast, Quinn surprised her with a night on the town in New Orleans. They had even taken the motorcycle—an exhilarating ride, and something she'd never before experienced.

Now, she clutched his arm as they walked up the stairs of the Saenger Theater, but not because she needed him for support. "This is so exciting!" She hung on to his arm and squeezed. "I can't believe you got these tickets!" She hadn't even mentioned the name of her favorite band, but apparently he'd been paying attention.

She liked a man who paid attention, not only under the sheets but outside them. She gave his bicep another squeeze. His hard-muscled arm felt like a fortress under her fingertips. She didn't need protection, but if she ever did, she knew where to go.

After the concert, they had dinner at Muriel's on Jackson Square, then noodled through the French Quarter. After picking up a couple of five-dollar hurricanes, they walked hand in hand along the paved sidewalk that bordered the Mississippi, then settled on a bench where they could watch the river's wide brown waters cruise past. "How's your foot feeling?" Quinn asked. "I'm not tiring you out too much, am I?"

"My foot's fine," she answered, leaning her head against his shoulder. Actually, her foot ached a little, but she wasn't about to admit that. A horse-drawn carriage clopped along the street; a backup plan for getting back to the parking garage if her foot failed her. "But if I start to feel faint, you might have to take me to the Café Du Monde for a pick-me-up."

Quinn smirked. "Beignets and café au lait cures everything, right?"

"Might not fix everything, but I can attest that sugar and caffeine work for a variety of ailments."

Quinn rested his arm along the bench's metal back, and Abby leaned into the curve of his arm. "This is nice."

He brushed her shoulder with his fingertips. "I'm going to miss spending time with you at the farm."

A pang of disappointment tugged at Abby's heart. She had known, of course, that once she got the cast removed, Quinn would go back to doing his thing, and she'd go back to doing hers. But she had gotten used to having him around, and she hoped he felt the same, at least a little. She tipped her head back to look at him. Moonlight—or the streetlight behind them—brushed the strong planes of his face in gold and made his blue eyes shine dark as midnight. She could almost imagine herself saying *I love you*. "Maybe you could still eat dinner with me and spend the night? At least some of the time? Aunt Reva won't be back for another four weeks, unless she comes home early for the town hall meeting."

He smiled, a gentle softening of his lips. "I'd like that."

She snuggled into his side again. "That's good."

A lonely trumpet in the distance played a bluesy jazz tune, and Abby reflected on the strange thought she'd had about saying *I love you* to Quinn. *Did* she love him? She loved having him around. She loved having him in her bed. She loved his many good qualities— his work ethic, his kindness to her and the animals at the farm, the love he showed to his son, and even the respect he gave his ex-wife.

"You've gone quiet," he said. "You're not worried about the next meeting, are you?"

"I worry about everything, Quinn." She even worried about the possibility of falling in love with him. What if she let herself love him? What if she already did? "I even worry about things that most people wish would happen."

"Tell me." He tucked her closer and put his chin on the top of her head. With her head on his chest, she could hear his slow, even breaths, feel his ribs expanding against her side. "Whatever it is, we'll work it out."

He always said that: *Whatever it is, we'll work it out*. And whenever he said it, she always felt better. Like nothing that could happen was insurmountable as long as they handled it together. She looked out at the Mississippi River, its whitecaps silver in the moonlight as it churned past, a silent, mysterious sheet of dark water, ever moving toward some unseen end. "I'm worried that I might be falling in love with you, and I don't know if I want that. I'm not sure I want to be that vulnerable again."

His slow, even breathing didn't change. She could feel his mind turning her words over in his head. "I understand. I feel the same way myself sometimes." His fingers idly stroked her shoulder, a subconsciously self-soothing motion that soothed her, too. "I wasn't looking to fall in love, either. In fact..." He gave a little huff of laughter. "The timing couldn't be worse. I mean, shit; I have nothing to offer you. If you had any sense, you'd run screaming."

"Not running." She patted his chest—his gloriously hard-muscled chest—then hugged him tight. "I'm worried about losing my heart, but I'm still right here."

He snorted. "Yeah, maybe you're not running now because the doctor said to take it easy on that foot. But what about two weeks from now?"

"I don't see how you can say that you have nothing to offer. You're a wonderful person, an amazing lover, an exceptional father... You're even a decent ex-husband, which says a lot to me about your character. And, you're a hard worker. What else is there that you think would make me run screaming?"

"I can think of three things offhand." He tapped a finger on her shoulder. "One: I'm broke as a haint because I've spent all my money to buy and renovate that estate." He tapped another finger. "Two: I'm in financial limbo because I lost my job and my reputation as a contractor when I trusted my business partner and got sold down the river."

"It's not wrong to trust people, Quinn."

He looked away from her and gazed out over the Mississippi. "Even if the person I trusted was JP?"Abby gasped.

"JP?" He was Quinn's ex-friend and business partner? Quinn had said they'd worked together, but Abby hadn't snapped to the connection. Of course, it seemed so obvious now. Why had she only just now put all this together? "JP is the ex-business partner who sold you down the river?"

He closed his eyes. "Yes. I'm sorry I didn't tell you before. There just wasn't a good time to do it."

She scooted closer. "It's okay; I understand. Tell me the third thing."

He tapped a third finger. "And three—something I haven't told you yet, but I think I need to—I had planned to sell the estate to raise enough money to build my own construction business, but this stupid fantasy keeps running through my head, even though it's the worst possible financial decision I could make."

"Yeah?" She snuggled close and ran a hand down his arm. "Tell me about this fantasy."

"I can't stop thinking of keeping the estate and living there— with you, if you'll have me."

"Quinn, I—" The thought of moving in with Quinn took her breath, like jumping from the high dive into cool, deep water on a hot summer's day. To live with him, and to be living next door to her aunt Reva, made a blossom of hope bloom inside her heart. To have a place, a home, a man to love, and an extended family to depend on… "I don't know what to say."

The seductive pull of that dream made her even more afraid. The bigger the potential prize, the harder the fall when it didn't happen—or worse, when it happened but then got snatched away.

"Calm down." Quinn soothed her by stroking her shoulder

again. "I'm not asking—not yet—because unless I can figure out another way to more than recoup my investment, I do need to sell that place, no matter how much I'd like to stay. And I have a lot of shit to work through before I'd ask you to start thinking about forever. I know I said making love would mean the start of something—and it did." He stroked her shoulder again. "It does. But I have to get right with my past before I can plan my future. Does that make sense?"

Abby nodded. She felt the same way. She had to let go of past hurts before she could put her heart on the chopping block again.

BAYSIDE BARN OPEN HOUSE TODAY!
11:00 a.m.–5:00 p.m.
Welcome, welcome. Come on in!

Abby zip-tied the brightly colored hand-painted sign to the open gate, along with a half-dozen helium-filled balloons that bopped together and bounced in the hot breeze.

Quinn and Edna were out right now, putting more signs and balloons in strategic locations to draw in random Sunday drivers and to point the way for people who may have seen the announcement in the Magnolia Bay flyer but weren't sure of the location. (Out here in the boondocks, some GPS guidance systems tended to fall short.)

Georgia danced excitedly at Abby's feet all the way back to the house. She'd been all up in everybody's business all morning while they were setting up the bouncy house, the popcorn machine, the iced tea and lemonade and water dispensers, and everything else. Crepe paper streamers draped every reachable eave and limb and handrail on the farm, except of course the goat yard fencing, on which anything made of paper would be considered a food item.

It seemed to Abby that everyone, animals and humans alike, was feeling excitement and anticipation for the day's fun.

All except Wolf, poor guy, who was hiding out under the porch. Hopefully, he felt safe there from all the commotion that had been going on since just after dawn. Abby sat in one of the folding chairs that were scattered randomly around the yard and tried to connect with Wolf telepathically. She wasn't sure she was getting through, but as Reva kept telling her, it didn't hurt to try. She got the sense that he knew what to expect and planned to stay hidden until the place quieted down, though maybe she was just kidding herself in an effort to feel better about his obvious distress. In case he could hear her, Abby promised that it would all be over before dinnertime, and that she'd save a hamburger patty for him to have as a treat.

"Abby, hey!" She opened her eyes and saw Seàn coming toward her at a slow jog. "Where do you want me?"

"You want to be in charge of the kiddie rides?" Sunshine and Midnight were saddled for pony rides, their lead ropes tied to a metal round pen at the back of the yard. Their manes and tails were braided with ribbons and flowers, their coats and hooves glossy and clean. Elijah and Miriam were dressed up and saddled, too, wearing flower-bedecked straw hats—with strategically placed holes for their long ears to stick through—and matching bouquets tied to their tails.

"Sure. I can do that, just tell me what the job entails."

Abby explained that he'd be ensuring that parents helped their kiddies on and off the equines and walked beside them for safety during the ride. (Volunteers would lead the animals along the fence line and then back again; it was more about the photo op at the end of the ride than the ride itself.) He'd also have to schedule several minutes between each ride to give the critters time to rest under the shaded awning and drink water from the portable trough.

"The girls from the high school will be taking turns leading the ponies and donkeys." Abby tilted her chin toward a clutch of pretty girls standing by the goat yard and petting Gregory, who hadn't been invited to participate because of his penchant for wandering off in search of adventure. "You'll have to make sure that the girls take breaks and stay hydrated, too. You think you can handle all that?"

Sean grinned. "You bet."

"Thanks." Abby glanced at her watch: 10:40 a.m. More than a dozen volunteers had shown up to help, and they all stood around chatting, but when visitors started streaming in, they'd take their places. Abby could tell by the smell of charcoal in the air that Mack was already grilling hot dogs and burgers in the pavilion. The buttery scent of popcorn floated her way, too, reminding her that she'd hardly eaten anything for breakfast.

Quinn and Edna were back, walking toward Abby with a willowy redhead and a young kid with the same bright hair. Edna waved at Abby and shouted, "Yoo-hoo!"

Abby met them by the extra-large round pen—this one reinforced with a layer of fence wire—that held the cuddle critters: two spring lambs and a few of the friendliest goats, three of the big Flemish giant bunnies, and an assortment of chickens and ducks. Arnold, the potbellied pig, had managed to squirm out of his bow tie twice and was finally allowed to be naked, but most everyone else wore some sort of adornment; ribbons, flowers, whatever nontoxic folderol they would tolerate (and hopefully refrain from eating). Several extra-large wire crates were lined with hay and placed inside the enclosure so any of the animals who weren't interested in cuddling could decide to take a time-out from the festivities.

"Abby," Edna said, "I'd like you to meet Sara Prather and her son, Max. Sara is the editor of the Magnolia Bay newspaper."

It wasn't an actual newspaper—Magnolia Bay didn't have a local newspaper anymore because it had long since gone bankrupt—but the chamber of commerce issued the small advertising circular that was printed free of charge by a local company and delivered to every address in Magnolia Bay. Aside from the coupons and advertisements from local businesses, it did contain some interesting articles and announcements of the town's current events. Abby wouldn't have known any of this if Wolf hadn't started delivering the paper to her doorstep; she'd have chucked it into the bin after running over it a few times. But since he had, she felt obligated to honor his effort by at least looking, maybe clipping a few coupons to use at the grocery store. She hoped that on some level, he knew that she appreciated his offering.

Abby shook Sara's hand. "Hi, Sara. We spoke on the phone. Thanks for advertising this event for us."

"It's what I do," Sara said, her green eyes smiling. She held up her camera. "Do you mind if I wander around and take pictures today for the flyer?"

"That'd be great, thanks." Abby set aside her reluctance to ask for help and asked for what she wanted. "Sara, do you think you could also do a little write-up about Bayside Barn? Let people know how important it is to the community? Maybe tell them where they can sign the petition to help us keep our animals? Mack has said he'll keep a clipboard of blank petitions at his office."

"Of course. There's one at the chamber of commerce, too." Sara put a hand on her son's shoulder to keep him from squirming while the grown-ups talked. "Maybe if you're not too busy all day long, we can find time for a quick interview?"

Abby nodded. "I'd love that."

"Welcome, Bayside Buddies," someone screeched from across the yard.

Abby jumped. "Oops, I forgot all about Freddy." And guests were beginning to stream through the gates.

"I'll get him," Quinn volunteered. Abby watched him walk away, all lean grace and hard muscles under a plain T-shirt and cargo

shorts. He'd come a long way since he moved next door, she realized. He still didn't mess with the Amazons after the bite one of
them gave him, but he'd made friends with Freddy the macaw. And
Abby had seen him feeding his granola bar snacks to Elijah, but she
hadn't let on that she knew. That could remain their secret.

Reva called the afternoon of the next town hall meeting, when
Abby was busy changing from one outfit to another. She'd given
up on her own clothing and was now rifling through Aunt Reva's
closet.

"Hey." Abby put the phone on speaker and whipped off the
dress she had just tried on. Cute, comfortable, colorful, but maybe
a little too hippie-earth-mother for Abby.

"I'm calling to wish you luck in the meeting tonight. I kind of
wish I'd decided to come home for it, but I'm also kind of glad I
didn't. I'm learning so much every day that I do hate to miss any of
it. I called Edna, and she assured me that I wouldn't be able to do
anything y'all aren't already doing."

"Edna is right, as usual," Abby agreed, hoping she wasn't lying.

"I called Mack, too. He says I should trust the process, so that's
exactly what I plan to do, hard as it may be."

"I know it's hard." It was hard for Abby, too. She tried not to
think about it too much. "How's class going?"

"You won't believe the cool stuff I got to do..." Reva launched
into a detailed account of the classes she'd had that week.

Georgia watched from the bed as Abby pulled another dress off
the hanger and slipped it on over her head. Quinn was working in
New Orleans today, but would be here to pick her up in less than
an hour. But nothing she tried on looked right. How was it that
some days, everything she tried on looked hideous, even the same
clothes that usually looked just fine?

Conversation wasn't required beyond a few well-placed exclamations of surprise and appreciation. Abby turned in front of the mirror and frowned at herself. She knew the dress wasn't the problem. She was the problem. She tried on another one—emerald-green linen—that wasn't too bad. *This will have to do.*

"How's Wolf coming along?" Reva asked.

"Still living in his den under the porch, but I think he sleeps on the pool patio at night."

"Inside the gate is an improvement," Reva said. "Is he still delivering the paper?"

"Yes." Abby selected a pair of earrings from Reva's jewelry box—tiny emerald studs to match the green dress. "Still trying to earn a sense of belonging." *There seems to be a lot of that going around.*

"Has he let you touch him yet?"

"Just once, for so brief a time I'm beginning to think I imagined it." Abby poked through the box looking for a matching necklace. "He loves Sean and even plays with him. He has come up to Quinn a few times. He ignores me." She settled for a simple gold cross.

"Have you asked him why?"

"Who, Quinn?" Abby struggled with the latch for a second before managing it.

"No, silly. Wolf."

"I haven't." She glanced at the clock. "I'll try talking to him tonight."

"Why not now," Reva pressed. "I'll connect in, too, and validate what you get. You have time before you have to leave, right?"

Yes, she had time, if she could quit obsessing over every detail of her appearance. With one last glance in the mirror, Abby started hanging up all the dresses she'd tried on. "Let's do it."

"You need to sit down and relax first," Reva insisted. "I can hear you rattling around. You won't be able to connect with him until you're more centered and grounded."

Abby suppressed a sigh. Reva was right; Abby needed to take a few moments to calm herself before the meeting, anyway. She moved the dresses aside and sat on the bed, leaning against the headboard. "Okay. I'm relaxed."

Reva laughed. "No, you're not. I can hear you breathing, and those are not relaxed breaths you're taking."

Georgia inched over to align herself with Abby's leg. Abby stroked the dog's thick fur and focused on breathing in and out, in and out, in…and…out… She released a sigh, and felt the tension she'd been holding onto seeping away.

"Good," Reva said. "Okay, now. Imagine Wolf walking toward you. See the expression on his face, his ears pricked forward, his gaze on you. See his tail waving slowly back and forth as he comes closer. Let me know when he sits in front of you."

Abby imagined Wolf sitting in front of her. She saw his face, not relaxed and happy with his tongue lolling, but with his eyespots drawn together as he panted with anxiety. "He's sitting. But he looks worried." She imagined Wolf looking aside, refusing to meet her gaze. He darted a glance over his shoulder. It looked as if he was planning a potential escape route. "He's thinking of running."

"He feels threatened by you. Ask him why."

"Why would he feel threatened?" Abby struggled with a flood of hurt feelings, the pain of being unjustly rejected. "I've only ever been nice to him. I've tried harder than anyone to earn his trust."

"Those are *your* feelings. You have to set them aside before you can hear his. Can you put those feelings in a box, just for now, and close the lid?"

Abby swallowed. "Yes." She imagined her feelings like the jumble of clothes on the bed beside her. She imagined herself folding them neatly and putting them in a box, then closing the lid and setting the box aside.

"Breathe," Reva coached. "Reconnect with Wolf."

She imagined the dog in front of her again, and gasped in

surprise when she saw herself wrapping a heavy chain around his neck. He struggled to break free, but she pulled the chain tighter. "He thinks I'm going to capture him! He thinks I'll put a chain on him and make him stay here whether he wants to or not."

"Ask him why he thinks that."

"I would never put a dog on a chain."

Reva didn't respond, but her patient silence sent its own message. *Ask.*

Abby went back to her imagined image of Wolf sitting in front of her. She asked the question, and got nothing. "I'm drawing a blank."

"Maybe you're asking the wrong question. Try wording it differently. And for God's sake, take the chain off first."

"Oh." Abby played the movie clip in her head, watching herself take the chain off Wolf's neck and tossing it aside. She watched herself sit a little farther back, not close enough to touch, not close enough to threaten. Wolf stopped panting, and his mouth looked more relaxed. *I won't hurt you*, she imagined herself saying. *I won't try to catch you or hold you captive.*

And just like that, the answer came to her.

"I'm trying too hard. He thinks I want to tame him, to own him, to make him mine. He feels my desire to lure him closer, and because I want something from him, he doesn't trust me. He only came up to me that one time because my eyes were closed."

"So what are you going to do now?"

"I have to be neutral. I have to let him come to me on his terms."

"Yes." Reva's tone was soft and approving. "Very good, young grasshopper."

Quinn tapped on the sliding glass door and Georgia leaped up, barking. Abby looked at the clock. "Damn, I'm sorry, Reva. I have to go. I was supposed to meet Quinn outside five minutes ago, and now he's knocking on the door."

"Okay, bye. Thank you, thank you, and good luck. Call me later?"

"Yep, yep," she answered. "I'll call later tonight." And hopefully, the town hall meeting would go so well that Abby would have good news to share.

———————

Abby ended the call, then looked up at Quinn. "Sorry I'm late. Aunt Reva called to wish us good luck."

"No problem." Actually, it would be a problem if they got there late and had to park a long way from the courthouse. But telling her that wouldn't help the situation any. He jingled his keys. "You ready?"

"Yes." She followed him to the back door. "No... Wait. Where's my purse?" She scanned the kitchen, then widened the search to the living room, anxiety apparent in her stiff posture and frantic movements.

He knew she must be worried about getting up in front of the city council and speaking at the town hall today. "You know, you really don't have to say anything at the meeting, if it makes you this nervous. Edna will be there, and she'll be happy to go to bat again. Plus, after the article Sara wrote in the flyer, we have almost a thousand signatures of people who want Bayside Barn to stay open. I think we've done everything we can do."

Abby ran her hands through her hair and came back into the kitchen where she picked up a stack of mail and put it down again. "I can't find my purse."

Quinn glanced at his watch. They should've left by now. "Where did you see it last?"

"If I knew that, I wouldn't be looking for it," she snapped. "Would I?"

He pocketed his keys and took her in his arms. Her heart thundered against his. "Calm down a second and think."

She took a breath. "Oh." He felt a flood of relief go through her body. She relaxed and smiled, then gave him a quick kiss. "I remember now."

She retrieved her purse from Reva's bedroom, and they headed out after closing the dog door to keep Georgia in the house. As Quinn drove to the courthouse, he noticed Abby's hands twisting in her lap. He reached out and took her left hand in his. "Why so nervous?"

She clutched his hand. "I don't know. I have a bad feeling about this."

"It'll be fine," he assured her, though he was far from feeling that way himself. Yes, they had a boatload of signatures, and Edna had drummed up a bunch of concerned citizens to show up and cheer for their side. But JP hadn't been sitting around doing nothing all this time, either. God only knew what kind of production he'd put on at the meeting.

"What if it's not fine?" With her hand in his, Abby couldn't wring her fingers in her lap, but she chewed on a fingernail instead. "Maybe we should've told Reva to come. What if we need her here? What if it all goes wrong?"

"If it goes wrong, we'll find another way to fight." He knew enough dirt on JP to smear his reputation, but since they'd once been business partners, any dirt he slung would blow back on him. He hoped it wouldn't come to that.

Quinn drove around the courthouse block looking for a parking place. As he'd feared, he would have to go farther afield. People stood in clusters on the sidewalk outside the building, and it looked like a line was forming to get inside. Abby squeezed his fingers. "Oh, no."

He squeezed back. "It's a good thing. These people are all here to support Bayside Barn." Some of them even had signs: *Save Bayside Barn,* and *I'm a Bayside Barn Buddy!* and *Bayside Barn Buddies, Unite!*

By the time he parked and they walked a couple blocks to the courthouse, the doors had opened and the most of the crowd had streamed inside. "What if we can't get in?" Abby worried as they took their place at the end of the line.

"We'll get in. Hand me your phone. I'll text Mack." He didn't have Mack's info in his phone, but he knew it was in hers. She was shaking visibly, her arms crossed over her purse. He gently took her phone from the side pocket. "What's the code to unlock your screen?"

At the X-ray machines, a reply came through from Mack: Edna is saving your places in the front row When they made it past security, Quinn held Abby's hand and began to thread their way through the crowd toward the courtroom. Inside, Tammy Goodson, the city council president, was praising the high turnout of Magnolia Bay citizens and welcoming newcomers from an out-of-town investment group who would be making a presentation.

Quinn led Abby down the packed center aisle where people were still standing and whispering as they tried to figure out where to sit. The front row had a printed sign taped to the end of the pew: Reserved for Speakers. Edna hadn't taken any chances, though. She had her voluminous purse and a briefcase bag spread out around her to save room for them.

A flush of shame and foreboding prickled Quinn's skin when he saw JP and several dark-suited minions on the other end of the front row. Quinn subtly pushed Abby ahead of him and made a motion for Edna to scoot down; he didn't want to be sitting any nearer than necessary to his old nemesis.

Quinn wondered whether he should have called JP and confronted him before now. Quinn had kept his promise to call his contacts in the construction business, but none of them knew anything about JP's plans beyond what he'd told the whole town at the last meeting.

Abby patted Edna's thigh and waved discreetly to Mack, who sat across the room with the other city council members. Now that they'd made it into the courtroom, her anxiety seemed to have subsided. Quinn took her hand, and she looked at him with a tremulous smile. Still nervous, that smile said, but holding steady and feeling hopeful.

President Tammy invited proponents of Bayside Barn to step forward and talk. Abby hopped up as if she'd been stung and took a stack of index cards from her purse with shaking fingers. As President Tammy introduced Abby to the crowd, Abby hurried to the podium—clearly terrified, but just as clearly eager to get it over with.

"My aunt, Reva Curtis, along with her husband, Grayson, opened Bayside Barn twenty years ago, making it their life mission to teach children—from Magnolia Bay to as far away as New Orleans—the importance of respect for the animals with which we share this earth." She took a deep breath, squared her shoulders, and settled in. "Together, they built the barn and renovated the old farmhouse on the property he inherited from his grandparents. Sadly, Grayson passed away two years ago, but Reva has continued to fulfill their mission at Bayside Barn.

"Not only does the barn offer valuable educational opportunities for the children of Magnolia Bay and surrounding parishes, but it serves as a safe haven for lost and abandoned animals of the community. Though Magnolia Bay lacks an official animal shelter—something Reva has long been advocating for—Bayside Barn has fulfilled that need." Abby took a shuddering breath and sent Quinn a panicked look. He gave her a thumbs-up sign and an encouraging nod.

"Whenever my aunt Reva sees a need, she doesn't wait to be told how she can help. She always takes it on herself to do the next right thing. That's why she can't be here today, because she is on sabbatical this summer in order to complete her education and certification in wildlife rehabilitation. So you see, even now, as some people are trying to take away her ability to help this community through the education and outreach opportunities offered by Bayside Barn, Reva is still working to improve her knowledge and to expand the ability of Bayside Barn to serve this community."

She stacked her index cards and set them aside. Sweeping a glance around the room, she met Quinn's eyes and Edna's and—Quinn thought—JP's. Then she looked at the city council members, one by one. "I know that everyone in this room knows the right thing to do. I just hope you'll find it in your hearts to do it. Thank you."

Except for JP and his cronies, everyone in the courtroom applauded, and many of them stood. Some in Abby's path back to the bench patted her shoulder, and a couple even leaned close to kiss her cheek. Flushed with relief, she sat next to Quinn and grabbed his hand, squeezing hard. He held her hand to his lips and kissed her knuckles. "Proud of you."

Quinn could feel JP shooting daggered glances his way from the other end of the bench. If JP hadn't known he was here before, he did now. Knowing JP's vindictive streak as well as he did, Quinn felt his skin prickle with apprehension.

Edna squeezed past and gave a speech, this time handing out dozens of slick-looking photos she'd had laminated onto card stock. She presented a thick sheaf of the signatures they'd gathered from hundreds of people who agreed that Bayside Barn should continue to be exempt from the no-farm-animals-within-city-limits rule, even though the city's limits had sprawled over the years to encompass the farm within its boundaries.

At least a dozen more people got up and talked about the positive impact Bayside Barn had made on them, their children, or their grandchildren.

Then, JP stood. Straightening his tie, he swaggered to the podium. His minions silently followed, carrying framed posters that they set up on easels around the room. Quinn's heart thumped against his chest like someone hammering at a closed door.

Holy crap.

They'd brought architectural renderings of a huge hotel and marina complex. One of the minions set up a projector screen that showed a map of the area as it existed now, with a drawing of the proposed complex superimposed over it.

Quinn heard a buzzing in his ears as JP used a PowerPoint presentation to illustrate each point. He explained that under his plan—for which he had now secured ample funding from out-of-state investors—the handful of estates on Winding Water Way would be leveled and the high ground built up even higher for a hotel complete with restaurants, shops, bars, and conference spaces to rival that of the finer New Orleans hotels. The cat's-claw forest—once acquired—would be the site of an exclusive golf course that would bring in plenty of tourists with money to spend. The bayside acreage would be the site of a marina large enough to house thirty large yachts, with dry storage for twice that number. The marshy inlets along the shore would be dredged to accommodate the large vessels.

JP talked about the millions of tourist dollars that would be added to the economy of Magnolia Bay, the hundreds of jobs that would be created. "So, you see," he concluded, "it's not so much about whether Bayside Barn should have its cute little furry animals within the city limits; it's about whether Bayside Barn should exist at all.

"Yes, it's been wonderful all these years. Yes, we all love it. But how many of you sitting out there would rather live in a thriving community with the ample jobs and infrastructure and shopping opportunities this complex will bring? Right now in Magnolia Bay, downtown stores are closing and college graduates are moving away to get jobs elsewhere. This town, my friends, is dying, and I am proposing a plan to resuscitate it.

"We have it on good authority that the owners of the bayside property and the acreage across Winding Water Way are eager to sell. I have also spoken to the owners of the two properties adjacent to Bayside Barn, and they've both agreed to consider an offer." Heat flared in Quinn's face at the innuendo that he'd secretly been negotiating with JP, and he felt Abby stiffen beside him.

JP looked right at Quinn and delivered the zinger: "One of those landowners is even a local contractor, and I've chosen him to oversee the project." Abby jerked her hand from his and glared, crossing her arms. Edna stared at him wide-eyed, a disbelieving look on her face.

"All that remains, good people," JP said, rubbing his palms together, "is for us to settle on fair terms with the landholders, which we will, of course, extend to the owner of Bayside Barn. Or…" He shrugged and spread his hands wide, sending a charming grin to the city council members. "We can buy up everything around them, then claim eminent domain for the good of the community and force them out."

Chapter 22

ABBY WAITED TILL THEY GOT OUTSIDE THE BUILDING TO FLY AT Quinn, barely restraining herself from shoving him in the chest. "What the hell was he talking about? You're in negotiations to sell your estate to that slimeball? And you're planning to *work* for that snake? After he sold you down the river? What the hell, Quinn?"

Edna stood beside Abby, a stalwart pillar of strength with her arms crossed over her ample bosom.

"No, it's not true." Quinn's handsome face held a sincere, pleading expression. "I did talk to JP, but it wasn't at all the way he described."

Abby wished she hadn't seen enough pleading expressions on another handsome, lying face to know better than to fall for it. "Are you saying that you told him to get lost, and he misunderstood that to mean, *Let's talk money*?"

"He offered to buy the estate. I didn't accept."

"But you didn't refuse, either, did you?"

He winced. "Not exactly, but—"

"And what about the contractor job? Big-shot overseer of the whole operation? That's a huge step up for you, isn't it?"

"I didn't accept—"

"Yeah, yeah. You didn't accept, but you didn't say no, either, right?"

Quinn hesitated just a tick too long.

"That's it," Abby said. "I'm done."

"Abby, it was a long time ago. He called out of the blue, and—"

Abby turned away from Quinn. "Edna, can you give me a ride home?"

"Sure thing, honey."

Quinn touched Abby's arm, and she shrugged him off. "I really don't want to look at you right now," she said over her shoulder. "Much less hear your excuses. Please go away."

He didn't, but she did. She left him standing on the sidewalk in front of the courthouse. Edna, bless her heart, hooked her arm in Abby's and towed her in the direction of Edna's car.

They didn't talk much on the way to the car, or even once they got in.

Edna started the car. "If he's consorting with the enemy, you're well shed of him. Fasten your seat belt."

"I know," Abby replied. "But it still hurts."

"I know it does." Driving like the old lady she was, Edna backed slowly into the line of traffic leaving the courthouse, making all the cars behind her stand still for far too long. "It'll hurt for a while, and then it'll hurt less, and after that it'll stop hurting. That's the way life goes."

That was about all they could find to say about that.

Edna steered around the town square and headed toward Bayside Barn. "Are you gonna call your aunt Reva and let her know what happened?"

"God, I don't know." Abby flung her head back against the headrest and plowed her fingers through her hair. She felt like a failure and an unwitting coconspirator who'd unknowingly invited the enemy into their camp. Not only that, she'd had sex with him. "What will I say?"

"Well…" Edna stopped at a light and put her blinker on. The *ticky-ticky* sound emphasized the silence while she thought. When the light changed, she made the left turn and spoke. "I think you should tell her exactly what happened. We presented our case, and the opposing side presented their case, and now we'll have to wait till the next meeting to see what the city council decides."

"And what about Quinn, and what he did?"

"We don't really know what he did, do we?" They had reached

the county road leading out of town, and Edna set the cruise control for about fifteen miles under the speed limit. "We've heard some alarming innuendoes, but what do we know for sure? I think we should stick with what we know and wait till we figure out the rest. Why bother her with supposition?"

"I guess you're right."

"Why don't you call her right now? Get it over with. I'm sure she's anxious to hear what happened."

Abby tried to call, but only got to leave a voicemail. "Hey, Reva. The town hall thing went as well as could be expected. We presented our case, the developers presented theirs, and a bunch of people came to give their opinions. I think we had a lot more people on our side than they had on theirs, so that was good. The council will discuss it at their next meeting, and they'll tell us what they decided at the next town hall. Mack said he'd call you later tonight and tell you more. Okay, that's it. Love you. Talk to you soon."

She ended the call and sighed. "Done."

Edna reached over and patted her leg. "There. That wasn't so bad, was it?"

Quinn picked up Sean after the town hall meeting as planned. They didn't have dinner with Abby as planned. Quinn had gathered the courage to text Abby to ask if they were still on for dinner, and he got his answer in her decision to ignore his text. So he'd taken Sean out to dinner instead, and they spent the evening at the pool house killing zombies on the Xbox while Quinn watched the lights go out next door.

"I kind of miss seeing Abby," Sean said, keeping his eyes on the screen and his thumbs working the controller. "Maybe we should go over there and say hi or something."

Quinn cleared his throat. "I think she's gone to bed already. The lights are out." Since Sean was sleeping over, the plan had been for him and Quinn to spend the night at the pool house. But they'd both gotten used to sharing meals with Abby. "She was pretty tired after that town hall meeting." That was the excuse he'd given, and Sean had accepted it, saying, "Just us guys, then," with an easygoing grin.

Quinn wondered whether Abby had made the big pot of spaghetti they'd shopped for.

A small shadow scratched at the glass door. Sean dropped the controller and hopped up. "Griff! Can he come in, Dad? Can he sleep in my bed? I'll fix him a litter box full of sand—I can use the pan you mix grout in and some of the mortar sand you have out back. He won't be a problem, I promise."

Without Sean's help, the zombies won, and Quinn turned off the Xbox. "I don't guess Abby would mind."

Sean opened the door and scooped up the heavy cat, who immediately started purring. "Text her and let her know," Sean said as he stroked Griff's broad head. "I don't want her to worry."

After that first text was met with silence, Quinn had hoped to give Abby some space before communicating with her again. He figured he'd stay busy with Sean through the weekend and try again on Monday. But Sean was right; if they were going to keep Griff inside, he should let Abby know. Anyhow, the lights were out, so she wouldn't see the text till morning, unless for some reason she woke in the night and wondered where the cat was.

Hey, Abby, he typed. Griff wanted to come inside, and Sean wants him to spend the night. Hope that's okay. He hesitated a second, then typed another line. Hope you're okay.

Sean made up the promised litter pan, then took a bowl of water and another bowl of chopped-up lunch meat to his room. He picked up the hefty, loud-purring feline and hovered in the living room doorway. "G'night, Dad."

"Good night, Sean. Close your door, please. Griff has a bad history of peeing on my stuff, and I don't want him to repeat it. If he pees, it better be in that litter box."

"Yup," Sean answered. "I'll keep my door closed. But he'll be good." He rubbed Griff's head and walked away, talking in a low, baby-talk tone. "Won't you be good, Griff? Yes, you will. You'll be a very good boy."

Quinn got ready for bed and filled a big glass with ice and water. But no matter how much water he drank, he couldn't get rid of a bad taste like old dust in his mouth. He probably should've told Sean that he and Abby had argued. Because Sean would expect to help out at the farm tomorrow; he had always enjoyed doing the barn chores and hanging out with the animals, especially since Quinn paid him a small wage for the time he spent helping out.

Saturday morning, Quinn heard the donkeys braying at daylight, and wished he still had the ability to go over there and feed them. He and Elijah had developed a relationship; he'd started giving the donkey a bite of his granola bar every morning, and that gesture of goodwill had won over the strong-willed, spirited equine who would now follow him anywhere.

As Sean slept in and Quinn sipped substandard coffee by the pool, he didn't know whether to be pissed at Abby for not listening to his explanation, or pissed at himself for creating this situation to begin with. He decided to go with a little of both. He had definitely screwed up, but she should have heard him out and let him explain. Melissa had perfected the art of walling herself off and refusing to listen to reason. He hadn't thought that of Abby, but maybe he was wrong. Maybe every woman alive had a tipping point past which no man could crawl with an apology for bad behavior.

Maybe he had a knack for finding that tipping point.

Abby stepped outside and reached for the morning's paper delivery, then squeaked in surprise when Wolf leaped down from one of the pool chaises, where he'd apparently slept last night. They stood staring at each other, until Georgia charged past Abby and leaped up to lick Wolf's mouth.

Abby picked up the paper and held it to her chest. "Thanks for this," she said quietly. "You're a good dog, Wolf." And remembering what Reva had said about Wolf's suspicion of Abby's ulterior motives, she turned and went back into the house to pour a cup of coffee.

She sat at the kitchen table and opened the paper, laying aside the rubber band that had held it in place. A double-page spread in the middle of the paper made her take a breath—and choke on her coffee. Eyes watering, she coughed helplessly while the headline that took up half a page swam before her:

Citizens Clash with Developers over Plan to Build a Hotel and Marina Complex with Golf Course on Bay

Abby scanned the article—at least, she started to scan the article—but in no time, she was reading, absorbing every word, every nuance. The article read like an in-depth investigative journalism piece that dug deep and presented an unbiased account of both sides. It listed pros and cons. The author—Abby skipped down to find the byline…Sara Prather, of course—delved into facts, figures, and projections. She wrote about the potential of financial gains for the community, but also about the potentially negative impacts on the environment. She called on city officials to conduct environmental impact studies and background checks before relying on the word of an unknown group of investors.

Jefferson Pearson, the real estate developer heading the project, was quoted as saying that he was given an anonymous tip about a strip of bayside land that would soon be available for sale between the old boat ramp and Winding Water Way.

Anonymous tip. Jefferson Pearson, otherwise known as Quinn's friend and ex-business partner. The same Jefferson Pearson who had offered Quinn a cushy job after he had received an *anonymous tip*. Abby felt a tornado of anger swirl up from the soles of her bare feet to career through her body and explode through the top of her head. Quinn hadn't just considered being involved in JP's plans; he had instigated them himself.

"That fucker!" Abby jumped to her feet and yelled the words out loud. "That fucking fucker!" Anger propelled her out the back door with such force that Wolf scrambled around the side of the house to his safe den under the porch, and even Georgia tucked her tail and crouched as if under attack. Abby had every intention of storming next door and giving Quinn a heaping helping of what for until she heard Sean yell, "Cannonball!"

A huge splash in the pool next door followed by the sound of Quinn and Sean laughing together brought Abby to her senses. Yes, it was bad that Quinn had probably told JP about the bay-side land. But Quinn couldn't have known what JP would make of that tip. He couldn't have known JP would go so far as to start that petition against Bayside Barn. Quinn wouldn't have put so much time and money into renovating that estate if he'd known all along that it would be razed to the ground. He'd been stupid, and he'd done wrong, but he wasn't evil. Abby needed to cool her jets, give herself the weekend to calm down and think rationally. Maybe Quinn's involvement in JP's scheme wasn't as bad as she thought.

Quinn loaded a small, soft-sided cooler with soft drinks, bottled water, not-quite-stale chips, and cold pizza left over from lunch. Then he and Sean hauled the paddleboards and all the related paraphernalia to the boat landing. They got all the gear situated under the bungee nets on the front of the boards, then put the boards in and started paddling out. A bank of dark clouds hung over the distant horizon, but the weather report claimed zero chance of rain.

"Dad," Sean said, his voice thoughtful. "Do you think they'll really build a hotel here?"

"I don't know, Son." Quinn thought of all the damage construction would do to this wild and beautiful space. The developers would fill in the marshes and build high retaining walls along the bayou, which they'd dredge out to allow large, deep-drafted yachts to come in. "I hope not."

"Look, Dad!" Sean pointed up into a tree on the far side of the bank. A bald eagle sat on the highest branch of a towering cypress tree. The nest she guarded was a flat platform built from thick twigs and long, woody reeds. "Is that an eagle?"

Quinn treasured the sound of Sean calling him Dad in the same tone he'd used back when he was a young kid whose father was someone he looked up to and admired, but more than that, truly loved. "Yes, that's a bald eagle."

He pointed to another eagle who glided effortlessly in the sky high above them. "That's one, too, flying overhead. He's young, so his head hasn't gone white yet, but it will. Eagles have been making a comeback around here, especially along these marshland inlets where the fishing is good. Eagles love to fish."

Sean watched the eagles in awe. He sat relaxed on his board, his attention on the world of plants and animals that went on about their lives, unconcerned with the two humans drifting past in the dappled shade of the small bayou. Sean let the paddle rest on his crossed knees. "I bet they'll leave if a hotel gets built here."

"Not just the eagles, but all the animals who live here now. Even old Goliath, who's probably been living here for the last umpteen years." Quinn felt a long-fingered grasp of breathtaking fear clench around his heart. "I'm afraid you're right, and I hope it never happens. Because if developers move in, the animals will have to move out."

Move out sounded like the animals had a choice, another place to go. When the stark truth was that they wouldn't move out, they'd just die, because the ecosystem that sustained them would be destroyed, and they'd have no place else to go. If that happened, Quinn hoped to God that Sean would never find out that the daddy he was once again beginning to look up to had helped JP get his clutches on this unspoiled land that abounded with life.

Sean pointed to a long, black snake that draped like a Christmas tree garland over a low-hanging branch that hung out over the water. "What kind of snake is that?"

Quinn paddled closer to get a better look. "It's a black racer. You can tell because his body is long and slender, and he's all black except for a white chin."

Sean paddled closer, too, but kept behind Quinn's board when he examined the snake. "Is it poisonous?"

"Well, snakes aren't poisonous. Plants are poisonous; snakes are venomous. But no, he's not venomous. He's harmless to humans, but he eats frogs and bird eggs and even small venomous snakes. He's a good snake."

"Mom says that only a dead snake is a good snake."

Quinn nudged Sean's board and turned them both back into the bayou's central flow. "Your mom isn't wrong about much, but I'd beg to differ with her on that point. Even venomous snakes have their place in the world, and they won't bother you if you don't bother them."

"Uncle Jim says that a water moccasin will come after you. He says they're aggressive and territorial."

Quinn's older brother, Jim, was a hunter and outdoorsman who loved to tell tall tales of daring and adventure, and Jim's tales got bigger with each retelling. The story Jim liked to tell about that event bore little resemblance to what actually happened, and Quinn knew because he'd been there, an unwilling witness to a soul-sickening attack that he, as the younger brother, had no power to stop. "Something you should probably know about your uncle Jim: he'd climb a tree to tell a lie when he could stand on the ground and tell the truth."

"He said that when he was hunting in a swamp one day, a water moccasin came after him and tried to bite him."

They hadn't been hunting so much as traipsing through the woods with the air rifles they'd gotten for Christmas. And when Jim saw the snake and decided that its skin would make a good hat band, all Quinn had been able to think at the time was that the poor snake was standing its ground in an effort to defend itself when fleeing didn't work. "Any animal will fight back when you're trying to kill it."

"I get that," Sean replied. "People want to kill what they fear, and any animal that's being attacked has a right to defend itself."

They drifted along with the current, and the serenity of the slow-moving water under the floating clouds seeped into the open pores of Quinn's spirit. He realized that he could see himself as the snake, being attacked and forced to fight back. He could also see himself as a human driven by his internal fears to kill anything he couldn't conquer. He wondered if Abby's animal communication bullshit was getting to him; then he decided that if it was, that was okay with him.

After a half hour of silent paddling through the lush bayou, Sean spoke up. "Is Abby expecting us for dinner? It seems like feeding time for the barn critters."

Abby had always used the term *critters*. That reminded Quinn too much of the steeped-in-the-South colloquialisms he'd spent a lifetime trying to escape. "She doesn't need so much help since she had her cast removed."

"But I miss the animals. And I miss Abby—especially her cooking."

Quinn paddled around the corner of a spit of land, avoiding a fallen tree that stuck up out of the shallow water at the edge of the boggy island. "I miss her, too. But she doesn't need our help anymore since her foot is better." A couple of turtles plopped off a dead branch into the water. "I thought you and I would hang out, just the two of us, and work on the estate's renovation this weekend."

Sean paddled harder to catch up. "But I want to see Wolf before I go home."

Go home. Those two words speared Quinn's heart. His son's home should be with *him*. But what he wanted more than having his son with him was having his son happy. "I'll text Abby and see if she can use your help with the evening feed."

"Yeah, sure. Text her now, so she'll know we're almost there." They skimmed along the coastline of the boggy island, where the mingled scent of wild azaleas and honeysuckle filled the air. Sean paddled hard to pass Quinn and take the lead. "Maybe we can both do the evening feed and then have dinner with Abby like we've been doing. If she doesn't feel like cooking, we could bring some takeout."

"If it's all right with you, I'll stay next door and get ready for tomorrow's project." Quinn knew it'd be awkward between him and Abby until they'd had a chance to talk, and he didn't want Sean to pick up on any angst. "But I'll see if Abby can use your help." Quinn dug his phone from the bungee net and sent a text to Abby: Sean wants to help with the evening feed.

A second later, he got an answer:

Sean is welcome to come to the farm anytime, and his help is much appreciated. I won't mention anything about what's going on between you and me. If he wants to stay for dinner, I'll make spaghetti. Make any excuse you want about why you can't come. I'll send him home with a plate for you.

He texted back. Excuse made. Thanks for letting Sean come. It means a lot to him—and even more to me. I hope we can talk on Monday.

She didn't respond at first, but after a while, a terse message pinged through. I'll be busy till 7:00 p.m. on Monday. I guess you can come then.

Chapter 23

EARLY MONDAY MORNING WHILE ABBY WAS IN THE BARN feeding critters, she heard Quinn's motorcycle rev up and roar down the drive. The sound reverberated off the barn walls as if the motorcycle was inside the barn instead of on the patio next door. No wonder the animals always yelled whenever Quinn drove up on his annoying, loud Harley.

Too bad his hot bod in those motorcycle leathers—and also outside of them—had convinced her to let him into her bed. Too bad his attentiveness in bed—and also outside of it—had convinced her to let him into her life. Too bad he'd lured her into trusting him before she'd received convincing proof that he wasn't trustworthy.

She knew from his early-morning text (which she'd ignored) that he was going into NOLA to measure a kitchen for a new custom cabinet project. He planned to come back in the afternoon and was looking forward to seeing her that evening.

But she didn't care where he went or what he did or when he came back or what he was looking forward to, because she had vowed two days ago to cut him out of her life, and she meant to stick by her resolution. She would hear him out—because she had agreed to in a moment of weakness—but then she would show him the door.

Sean, on the other hand, would be welcome as long as he wanted to keep coming around and helping out at the farm. He loved the animals and seemed to need the nurturing they provided. Plus, he liked Abby's cooking, and she enjoyed cooking for someone who enjoyed it.

In the barn's open doorway, Georgia gave Wolf's ears a thorough cleaning while he stretched out on the concrete in a patch of sunlight. When his ears were done, she moved on to give tender attention to the large, scabby wound in his side. "Get a room, you two," Abby groused.

As usual, they ignored her.

She shoveled another load of steaming pony poop into the wheelbarrow and tried to hate Quinn and his loud, annoying Harley. And she knew that she should hate them both. But her downfall now, as before, had nothing to do with reality and everything to do with her stupid, unrealistic, romantic wishes of what could be, which always stopped her from seeing the undeniable, realistic, verifiable truth of what actually was.

Georgia leaped to her feet and barked at a battered pickup coming down the drive. Wolf fled for the safety of his den. Abby brushed her hands on the back pockets of her shorts and went out to greet Mack. "Hey, what's up?"

"Nothing good," Mack grumbled, his voice deep and dark and disgusted. "I've come to give you a heads-up about something that's brewing down at City Hall."

Abby's heart fluttered like a panicked chicken fleeing from a fox. She put a hand on her chest to calm its hectic beating. "What?"

Mack ran a hand through his short dark hair, making it stand on end. "Can we go inside?"

"Sure." Abby led the way to the house. Inside, she took down two glasses and filled them with ice and water. "Let's sit at the bar."

"I'm kind of dusty," he protested.

"These barstools can take it." She set their water glasses on the counter. "I'm dusty, too, from shoveling stalls."

Her nerves had calmed a bit from doing the small, homey chore of filling glasses for herself and her guest, but the second she sat at the bar, the panicked chicken in her chest started fluttering again. Mack perched his butt on the barstool next to hers and turned the water glass in his hands. He cleared his throat and gave her a mournful look full of pity and regret.

"Go ahead." She sipped her water and swallowed to make it go down past the lump of fear in her throat. "Tell me."

"The city council is all—pretty much all—on your aunt Reva's side." He cleared his throat again and took a sip of water. "The mayor, however, believes that the presence of farm animals in the city limits could present a health hazard for the citizens of Magnolia Bay."

Abby scoffed. "That's bullshit. First of all, the farm is inspected yearly by the USDA. Second, the only people who might possibly live near enough to care are the Grants next door, who signed the petition to allow us to keep the animals. And Quinn, who's planning to sell out, but at least he signed the petition."

Mack winced at the last part of Abby's statement. "Well, here's the thing…"

Abby's neck prickled. "What thing?"

"I did some digging around, trying to figure out how the petition to rescind got started." He cleared his throat. Again.

"Are you coming down with something?" Abby snapped. "Drink some water and spit out whatever you came here to say."

One side of Mack's mouth quirked up in an almost-smile. "You sound just like your aunt Reva."

"Out with it," Abby repeated.

"It looks like Quinn complained to his real estate agent about the noise over here when y'all were still doing school field trips. He was worried that having a farm next door would impact the resale value of his property, so he told her to do whatever it took to fix the problem."

Abby pursed her lips and nodded, her back teeth clenched against the angry words that wanted to spew out. "So Quinn started the petition."

"Not directly. He complained to his real estate agent, and she talked to JP, giving him the idea of buying up the land around here and building that complex. JP took the ball and ran with it. Getting rid of Bayside Barn was the first step in his plan, step two being the quiet buyout of your elderly neighbors on the other side, step three being, of course, making Quinn an offer he'd be a fool to refuse."

"And step four being that if Reva couldn't keep the farm animals, she'd be forced to sell out and go somewhere else?"

"If she wanted to keep her farm animals, she'd have to move. And everyone knows Reva well enough to know that she wouldn't rehome her animals. They mean more to her than the land."

"Even though she loves this place and it has been in Grayson's family for generations."

Mack nodded. "Even so."

"And I guess that once JP owned this block, he'd be able to force the owners of the bayside land to sell?"

"He wouldn't have to force them. The old man isn't long for this world, and his wife won't let her shirttail hit her back before she sells everything they own. She hates it here."

"So Reva's the only one who needed a little extra nudge, and because of Quinn, JP knew exactly how to do that."

"True. And if Edna hadn't stood up at the town hall and made such a fuss, the mayor would've quietly pushed it through despite the council's objections."

"He can do that?"

"Yep. He can veto any decision the council makes. He would've preferred to do it without a lot of opposition from the townspeople, but you know what they say about money talking."

"Well, shit." Abby's nervous heart had stopped fluttering; it seemed to have stopped beating entirely. "What can we do?"

Mack shook his head. "I wish I knew. I guess you'd better call Reva, though. Let her know all this is happening."

Abby put her head in her hands. "I feel like this is all my fault."

"Naw." Mack patted her back. "Of course it isn't. How could it be?"

She pulled her hair back off her face and let it fall again. "I let the donkeys get loose. I let the cat pee in Quinn's toolbox. I let a bad kid climb over the fence during a field trip. Quinn complained about the noise when we had field trips, but I didn't do anything to address his concerns."

"What the hell could you have done? Tell sixty kids to be quiet all day long?"

She shrugged. "More like ninety kids most days, but yeah."

"This is not your fault. The same thing would've happened if Reva had been here."

"Maybe, but I still feel bad." She didn't elaborate on the main reason she felt bad—because she'd slept with the enemy.

———

Monday evening at 6:59 p.m., Quinn stood at Abby's door wearing clean jeans and a crisply ironed shirt, his hair still slightly damp from the shower, carrying a perfectly chilled bottle of expensive wine just waiting for the cork to pop. She'd had the entire weekend to fume, and he hoped that after a couple of glasses of wine, she'd be ready to listen to reason.

He tapped on the sliding glass door. Wolf came slinking around the corner of the house to sit beside him. Quinn reached down and caressed the dog's head. "You need to let somebody give you a bath," he advised the dog. "I hope you won't take this the wrong way, but you smell like a dog."

Wolf grinned a canine grin while his long, plumy tail swished back and forth along the concrete patio. Quinn tapped on the door again, then peered inside. The living room and kitchen lights were off. A light shone from Abby's bedroom, but the door was closed, which would explain why Georgia hadn't rushed out the dog door to greet him.

"Maybe Abby's in the bathtub," he said to the grinning dog. "Maybe she's still getting dressed." But something about the lights being off in the main part of the house made Quinn's skin shiver. He glanced at his watch; he wasn't early. He was spot-on, exactly on time.

He thought about going inside; he even tried the door, but it was locked. He checked the text from Abby inviting him—well, okay, grudgingly giving him permission—to come today. Surely he hadn't made a mistake on the timing.

A new text had come through. He read it, and everything behind his ribs—heart, lungs, everything—dropped through his rib cage and hit the concrete with a crash: Don't come.

Abby's incomprehensible message read the same way the second time he scanned the terse line. *Don't come.*

He set the bottle down on the patio and texted back: Why not? Is everything okay? Are you okay?

He had enough sense to figure out the answers to those questions. But he hoped to God there was some other explanation. Maybe she was sick. Maybe she'd come down with a cold or something that she didn't want him to catch. His immune system was working just fine, and he wasn't afraid of catching whatever little bug she might have. Already imagining the scene in which he had to walk away from Abby with nothing but an uncorked bottle of wine in his hand, he knocked on the door, harder this time. And when nothing happened, he knocked on the laundry room door, the one with the dog door in the bottom, the one closest to the guest bedroom.

Georgia barked from the bedroom, her high-pitched alarm yodel. Something could really be wrong with Abby. Meningitis, food poisoning, a virulent flu—okay, it wasn't flu season—but… Something *could* be wrong. He tried to convince himself that anything could be wrong.

Anything but the distinct and maybe unavoidable possibility that she was done with him.

He banged on the door. Georgia's alarm yodel rose in frequency and tripled in volume. After a second, he heard a door slam and pounding footsteps coming his way before Abby yanked the door open. "Did you not get my text?"

"I got your text. I'm worried about you. Are you okay?" She didn't look okay. Her eyelids were puffy and red-rimmed, her nose was pink, and her skin was flushed as if she'd been sleeping hot. Her wavy hair was even crazier than usual, the waves ending in little corkscrews on the ends. She wore a stretched-out slouchy tank top over Daffy Duck boxer shorts. "Are you coming down with something?"

She put a hand on her hip. "I'm coming down with a bad case of getting over your stupid, lying, betraying ass. That's what I'm coming down with."

"Oh." So just as he'd feared, she wasn't sick, just sick of him. He took a step back, into the haze of mosquitoes and gnats and all manner of flying bugs that circled around the porch lights. "Can I come in so we can talk?"

She took a step back and slammed the door in his face. Wolf whined and crouched low to the ground, but stayed by Quinn's side. "Thanks for the backup, buddy," he said, reaching down to stroke the dog's ears. "I think I'm gonna need all the help I can get."

He knocked on the door again. "Abby, please let me in," he called through the closed door. "I understand that you're mad at me. I think I understand why. But I know you're not the kind of person who'd turn me away without giving me a chance to explain."

"You don't know what kind of person I am," she challenged in an angry, loud voice he heard easily. He was surprised it didn't rattle the windows. "But if you keep standing there, you might just find out."

"Just give me five minutes," he pleaded. Wolf's furry body pressed against his leg, giving comfort. "I don't know what you've heard, but—"

She opened the door and speared him with a look so filled with hatred that he gasped.

"I know everything." Her face was tight with anger, her voice filled with bitterness.

Shit. He should have confessed before, when they could have laughed—okay, maybe not laughed, but… "I know this looks bad, but—"

"I don't care what you have to say." She stepped forward and poked him in the chest with her finger. "You don't get a chance to explain." She poked him again, probably wishing that her finger was a gun driving a bullet into his heart. "Because of you…" She poked him again, pushing him back a step. "Because of you, my aunt is going to lose everything."

She didn't have to poke him again; this time, he stepped back, feeling her anger pour over him like a raging flood. "Because of you, my aunt will have to rehome her animals—which she won't do—or sell the farm that she and her husband built together on the property that has been in his family for generations."

"I'm sorry. I know I—"

She backed up and braced her hands on the doorframe. "I don't need your excuses, Quinn. If you have anything to offer, anything at all, it had better be solutions, not excuses. If you can't do something to reverse this disaster you created, I never want to see you again."

She slammed the door, then turned the dead bolt with a decisive click. "Fix it," she yelled through the closed door. "Fix it, or don't ever step foot on this property again."

Then all the porch lights went out, leaving Quinn alone in the darkness.

But not entirely alone, he realized. Wolf sat beside him, a stalwart companion emanating comfort and acceptance. The glow from the bedroom window gave Quinn just enough light to see the gleam of the wine bottle he'd left sitting on the patio. He picked up the bottle, then petted Wolf on his furry head. "I guess it's just you and me and the wine now, buddy."

Wolf panted agreement.

"You want to come home with me?" He patted his leg and took a step toward the driveway. "Come on, pal." Wolf hung back and looked toward the lighted bedroom window.

"Come on, Wolf." More than anything, Quinn didn't want to be alone tonight to contemplate his many mistakes that had ruined his life up until now and eventually culminated in this moment. He'd been shortsighted and selfish, maybe not just recently; maybe he'd been that way all his life. He probably deserved to be alone, but he didn't want that. Not tonight, and not ever again. He patted his leg, this time adding a little whistle of encouragement. "Come on, buddy. We can have steak for dinner."

Wolf took a couple of steps, then looked back again.

"Fine. Never mind." Quinn didn't deserve companionship, not even that of a stinky half-wolf that smelled like a dog.

Abby's bedroom light went out, plunging everything, even the air in front of Quinn's face, into complete darkness. He fumbled for his phone and used the flashlight function to light the way back to the pool house.

He'd made it some distance down the driveway when he heard the faint sound of Wolf walking behind him, panting and whining softly. Clearly anxious about leaving the farm to follow Quinn, Wolf kept going, even when they left the farm's open gate and turned the corner onto Quinn's property. When Quinn opened the sliding door to the pool house and invited Wolf inside, the dog dropped to his haunches on the concrete and looked back at the dark house next door.

"You don't have to stay," Quinn said. "I get it. I'd rather be there, too, but I'm not welcome anymore."

Wolf lowered his elbows to the ground and put his head on

his paws with a groan. He seemed to understand how it felt to be banished from the lives of people he loved.

———————

Quinn hardly slept that night, and what little sleep he got was riddled with nightmares of driving a pickup downhill with no brakes around hairpin turns—with a load of alligators in the back and Wolf in the passenger seat.

Exactly what his life felt like right now: out of control with a truckload of problems and only one friend in the world, a smelly wolf dog who didn't even trust him enough to come inside the house and get a much-needed bath.

While Quinn twisted in his sheets, he at least had time to twist and turn his Rubik's Cube of problems around and examine potential solutions from every angle. When the prospect of sleep went from elusive to impossible, he turned on his light and got out his legal pad. He hadn't made a list in a long while, but now it seemed imperative. He had to sort out his thoughts and consider his options, so he uncapped his pen and made a list.

1. Sell out now; list the place as-is and be done with it.

But if he did that, JP would snap it up, so he might as well...

2. Call JP, negotiate a high price for the estate, take him up on his job offer, and insist on an advance so I can move away from here immediately.

But if he did that, he'd lose his time with Sean, along with any chance of reconciling with Abby.

3. Call Reva, apologize profusely, beg her to intercede with Abby, and promise to...

But he didn't know what he could promise that would make things right, and besides, he didn't know Reva's cell phone number.

4. Call Mack, get Reva's number, do #3 above.

But he still didn't know what he could promise that would make things right.

5. Continue to renovate the estate and promise Abby the moon if she'll forgive me and move in with me and live happily ever after.

But that wouldn't work unless her aunt Reva still lived next door. And Abby had said that she never wanted to see him again—unless and until he fixed the problem he'd created. Which left him with...

6. Find a way to make sure that Reva's animals can stay at Bayside Barn.

Frustrated and entirely too frazzled to go back to sleep, Quinn got up, got dressed, and made coffee. The shadow of Wolf's form lying just outside the glass door was only slightly darker than the darkness beyond. In another hour, the bay would become visible through the darkness, a pale-gray shimmer in the distance. After that, the sky above the trees would turn a soft pearl pink.

Maybe by the time all that happened, Quinn would've come up with a plan. He sat at the kitchen table, sipped his hot black coffee, and underlined the only possible solution he'd come up with:

6. Find a way to make sure Reva's animals can stay at Bayside Barn.

The solution was unfortunately short on details, and no matter how much he thought and doodled and wrote stupid ideas that he ended up crossing out, he couldn't come up with a viable plan.

What he needed was a change of scenery, something to occupy his mind and his hands just enough to allow his thoughts to sort themselves out. The sky was beginning to turn pink when he took a fresh cup of coffee and his legal pad—in case inspiration struck—out to the main house.

Wolf followed until Quinn went inside. It seemed from the way he acted that he'd never been inside a house before. "Come on, Wolf. It's okay." Quinn snapped his fingers, he whistled, he slapped his leg; none of it was convincing. "Fine. Suit yourself." He went inside and left the door open so at least Wolf could see him.

He was already set up to paint, so he plugged his phone into the Bose speaker, uncapped a five-gallon bucket of paint, and dipped the lightly textured paint roller in. His renovation plan was roughly a top-down model; he had painted all the upstairs rooms and installed new light fixtures throughout. Downstairs, he had installed can lights and painted the ceiling. Now, he was painting the downstairs walls an innocuous warm tan color. The trim and baseboards would be a creamy almost-white, but that would be the last thing he did after refinishing the hardwood floors.

The flooring project would be the most time-consuming, but the paint made the biggest visible difference. This old house was beginning to look like a home, and with every stroke of the paint roller, Quinn imagined what it might be like to live here with Abby.

He took a step back to survey the wall he'd just finished and noticed a flash of movement from the corner of his eye.

Wolf had commando-crawled into the room and now sat like a sphinx, watching Quinn intently. "What?" Quinn asked. "You need an award for coming inside?"

Wolf put his head on his paws and blinked.

"I'll get you something later."

Quinn had just turned to dip the roller again when he heard a footstep on the dusty wooden floor.

"There he is." Abby came into the room and hovered near the door. "I was worried." Georgia whined in delight and rushed up to Wolf, happily licking his face.

Quinn looked around at Abby and tried to keep his face expressionless, even though it hurt like hell to see her being so standoffish. "You're up early."

"Georgia woke me up and insisted that I follow her over here."

Quinn wished he knew what to do or say. Abby seemed just as spooky and afraid as Wolf had been about coming in here. If he turned around, or even said anything about the big-ass elephant standing between them, she might bolt and run. So he turned his back to her and kept painting, and came up with something to say that he hoped would be as neutral as the wall paint. "He followed me back to the pool house last night. Slept outside even though I tried to invite him in."

"He won't come inside my house, either."

He kept painting, sliding the roller along the walls one neat row at a time. "He's in here now though," Quinn said. "Maybe this is a turning point for him."

"I hope so." Abby's voice, Quinn noticed, was just as carefully expressionless as his.

"I guess I should've sent you a text to let you know he was here." But she'd been ignoring most of his texts anyway, so even if it had occurred to him, he probably wouldn't have done it. "Sorry you were worried."

"Not your fault." Her unsaid words, like everything else, hung in the vast void between them. Meanwhile, Georgia and Wolf were all over each other, practically moaning with delight.

"Get a room," Quinn and Abby both said at the same time.

Quinn paused in his painting, but only for a heartbeat.

"Snap," Abby said, her voice sounding weak.

He emptied the roller, then stood with his back to her, wondering what to do next. "This is ridiculous," he said under his breath.

"The walls look good," she said at the same time, not much louder.

He turned around and hung the roller on the edge of the bucket. "Abby, I know you don't want to have anything to do with me, and if that's your decision, I'll have to live with it. But no matter what you decide, we need to talk first."

She crossed her arms, and her luscious, always-smiling mouth went hard. "I don't have anything to say to you until you fix the problem you created for my aunt."

Moving slowly, he reached for a painter's rag and started methodically cleaning his hands. "I understand that's how you feel. However, even though I sat awake most of the night trying to figure out how to do that, I'm coming up empty. For your aunt's sake, if not for mine or yours, I need your help."

Chapter 24

MUCH AS ABBY HATED TO ADMIT IT, QUINN WAS RIGHT. THEY did need to talk. "So talk," she invited. Not very graciously, she had to admit.

"Let's go where we can sit." He gestured toward the pool house, and she led the way, keeping as much space between them as possible. On the patio, he slipped past her and opened the sliding door, then stood aside to let her go in first. So polite. So stilted.

So sad.

Abby's eyes stung with tears she wouldn't allow to fall. She'd cried enough already. How could he have betrayed her the way he did? She'd been closed off, locked up, her wounded heart armored against any further pain. And he'd slowly and methodically dismantled all her efforts at self-protection. Even making her open her heart to his son, whom Quinn could snatch away from her on a whim.

She sat in the center of the small couch, leaving no doubt that Quinn wasn't invited to sit next to her.

Thank God she hadn't let Sean get *too* close.

And at that thought, she heard her indrawn breath stutter. Because she *had* let Sean get too close. She cared what happened to him, and she cared whether she ever got to see him again. Quinn held not only one, but two giant slices of her heart.

"You want water?" Quinn asked from the kitchen. His voice sounded almost—but not quite—normal.

"Yes, please." It would give her something to do, some small shield to hold between herself and Quinn. Between herself and her own feelings, which seemed to be expanding inside her and trying to break out.

Instead of handing the water glass to her, he set it down on the table in front of her. He could tell that she didn't want to touch him.

He'd left the door open for the dogs, but they didn't come in. They lounged by the pool, being obscene with each other. All that unconditional love made her want to... Well, she didn't know what it made her want to do. Forgive him? No. Smack him? Maybe. She couldn't decide.

He sat across from her in the matching chair. "So. You wanted to talk." She agreed it was necessary, but she wasn't about to make it easy for him. "You go first."

"I fucked up." He leaned forward, his forearms propped on his thighs, his fingers linked in front of him. "I complained to my real estate agent about those loud, annoying field trips when I first moved in here, before I'd even met you."

"You complained." She leaned back and crossed her arms. "And your Realtor just decided to take it upon himself to make your problem neighbor disappear."

"Herself."

Abby waved that stupid detail away with a flick of her fingers.

"And no," he continued, his expression earnest. "She didn't just decide to take it upon herself. I told her to do whatever it took to make the problem go away, and I promised her a signing bonus once she helped me sell this place."

Abby crossed her legs and swung one foot, struggling to contain her anger. "And then what? You called your ex-boss—"

"Business partner," he interrupted. "But I—"

"Whatever." She flicked her fingers again and swung her foot harder. "You called JP and cooked up—"

"I didn't—"

She scowled at him and he shut up. "And y'all cooked up a scheme to get rid of Bayside Barn, a scheme you backed out of after you convinced me to have sex with you?"

"Well, in my defense, you didn't take much…" His voice trailed away, probably when he noticed the angry smoke coming out of her ears. He cleared his throat. "I didn't call him; he called me. And we didn't scheme or cook up anything. I told him I would think about what he said and get back to him, just to get him off the phone."

"And you knew all this was about to happen, and you knew that you caused it, but you didn't say anything to me. You lured me in with your helpful-nice-guy act and let me make a fool of myself over you. You lured me in, and all the while, you were lying to me."

"No." His voice sounded gentle and sad. "It wasn't like that." He spread his hands, an unspoken plea for her to listen. "I swear, I didn't put the two things together in my mind. I had blown off steam to my real estate agent, and when I didn't hear back from her, I figured she had ignored me. I had no idea she had spilled everything to JP."

"Well, why didn't you tell me he wanted to buy all the land around us? Didn't you think my aunt had a right to know that?"

"JP's always full of grandiose plans. I didn't think anything would come of it."

"Humph." She swung her foot, percolating on what he'd said. She could see how Quinn might have been too self-involved to have noticed what was going on all around him, or to care how it might impact her aunt. "Okay. I've heard you out." She stood. "I'm going now."

He jumped up and put a hand on her arm, a gentle, don't-go touch. "Can we please try again?"

She shrugged away, and his hand dropped to his side. "You have a big problem to solve before I'll think about that. You can keep me posted on your progress, and I'll help out if I can. And Sean is always welcome at the farm. You can tell him you're too busy to stop what you're doing, and I won't say anything about the current situation. That's the best I can do for you right now."

He put his hands in his pockets. His eyes were serious and sad. "I understand."

She walked out through the open door, and he followed. Georgia put her front paws on Quinn's leg and smiled her snarly grin, wagging her tail. It seemed to Abby that Georgia was asking him to come back to the farm with them. He petted her head, a reluctant no.

Abby turned her back and crossed the pool patio. After a second, she heard Georgia's nails on the concrete as she trotted to catch up.

"Can Wolf stay here with me?" Quinn called out.

"Sure," she called back over her shoulder. "He's not my dog anyway. Never has been."

———————

Quinn tried to go back to painting—and he did; he painted another wall and the stairwell—but he had a hard time settling in. His heartbeat seemed to reverberate under his skin, making him feel jumpy and disconnected. Antsy. Like he needed to be doing something else. "Screw it." He put the lid back on the paint bucket and took the roller and brush outside to rinse with the hose. He had to get out of here and do something different. Get on his motorcycle and let the wind blow through him with a fresh perspective.

Anyway, it was past lunchtime, and his stomach was growling at him.

He ended up at a bayside pub he had ridden past but never had time to stop at. From the outside, the place looked festive but relaxing, with rows of multicolored triangular flags fluttering from the edges of a vine-covered arbor in the morning breeze. Lights that hung from the arbor's beams were turned off now, but the sun sparkled off the bulbs. As he got off his motorcycle, a wind chime he couldn't see made a happy, high-pitched clanking sound.

It took a second for his eyes to adjust to the dim interior. The hostess looked up from her station near the entrance. "Table for one?" She cocked her head, her ponytail swinging. "Or would you rather sit at the bar?"

He glanced at the long bar that faced a wall of windows overlooking the water. A few people sat with their backs to him, but the bar wasn't crowded by any means. "I'll sit at the bar."

She led him to a seat and handed him a menu. While he surveyed the menu, he felt a steady gaze on him and looked to his right.

"Hey, Quinn," Mack said. "How's it going?"

"Abby dumped me." He closed his menu. "How you doing?"

"My wife kicked me out."

Quinn gasped. "Dude. I'm sorry to hear that."

Mack shrugged. "I guess it's just as well. Neither of us was very happy."

"Still, man. That's raw. I'm so sorry. If you need a place to stay, I've got room."

"Thanks, but I'm okay."

"Where you staying?"

"The vet's office. Good thing we kept a full bath and bedroom at the back of the building when we renovated. Figured they'd come in handy if I had to stay overnight to monitor a critical case." He took a swig of his drink. "Didn't figure I'd have to move in."

The bartender came up with a notepad in hand, his pen poised to write. Quinn ordered a loaded burger and fries, then looked over at Mack. "You want another drink?"

Mack nodded, his face glum. "Sure. Straight-up bourbon."

Quinn held up two fingers. "Another for him and one for me, please." He looked at Mack again. "You had anything to eat yet? You gotta eat. Whatever you want; I'm buying."

"Thanks." Mack gave an almost-smile and spoke to the waiter. "I'll have what he ordered."

The food arrived, and while they ate, Quinn told Mack

everything that had happened—everything he'd done—to ruin his relationship with Abby.

"Yeah, I knew already. That was boneheaded," Mack said, his tone neutral and nonjudgmental. "I have to 'fess up that I'm the one who told Abby about the petition. I thought that she and Reva had a right to know what they're up against and why."

"Yeah?" Quinn did a gut check to see how he felt about that news, and decided that he didn't feel any sort of way. Mack was a good guy doing what he thought best. "I guess it was bound to come out sooner or later. How'd you find out?"

"I asked JP how he knew about the land, and he didn't mind telling me. In fact, he didn't mind telling me everything."

"Of course he didn't." JP didn't care about anyone but himself, and he loved to stir up drama and strife.

"What are you gonna do to get back in Abby's good graces?"

"I don't know." Quinn swirled the bourbon in his glass, making the ice cubes clink. "I've got to find a way to convince the powers that be not to force Bayside Barn to shut down."

"The city council is on your side. But the mayor's eyes are dollar-sign green."

"Hard to beat the lure of money." Quinn finished his drink and signaled the bartender for another. "You want another one?" He asked Mack.

"Naw. Two's my limit."

"You gotta go back to work?"

Mack shook his head. "Not unless I get an emergency call. I figured since I lost my wife *and* my office manager this morning, that was cause enough to close early today."

"Both?"

Mack gave Quinn a droll look. "Same person."

"Welp, I can help you with part of your problem. Abby used to be an office manager, and she's looking for a job, or at least she will be once Reva comes home. You should call her."

Mack's eyebrows went up. "Thanks for the tip. I will."

The bartender brought Quinn's second drink. He raised it to Mack before taking a sip. "Here's to new beginnings, whatever they look like."

Mack raised his nearly empty glass. "Here's to the endings that have to come before the new beginnings, whatever that looks like."

"I'm not ready to give up yet," Quinn said. "There has to be a way to salvage the situation with Bayside Barn."

"JP dangled a baited hook in front of the mayor," Mack said. "But as bait goes, this one's pretty slippery and liable to wiggle off before the big fish they're hoping for comes along. JP's idea has a lot of potential, but there's also a lot of risk. They'll have to do environmental impact studies that could take years, and buying up all those separate properties may not be as easy or cheap as JP makes it out to be."

"Okay, so…" Quinn made a come-along gesture with his fingers. "It sounds like you have an idea. Let's hear it."

"Maybe you could dangle some bait that's less likely to slip off the hook. A sure thing that would pay off quicker. Elections are coming up in the fall. Mayor Wright might trade the potential of money in the future for a better shot at job security right now."

"Yeah? Like what?"

"I dunno. Whatcha got?"

The bartender walked past, and Quinn motioned for the check. "All I've got is that estate I'm renovating. And to be honest, I was kind of thinking about moving in there myself. With Abby, if she'll have me."

"Well, she ain't moving in with you if you don't fix the problem you caused, so maybe you ought not put the cart before the horse. Especially since the horse ain't even broke yet and is just as liable to kick you as to look at you."

Quinn finished his drink and set the glass on the inner rim of the bar. "Point taken. So given that all I've got to bargain with is the estate, how can I use that capital to bait my hook?"

"The town's been needing an animal shelter since forever. If you donated your estate—"

"Donate!" The word burst out of Quinn's mouth before he knew it, and several people near them turned to look. "Donate," he said more quietly. "It's all I have. If I donate it, I'll be throwing away all the equity I put into buying the place. I won't even have a place to live."

"Well now, hold on." Mack's wide brow furrowed in thought. "What if you donate the land to the city for the shelter, and offer to renovate the house and property to that end? You could stipulate that the city would have to pay you for the renovations—they'd have to pay anyone else they hired—and you could further stipulate that you want to live in the pool house while you do the renovations. That'd give you a steady income and plenty of time to find another place to live."

"Shit, Mack." *Crazy. Reckless. Stupid.* Those words flew through Quinn's head as he took care of the bill. Why would he give away every ounce of financial security he'd managed to hang onto after the divorce and the collapse of his career? If he did that, he'd have nothing, no safety net.

But maybe if he threw everything he had down the well, he'd get to keep his relationship with Abby—or at least a chance to try again. "It might work."

Mack stood. "I came in on my boat; it's tied up to the dock. I'm gonna hang out on the water a while. You're welcome to join me if you've got nothing better to do."

"Thanks, but I think I'll go back home and think about your idea." Quinn stood, too, and slipped his wallet into his back pocket. They walked out of the restaurant into brilliant afternoon sunlight. Quinn slipped his aviators on.

Squinting, Mack clapped Quinn on the shoulder. "Thanks for lunch. Let me know if there's anything I can do to help."

Quinn waited till Mack's battered old fishing boat puttered

away from the dock, then put on his helmet and headed home. As the wind blew through his hair—metaphorically; he was wearing a helmet—and his mind, Quinn let Mack's idea spin around in the mental whirlwind. All the pros and cons fluttered like bits of paper set loose in a hot Louisiana breeze. By the time he'd made it back to the estate's driveway, all but two of those bits of paper had fallen to the ground.

Con: Lose everything—not just lose it, but give it away.

Pro: Have another shot at making a life with Abby.

By the time he stepped on the kickstand and took off his helmet, he'd made his decision.

The Pro won.

———

After talking with Mack—and then with Quinn—Abby decided that Reva deserved to know that Quinn's complaint to his real estate agent was what started this entire mess. This flaming snowball of shit was getting bigger by the minute, and it had gathered enough momentum that nothing could stop it from rolling straight to hell. Somebody had to do something, and Abby was at a loss. She and Edna—and Quinn, too, she had to admit—had done everything they could. Quinn had no influence over JP, and if he could have stopped the impending disaster, he would have done it already. They needed everyone brainstorming together to figure out what to do before it was too late.

Abby sent a text telling Reva that she'd call the dormitory phone that evening at seven, and Reva responded with a thumbs-up icon. At the appointed time, Reva answered on the first ring, her voice breezy, happy, and just a little bit out of breath. "Hello, love. How is everything at the farm?"

Terrible? Horrible? Dealing with impending doom? Abby cast about for an appropriate answer. "The animals are all fine."

"Oh." Reva's joyful-sounding voice crashed to earth. "What's going on?"

Abby sat at the kitchen table and poured out the whole sad story. When she finished, the connection went silent for a couple of ticks. "Reva? Are you still there?"

"Yes, honey. I'm still here. Just thinking. Give me a sec." After hearing this kind of news, most people would be screeching loud enough to burst Abby's eardrums. But Abby could visualize Reva at this moment, because she'd seen it so many times before. When other people would be pacing the floor with steam coming out of their ears and blood pulsing behind their eyes, Reva would sit quietly with her hands clasped and her eyes closed, listening to someone or something beyond the veil between this world and the next. "Where's Wolf? Have you communicated with him lately?"

A swift change of subject. "No. But when Quinn left, Wolf went with him."

"Two outcasts who've been betrayed by those they loved."

"But I didn't betray Quinn; he betrayed me. And you. He betrayed us."

"No, he hasn't betrayed you, because the farm isn't yours. And he didn't betray me, because he doesn't know me at all, let alone well enough to betray me. The important point to remember going forward is that you haven't betrayed him yet. But you might be next in line, because you also haven't given him the benefit of your understanding and compassion, have you?"

Understanding and compassion. When had either of those virtues done anything other than break her heart? "But Reva," Abby sputtered, "you should be angry at him. He started something that might... I mean..." Abby could feel Reva's patience on the other end of the connection, and she pulled her thoughts together. "Everything you've worked for all these years, everything you're working for now—"

"Won't be wasted."

Abby felt the wind in her sails die down. "But what if you lose?"

"What if," Reva replied in a gently mocking tone. "Maybe we should forget about what ifs and think about what is."

Abby's mind felt scrambled, and she wished she had called Reva much sooner. "Please tell me what is, Aunt Reva. I think I need reminding."

Reva took a deep breath, and Abby knew she was connecting into some other consciousness, maybe an animal or maybe an angel or maybe someone's spirit guide. "Wolf tells me that Quinn loves you dearly—"

"Well, he hasn't said so yet," Abby responded with a huffy tone she couldn't keep out of her voice.

"—And he is brokenhearted over what happened." Reva didn't pause or acknowledge Abby's outburst. "He didn't mean for his... Hang on—I'm searching for the right word...his unthinking actions...no, his hasty actions...to have any effect other than blowing off steam."

That was almost exactly what Quinn had said.

"Wolf says that Quinn has come up with a plan to reverse the impact of his bad decisions, and he is already acting on the plan. Your hostility—"

"I'm not hostile!" Abby butted in.

"Your hostility," Reva repeated patiently, "is reducing Quinn's power in creating this change he's working toward. You need to stop sending anger and start sending love. You need to release your frustration at the world's unfairness and recognize that most people—like maybe sixty-one percent—are doing the best they can, given their circumstances. And I'm telling you that Quinn is part of the sixty-one percent."

Reva's words surrounded Abby like a warm blanket. "Should I go over there and apologize?"

"Leave it be tonight. Tomorrow is a new day, and when all is well, Quinn will come to you. Meanwhile, you have some inner work to do. Talk to Wolf; he has advice for you. Write in your journal; your higher self has advice for you, too. And once you've done all that, sit with Georgia and meditate on what you want to manifest for your future. She'll help."

Abby sighed. "But what about your future? What about the future of Bayside Barn?"

"Those are my concerns, not yours. Ever since this controversy started, I've been doing the inner work I'm advising you to do, and I'm certain that whatever happens will be for the greater good. Now. I want you to take the rest of the evening to journal and meditate. Will you do that?"

Abby's conversations with Reva always ended up with a list of marching orders. "I will. Anything else I need to know?"

"Aside from the fact that I'm coming home this weekend?"

"Oh, shit." Abby glanced at the calendar on the wall above Reva's desk. Reva's course was ending on Friday, and Abby would be picking her up at the airport in New Orleans late that evening. "Yes, of course. I hadn't forgotten." Not exactly. She would have looked at that calendar sooner or later.

"When's the city council meeting?" Reva asked.

"Not this Friday but next," Abby supplied. "That's when they'll make their decision—and if it's in our favor, we have to hope that the mayor won't veto. That's honestly my worst fear, that we'll have everyone on our side but the mayor."

"And what is fear?" Reva asked gently.

"False evidence appearing real," Abby answered dutifully. "I'll try to remember that."

"Please do," Reva said. "And stop worrying. Let's not put any energy into projecting outcomes other than those we want."

"Yes, ma'am."

"Okay, so. You have your marching orders?"

Now that Reva knew everything, Abby felt more settled and confident than she had in days. If Reva wasn't freaking out, then maybe Abby shouldn't be, either. "Yes, ma'am. Thank you so much for not blaming me for everything that's happened on my watch. I'm really sorry, and I hope you'll forgive me for letting this situation get so out of hand."

"Honey, if you needed forgiveness for anything, I'd have already given it to you. But there's nothing to forgive."

"But—"

"Do me one more favor before you go to bed tonight, please," Reva added.

"Anything," Abby answered.

"Forgive yourself."

─────────────

Quinn tried to see the mayor that day, but the best he could do—after wasting over an hour getting cleaned up and dressed up and driving into town—was to make an appointment for the following day and go home. Sean was at his mom's and Abby wasn't speaking to him, but at least he had Wolf, who'd been lying by the pool house's sliding glass door when Quinn parked his bike on the patio. "Hey, buddy," Quinn said. "You want to come in this time?"

Wolf looked up at him sideways without lifting his chin off his paws.

"Well, okay, then." Quinn stepped over the dog to enter the pool house, but left the door open in case Wolf changed his mind. "In case it matters, I'm grilling steak for dinner."

Wolf declined to come inside, even when Quinn put a big, juicy steak out on the kitchen counter to marinate. Griff snuck in and hopped onto the counter, but Quinn caught the cat a split second before he could steal a taste of homemade steak marinade. (Abby's cooking prowess had somehow sparked some culinary creativity in Quinn, but he planned to confine his newfound talent to grilling.)

Quinn tossed the cat out and took a cold beer out with him onto the patio. When he fired up the grill and put the steak on, Georgia showed up. She hung out until Abby called her, and it broke Quinn's already-battered heart to see her and Wolf parting after each tried to convince the other to stay together. But Wolf refused to budge, and Georgia had to leave.

Griff tried to cuddle with Wolf, to offer him some consolation, but Wolf looked away and growled softly. When the steak was perfectly browned, Quinn dished up a delicious but lonely dinner, wishing Abby or Sean—or Abby and Sean—were there to share it with him. Wolf still wouldn't come inside, and mosquitoes were starting to drift in, so Quinn admitted defeat and closed the door.

After dinner, he went to bed early, since there was nothing better to do. He had that same dream he'd had before in which Abby was a mermaid in the frog-green pool. As before, the dream started out erotic and turned out dark. But this time, she wasn't dragging him down. This time, she was stuck underwater, unable to breathe, and hopelessly tangled in a net he'd thrown over the pool before he knew she was down there. And no matter how hard he swam, he couldn't get past the net's sturdy mesh to save her.

When Wolf's lonely howl outside the door woke Quinn at 2:00 a.m., he was almost relieved. He wouldn't get any sleep tonight, but at least he could stop dreaming.

Georgia's high-pitched howl woke Abby from a dead sleep at 2:00 a.m. She bolted upright. "What?"

Georgia howled again. Abby listened to the sounds outside, alert for signs of an intruder breaking in. But all she could hear was the familiar nighttime chorus of tree frogs and crickets. "What is it, Georgia?"

The little dog howled again, the sound mournful and distraught. And then, Abby heard Wolf's answering howl coming from next door. "Oh, girl." Abby stroked Georgia's fur. "Are you missing Wolf?"

Georgia howled again. Of course she was missing her friend. But she and Wolf had chosen opposite sides in this ongoing war between Abby and Quinn. "I'm sorry," Abby said. "You can go over there if you want to."

But Georgia only lifted her face to the ceiling and howled again.

"Come here." Abby hauled Georgia up close and tried to snuggle her back to sleep, but Georgia's body remained taut with tension. Abby held Georgia still and managed to drift off into dreamland herself, but Georgia bolted upright at 3:16 a.m. and started howling again.

Abby took the little dog's face in her hands and stared into her worried brown eyes. "Georgia. If I promise to talk to Quinn tomorrow, will you please let me sleep?"

Georgia pulled away and howled again. Wolf howled back, and Abby almost considered going to Quinn's right away. But thoughts of the swarms of mosquitoes that would attack her between here and there held her off. "I promise, I'll talk to Quinn tomorrow if you'll just let me sleep tonight."

After few minutes more of singing the songs of her people while Wolf sang back from Quinn's side of the fence, Georgia quieted down and seemed to relax. "That's it, girl," Abby crooned and massaged Georgia's tense muscles. "You just relax and go to sleep. Tomorrow is a new day, and we'll all do better tomorrow."

With a groan, Georgia stretched out and aligned herself along Abby's leg. Did they have an agreement? Abby couldn't be sure. But at least Georgia finally fell asleep.

Even more important, she let Abby fall asleep and stay that way until morning.

The mayor of Magnolia Bay stepped around the massive mayoral desk to shake Quinn's hand. The man didn't look at all like Quinn expected; not a portly politician in a slick-looking suit, but a tall, vigorous-looking man in his early sixties wearing a golf shirt and khaki pants. "Hello, Mr. Lockhart," the mayor boomed. (At least his voice sounded like Quinn had expected it to.)

Quinn extended a hand. "Mayor Wright, thank you for making time for me."

The mayor clasped Quinn's hand and shook it with firm determination. "What can I do you for?"

Quinn ground his back teeth at the mayor's classic southern penchant for turning grammar on its head in a cutesy way. "I'd like to propose a business deal to counter the one you're currently considering regarding the bayside marina development."

"Ah, yes." The mayor indicated that Quinn should take a seat across from the desk. "Mack put a small bug in my ear about your idea." He folded his lanky frame into his fancy leather desk chair, scooted the chair up close, and steepled his fingers in front of his lips. "I'm listening."

Quinn relayed the list of pros and cons he'd come up with last night. The pros of taking a sure-bet deal to build an animal shelter for the city on Quinn's land versus the cons of letting developers build a hotel and marina complex that, even if the environmental impact study came in on their side, would still take upward of five years to start making a profit.

"But the animal shelter won't make a profit at all, will it?" Mayor Wright asked. "It'll be a drain on the economy."

"You are correct that the shelter won't make a profit. But it will provide a vital service to the community that your constituents will appreciate come election time, and it won't be a drain on the economy."

Quinn thanked God that he and Mack had brainstormed with Reva over Skype about how the shelter's renovation and build-out could be paid for, and what the likely operating expenses would be once the shelter was up and running. He explained the plan. They would apply for a grant to fund the construction, then use several potential income streams—such as government grants, private endowments, local business partnerships, local fund-raising efforts, and adoption fees—to fund ongoing operations.

Most important, he made it clear that Bayside Barn would be an integral part of the shelter's operations. They would house any abused or neglected farm animals or equines that were brought into the shelter. That would, of course, require them to maintain the ability to keep farm animals within the city limits.

"I'll definitely think about it," the mayor promised, standing. This time, he stayed behind his desk, but extended his hand across the desk. "Thank you so much for coming in."

An offer to think about it wasn't what Quinn had expected, either. He had expected—or at least hoped for—an enthusiastic acceptance. He stood and shook the mayor's hand. "When will you make your decision?"

"I'll probably wait to hear both sides' arguments at the next city council meeting. Once the council makes its decision, I'll decide whether to veto or not." The mayor sat back down, scooted his chair up, and pulled a stack of file folders close. A clear dismissal.

Quinn walked out, disappointment weighing his steps. He knew from Mack that the city council would be on their side. But if the mayor wasn't on their side, too, Bayside Barn was doomed.

Chapter 25

WOLF WAS WAITING OUTSIDE THE DOOR WHEN ABBY WENT TO feed the critters that morning. "Hello, you," she said, reaching down to pet his head. This time, he didn't flinch or back up; he stood still and allowed her to stroke his soft fur. "That's a good boy."

Georgia seemed to know that Abby and Wolf were sharing a moment, so she trotted off in the direction of the barn. The farrier had come the day before; she was probably hoping to find some leftover hoof trimmings to chew on.

"How's Quinn doing?" Abby asked Wolf, not really expecting to receive an answer.

Sad. Lost. Missing you.

The words popped into Abby's mind like tiny bubbles that floated up and then exploded one after the other, leaving her with the same feelings.

Sad. Lost. Missing him. All that, along with a heaping helping of guilt. She shouldn't have shut him out without listening to him, without at least giving him a chance to explain. She shouldn't have given him an ultimatum to fix the problem he'd caused or else. She should have understood and offered to help.

It's not too late. Wolf leaned against her leg and looked up at her with his expressive golden-brown eyes. He seemed...approving, as if she had turned some sort of corner, and he had finally accepted her.

"Bet you won't let me give you a bath, though."

Georgia barked from inside the barn, breaking the spell. Wolf bolted ahead and Abby followed, her heart feeling lighter than it had since she'd cut Quinn out of her life.

Wolf and Georgia lounged in a patch of sunlight and munched

on hoof trimmings while Abby did the morning feed. She finished the barn cleaning, raked out the chicken coops, and hosed down the aviary, humming to herself.

Joyful. Despite everything that was going on, today she felt joyful. Wolf was right; Abby had turned some sort of corner. After the farm chores, Abby sat by the pool to do more of the inner work Reva had asked her to do yesterday. She took out her seldom-used journal and wrote another page of what felt like random ramblings, but it really did seem to help Abby get in touch with some latent inner wisdom she didn't often take the time to connect with.

Processing and percolating, Reva called it; writing questions to herself, then writing the answers. She turned that page and started a new one, where she took notes on a new conversation with Wolf. While he sat beside her lounge chair and stared at the horizon, she wrote a question: Have I turned a corner?

He looked back at her briefly. *Ask me something you don't know.*

What advice do you have for me?

My advice for you is the same you would give to me: Let love in. Trust in love. Love will heal you. Maybe we can help each other to have that kind of courage.

A shadow fell over her notebook, and Abby shaded her eyes with her hand to look up. "Quinn." Her heart did a quick little dance before settling down again. "Hey."

He stood there looking uncertain. "You gonna tell me to leave?"

"No, I'm not." She patted the empty lounge chair next to hers. "I'm gonna tell you I'm sorry. I was wrong to shut you out the way I did."

"I don't blame you for hating me. I was an arrogant, selfish asshole."

"I don't hate you, Quinn. I—" *I love you.* "I don't hate you."

He sat in the chair and stretched out his legs. Leaning back with a heavy sigh, he took off his sunglasses and closed his eyes. The hot sun picked out the highlights in his brown hair and revealed lines of stress beside his eyes and mouth that Abby hadn't noticed before.

"You making a list?" He asked the question without opening his eyes or turning his head.

"Sort of." She closed her notebook. The subtle sense of joy she'd been feeling all day expanded in her heart when she looked at his beloved, tired features. Wolf walked up to Quinn and brushed against his arm. He reached out in a weary motion to stroke the dog's head. "Are you okay?" she asked. "You look worn out."

"Haven't been sleeping," he murmured, sounding drowsy.

Abby set her notebook aside and stood. "Come inside. I'll tuck you into my bed, and I promise that you'll be able to sleep."

He groaned. "I'm comfortable here."

Tiny beads of sweat glistened on the hard planes of his tanned face. "Yes, but in fifteen minutes, you'll be sweating down, and in another half hour, you'll be working on an interesting sunburn." She took his hand and pulled at it. "Come with me."

He grumbled but allowed her to tug him upright. She turned toward the house, but he pulled her back and wrapped his arms around her. With his face in her hair, he inhaled deeply. "You smell"—he inhaled again—"like horses."

She laughed and gave his hard waist a tight squeeze. "I'm sure you're right. You could probably get a whiff of bird, too, if you tried. I promise I won't get in bed with you smelling like this."

He nuzzled her neck, making her shiver. "Nah, that's okay. I like the smell of horses."

She patted his butt. "Come on, Quinn. It's nap time." She led him through the house, then released him at her bedside. Tossing the throw pillows onto a chair, she turned down the covers. "You can keep your underwear. Take the rest of it off," she commanded. While he undressed, she went to each of the windows and closed the blinds. He got into bed, his eyelids at half-mast, sleepy and sexy at the same time. She covered him with the quilt and sat on the edge of the mattress. "I'm sorry I was so hard and unforgiving. I take it all back."

He took her hand and brought it to his lips, kissing her knuckles. "I've been talking with Reva and Mack, and together we've come up with a solution that we think the city council will vote yes on. I talked to the mayor this morning, but I don't know if he'll agree. We'll have to make our case to the council before he'll decide. I wish I knew something more to do, but—"

Abby leaned forward and kissed him, effectively shutting him up. "Whatever happens, we'll handle it together."

—————

Quinn drove Reva's car to pick Reva up at the airport. On the way, he told Abby about his plan to save Bayside Barn.

"Quinn," she protested, "you can't do that. You can't give away all your assets. You'll be left without any working capital to build the construction business you wanted."

"Yeah, but I'm almost making enough to live on with the cabinetry work I've been doing, and I'll be getting paid to complete the renovation for the shelter. Besides, maybe I don't want to be a contractor anymore anyway. The only thing is…" He let his voice trail away. He didn't know how to say that next part.

"The only thing is…?" Abby prompted.

He glanced at her, then trained his eyes on the road. "I won't be making a lot of money. I won't be able to offer you a big fine house or an unlimited credit card account or—"

"Whoa." Abby turned, her back against the car window, her knees angled toward him on the seat. "Quinn, what are you talking about?"

He gripped the steering wheel as if the car was about to spin out of control. "I want us to be together." He squeezed the steering wheel even tighter. "I want to make a life with you. I just don't have much to offer you right now."

Abby loosened her seat belt and scooted as close as the console would allow, then leaned her head on his shoulder, both her hands wrapped around his bicep. "I don't care about all that. I'd like to be with you, too. It doesn't matter to me where we live or how much we have. I can get a job, too, once Reva is back home to take care of the farm. We'll build our future together. You don't have to do it all by yourself. There's only one problem I can see."

He felt his whole body tense up. "What's that?"

"You haven't told me yet that you love me."

He jerked back in surprise. "Of course I have. A few times, I'm sure."

She shook her head. "Nope. You've never said it out loud. Neither have I, by the way; I didn't want to say it first and put you in the awkward position of having to respond."

He squeezed her clasped hands against his side. "I love you, Abby."

She squeezed his bicep and snuggled closer. "I love you, too, Quinn."

Reva's suitcase weaseled behind her in a zigzagging motion. One of the wheel's housings had cracked, so the wonky wheel whirled and spun on the polished marble floor of the airport's baggage claim, knocking the suitcase off-kilter on an irritatingly regular basis. She felt the phone in her purse buzz with an incoming text, but ignored it until she had dragged the suitcase outside.

Standing at the curb, she read the text from Abby: We're parked in the cell phone lot. Let us know when you've got your bags and we'll get in the pickup lane.

She texted back: I'm here.

When she saw her car inching along the curb some distance away, she stepped off the curb—just barely—and waved to get

Abby's attention. A car going past blared its horn, and someone gripped Reva's arm firmly from behind. She stepped back onto the curb and looked way up to meet the man's gaze. "You," she said, feeling her voice soften. It was the tall, good-looking man who had saved her from the escalator in the Miami airport. "You must be some sort of guardian angel or something."

He grinned. "Nope. Just spend a lot of time at airports. A long-distance love affair will do that to you."

"I remember. Your girlfriend was flying into Miami before. And now...?"

"She's coming to New Orleans for a conference, and I took time off work to be with her. I just parked the rental car, and now I'm headed to baggage claim to meet her."

"Young love," Reva sighed. She remembered Grayson and her being that way, spending every available moment together. Getting out in the world always reminded her of how much she missed him. "Don't ever take it for granted. Don't take *her* for granted."

"I won't, believe me." The young man winked, reminding her so much of Grayson that it took her breath. "Whenever she needs me, I'll find a way to be there."

Another horn honked... Abby this time—or, rather, Quinn. He was driving Reva's car and Abby sat in the passenger seat. Quinn parked at the curb and popped the trunk. In the whirl-wind way of curbside pickups, he grabbed Reva's suitcase and put it in the car while Abby hopped out to give Reva a quick hug. Quinn slammed the trunk and came around to open the doors for her and Abby. "I feel like I know you already," he said, taking Reva's hand. "Abby has told me so much about you. So has Mack."

She pulled him into a hug. "I'm so happy to meet you, Quinn. I'm looking forward to meeting your son, too. Abby has spoken fondly of you both."

The introductions took no more than a minute, but by the time she turned around to introduce her tall, handsome friend to Abby and Quinn, he had already melted away into the crowd.

On the drive back to the farm, Reva sat in the back seat and napped. And she was glad she'd taken that opportunity to rest up, because Abby had planned a big welcome-home dinner for Reva at the farm. All the barn's volunteers were already there when they pulled up, and so was Reva's friend Heather. Mack pulled in right behind them, and Sean's mother dropped him off a few minutes later.

Fueled by an enormous salad, a big pan of lasagna, and three loaves of garlic bread, the conversation soon evolved into a lively brainstorming session on the future animal shelter and Bayside Barn's role in it. Quinn kept looking at his phone, so much so that Reva felt compelled to comment. "Are we boring you, Quinn? Or maybe you've got somewhere else to be?"

Quinn grimaced. "I invited a friend to come and help us brainstorm about the new shelter. I knew he couldn't make it for dinner, but I thought he'd be here by now." He pushed his chair back and stood. "I'm just gonna step outside and try to give him a call. I hope he's not lost on a back road without a cell signal."

"While you're at it, make sure the porch lights are on so he can see the house from the road."

When people started clearing the table, Reva stood and tapped Sean on the shoulder. "Hey, wanna help me with something?"

"Yes, ma'am." He followed Reva through the house into the supply closet.

"You start on this side, and I'll look on the other. We're looking for a big pad of poster-sized Post-it notes. I know they're in here somewhere."

While they dug through the dusty shelves, Sean accidentally knocked down a box that popped open when the corner hit the floor. "Oops, sorry." He knelt down to pick up the scattered contents, then stood with a plastic star in his hand. "Oh, wow! I have one of these from when I visited here in the third grade."

"Oh my goodness." Reva thought they'd long since used all those plastic stars; now they used stick-on ones, because kids these days couldn't be trusted with a stick-pin. "I didn't know we still had any of these left."

Sean reached up for the next same-sized box on the high shelf and brought it down. "You have bunches of them."

"Could you check if that other box up there…?"

Sean brought down a third box and lifted one of the flaps. "Yep. Stars in here, too."

"Awesome. Set those over by the door, please. I'll figure out what to do with them later."

She found the pad of poster Post-its and handed it to Sean, then picked up a box of colorful Flair pens.

In the dining room, she put the pens in a coffee mug on the table. "Sean," she instructed, "stick one of those poster sheets on each of the sliding glass doors and the windows facing the pool; enough for everyone here to have their own page to draw on."

Georgia gave a high-pitched warning bark and rushed out through the dog door.

"Put up one for Quinn's friend, too. That must be him arriving."

Heather came up, drying her hands on a dish towel. "Kitchen's clean." Her round cheeks were pink, and the humidity had coaxed her shoulder-length blond hair into gentle waves. "What else can I do to help?"

Reva hugged her friend. They'd met a year ago at a grief support group right after Heather's husband died, and despite the difference in their ages, they'd developed a true friendship. Reva might even say that Heather was her best friend. "You don't need to do a thing, honey. Unless you need me to give you a job so you won't hurry back home to the kids."

Poor Heather, suddenly left with three kids to raise by herself. At least Dale had left them with enough money that Heather—a stay-at-home mom—hadn't had to sell the house or find a job right away.

"I'm not in a hurry to get home." Heather grinned, her green eyes crinkling at the corners. "Erin made me promise not to come home until after the twins' bedtime. She's saving up for a new phone."

The back door opened, and Quinn—typical man—brought his friend into the house through the laundry room (which at least was blessedly clean except for Reva's suitcase of dirty clothes on top of the dryer). Heather, standing beside Reva, didn't move or make a sound, but something about her energy shifted. Reva looked over to see Heather's always-pink cheeks get even pinker. Surely not hot flashes… Heather was much too young for those.

"Hey, everybody," Quinn said, diverting Reva's attention from her friend. "This is my old college buddy, Adrian Crawford. He's a business consultant, so I thought he might be able to give us some advice on getting the shelter going."

"I hope y'all weren't waiting on me. I had another meeting that ran late." Completely at ease as Quinn introduced him around, Adrian looked like Hollywood's impression of a business consultant, with his black slacks and rumpled business shirt over Superman muscles, topped by an almost too-pretty face and a two-hundred dollar haircut. "Then I got lost. I drove past here twice before I noticed the porch light."

Quinn introduced Adrian to Reva, and then to Heather.

Adrian took Heather's hand and smiled a smooth and easy smile that warmed the depths of his deep blue eyes.

Ohhh. Reva looked at Adrian, and then back at Heather. No wonder she was blushing. Adrian was the kind of guy who could make any woman feel a little hot-flashy, and Reva knew that Heather hadn't dated at all since her husband's death.

Georgia jumped up to welcome Adrian, spreading joy and dirty paw prints and stray white hairs everywhere. Adrian released Heather's hand and knelt to give Georgia his full attention, seeming not one bit concerned about the state of his expensive slacks. "Hey, little dog," he crooned. "I haven't met you yet. What's your name?"

"It's Georgia," Reva supplied, looking at Heather over Adrian's chestnut-brown head and those broad shoulders that challenged the seams of his tailor-made shirt. "Don't let her get your pants dirty."

"Aww," Adrian drawled without looking up, "we aren't gonna worry about that, are we, Georgia?" It almost looked as if he was avoiding further contact with Heather as he ruffled Georgia's fur and rubbed her ears, causing her to moan in joyful surrender. Heather's cheeks had gone back to their normal rosy pink, but her wide eyes still looked slightly stunned.

Quinn clapped his hands. "Let's get busy, shall we?"

Adrian stood, and he didn't even brush the dog hair off his slacks. Points to him. He glanced at Heather and smiled his easy smile but looked away too quickly. This guy with such polished social skills seemed almost nervous around Heather, who abruptly folded the dish towel she was still holding onto and hustled off to the safety of the kitchen.

But Reva wasn't about to allow Heather to make herself scarce just because the presence of a fancy new rooster in town was ruffling her feathers. "Heather, since you're in the kitchen, would you please bring us a pitcher of lemon water and a stack of cups?" It was high time Heather's feathers got fluffed.

No point in letting him off easy, either, she decided. "Adrian, would you mind giving her a hand? We might need two pitchers of water, now that I think about it."

Leaving those two to stew in their own juices, Reva handed a black pen to Quinn. "Assuming that the edges of the page are the boundary lines of your estate, can you draw roughly where the existing structures are on each of those pages?"

"Sure." While he did that, Reva stuck another sheet onto the wall and wrote: *Dog runs. Fenced play yards. Cat room with attached outdoor enclosure. Puppy room. Laundry. Office.* She turned to the group of people who had settled at the table again. "Everybody grab a pen and use those posters to draw your ideas of what should go where at the new shelter. I'm making a list of things you'll want to consider." She looked at the list she'd written so far and chewed on the cap of her pen. "Y'all help me out. What else do you think the shelter will need, and how can we make the best use of what's already there?"

"Kitchen," Edna yelled out. "Gotta have a kitchen."

Reva wrote *kitchen*.

Mack said, "Infirmary with a quarantine area. You'll want to keep any sick animals away from the others."

She wrote that, too. "Great idea, Mack."

Quinn handed over the black pen. He had drawn outlines for the pool, the pool house, and the main house on each of the other pages. "We need to decide what to do about the pool. It's leaking around the steps, so it'll need to be fixed if there's a reason to keep it. Otherwise, we'll need to fill it in."

"Oh, we're keeping it," Reva said. "We can use it for rehab when injured dogs come in."

"And for playtime, too," Abby said. "I've seen videos of a bunch of dogs playing ball in a pool together. It'll be great for exercise and socialization with other dogs."

"I dunno," Quinn said. "I've tried to patch those steps, but they still keep leaking. We might need to go so far as to tear them out and put in new."

Mack got up and started drawing on one of the sheets. "You could extend the pool's shallow end to make a beach-style entrance. A lot of dogs won't go in the pool if they have to walk down steps, but they will if it's a gentle slope."

Edna started drawing on another sheet. "You'll have to put a fence around the pool, for safety."

Sean stood next to Edna and drew a bunch of dogs playing ball— not exactly Reva's idea of architectural planning, but fun. "We'll get the dogs a tennis-ball launcher," he said. "That way, they can play all day long whether there's someone to throw the ball or not."

Before long, everyone was standing together at the windows, tossing out ideas and drawing their vision for the new shelter on their posters. Reva stood back and watched, hugging herself to contain her excitement. Seeing everyone's ideas on paper made the dream feel more real than it ever had. Maybe this time, it would really happen.

"Reva," Edna said, "I know that in the past, you and Grayson offered to run the shelter, if the city would build one. But I don't know how you'll be able to do all that by yourself and still run Bayside Barn, too."

"Let Abby run the shelter," Mack said, turning to look at Abby. "You have office management experience, right?"

"I do." Abby's whole face brightened. "Do you think I could get the job?" Then she looked over at Reva. "Unless you want it, Aunt Reva?"

Abby was clearly trying to dim her excitement in case Reva wanted the job for herself. But honestly, she didn't. She was more than happy to pass that torch along. Reva put a hand on Mack's burly shoulder. "That's a great idea, Mack. I don't know why I didn't think of it."

Then she smiled at her niece. "I'll be around to help out, if you need me. But I'm going to be busy with the barn and my new wildlife rehab thing, plus taking care of any farm animals that we're keeping for the shelter."

"And Abby," Mack added, "since Reva's back home now, and the shelter won't be open right away, I sure could use your help at the vet clinic. I'm short one office manager these days."

"Really?" Abby's smile lit up the room. "I'd love that, Mack. When can I start?"

"Yesterday would be good," Mack said. "That is, if Quinn doesn't need you on-site to supervise the building project."

Quinn put an arm around Abby. "I think I'll be able to let her go at least some of the time."

Lord, those two were so cute together. They reminded Reva of herself and Grayson back in the day. And look at Heather and Adrian, the attraction between them a palpable thing, though they could hardly bring themselves to look at each other. They'd chosen to draw their brainstorming ideas on Post-it posters at opposite ends of the room, and Heather kept slinking off to the kitchen to refill the water pitchers and bring out artistically arranged plates of cookies.

"We'll also have to hire someone to run the day-to-day operations," Mack said. "Feeding the animals, cleaning the enclosures..."

"I'll do it," Sean volunteered. "Let me."

Edna reached out and ruffled his hair as if he was five years old, but he didn't seem to mind.

"You're a little young for that job," Reva said. "But I'll need some help around the barn, if your mom doesn't mind you working here a couple hours after school each day. That'll free me up to help Abby get the shelter up and running."

"I know just the person for the daily operations job," Edna said. "Heather Gabriel," she called into the kitchen, where Heather had disappeared again. "If you don't want to be nominated for something, you'd best get back in here and speak up."

"I'm coming," Heather called back. "Just wiping down the countertops."

Reva smothered a smile. She couldn't wait to tease Heather about this the next time she saw her. She'd already wiped down the countertops so much that they'd need to be resealed.

"She'll be perfect," Edna said, "don't y'all think?"

"Heather is wonderful," Reva agreed. "And I know she has written grant proposals for the elementary school before, so she can help Abby with that." But she glanced at Mack uncertainly; the actual hiring would be done by the city council, and while he'd been the one to think of offering Abby the job as the shelter's director, Edna didn't have that power.

But Mack grinned. "That sounds great, Edna. If Heather wants the job, I'll put in a good word to the city council."

Reva squeezed Mack's shoulder. He was such a good man. "It feels like everything's coming together, doesn't it?"

As long as the mayor didn't shoot the whole thing down.

Chapter 26

THE CITY COUNCIL MEMBERS HAD AGREED THAT THE courthouse wasn't big enough to hold the huge crowd expected at the council meeting that would decide the fate of Bayside Barn. So it was in the town's auditorium that JP held forth on the benefits of building a huge marina complex. With the charisma of a talk-show host and the earnest conviction of a televangelist, JP made an argument that even Quinn wanted to buy into, and he knew better.

Quinn's palms started sweating when he realized that not only would his presentation follow JP's, but it would have to be even more convincing. This was their only shot. Abby squeezed his thigh, whether in warning or anxiety or comfort, he didn't know. He glanced over to see her encouraging smile. "Stop worrying," she whispered. "You've got this."

And when President Tammy introduced him and he stood behind the podium to present his case, any nerves he had been feeling melted away. The vision of the future animal shelter just felt right. It felt meant to be.

He clicked through the PowerPoint presentation he had prepared, with photos of the existing property along with renderings of the changes and additions he would make. Even the leaking pool seemed to be perfect for the animal shelter, because the new beach-style ramp would make the pool accessible to the shelter dogs.

"We'll build a concrete-block wall between the shelter and Bayside Barn," he explained, showing another slide, "so the shelter animals won't be bothered by field trip buses coming in to Bayside Barn. An access gate between the two properties will be large enough to accommodate any vehicle. Whenever the shelter receives any abused or abandoned livestock, they'll be housed at

Bayside Barn, at least until the shelter has its own barn space and fenced grazing pasture, which we'll build in phase two, about a year after the shelter opens."

When he finished his presentation, the packed crowd in the auditorium surged to its feet, whooping and cheering. Quinn felt himself blushing, his cheeks pulsing with his heartbeats. He had been so in the zone during his presentation, he'd almost forgotten how big the crowd was. He quickly gathered his notes and ducked back to his seat, while people he'd never met clapped him on the shoulder and congratulated him.

After a few minutes of quiet discussion among the city council members, President Tammy took to the podium. "The council unanimously agrees to allow Bayside Barn to keep farm animals, and indeed, any animals Reva Curtis deems appropriate for the education goals of Bayside Barn. We further decree that once given, this permission cannot be rescinded for any reason." She glanced at the mayor, who answered her unasked question with a brief nod.

She sat, and the mayor took the podium.

"Furthermore," the mayor boomed, "as the mayor of Magnolia Bay, I am delighted to accept Mr. Lockhart's generous donation of the animal shelter that this community has needed for so long. As you all know, I have worked tirelessly to…" And while the mayor unfurled his stump speech, giving himself all the credit for making this miracle happen, Quinn noticed a quiet disturbance happening at the edges of the crowd.

Reva, Abby, Edna, and all the other Bayside Barn volunteers were moving through the auditorium, each carrying a cardboard box through the audience. People were gathering around the women to peek into in the boxes, then reach inside.

Abby bumped into Quinn from behind with the sharp edge of the box she was carrying. "Want one?" she asked.

"One what?" He tilted the box toward him. "Awww." He sifted

through the multicolored plastic stars and picked out a blue one with gold lettering. "I'm proud to be a Bayside Barn Buddy," he read out loud.

"I'm proud you're a Bayside Barn Buddy, too," Abby said, her hazel eyes sparkling.

He pinned the star to his shirt and leaned in to give Abby a kiss. The big box of stars was in the way, so he took it from her and handed it to the nearest person. "Here," he said. "Give these out, please, so I can kiss my girlfriend."

The mayor finally ended his speech. President Tammy plucked the mayor's white cowboy hat off his head, stepped to the podium, and waved the hat in the air. She started the chant, and then the whole crowd joined in.

Quinn hauled Abby up close, but stopped kissing her long enough to join in the chant: "Go, Bayside Barn Buddies, go!"

―――――――――――

A mixed-up mass of emotions clogged Abby's throat, and tears prickled behind her eyes as she sat next to Quinn in the office of the title company and watched him sign away everything he'd salvaged from his previous life. He flipped to another flagged page of the document, signed his name again, then repeated the process, over and over again.

Giving it all away to save Bayside Barn.

He laid the pen aside and slid the sheaf of papers across the conference table toward the mayor, who stacked the documents and grinned. "The city of Magnolia Bay thanks you, sir."

"You drive a hard bargain." Quinn stood and offered his hand across the table. "But I'm glad we could come to an agreement."

The mayor had given Quinn until Labor Day to complete the building of the shelter and, as he so kindly put it, "get the hell out." Mayor Wright wasn't entirely happy about having to give up the prospect of the marina complex, so Quinn had been forced to sweeten the bait by promising that the shelter's grand opening would happen before the city's next mayoral election.

Abby stood, too, and Quinn took her hand in his. He squeezed her fingers. "We'd better go get to work."

We, because the city council had indeed hired Abby to run the shelter. While Quinn was supervising the construction teams, Abby would be setting up the shelter's office and interviewing potential staff members.

"Yep," boomed the mayor. "Time's a-wasting, clock's a-ticking. Y'all better get busy."

Abby waited for the familiar sense of worry to creep up behind her. How would they get everything done, even with the city's financial backing and a slew of helping hands pitching in? What if the pressure of working together proved to be too great a strain on Abby and Quinn's new relationship? But the worry and anxiety that had plagued her all these months seemed to have faded away. The what-ifs ahead would be challenging, no doubt. But she and Quinn would conquer them together.

Epilogue

"Abby," Quinn said from the bathroom doorway. "What in the world are you doing?"

"You mean, besides taking a bath?" She poured another cup of water over her head, then yelled, "Whoo! That was fun! I'm getting clean!" She repeated the process, but this time instead of yelling, she shook her head and splattered water all over the bathroom and the two dogs who sat by the bathtub, watching Abby's antics.

"Looks to me like you're putting on a show for these dogs." And for him, too; her wet, naked body and rosy-tipped breasts were a sight to behold.

"I'm really just doing it for Wolf." She reached out to the dog, who leaned forward just close enough to lick her fingers but no closer. "I'm trying to show him that a bath is a good thing."

She dunked the cup back into the water to fill it, then poured it out over her head, hollering with false glee and intentionally splattering the dogs. "I want Wolf to know that a little water won't hurt him."

"I don't know about Georgia," Quinn said, "but Wolf thinks you're crazy."

"I know." Abandoning the cup idea, Abby dipped a washcloth into the sudsy water and reached out to wipe Wolf's face. She got one good swipe in before he backed out of her reach. "But we've put up with his dirt-tracking, stinky self long enough. Now that he's coming inside so much, he needs to learn about baths. Also, he's scheduled to be neutered this week, and I refuse to take a dirty dog to the vet."

Quinn chuckled. "I understand your motivation; I'm just not sure you're going about it the right way."

Abby squeezed out the washcloth. "Let's hear your bright idea, then."

Quinn eased into the small bathroom and peeled his shirt off over his head. "Dogs," he ordered. "Out."

The dogs ran out and Quinn closed the door, turning the lock just in case. Now that Reva was back at the farm and the estate was a construction zone, privacy was hard to come by.

Reva, Mack, Edna, President Tammy, Mayor Wright, and a few other folks on the shelter's planning committee had all been known to just show up and walk on into the pool house, hollering for Quinn to show them the latest progress on the shelter. But they had an official tour for the shelter's planning committee scheduled in a few hours, so Quinn figured he and Abby were safe for now. But he jiggled the bathroom doorknob to make sure the lock was secure.

Abby held the damp washcloth to her naked breasts. "What are you doing?"

He skimmed his jeans and underwear down his legs in one motion and stepped out of them. "It's step one of my bright idea."

Her hazel eyes went round at his audacity—and hopefully his anatomy, too, which left no doubt of his intentions. "First, you and I take a bath."

"I know you know how to take a bath, Quinn." She scooted to the end of the tub. "It's the dog I'm trying to convince. And I'm not sure you and I will both fit in here."

"Oh, yeah," he promised, "we'll fit."

He climbed in, practically on top of her, sending a tidal wave of water over the tub's rim. She giggled. "How does this get the dog clean, exactly?"

"I promise I'll bathe Wolf later," he said in between kisses. He had planned to bathe the dog before the meeting, anyway. Abby's little peep show was just a happy accident. "I'm working up sufficient motivation, because I know it won't be easy."

Abby scooted down and adjusted their position; with her hips cradling his, he quickly found the opening he sought and plunged inside. His mighty thrust pushed Abby upward; her back skidded against the wet porcelain tub, making a squeaking sound. Her involuntary "Oof," wasn't quite the reaction he was hoping for, either. He held her shoulders still and tried again, but this time, even more water sloshed over the rim of the tub, and Abby laughed. "Maybe we should try the bed?"

An hour later, Abby snuggled under the covers and smiled at the sounds of Wolf whining, Quinn cursing, and water splashing in the bathroom. Georgia had trotted over to Reva's at the first sign of doggy bathtime.

Finally, the alarming sounds coming from the bathroom died down, followed by the more soothing sound of the hairdryer. Abby dozed a little, dreaming of the house plans she and Quinn had been brainstorming together. He hadn't exactly asked her to marry him, but they were definitely planning a future together. Now that the shelter's construction was nearly complete, Quinn's permission to live at the pool house would also be coming to an end. Reva had offered Quinn a half-acre out behind Bayside Barn that he could build a cabin on, but he and Abby had also been discussing whether to rent, buy, or build somewhere else. Nearby, but not quite so underfoot.

Abby had just drifted from dreaming of floor plans to dreaming for real when the bedroom door burst open. She sat up and clutched the bedspread to her naked breasts, then relaxed when she saw Quinn and Wolf standing there. Both wore satisfied grins on their faces, and Wolf—whose soft fur looked like a clean, fuzzy cloud after his bath, blow-dry, and brush-out—sported a new collar that jingled when he moved.

"Who's the most handsome boy ever?" Abby asked, holding her hand out to Wolf.

Quinn looked down at his wet jeans and bedraggled shirt. "Not me, I guess."

Abby laughed as she kissed Wolf's clean-smelling head. "Not you this time. Correct. But you're still welcome in my bed if you get out of those wet clothes first."

"Technically, it's my bed," Quinn said, but he quickly complied and slipped between the sheets.

Wolf, who'd only recently begun sleeping in the house at night and had never gotten on the furniture despite Georgia's bad example, leaped onto the bed and rolled onto his back, thumping his tail and grinning up at Abby. She obligingly petted his belly. "What are you doing on this bed, mister?"

"He wants you to admire his new collar and tags," Quinn said, leaning back against the pillows.

"Very pretty," Abby said, still rubbing the dog's belly.

"No," Quinn said. "He wants you to *really* admire them."

Abby sat up to get a better look at the cluster of jingling tags on Wolf's new collar. First, the new rabies tag Mack had given them when Wolf finally allowed him close enough to give the injection. Behind that, another tag shaped like a heart. Abby read the engraving: MY NAME IS WOLF. IF I'M LOST…

Abby turned the tag over, and gasped. "Oh, Quinn."

Behind the tag, a diamond engagement ring sparkled from the tag's O-ring.

And the other side of the tag read, *Please call my people, Abby and Quinn Lockhart* (followed, of course, by their phone numbers). "Oh, Quinn," she said again.

"I was sort of hoping for a more definite answer," Quinn joked. But a small, lost note in his voice reminded Abby that like Wolf, Quinn had only recently learned to trust those he loved not to betray him.

Abby worked the engagement ring off the O-ring and slipped it onto her finger. Then she shifted the sheets and climbed right on top of her fiancé's warm, naked body. "Yes," she said, straddling him. "Yes, I will marry you, Quinn Lockhart."

Then she kissed him, long and slow, before drawing back to stare into his beautiful blue-jean-blue eyes. "And do you want to know why I'll marry you?"

He grinned. "Because I'm extremely good-looking and independently wealthy?"

She shook her head. "Nope." She held her hand up and admired the way the diamond caught the light from the window and threw sparkles of colored light onto the ceiling. "Guess again."

"Because you love me?"

"Yes." And she would keep saying it, even after she knew for sure that he truly and completely believed it. "Because I love you."

———————

Wolf sat with Georgia outside the closed bedroom door, listening to all the sighs and giggles and groans coming from inside. Georgia sniffed his still-damp ears and gave a happy tail wag. "You'll have to go roll in something to get rid of that shampoo smell. I know where there's a dead frog one of the workmen ran over in the driveway."

Wolf smiled and swished his tail along the floor. "That's okay. I don't mind smelling like this, if it makes my people happy." My people. He still couldn't quite believe it, but the shiny new tags that jingled on his new collar made it feel at least a little bit more real. "And when you've been carrying around a bathtub full of dirt for as long as I have, it feels good to finally get clean."

"Yes, but…" Georgia shivered. "The smell of shampoo reminds me of baths, and I hate baths."

He licked her silly little face. "If you hate baths, you should try to stay clean instead of rolling in dead. I'm looking forward to sleeping in the bed now, like you do."

"Whose bed you gonna sleep in?" She sat up on her haunches to lick his lips. "You gonna sleep in my bed with Reva, or in theirs?"

She turned an ear toward the closed door. "Their bed is kind of loud and jumbly. Ours is quieter."

Wolf cocked his head to listen. There *was* a lot of squeaking going on in Abby and Quinn's bedroom. It sounded like they were hopping up and down on the bed. Why they would do that made no sense to Wolf, but then people were mysterious creatures who seemed to do a lot of strange things for no good reason. "Maybe I'll try all the beds before making a decision."

Quinn had installed a doggy door in the gate between the two properties and in the sliding glass door of the pool house, and Wolf could fit—just barely—through the dog door to Reva's house, so he could go where he pleased. No one ever chased him away anymore, and in fact, everyone in both houses told him often that they loved him, and that he was welcome to stay. It had been a long journey from fear to trust, and he knew he still had some work to do to fully understand with his mind what he already knew in his heart to be true.

He had everything a dog could want now: the safety and security of being welcomed into not just one family but two, and the freedom to go where he would within those boundaries drawn by love. He had a large extended family that loved and accepted him, including the heart of that family, a funny little dog who loved him beyond measure, even though she wouldn't always share the tennis ball. It didn't matter which bed, or even which house he decided to sleep in. He had time to decide. He had time to truly learn what Georgia had been trying to tell him all along.

He belonged.

He could stay.

*If you've fallen in love with the Welcome to Magnolia Bay series,
read on for a sneak peek at book two:*

Magnolia Bay
Forever

Coming soon from Sourcebooks Casablanca

ADRIAN CRAWFORD PARKED HIS NEW LEXUS LC 500
convertible at the loneliest corner of the new animal shelter's
gravel parking lot, far from the handful of other vehicles, and even
farther from the centuries-old oaks that draped their scaly, fern-
covered branches over the new chain-link fence.

The construction/renovation of the shelter had progressed
significantly since his last visit a week ago. The old craftsman-style
home's exterior facelift was complete. Quinn Lockhart, Adrian's
old college buddy and the contractor in charge of the project, had
already put up the new sign by the entrance. The sign, hand-made
with carved lettering painted bluebird-blue on a butter-yellow
background, matched the new paint and trim on the old house.

A bit bright for his taste, but as a business consultant working pro-bono for the non-profit shelter, it wasn't his place to argue
with the three women in charge of this project. And Quinn was so
crazy-in-love with the trio's leader, Abby Curtis, that he probably
wasn't thinking straight.

"*Furrever Love*," Adrian scoffed. "What kind of name is that for a
business?" The unfortunately cutesy name the women had chosen

for the shelter arched across the top of the sign in a curlicue font they had agonized over for hours. Beneath that, in more sedate lettering: MAGNOLIA BAY ANIMAL SHELTER.

Adrian pushed the button to close the car's top. He left the windows open a few inches to keep the car's interior from baking in the Louisiana summer sun, then exited the car, pointing the key fob to lock the car with a quiet but satisfying blip-blip.

"Gang's all here." Quinn's truck was parked by the outdoor dog runs, where the sound of heavy machinery droned. Reva—the organizing force behind the shelter even though her niece, Abby, was officially in charge—lived at the farm next door. Abby and Quinn were living on-site in the old estate's pool house until the shelter's grand opening, so unless Quinn was making a hardware store run, they were always here.

"Well, almost all here." Heather's car, he noticed as he walked toward the house, was conspicuously absent.

Typical. Heather Gabriel was just about always late. Adrian couldn't help but wonder why Abby and Reva thought they could trust her to be in charge of the day-to-day operations when she couldn't even make it to their weekly 4:00 p.m. meetings on time.

Reva's dog, Georgia, trotted across the parking lot, coming toward him with a proprietary air. She was a funny-looking combo of dog breeds—a short, long dog with a thick speckled coat of many colors and a white-tipped tail that curved over her back. Her brown eyespots drew together in a concerned frown as she sniffed his jeans and then the treads of his new Lowa hiking boots. When she had completed her inspection, she looked up at him with a *"State your business and I'll decide if you can come in"* attitude.

He bent to pet Georgia's head. "I'm here to brainstorm with the team about another grant proposal for funding, if you must know."

Then he scoffed at himself. Quinn, Abby, Reva, and Heather all talked to animals like they were human. Now he was doing it, too. "Assimilation is nearly complete," he told Georgia in his best imitation of The Borg.

Georgia stiffened and growled at something behind Adrian. He turned and looked, then bolted to his feet. The scruffy old black-and-white tomcat who'd been hanging around the area was walking tightrope-style along the top of the chain link fence near Adrian's car. "Don't you do it…"

He could tell by the direction of the cat's gaze that he was about to jump from the fence to the hood of Adrian's brand-new, never-been-scratched car. "No!" He started running, but the cat was already gathering itself for the leap. "Bad cat!"

Too late.

Georgia took off like an avenging army of one, galvanized into action and ready to tell the cat what-for, announcing her intention with a high-pitched, yodeling bark.

The cat was already in mid-leap with front paws extended, body stretched out, back toes spread, when he spotted the dog barreling toward him. Eyes wide, mouth frozen in a grimace of fear, the cat twisted in midair to go back the way he'd come. Too late.

His spine hit the hood of Adrian's car with a loud *thwump*, then his body twirled like a corkscrew, all claws extended as he scrambled to get his balance.

"No…" Adrian ran, but Georgia ran faster. She leaped up, scrabbling at the side of the car in an impossible effort to reach the cat. Never gonna happen; Georgia wasn't even knee-high. But she didn't know it, the cat didn't know it, and none of that mattered to the previously shiny, immaculate finish of Adrian's new car.

"No, shoo, bad dog," Adrian yelled. Why hadn't he used the perfectly good fitted canvas cover that he'd left in the trunk of the car? "Get down, right now." Why hadn't he bothered to toss it over the car the second he got out? "Hush, dog." He tried to push the dog away with his foot. "Get back. Go home."

The cat leaped up to the car's convertible top and hissed down at the dog, who barked even more ferociously, moving to scratch a different area on the side of Adrian's poor car. He snatched the little troublemaker up before she could do it.

The little dog whined and squirmed, but couldn't bark. The cat, frozen in a bowed-up caricature of a Halloween cat, stopped growling long enough to catch his breath. In the sudden cessation of noise, Adrian heard a sound behind him.

Reva rushed up, all flowing hair and patchwork fabric; a prematurely gray hippie gypsy. She snatched Georgia out of his arms. "I'll put her up," she said. "See if you can grab the cat and bring him inside. We've been trying to catch him for weeks."

As Reva hurried back across the parking lot with her Birkenstocks scuffing along the gravel surface, Adrian took off his sunglasses and stood with his hands on his hips, surveying the damage. These scratches were not the sort that could just be buffed out with a good coat of Minwax. "Son of a bitch."

But there was nothing he could do about it now. He heaved a sigh and plowed his hands through his hair, then applied his business-consultant problem-solving skills to the situation. "Okay." First things first. "Come here, cat."

He held his hands out to the cat and made kissy noises. The cat bowed up and backed away, growling low in his throat. "Naw, don't be that way." He softened his tone even further. "Come on, little man." The cat *was* scrawny, but also a fully-grown tomcat with a big jug-head jaw. "Here, kitty, kitty."

The cat glared at him, so he used one of the tricks he'd heard Reva mention when she was talking to the shelter girls about taming wild cats. He half-closed his eyes, looking sleepily at the cat and blinking slowly. The cat settled onto his haunches, his glowing amber eyes not as wide-open as before.

Well, fuck me, he thought. It worked.

He started humming, not a tune, just random low tones.

The damn cat started purring, and damn if he didn't start doing that slow blinking thing, too.

Which Adrian realized he had forgotten to keep doing, so he started it up again. His humming resembled a tune he'd heard his grandmother sing, so he added words to the tune: "What's up, stinky cat?" The cat did stink. He smelled like dirt, motor oil, and cat pee. "Whoa, whoa, whoa... Come here, stinky cat; whoa, whoa, whoa..."

The cat's body tensed, raising up a fraction off his haunches as if preparing to run.

Yeah, that shit wasn't working, so he went back to humming. The cat settled back down. He didn't seem inclined to move toward Adrian's outstretched hands, but at least he wasn't running or hissing or growling. So Adrian eased forward, then gently touched the cat, spreading his fingers lightly over the cat's bony ribs.

The cat's purring stopped. Adrian kept his fingertips on the cat's haunches, letting the skittish feline get used to him before he pushed the envelope any further. He did more of the blinking thing, still humming, and slowly began to stroke the cat's scruffy, greasy, black-and-white fur. It seemed peppered with tiny scabs.

No question, this dude was a fighter.

Adrian eased his fingers farther along the cat's back, then slowly, gently, dragged him forward. The cat resisted at first, but at some point in the process, he padded along the car's hood toward Adrian, assisted by the gentle pressure Adrian kept applying. They seemed to have reached some sort of unspoken agreement. Making soothing sounds, not even a hum anymore, but a vibration in his throat that he could feel but barely hear, he gathered the reluctant cat into his arms.

Cat let the man hold him close, only because the hands that held Cat didn't grab too tightly or try to force anything. Cat knew, somehow, that if he changed his mind about accepting help, the man would let him go.

Cat had never been given any other name, though he had been called many different versions of it. As he rode along in the man's arms—carried toward the building into which he'd seen other cats come and go of their own free will—Cat thought of the many names he'd been called.

Damn Cat. Fucking Cat. Asshole Cat. Go Away Cat.

But this man called him by a new name, one which Cat much preferred because of the tone in which it had been uttered. Stinky Cat. He liked that one. He decided that would be the name by which he would refer to himself, whenever he wanted to think of himself as a cat with a name.

The closer they got to the building, the more tense Stinky Cat felt himself becoming. He wanted to believe. He wanted to be like those other cats who seemed so confident, so unafraid. They even sat with the dogs—napped with them on the building's wide front porch!—and everyone seemed perfectly content. Even the bad little dog who'd come after him was nice to those other cats. She licked their ears the way mama cats licked their babies.

But Stinky Cat had a bad feeling that the dog he'd heard called Georgia wasn't going to lick his ears. She might not have used her teeth on him as she'd threatened to do, but she made it clear she didn't want him around. She had been ready to chase him right back over the fence he had climbed. He had wanted to see more of this strange place in which dogs and cats and people seemed to get along much better than the dogs and cats and people of his previous experience, who were more inclined to try to kill one another.

But now he wasn't so sure he was up for the challenge. He pushed his front paws against the man's supporting arm and leaned his head back against the man's chest.

"Shhh," the man said, "You're okay." Then he stopped walking and stood still, halfway between the metal hill Cat had been stranded on and the building where the dogs and cats came and went whenever they pleased. "Nobody's going to hurt you."

Stinky Cat didn't know what the words meant, and he was too worried about what might happen to understand the man's thoughts. But the tones of the man's voice soothed him, just as the man's fingers stroking his fur soothed him. He felt himself purring again, relaxing against the man's comforting bulk almost against his better judgment. He knew this human wouldn't harm him intentionally, as so many others had.

But he wasn't sure about the people inside that building.

Stinky Cat wanted to see if he could be one of those cats who seemed so happy and unafraid. But he couldn't bring himself to risk it. He'd been afraid all his whole life—or at least from the moment in early kittenhood when he woke with his siblings to find that their mother was gone. He even slept afraid—and lightly enough to wake completely between one breath and another, his ever-present fear fueling his ability to escape or fight for his life if a predator pounced.

Fear had kept him alive this long.

How could he give it up now?

———

Adrian had the damn stinky cat within ten feet of the shelter's front porch when he heard Heather's car coming. He knew it was hers, because of the loud rattling sound the old Honda's hinky motor made. She always brought her kids, and her badly-behaved dog. Knowing there was a high probability of mayhem about to ensue, he petted the cat and took another few, slow steps, hoping to make it inside the building before the car skidded into the parking lot. "What's up, Stinky Cat," he sang. "Whoa, whoa, whoaah."

Tamping down the sense of urgency that kept creeping into his head and infusing his tone, he took a few cautious steps closer to the shelter. Balancing the need to move in sync with the cat's fluctuating degree of compliance to the plan with the imperative of getting inside before...

Heather's car careened into the parking lot, scattering gravel. The dog's head hung out the window, barking as if he had something important to say.

The cat's claws came out like Wolverine's knives. Intent on escaping, the frightened feline dug those claws into Adrian's flesh, slicing effortlessly through his shirt. The back claws gained traction by digging deep into Adrian's abs, while the front claws latched on to his chest. The determined cat used his claws like grappling hooks to haul himself up to an unsteady perch on Adrian's shoulder, where with one last, mighty effort, he launched off Adrian's back and hit the ground running.

Before Adrian could gather the presence of mind to say, "Ow, shit," the cat had scaled the chain link fence and leaped into the thick underbrush on the other side.

Adrian watched Heather park her rattletrap car under the shade of a live oak whose trailing, fern-covered branches were as thick as a full-grown human body. She clearly had more trust in the universe—or her car insurance—than he did.

Since he no longer held the skittish cat in his arms, he might as well assess the damage to his car, which had lived in the dealership's lot not more than a month ago. He made it halfway across the lot when Heather's dog—a speckled gray Aussie with flashy copper and white markings—rushed up to greet him. Adrian reached down to pet the dog's head. "Hello, Jasper. You don't even realize that you just ruined everything, do you?"

Jasper panted with enthusiasm, wagged his whole back end, and grinned a doggy grin.

A second later, Heather's son, Josh, ran up to bombard Adrian with the latest news. "I got in trouble at school today. See?" He pointed to a small bruise on his cheekbone. His wheat-blond hair stuck up in clumps, and his navy blue polo shirt was gray from what must have been a sweaty altercation on the school playground.

"Wow, I bet that hurt." Adrian gave what he hoped was sufficient attention to the almost nonexistent but clearly exciting wound. "Did the teacher punch you?"

"No, silly." Josh grinned, revealing a gap where he'd recently lost a tooth. "Teachers don't get to punch kids."

Precisely why Adrian had never considered becoming a teacher. "What happened, then?"

"I pushed Kevin for calling me a crybaby, and then he punched me. We both got in trouble, and Ms. Mullins—she's the principal now—said we'll have to apologize to each other in the morning, but after that, we're gonna forget all about it."

"Uh-huh."

"…As long as it doesn't happen again," Heather added with a stern look at Josh. She and Josh's twin sister, Catrina, walked toward them hand-in-hand.

Adrian couldn't help noticing how cute Heather looked, even dressed as she was in baggy jeans and a cherry-red tank top that wasn't tight, but somehow still showed off her amazing curves. What seemed like a deliberate effort to hide her femininity wasn't working. Had never worked, in fact, at least as far as he was concerned.

The needy kid who now clung to Adrian's leg in an effort to regain his attention kept him from reaching out to touch the bright blond curl that had escaped Heather's haphazard ponytail to blow against her cheek. It wasn't that the little boy was physically in the way, because if Adrian wanted to touch Heather, no one would be able to stop him. What stopped him was the fact that she was a widow with kids.

Acknowledgments

I believe that every book possesses a consciousness of the story it wants to tell. Before a word has been written, the book already exists, both fully formed and formless. The story taps a writer on the shoulder and whispers in their ear. It conspires with the universe to bring together a team capable of bringing it into the physical world. The part where the author applies seat to chair and taps out 100,000 words is only a small part of the process. So many serendipitous events, people, and animals made this book happen, so I have many to thank. This book would not exist if not for:

Damon Suede, who said, "Talk to Deb."

Cat Clyne, who said, "Send a proposal."

Deb Werksman, my wonderful and supportive editor, who said "Yes!" and welcomed me to the Sourcebooks family with a warm smile, open arms, and a believing heart. Her confidence in me and the stories I am called upon to tell inspires me every day.

The incredible Sourcebooks team, who do the fingernail-biting work that makes me nervous just to think about. Georgia (my dog who inspired the character) thanks them too, because their dedication means that I have more time to write while she warms my feet. (Because as we all know, you can't write a good book if your feet are cold.)

Nicole Resciniti and Lesley Sabga at the Seymour Agency, who remind me that I can sail through the air and grab for the bar without worrying I might fall. Together, they neutralize my fear of heights.

Lisa Miller, whose Story Structure Safari class taught this pantser how to plot, and the Expedition Gang, whose brainstorming power helped me create a coherent plot for the entire series.

The Plotting Wenches, my tribe of fellow writers, plotters, and schemers, who supply advice and encouragement. When any one of y'all says, "this stinks, and here's why," I get excited because I know you'll help me figure out how to make the pile of whatever I wrote come out smelling like a gardenia.

My family, who inspires me and distracts me and loves me and reminds me on a regular basis that we have a pool in our yard, and that sometimes I need to step away from the computer.

My husband, Hans, who keeps my world spinning by taking care of me and this place and the animals who live here so I can write. (No thanks, BTW, to the Life 360 app for reminding him that I haven't left the property in the last two months. That might be none of his business, just saying.)

My sister (whom I have never called by her actual name but in the way of the south, she is, simply, Sister), who is a retired nurse. If anything I have written about medical subjects is wrong, it is her fault, not mine. (Sister, I'm just kidding. I'll take partial responsibility at least.)

My team: Jennifer Newell and Katrina Martin, for tackling technology on my behalf.

My tribe: friends who forgive me for writing instead of socializing; fellow animal communicators, students, clients, and animals (including mine!) who continue to teach me daily.

My readers: I wrote this book for each one of you. I hope you've enjoyed the journey, and maybe even recognized your own gift of animal communication within these pages. If that recognition feels like an invitation to explore and deepen your abilities, it is. Understanding breeds compassion, and that's something the world needs. Together, we can save the world, one happy ending at a time. Let's do it.